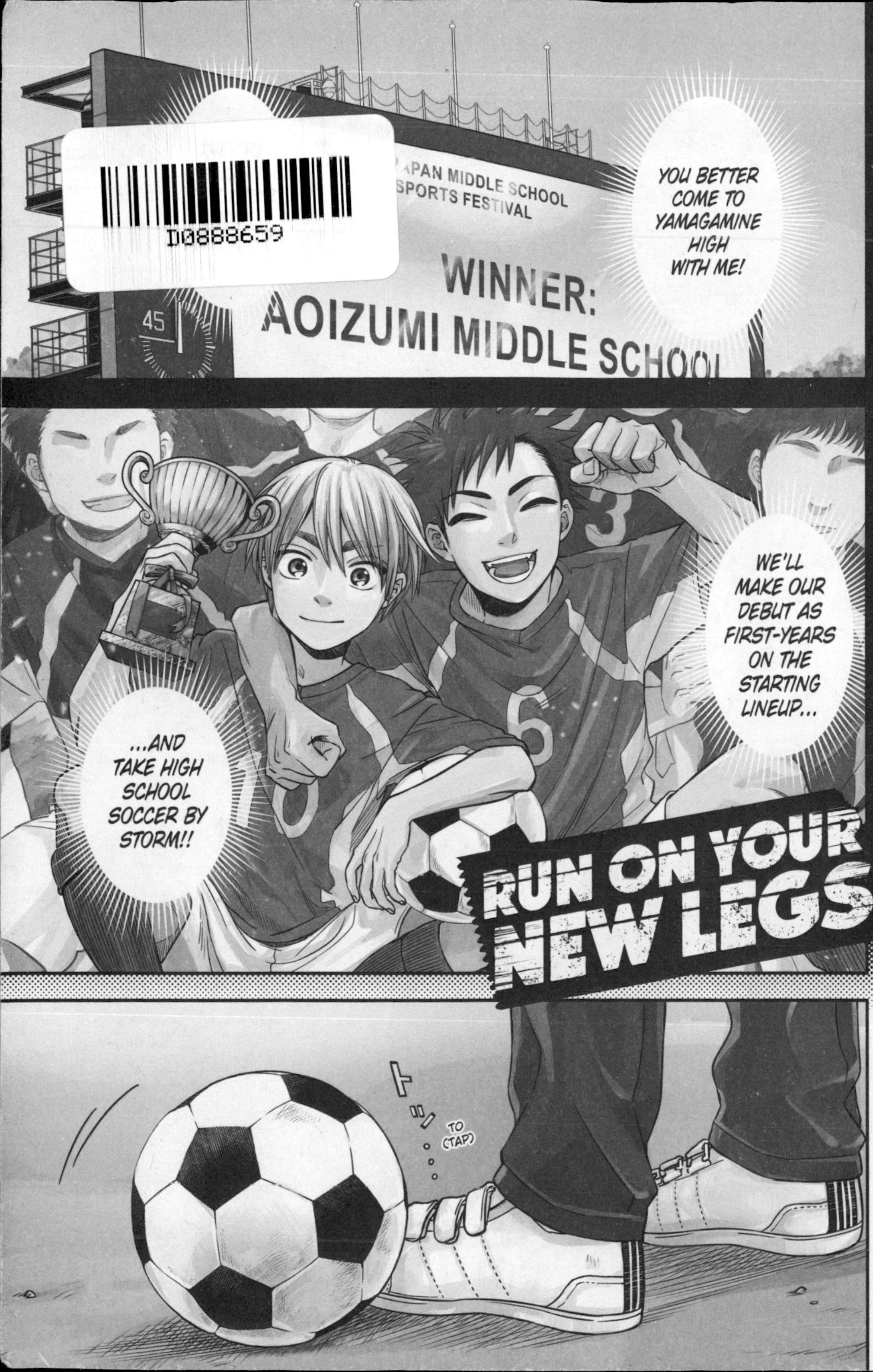

JAPAN MIDDLE SCHOOL SPORTS FESTIVAL
WINNER: AOIZUMI MIDDLE SCHOOL
45
YOU BETTER COME TO YAMAGAMINE HIGH WITH ME!
WE'LL MAKE OUR DEBUT AS FIRST-YEARS ON THE STARTING LINEUP...
...AND TAKE HIGH SCHOOL SOCCER BY STORM!!
RUN ON YOUR NEW LEGS
TO (TAP)

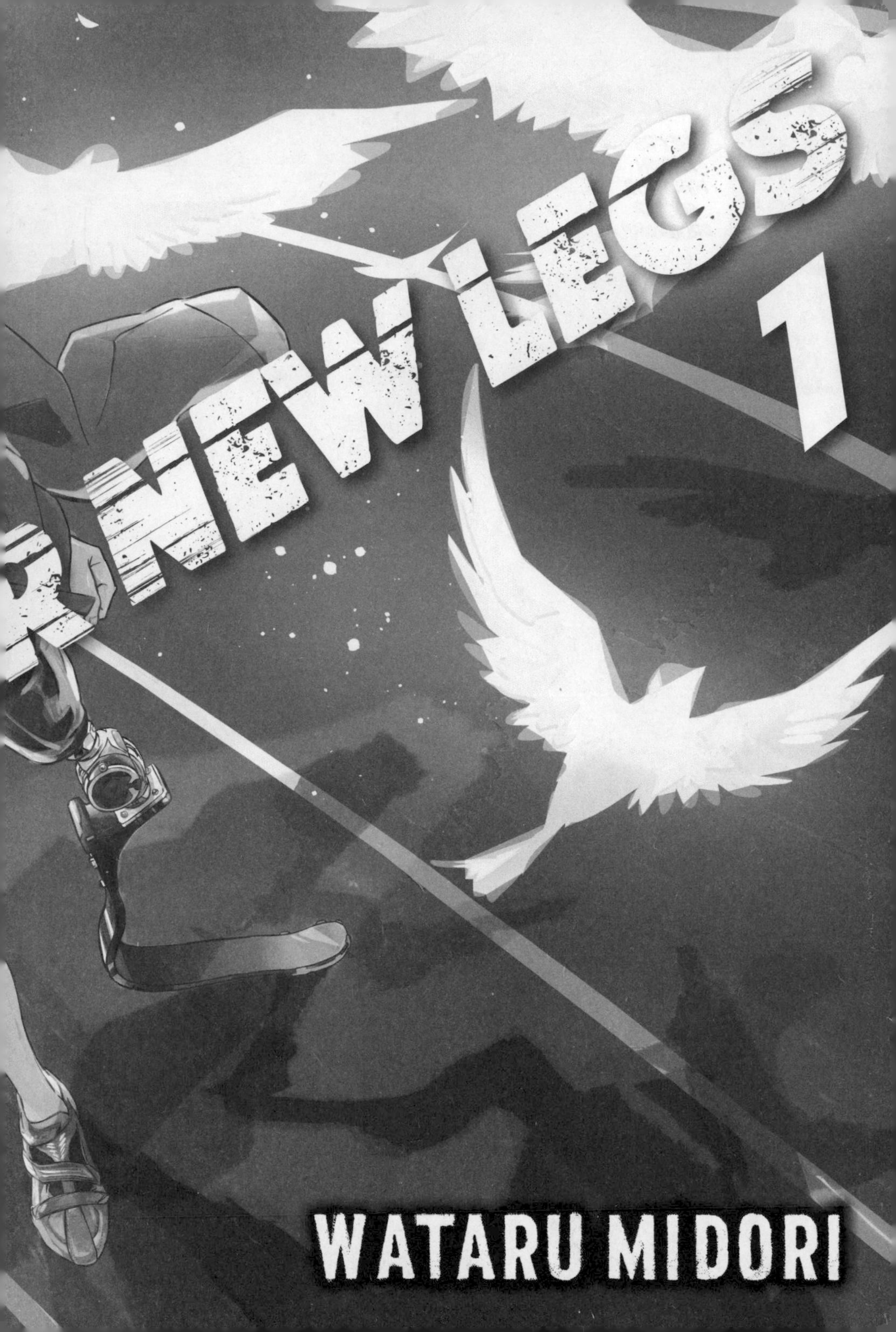
NEW LEGS
1
WATARU MIDORI

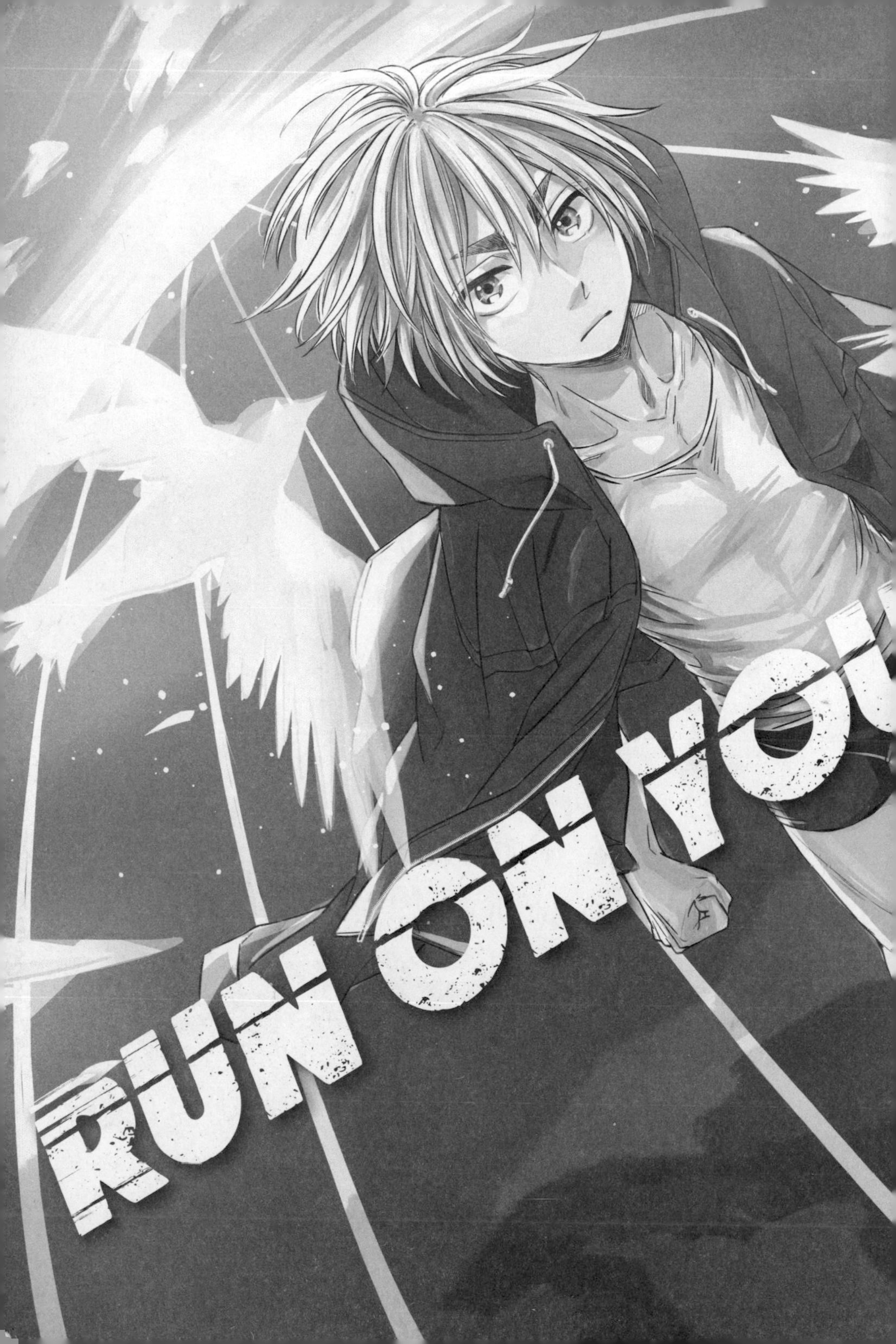
RUN ON YOU

TABLE OF CONTENTS

Chapter 1: What Can I Even Do?

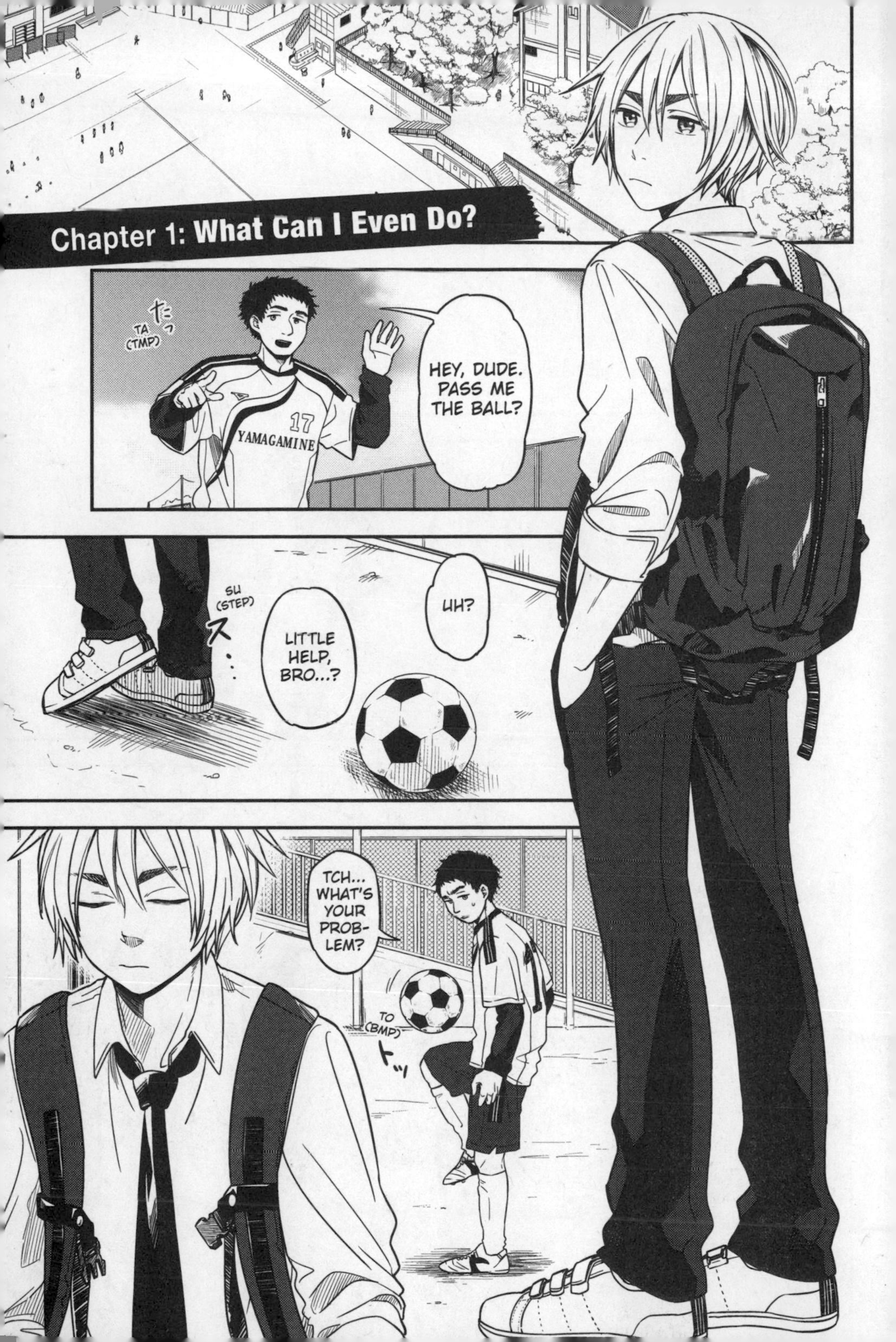
HEY, DUDE. PASS ME THE BALL?
TA (TMP)
YAMAGAMINE 17
UH?
LITTLE HELP, BRO...?
SU (STEP)
TCH... WHAT'S YOUR PROB-LEM?
TO (BMP)

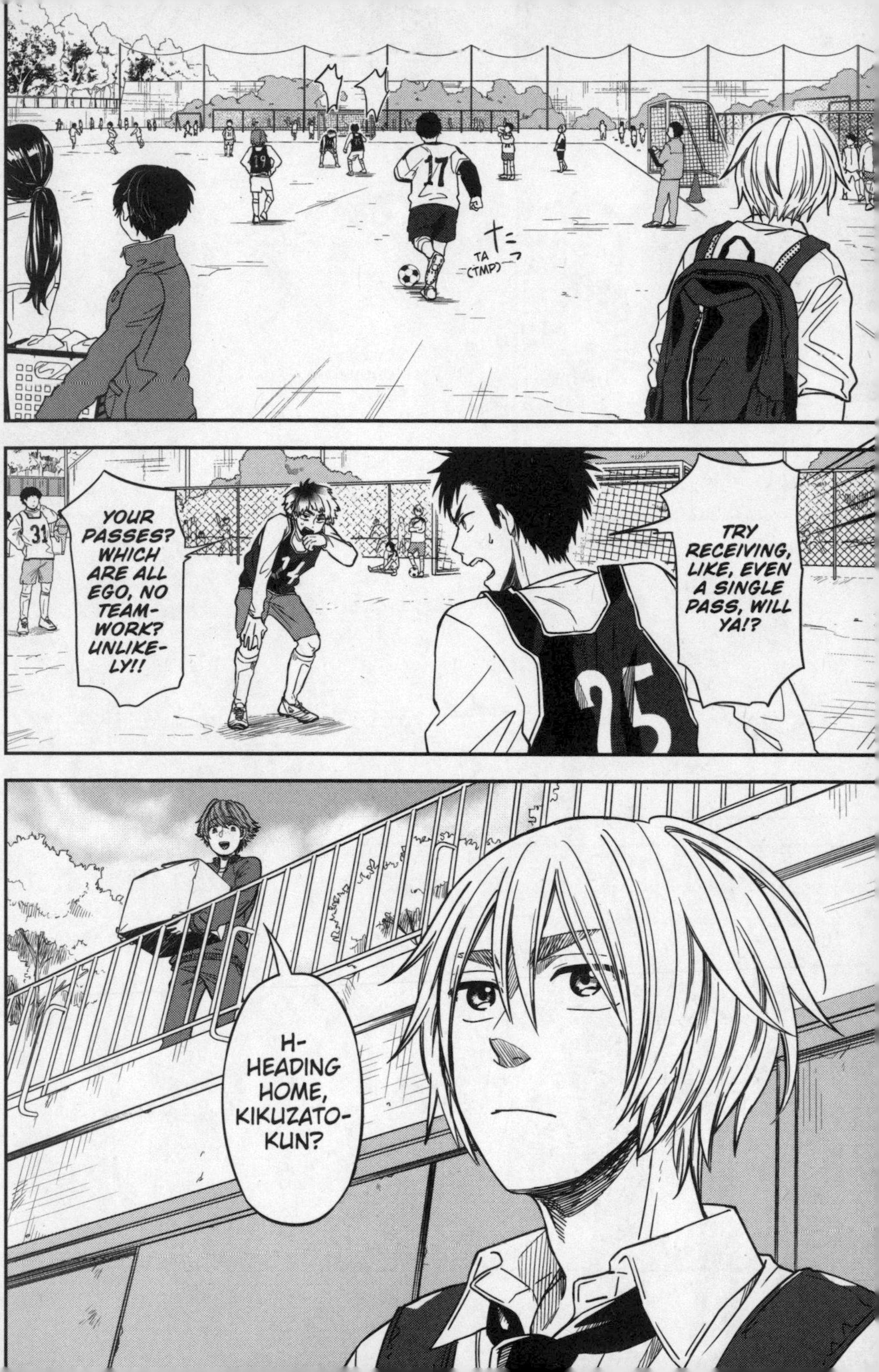
TA
(TMP)
TRY RECEIVING, LIKE, EVEN A SINGLE PASS, WILL YA!?
YOUR PASSES? WHICH ARE ALL EGO, NO TEAM-WORK? UNLIKE-LY!!
H-HEADING HOME, KIKUZATO-KUN?

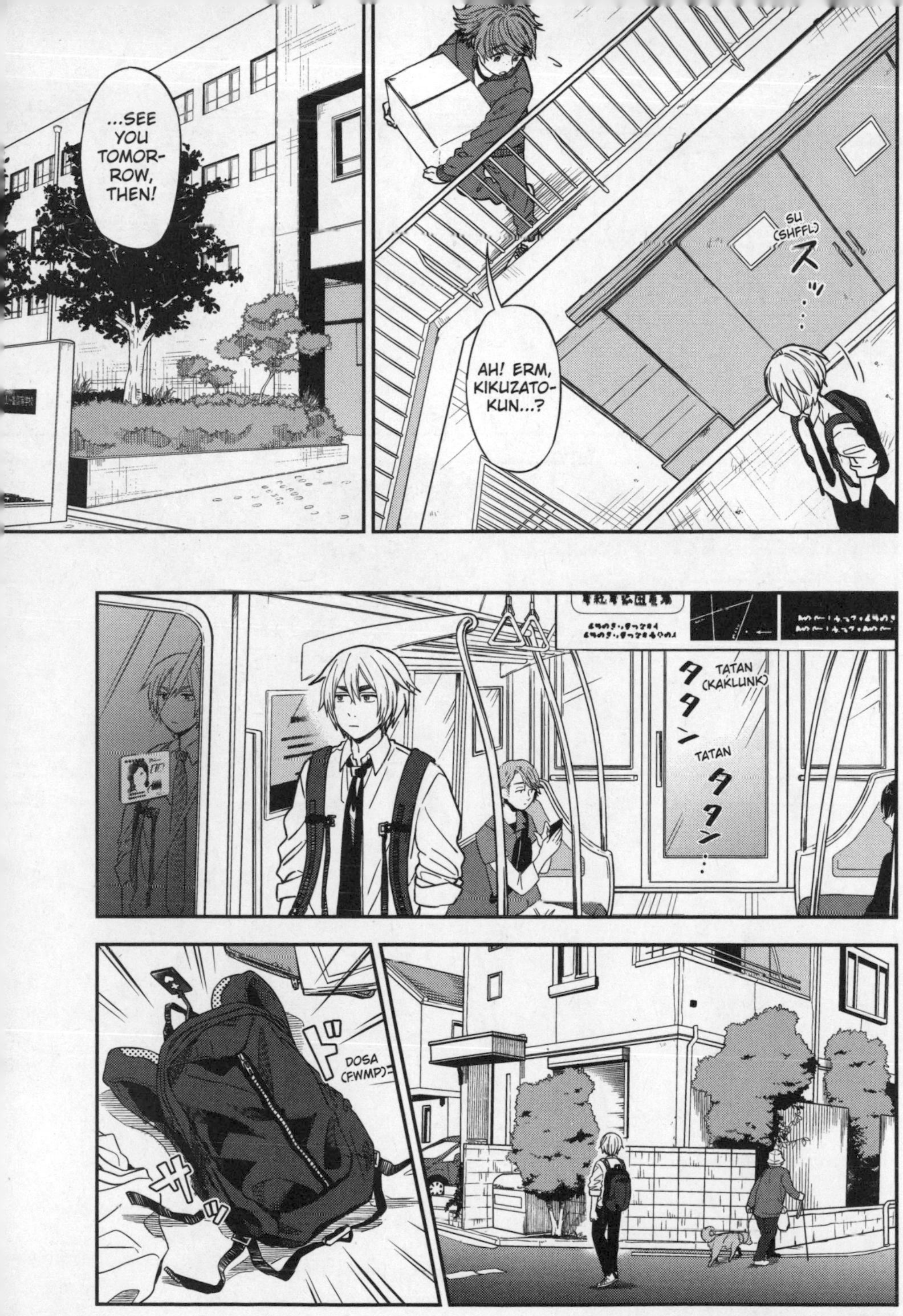
AH! ERM, KIKUZATO-KUN...?
SU (SHFFL)
スッ…
...SEE YOU TOMORROW, THEN!
TATAN (KAKLUNK)
タタン
TATAN
タタン…
DOSA (FWMP)
ドサッ

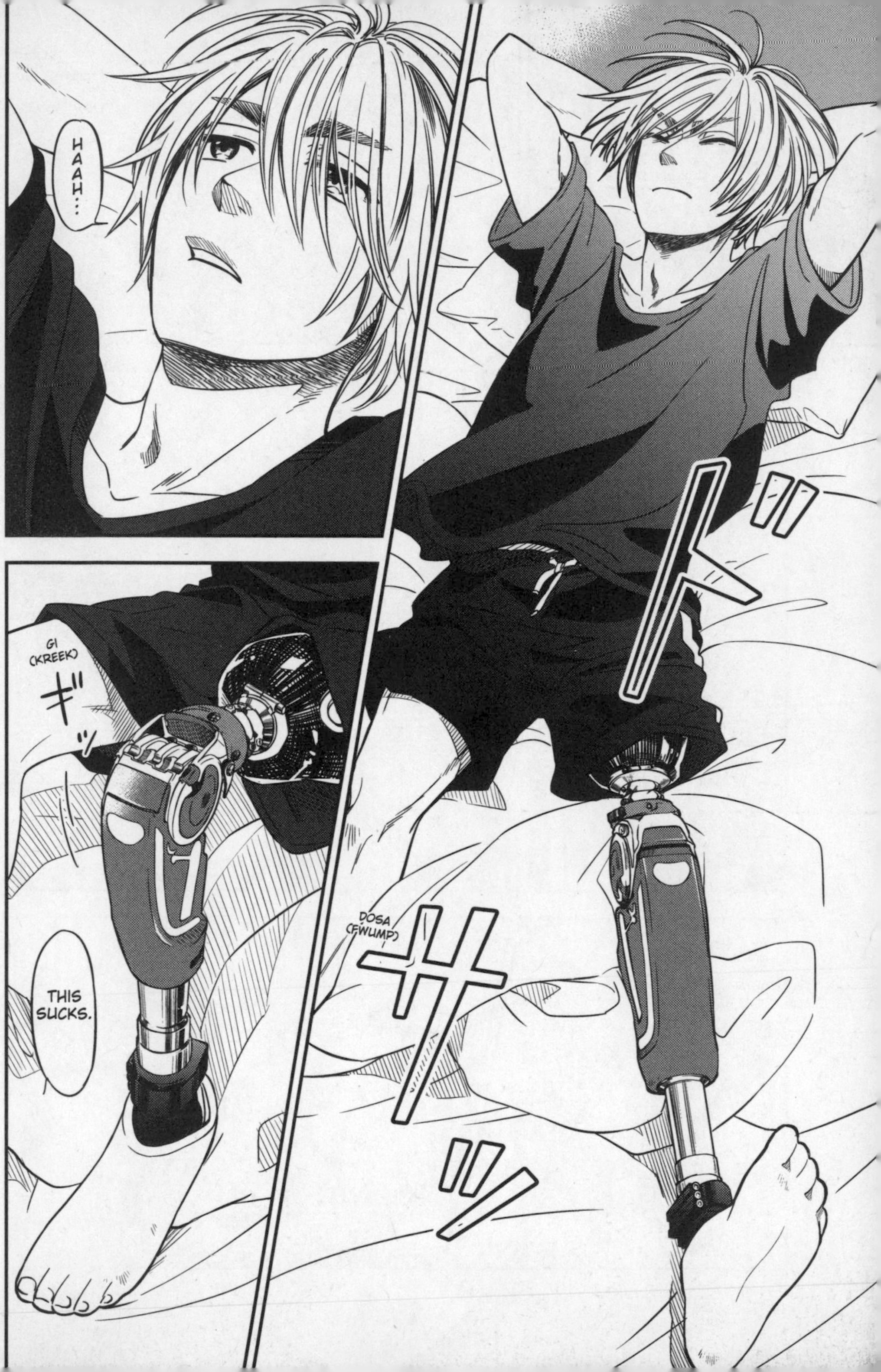
DOSA (FWUMP)
ドサッ
HAAH...
GI (KREEK)
ギッ
THIS SUCKS.

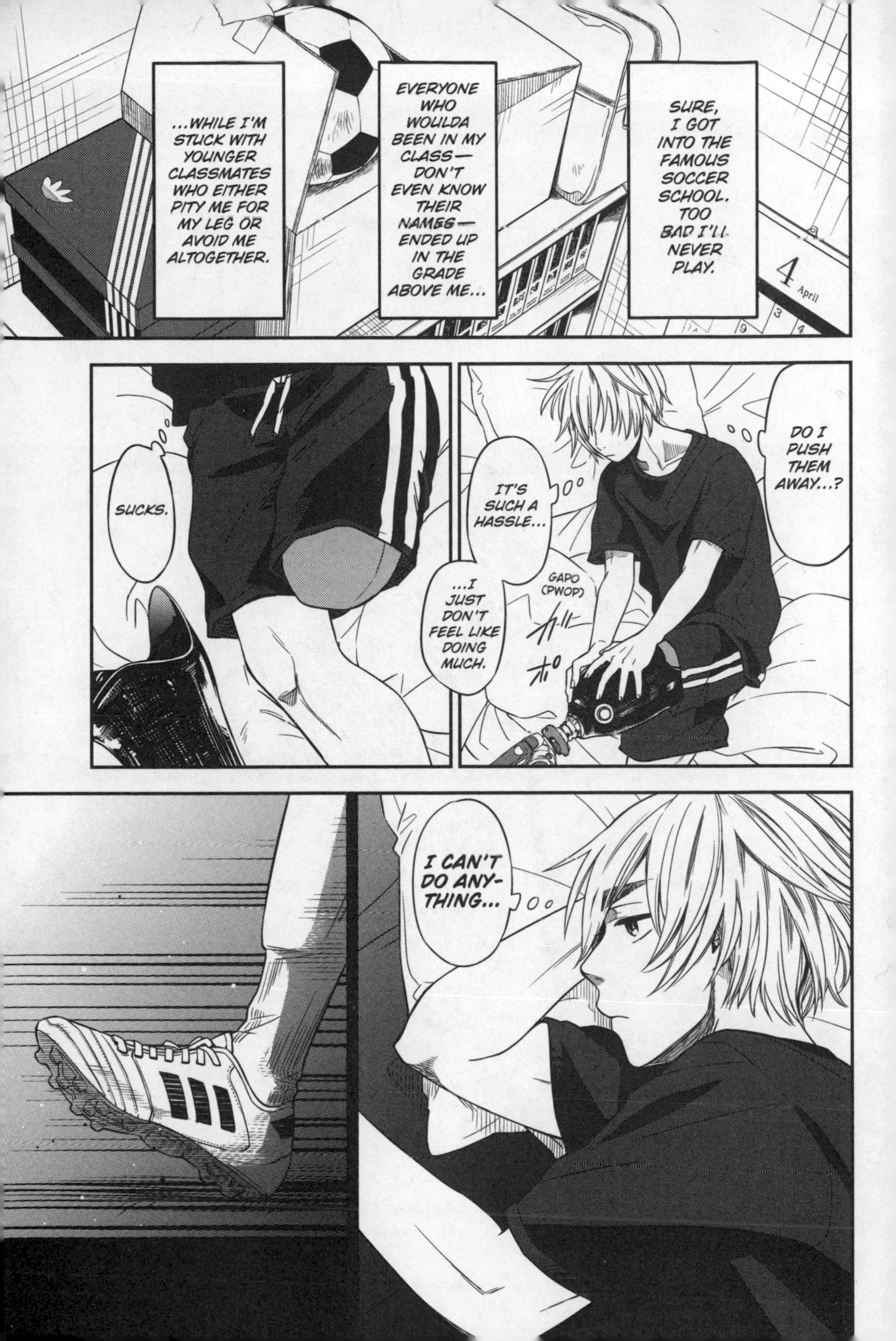
SURE, I GOT INTO THE FAMOUS SOCCER SCHOOL. TOO BAD I'LL NEVER PLAY.
EVERYONE WHO WOULDA BEEN IN MY CLASS—DON'T EVEN KNOW THEIR NAMES—ENDED UP IN THE GRADE ABOVE ME...
...WHILE I'M STUCK WITH YOUNGER CLASSMATES WHO EITHER PITY ME FOR MY LEG OR AVOID ME ALTOGETHER.
4
April
DO I PUSH THEM AWAY...?
IT'S SUCH A HASSLE...
GAPO (PWOP)
...I JUST DON'T FEEL LIKE DOING MUCH.
SUCKS.
I CAN'T DO ANY-THING...

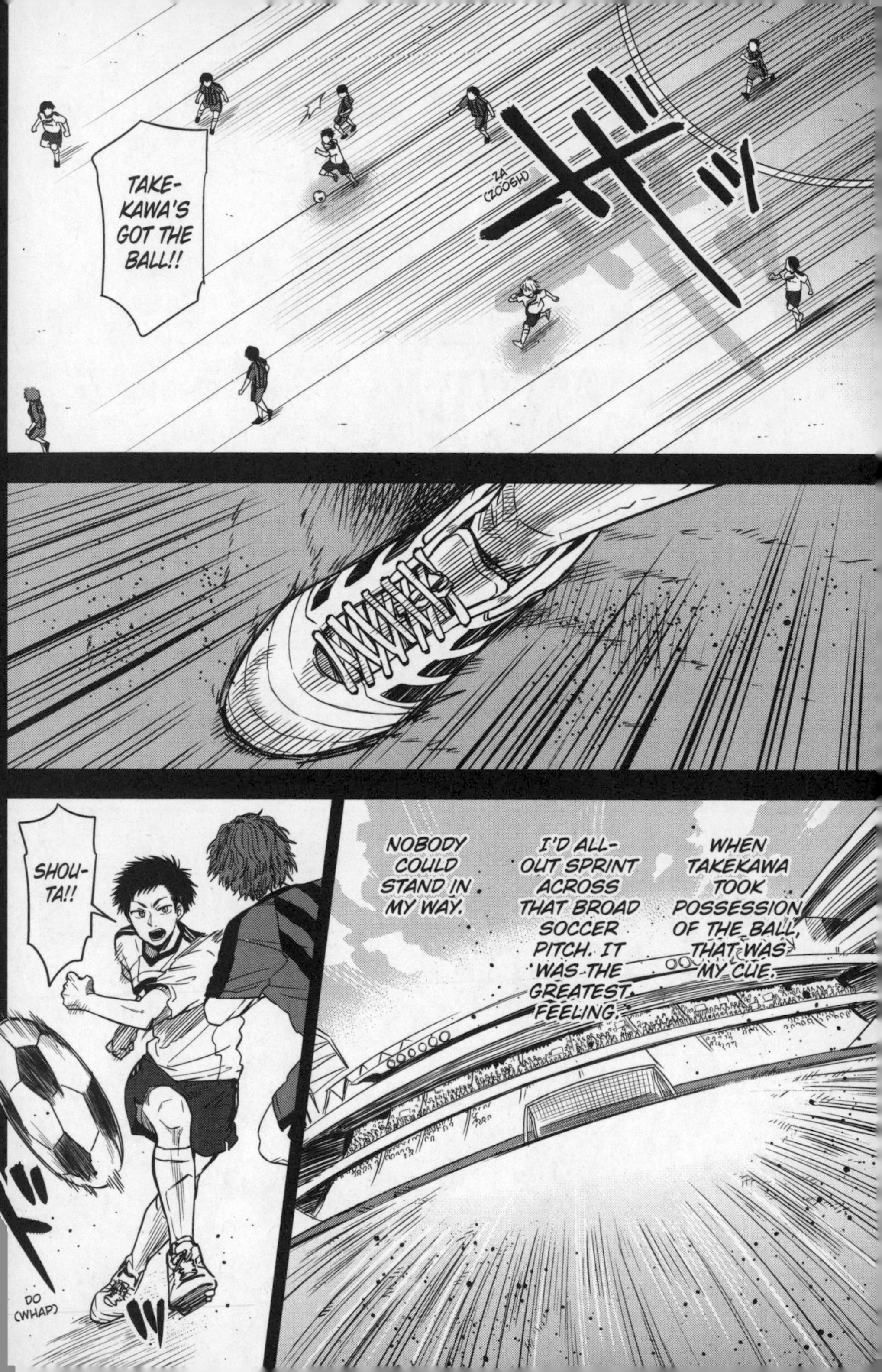
ZA (ZOOSH)
TAKE-KAWA'S GOT THE BALL!!
WHEN TAKEKAWA TOOK POSSESSION OF THE BALL, THAT WAS MY CUE.
I'D ALL-OUT SPRINT ACROSS THAT BROAD SOCCER PITCH. IT WAS THE GREATEST FEELING.
NOBODY COULD STAND IN MY WAY.
SHOU-TA!!
DO (WHAP)

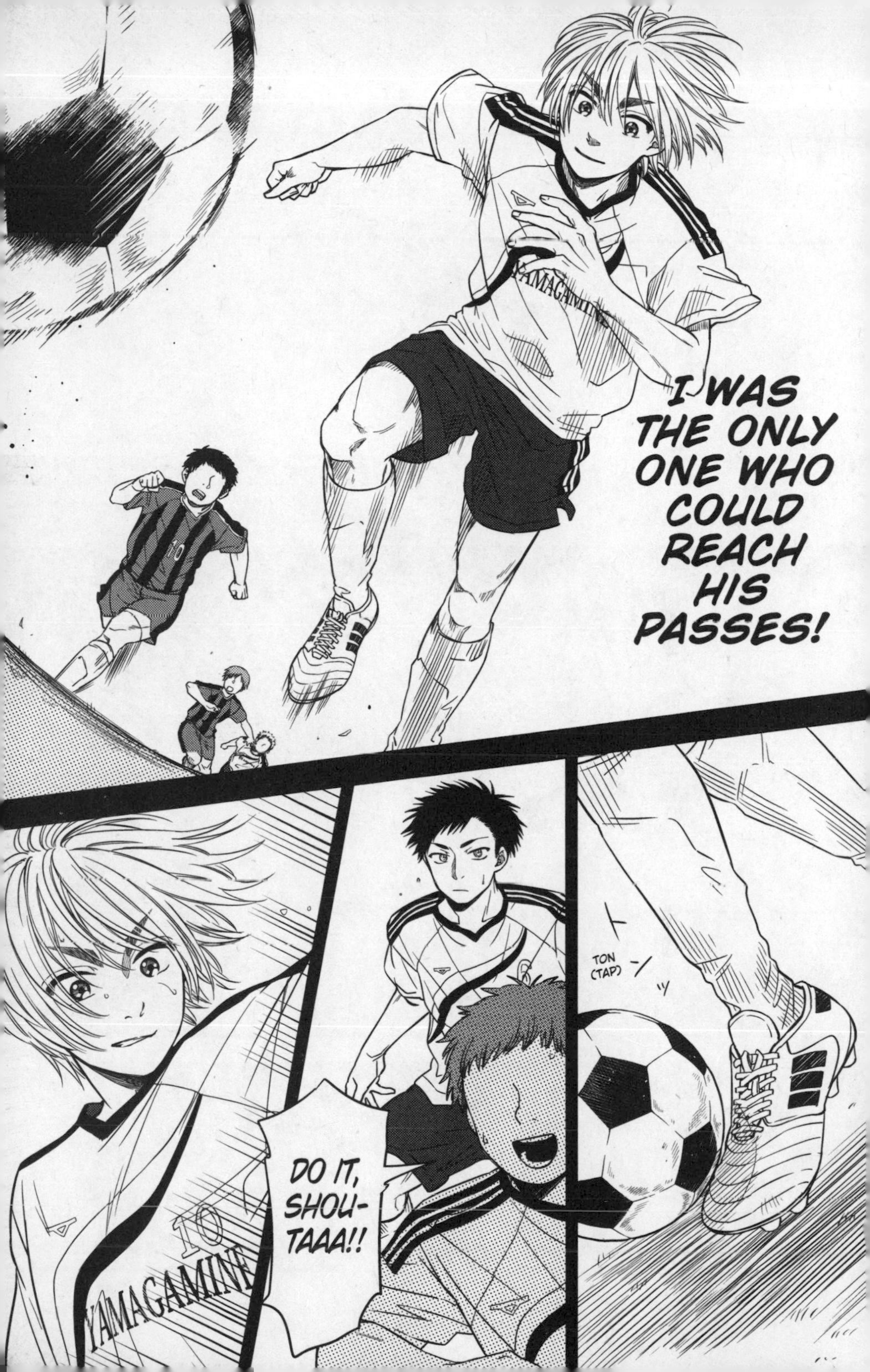
I WAS THE ONLY ONE WHO COULD REACH HIS PASSES!
TON (TAP)
DO IT, SHOU-TAAA!!

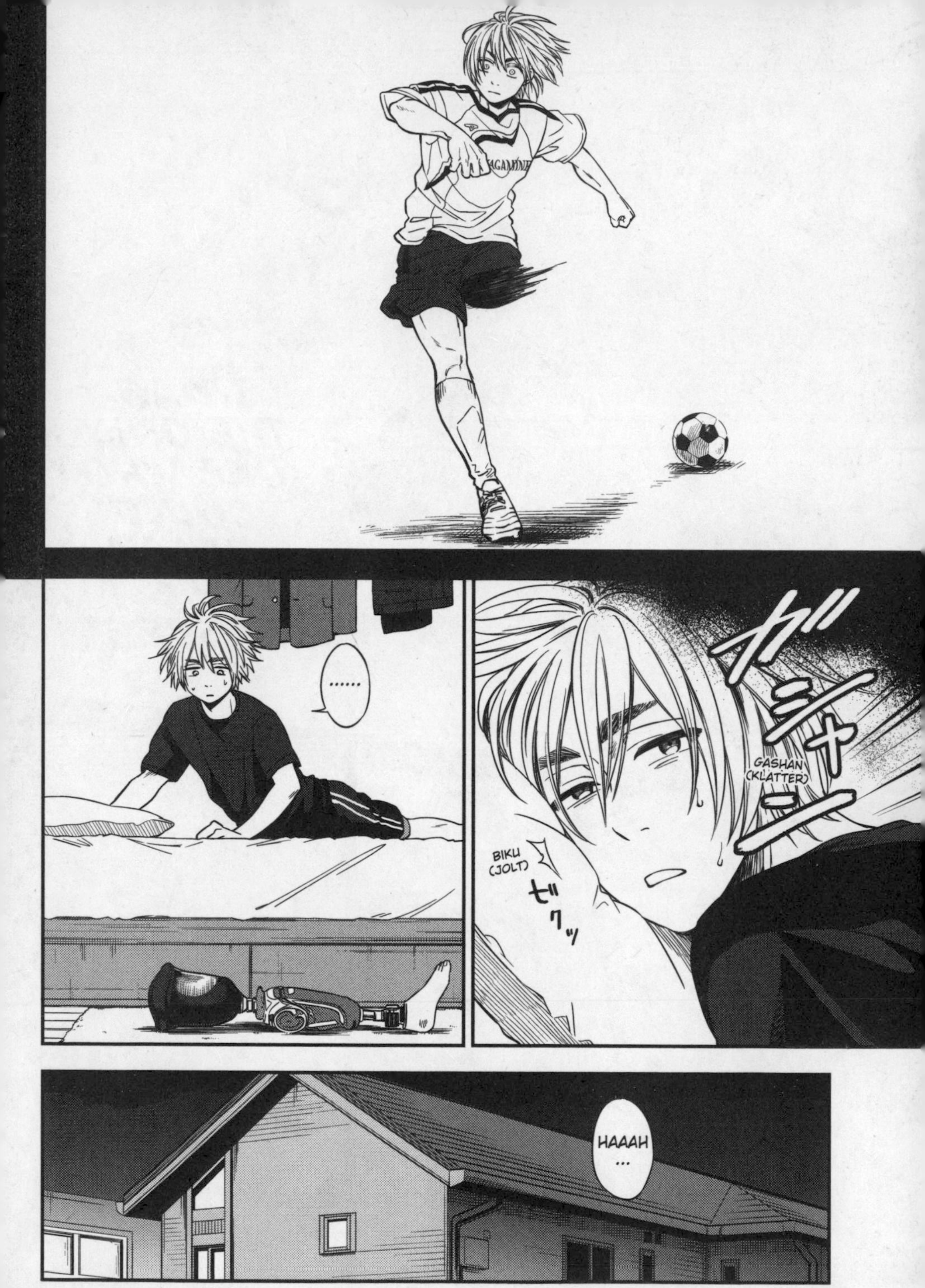
ガシャーン
GASHAN (KLATTER)
ビクッ
BIKU (JOLT)
......
HAAAH ...

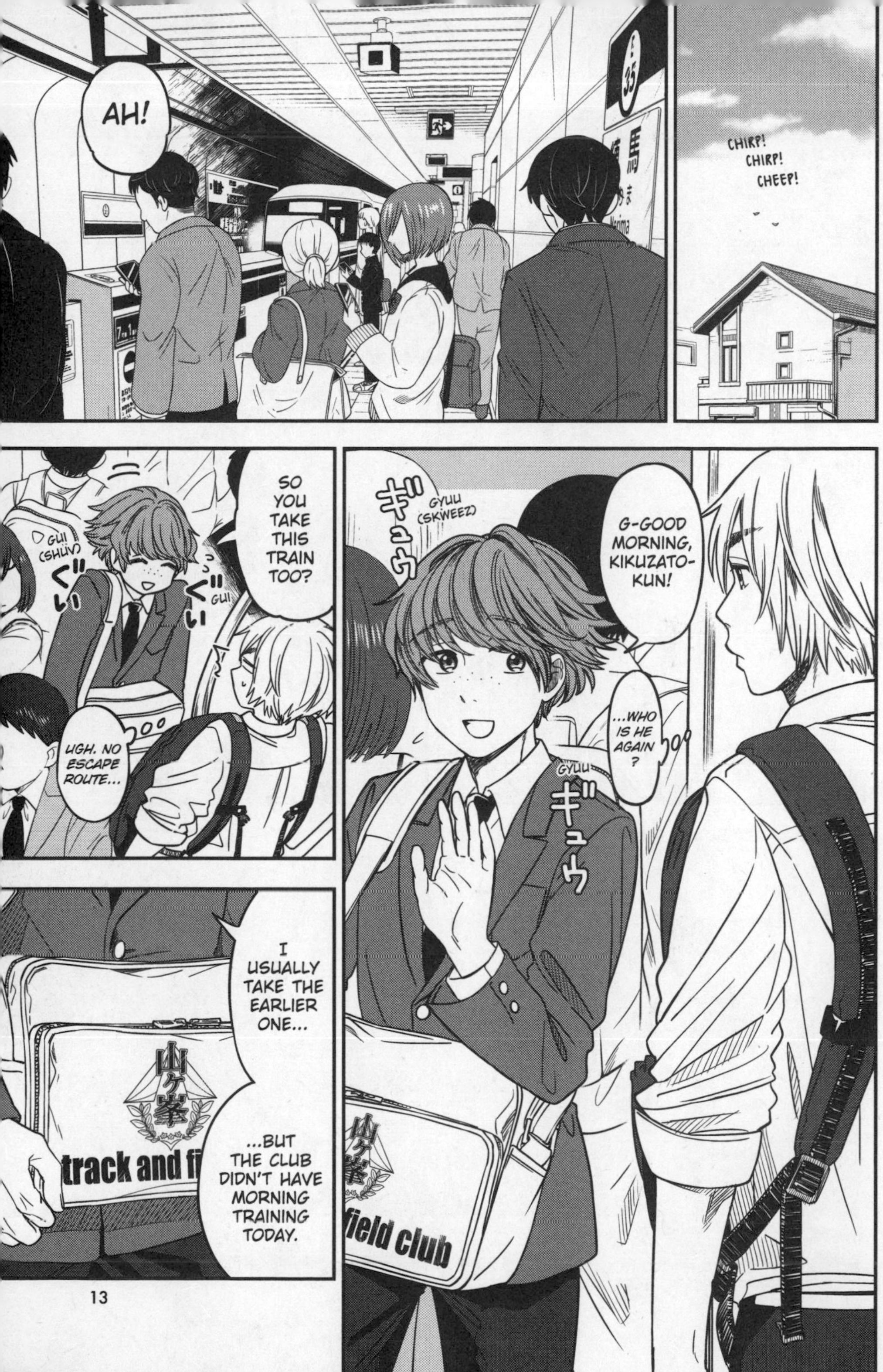
CHIRP!
CHIRP!
CHEEP!
AH!
ギュウ
GYUU (SKWEEZ)
G-GOOD MORNING, KIKUZATO-KUN!
...WHO IS HE AGAIN?
GYUU
ギュウ
field club
SO YOU TAKE THIS TRAIN TOO?
GUI (SHÜV)
ぐい
ぐい
GUI
UGH. NO ESCAPE ROUTE...
I USUALLY TAKE THE EARLIER ONE...
...BUT THE CLUB DIDN'T HAVE MORNING TRAINING TODAY.
track and fi

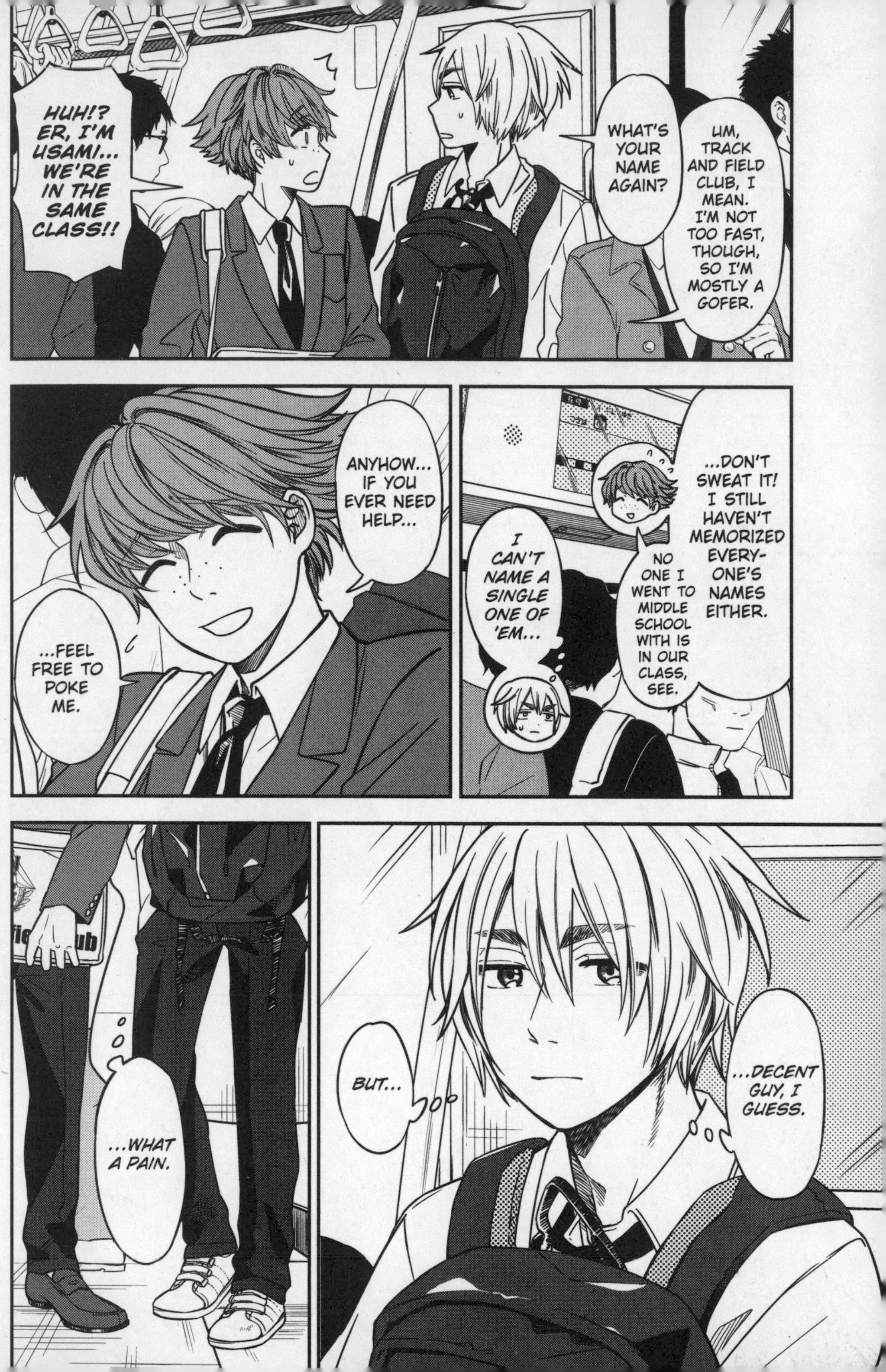
UM, TRACK AND FIELD CLUB, I MEAN. I'M NOT TOO FAST, THOUGH, SO I'M MOSTLY A GOFER.
WHAT'S YOUR NAME AGAIN?
HUH!? ER, I'M USAMI... WE'RE IN THE SAME CLASS!!
...DON'T SWEAT IT! I STILL HAVEN'T MEMORIZED EVERY-ONE'S NAMES EITHER.
NO ONE I WENT TO MIDDLE SCHOOL WITH IS IN OUR CLASS, SEE.
I CAN'T NAME A SINGLE ONE OF 'EM...
ANYHOW... IF YOU EVER NEED HELP...
...FEEL FREE TO POKE ME.
...DECENT GUY, I GUESS.
BUT...
...WHAT A PAIN.

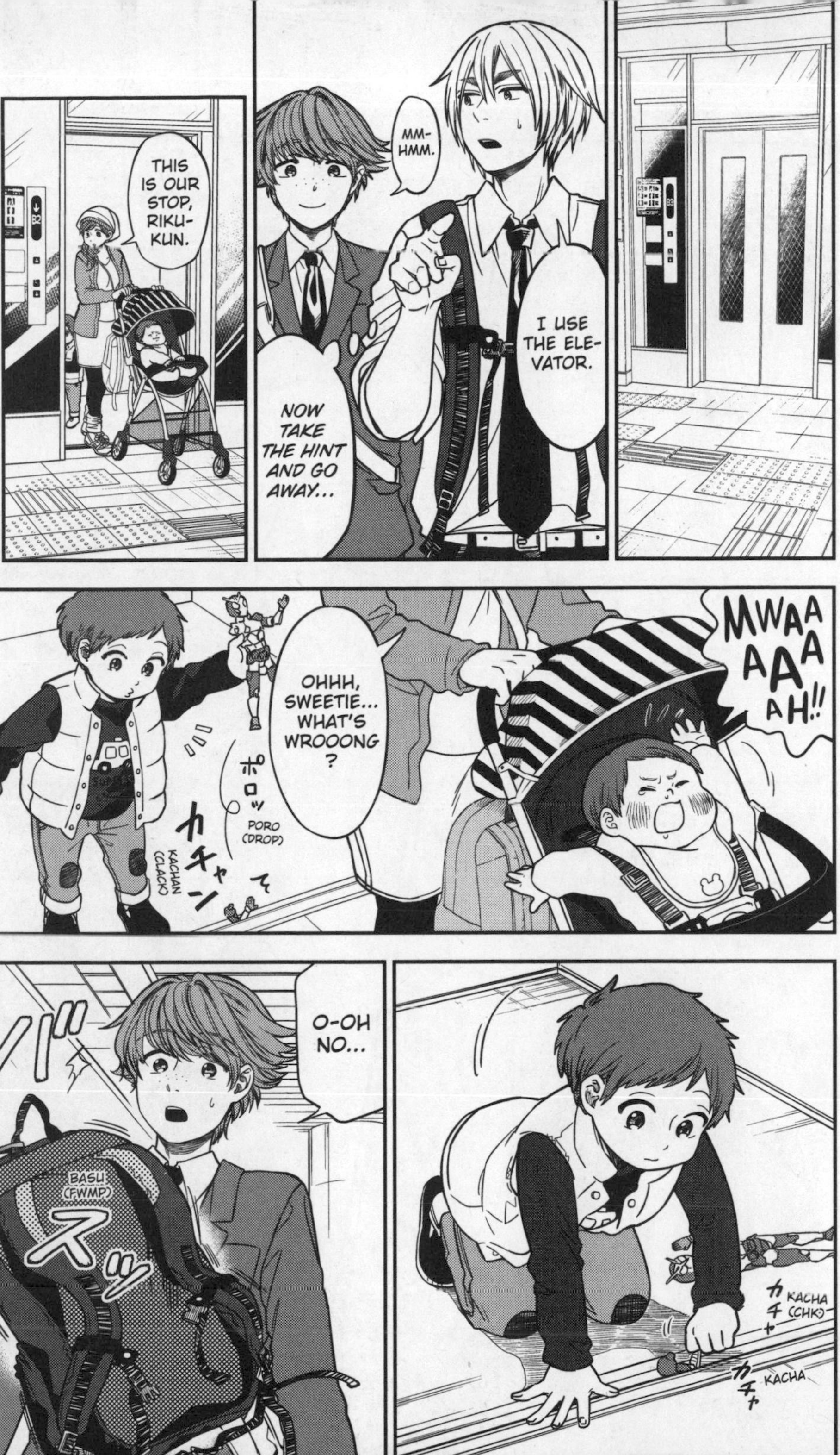
MM-HMM.
I USE THE ELE-VATOR.
NOW TAKE THE HINT AND GO AWAY...
THIS IS OUR STOP, RIKU-KUN.
MWAAAAAAAH!!
OHHH, SWEETIE... WHAT'S WROOONG?
ポロッ
PORO (DROP)
カチャン
KACHAN (CLACK)
カチャ
KACHA (CHK)
カチャ
KACHA
O-OH NO...
バ
スッ
BASU (FWMP)

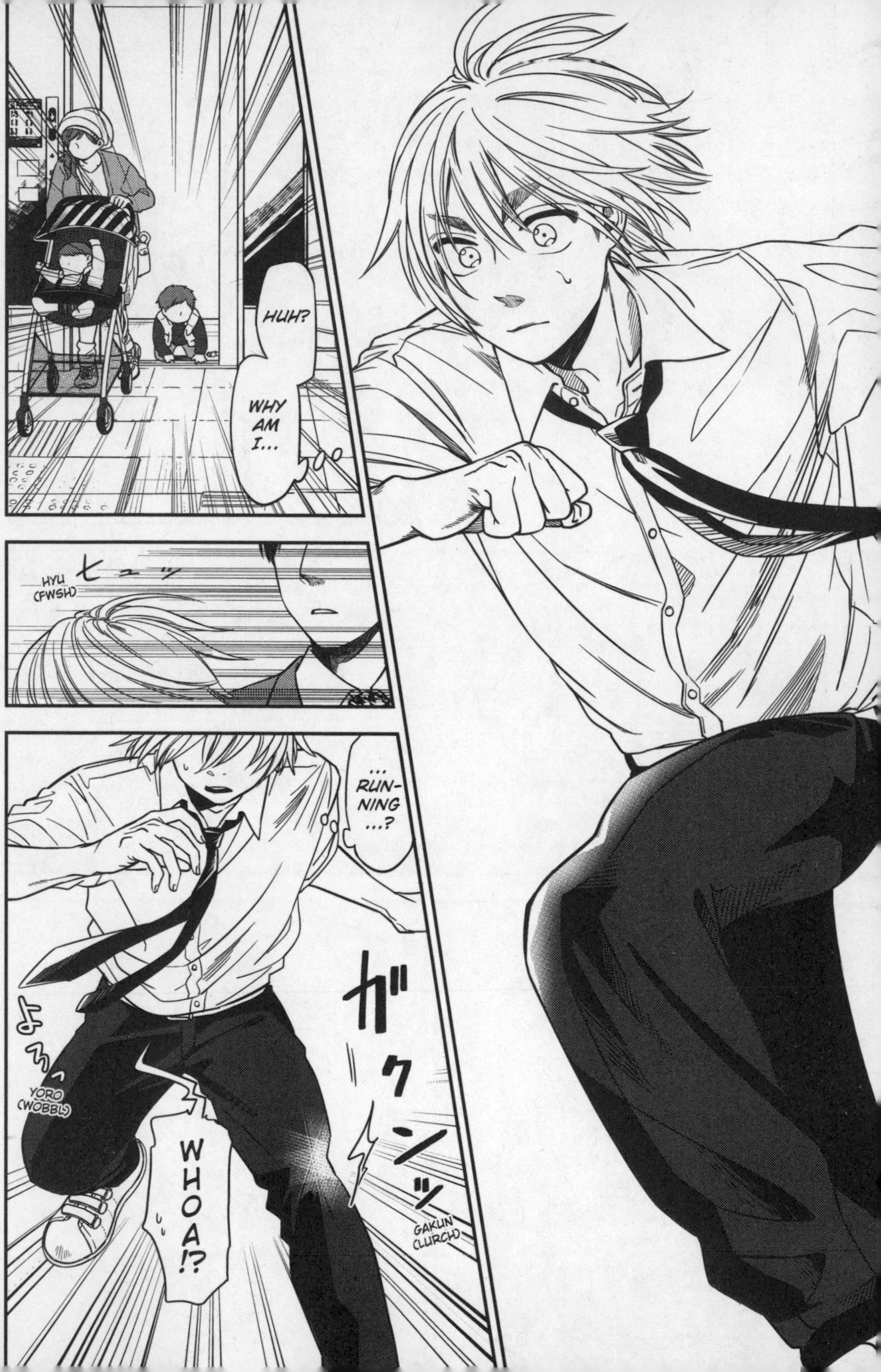
HUH?
WHY AM I...
ヒュッ
HYU (FWSH)
...RUN-NING...?
ガクンッ
GAKUN (LURCH)
WHOA!?
よろ
YORO (WOBBL)

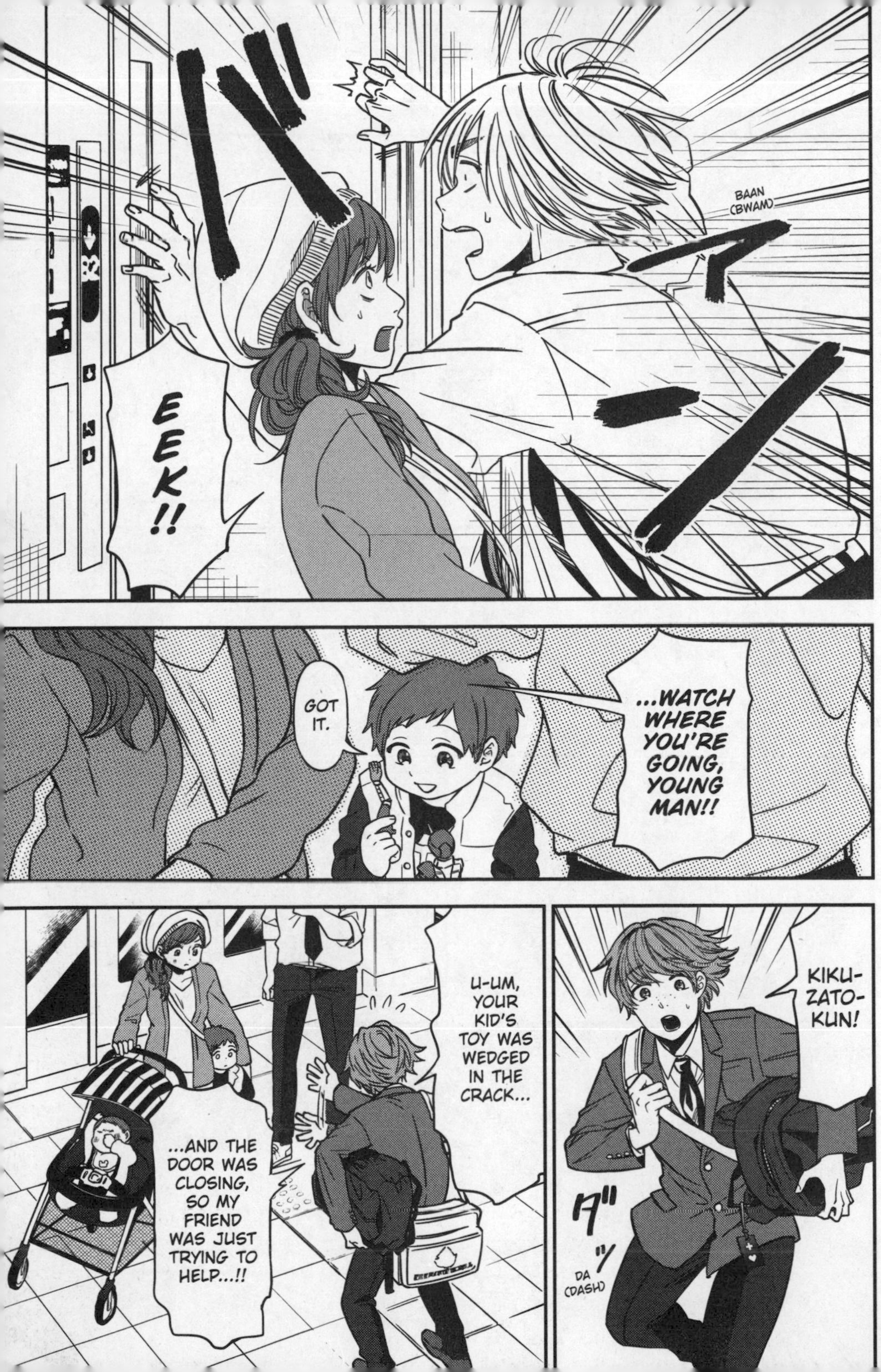
BAAN (BWAM)
EEK!!
...WATCH WHERE YOU'RE GOING, YOUNG MAN!!
GOT IT.
KIKU-ZATO-KUN!
DA (DASH)
U-UM, YOUR KID'S TOY WAS WEDGED IN THE CRACK...
...AND THE DOOR WAS CLOSING, SO MY FRIEND WAS JUST TRYING TO HELP...!!

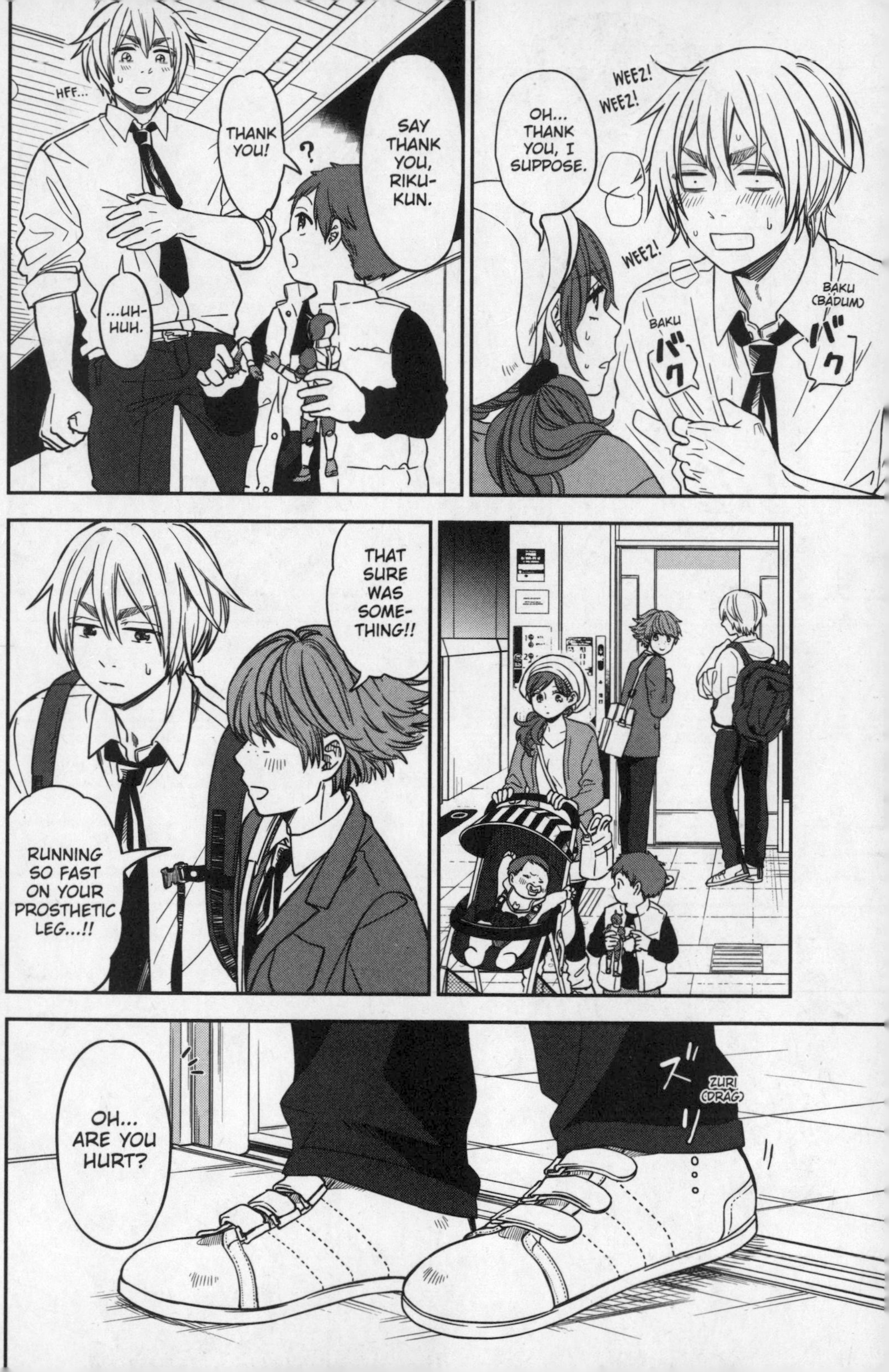
WEEZ! WEEZ!
OH... THANK YOU, I SUPPOSE.
WEEZ!
BAKU (BADUM)
バク
BAKU
バク
SAY THANK YOU, RIKU-KUN.
?
THANK YOU!
HFF...
...UH-HUH.
THAT SURE WAS SOMETHING!!
RUNNING SO FAST ON YOUR PROSTHETIC LEG...!!
ズリ
ZURI (DRAG)
OH... ARE YOU HURT?

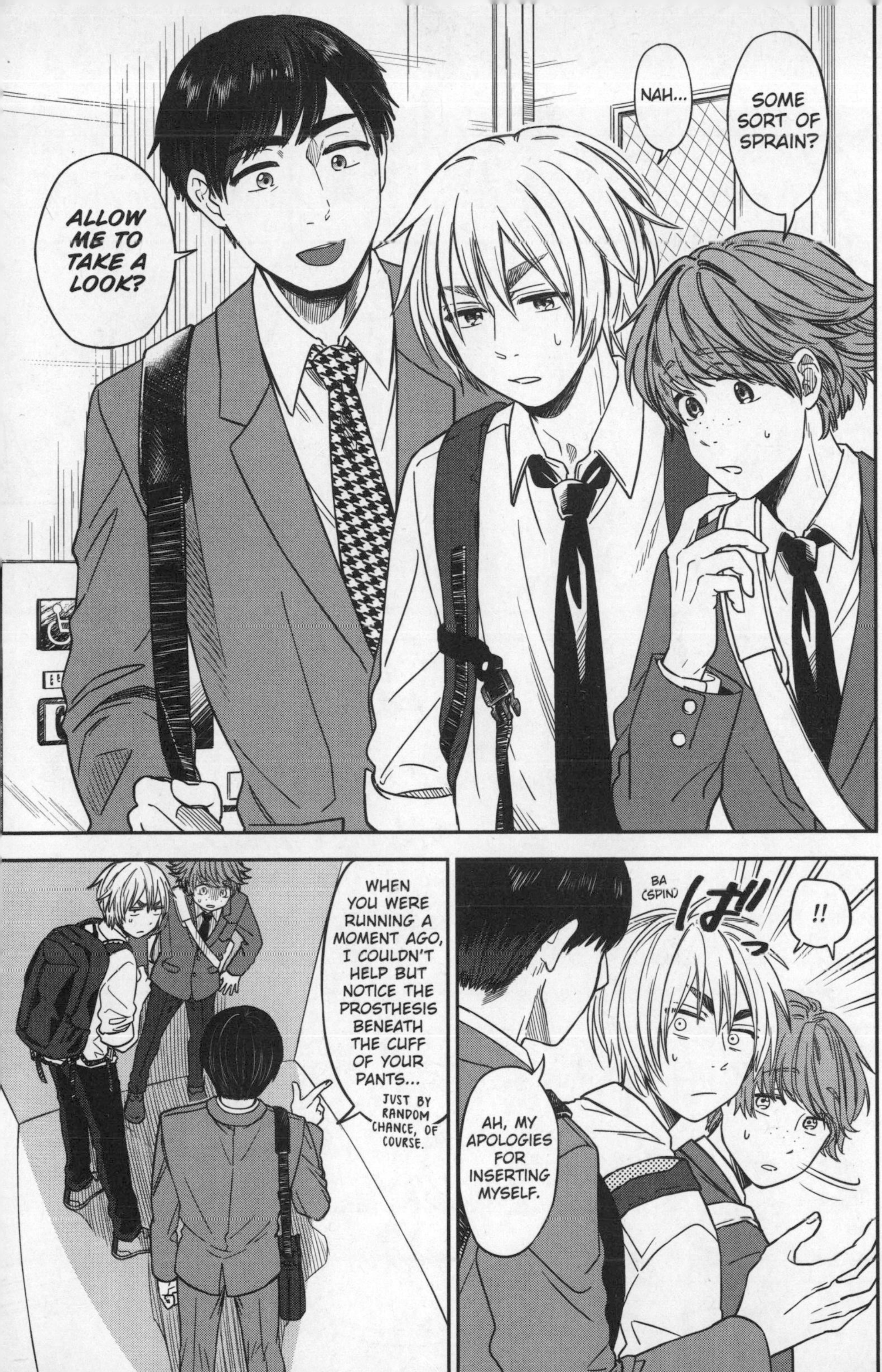
SOME SORT OF SPRAIN?
NAH...
ALLOW ME TO TAKE A LOOK?
!!
ばっ
BA (SPIN)
AH, MY APOLOGIES FOR INSERTING MYSELF.
WHEN YOU WERE RUNNING A MOMENT AGO, I COULDN'T HELP BUT NOTICE THE PROSTHESIS BENEATH THE CUFF OF YOUR PANTS...
JUST BY RANDOM CHANCE, OF COURSE.

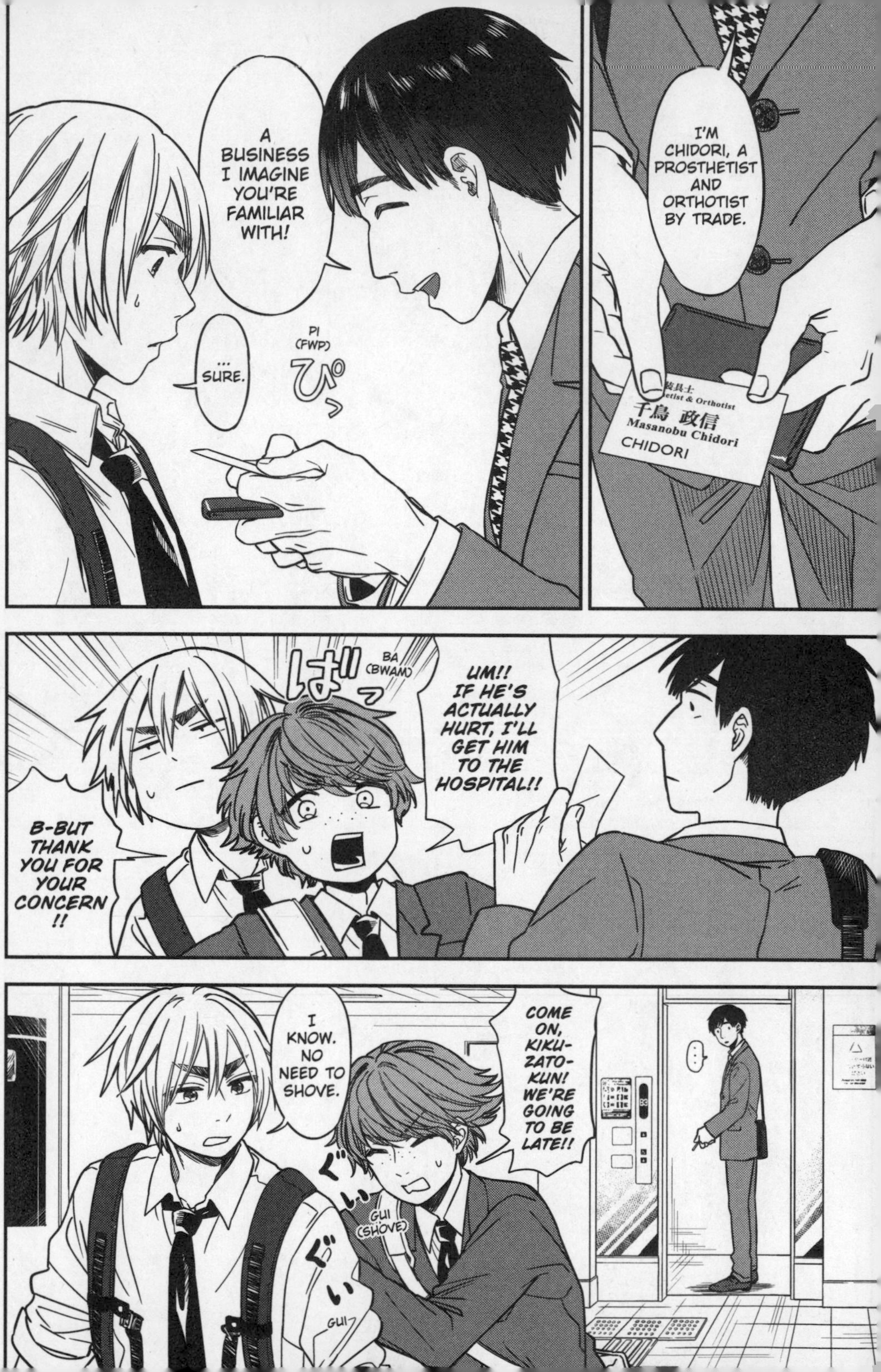
I'M CHIDORI, A PROSTHETIST AND ORTHOTIST BY TRADE.
千鳥 政信
Masanobu Chidori
CHIDORI
A BUSINESS I IMAGINE YOU'RE FAMILIAR WITH!
... SURE.
PI (FWP)
ぴっ
UM!! IF HE'S ACTUALLY HURT, I'LL GET HIM TO THE HOSPITAL!!
BA (BWAM)
ばっ
B-BUT THANK YOU FOR YOUR CONCERN!!
...
COME ON, KIKUZATO-KUN! WE'RE GOING TO BE LATE!!
I KNOW. NO NEED TO SHOVE.
ぐいっ
GUI (SHOVE)
ぐい
GUI

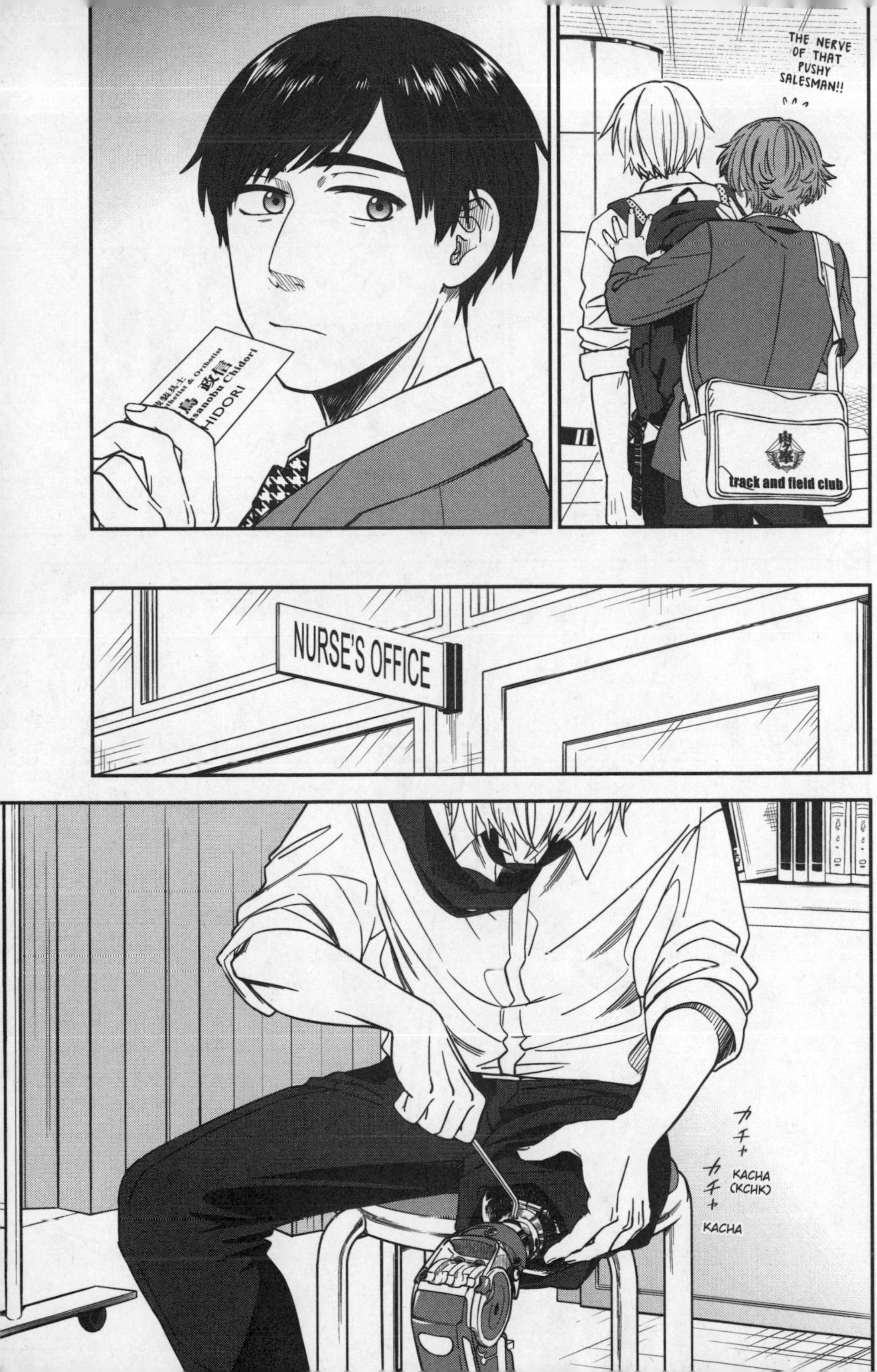
THE NERVE OF THAT PUSHY SALESMAN!!
track and field club
NURSE'S OFFICE
カチャ
KACHA (KCHK)
カチャ
KACHA

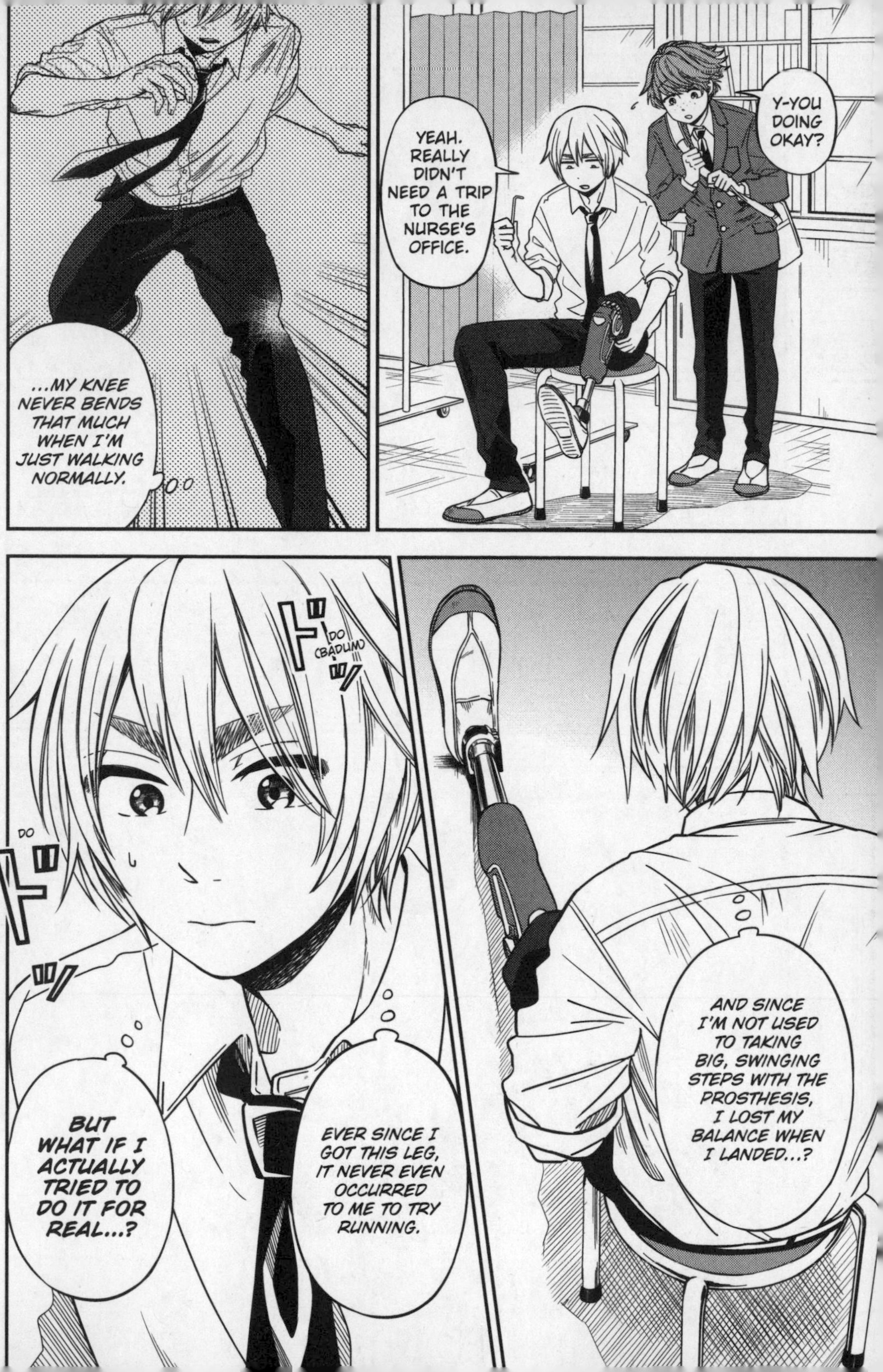
Y-YOU DOING OKAY?
YEAH. REALLY DIDN'T NEED A TRIP TO THE NURSE'S OFFICE.
...MY KNEE NEVER BENDS THAT MUCH WHEN I'M JUST WALKING NORMALLY.
AND SINCE I'M NOT USED TO TAKING BIG, SWINGING STEPS WITH THE PROSTHESIS, I LOST MY BALANCE WHEN I LANDED...?
DO (BADUM)
DO
EVER SINCE I GOT THIS LEG, IT NEVER EVEN OCCURRED TO ME TO TRY RUNNING.
BUT WHAT IF I ACTUALLY TRIED TO DO IT FOR REAL...?

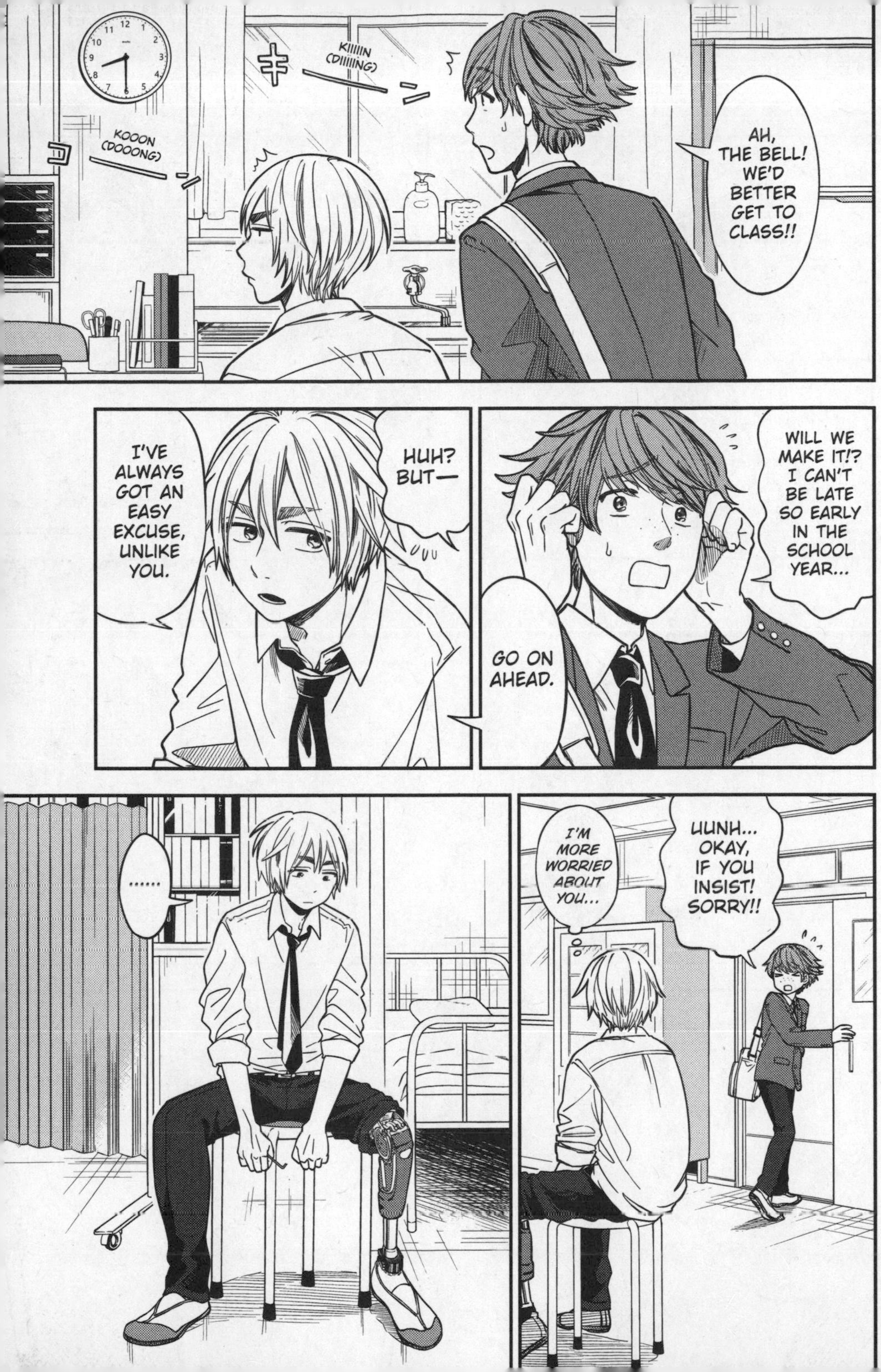
KIIIIN (DIIIIING)
KOOON (DOOONG)
AH, THE BELL! WE'D BETTER GET TO CLASS!!
WILL WE MAKE IT!? I CAN'T BE LATE SO EARLY IN THE SCHOOL YEAR...
GO ON AHEAD.
HUH? BUT—
I'VE ALWAYS GOT AN EASY EXCUSE, UNLIKE YOU.
UUNH... OKAY, IF YOU INSIST! SORRY!!
I'M MORE WORRIED ABOUT YOU...
....

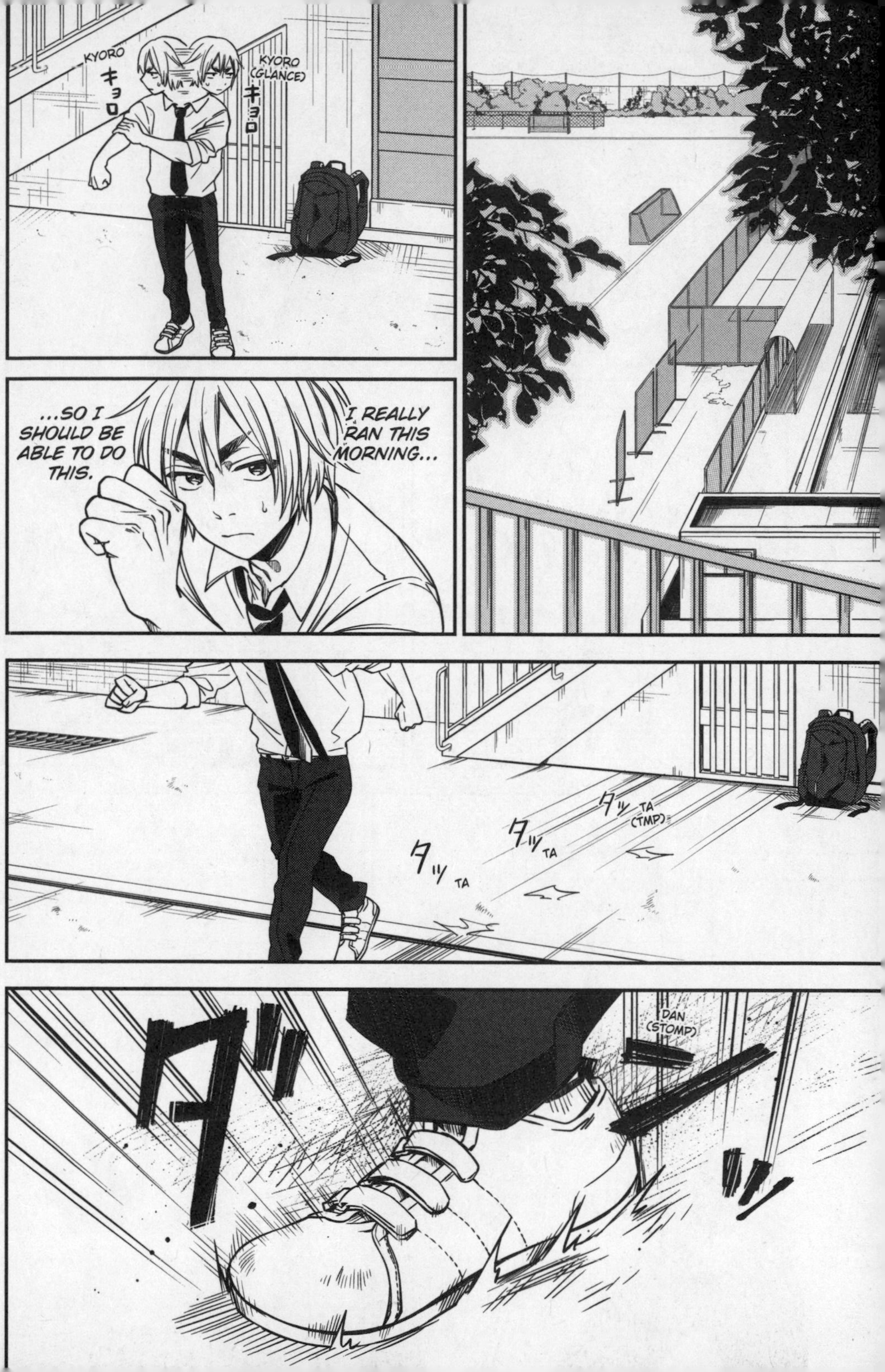
キョロ
KYORO (GLANCE)
キョロ
KYORO
I REALLY RAN THIS MORNING...
...SO I SHOULD BE ABLE TO DO THIS.
タッ
TA (TMP)
タッ
TA
タッ
TA
DAN (STOMP)
ダッ

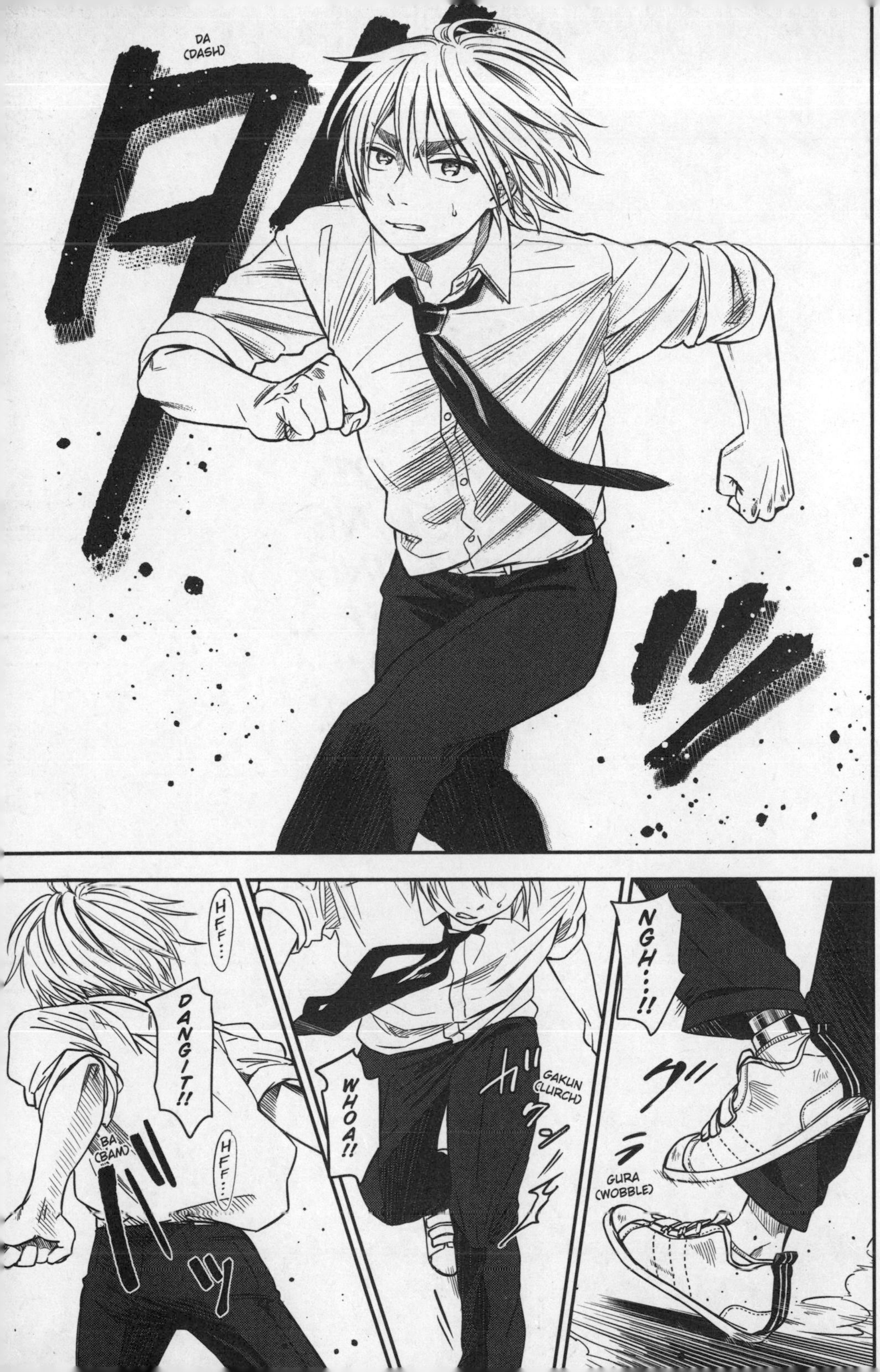
DA (DASH)
NGH...!!
GURA (WOBBLE)
GAKUN (LURCH)
WHOA!!
HFF...
DANGIT!!
HFF...
BA (BAM)

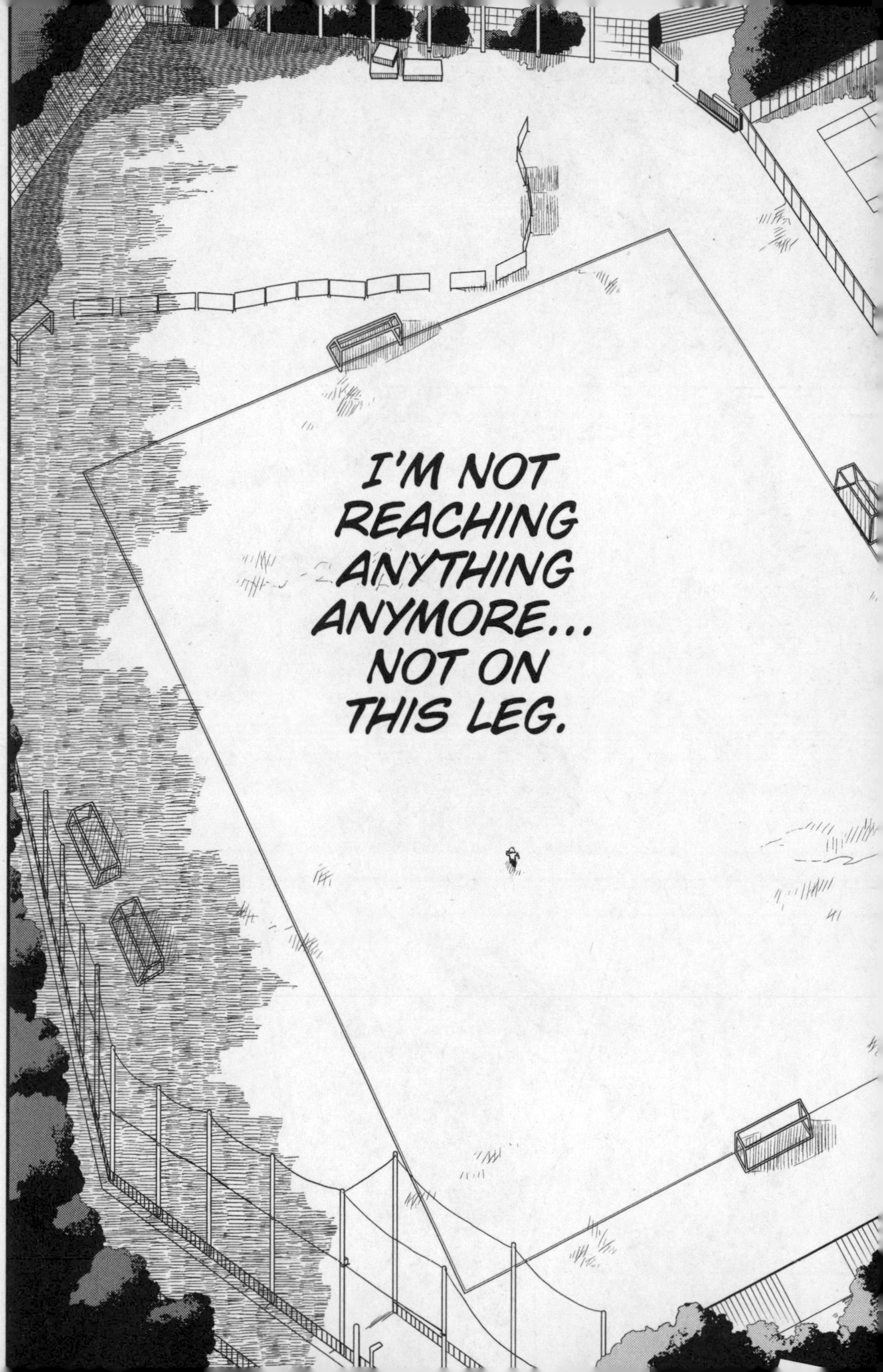
I'M NOT REACHING ANYTHING ANYMORE... NOT ON THIS LEG.

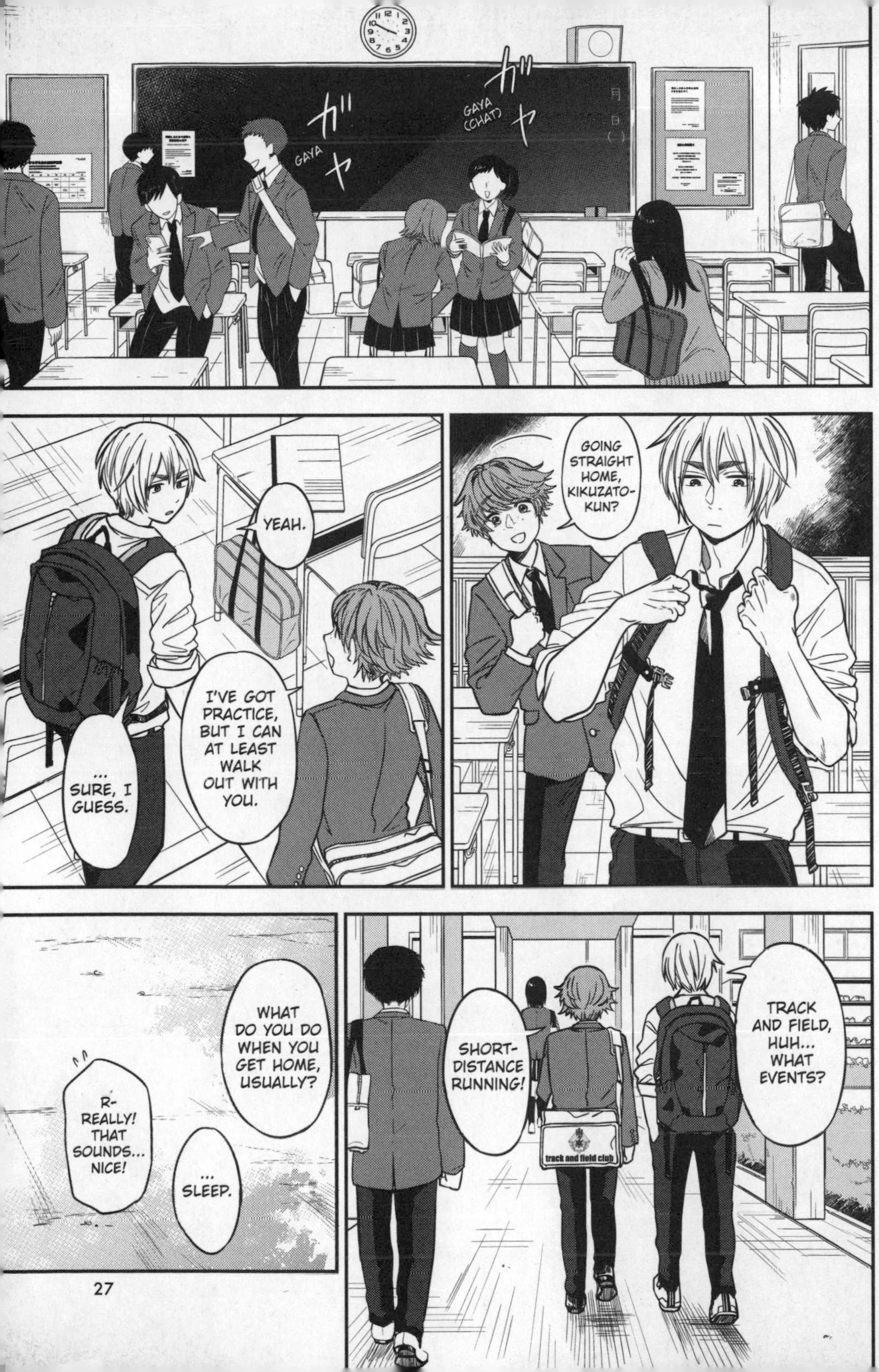
ガヤ
GAYA (CHAT)
ガヤ
GAYA
GOING STRAIGHT HOME, KIKUZATO-KUN?
YEAH.
I'VE GOT PRACTICE, BUT I CAN AT LEAST WALK OUT WITH YOU.
... SURE, I GUESS.
TRACK AND FIELD, HUH... WHAT EVENTS?
SHORT-DISTANCE RUNNING!
track and field club
WHAT DO YOU DO WHEN YOU GET HOME, USUALLY?
... SLEEP.
R-REALLY! THAT SOUNDS... NICE!

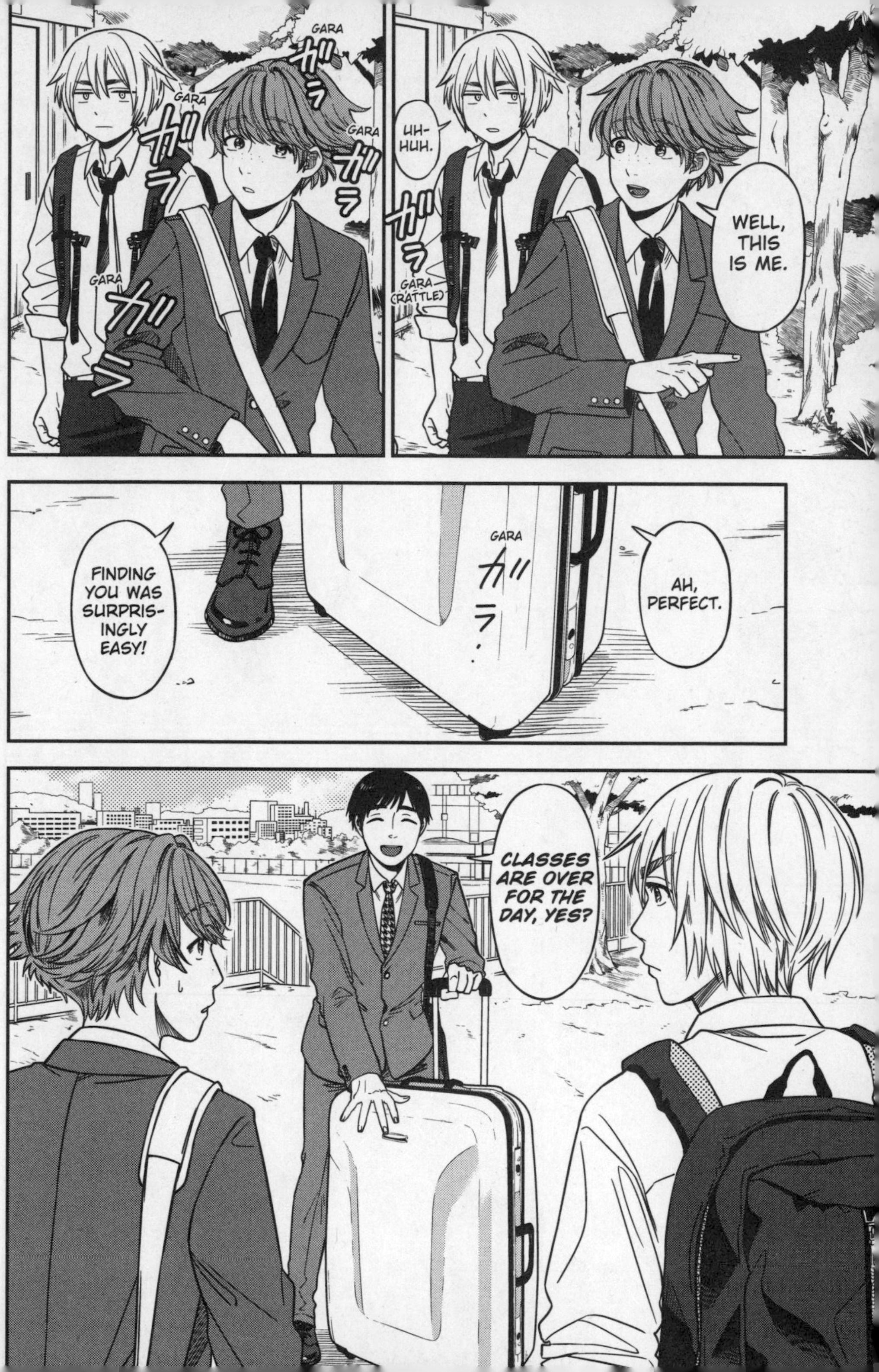
WELL, THIS IS ME.
UH-HUH.
GARA (RATTLE)
GARA
GARA
GARA
GARA
AH, PERFECT.
GARA
FINDING YOU WAS SURPRIS-INGLY EASY!
CLASSES ARE OVER FOR THE DAY, YES?

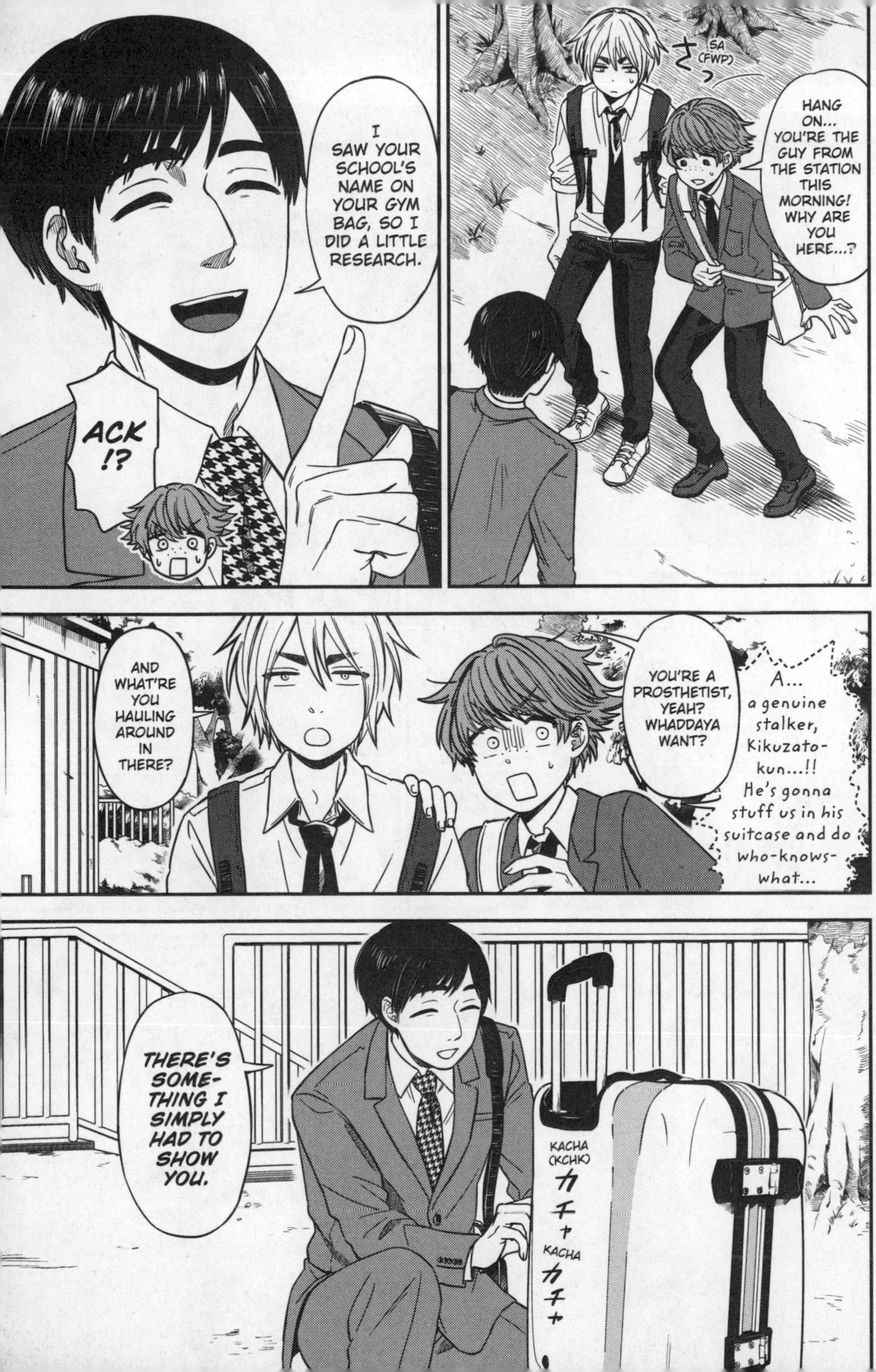
SA (FWP)
さっ
HANG ON... YOU'RE THE GUY FROM THE STATION THIS MORNING! WHY ARE YOU HERE...?
I SAW YOUR SCHOOL'S NAME ON YOUR GYM BAG, SO I DID A LITTLE RESEARCH.
ACK!?
A... a genuine stalker, Kikuzato-kun...!! He's gonna stuff us in his suitcase and do who-knows-what...
YOU'RE A PROSTHETIST, YEAH? WHADDAYA WANT?
AND WHAT'RE YOU HAULING AROUND IN THERE?
THERE'S SOME-THING I SIMPLY HAD TO SHOW YOU.
KACHA (KCHK)
カチャ
KACHA
カチャ

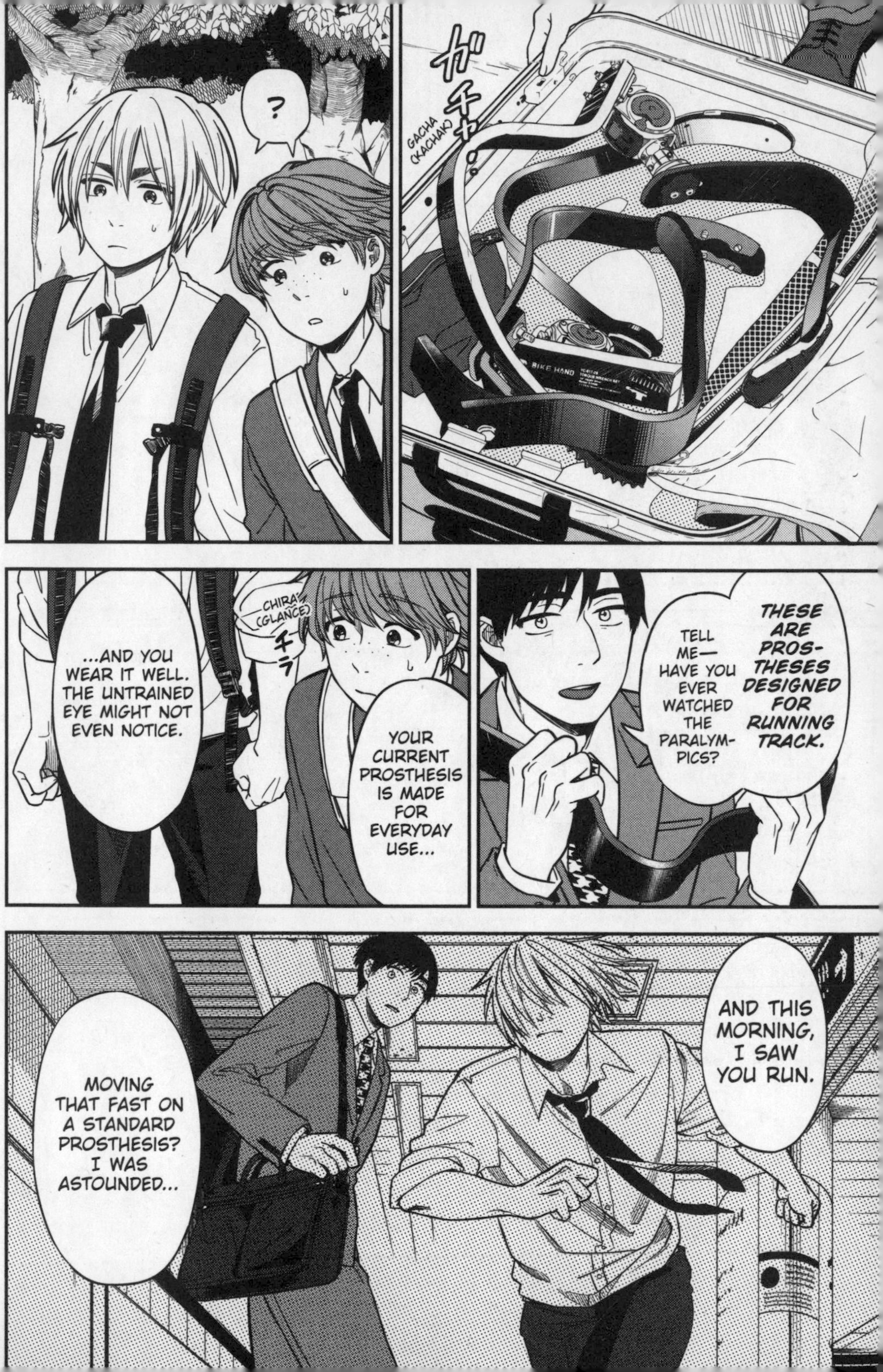
ガチャ
GACHA (KACHAK)
BIKE HAND
?
THESE ARE PROS-THESES DESIGNED FOR RUNNING TRACK.
TELL ME—HAVE YOU EVER WATCHED THE PARALYM-PICS?
チラ
CHIRA (GLANCE)
YOUR CURRENT PROSTHESIS IS MADE FOR EVERYDAY USE...
...AND YOU WEAR IT WELL. THE UNTRAINED EYE MIGHT NOT EVEN NOTICE.
AND THIS MORNING, I SAW YOU RUN.
MOVING THAT FAST ON A STANDARD PROSTHESIS? I WAS ASTOUNDED...

I'D LIKE TO HELP YOU RUN FASTER.

SINCE I'VE COME ALL THIS WAY, WON'T YOU PLEASE GIVE IT A TEST RUN?

ZUI
(ZWIP)
ずいっ

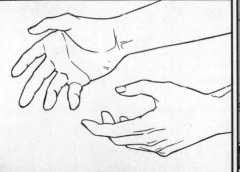

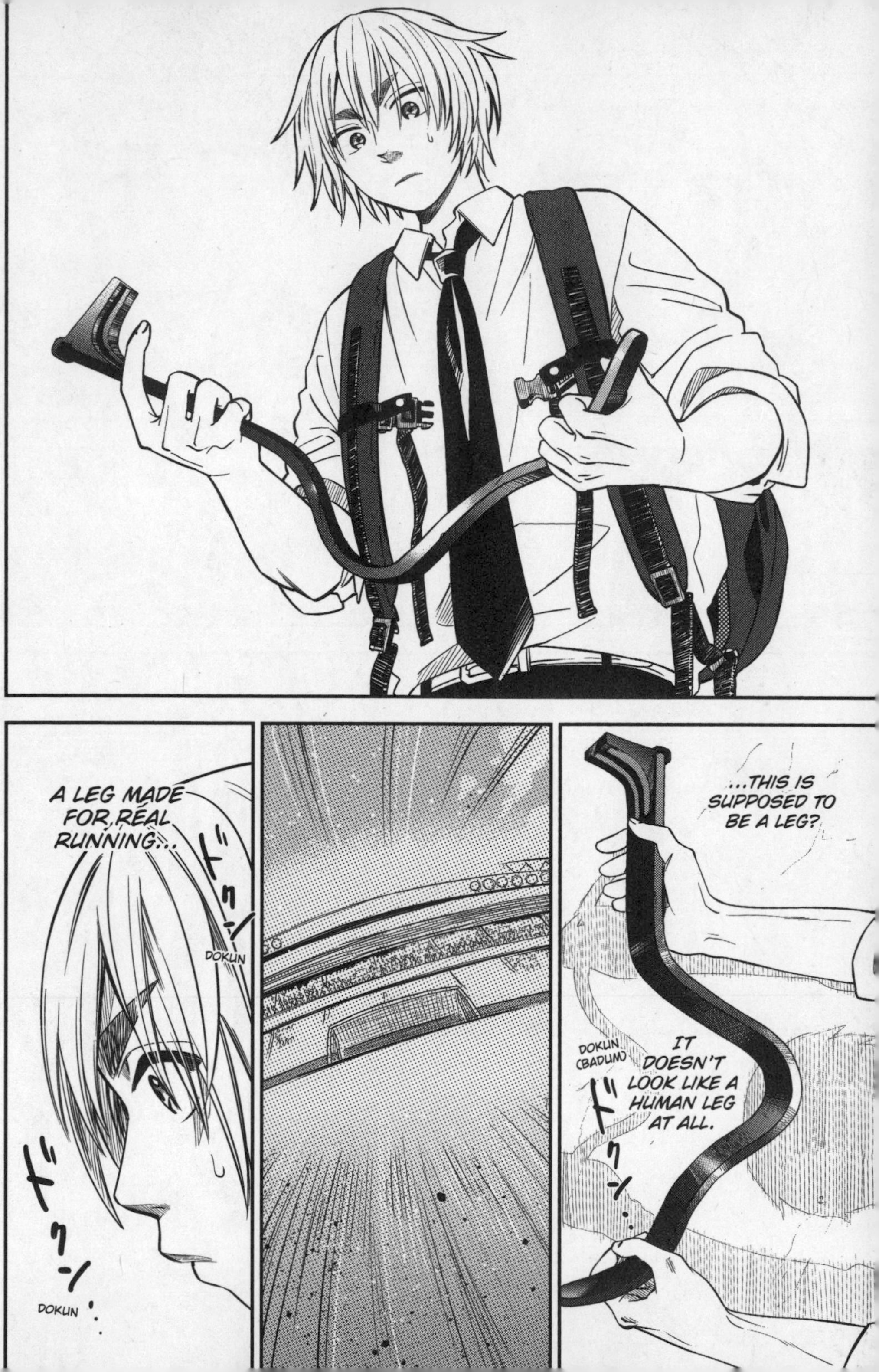
...THIS IS SUPPOSED TO BE A LEG?
DOKUN (BADUM)
IT DOESN'T LOOK LIKE A HUMAN LEG AT ALL.
A LEG MADE FOR REAL RUNNING...
DOKUN
DOKUN

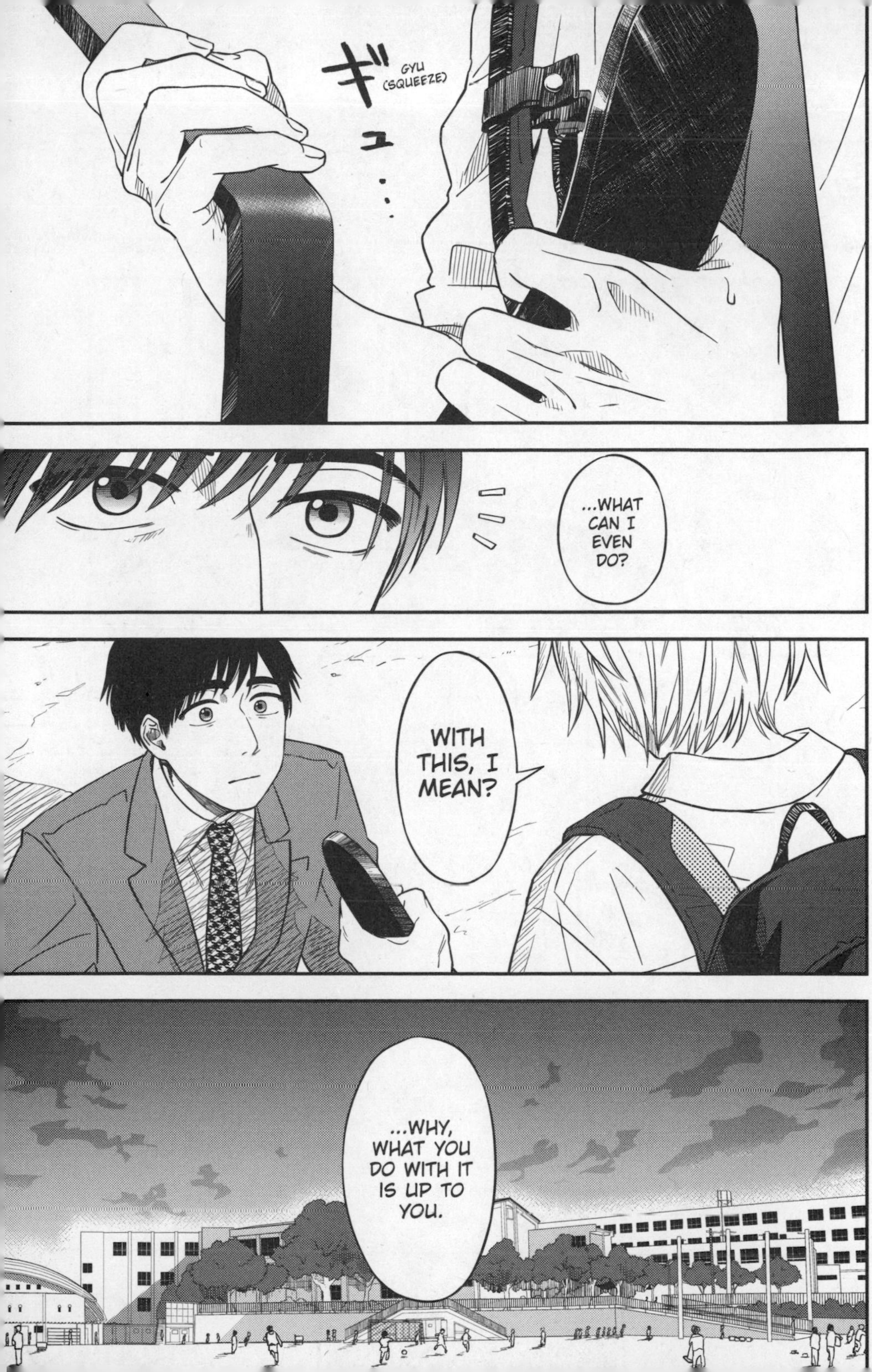
ギュ
GYU (SQUEEZE)
...WHAT CAN I EVEN DO?
WITH THIS, I MEAN?
...WHY, WHAT YOU DO WITH IT IS UP TO YOU.

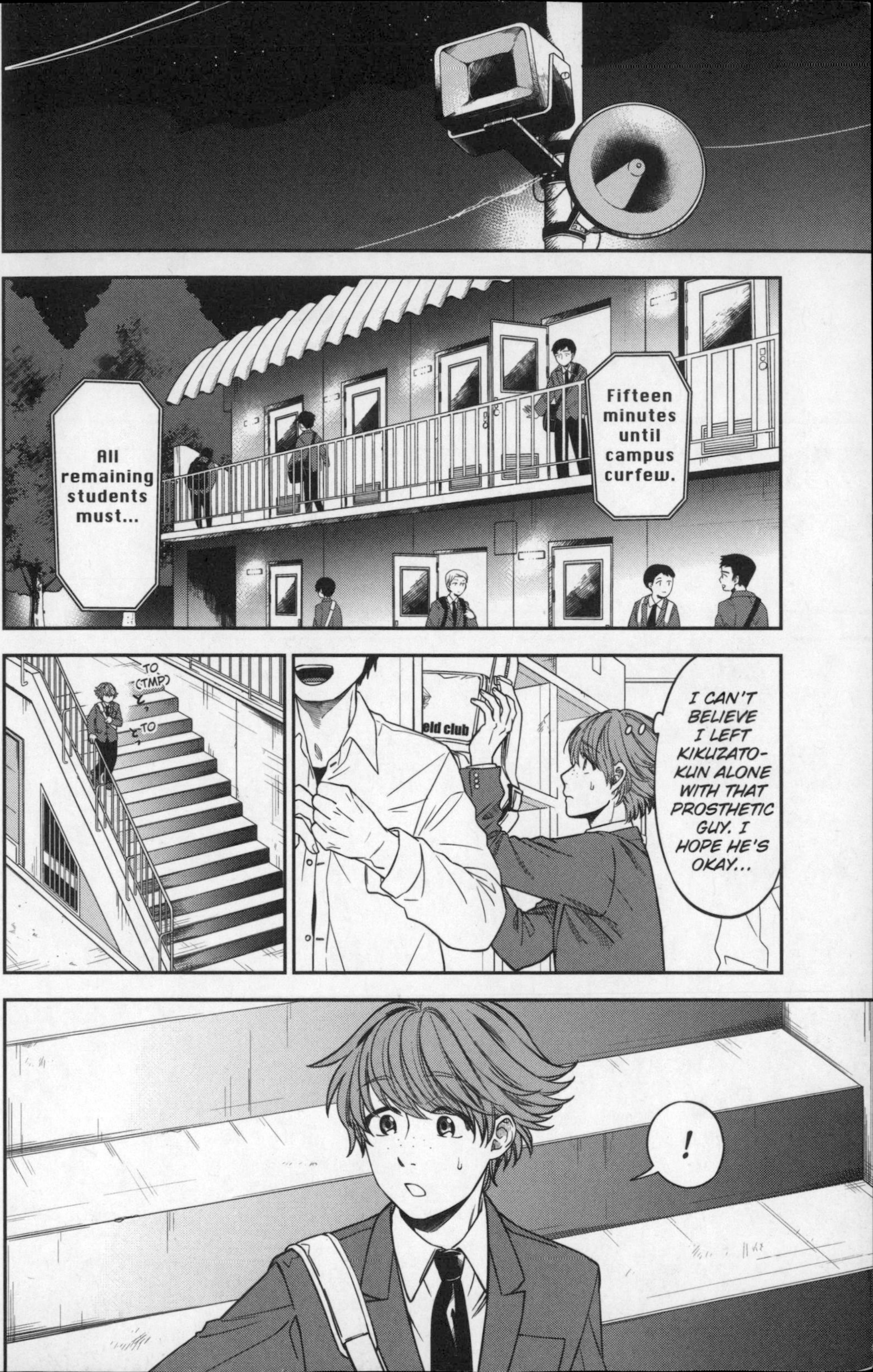
Fifteen minutes until campus curfew.
All remaining students must...
I CAN'T BELIEVE I LEFT KIKUZATO-KUN ALONE WITH THAT PROSTHETIC GUY. I HOPE HE'S OKAY...
eld club
TO
(TMP)
TO
!

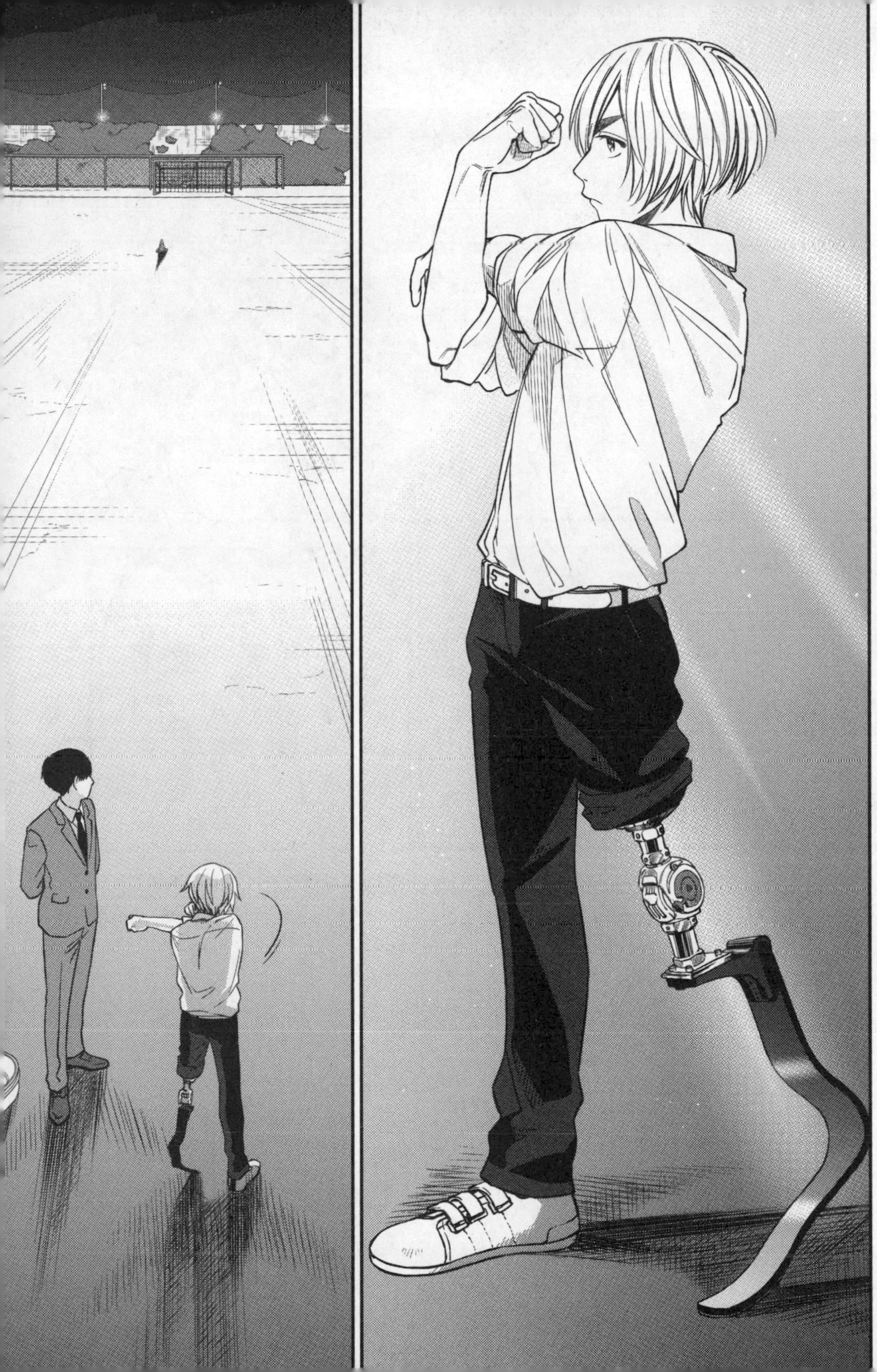

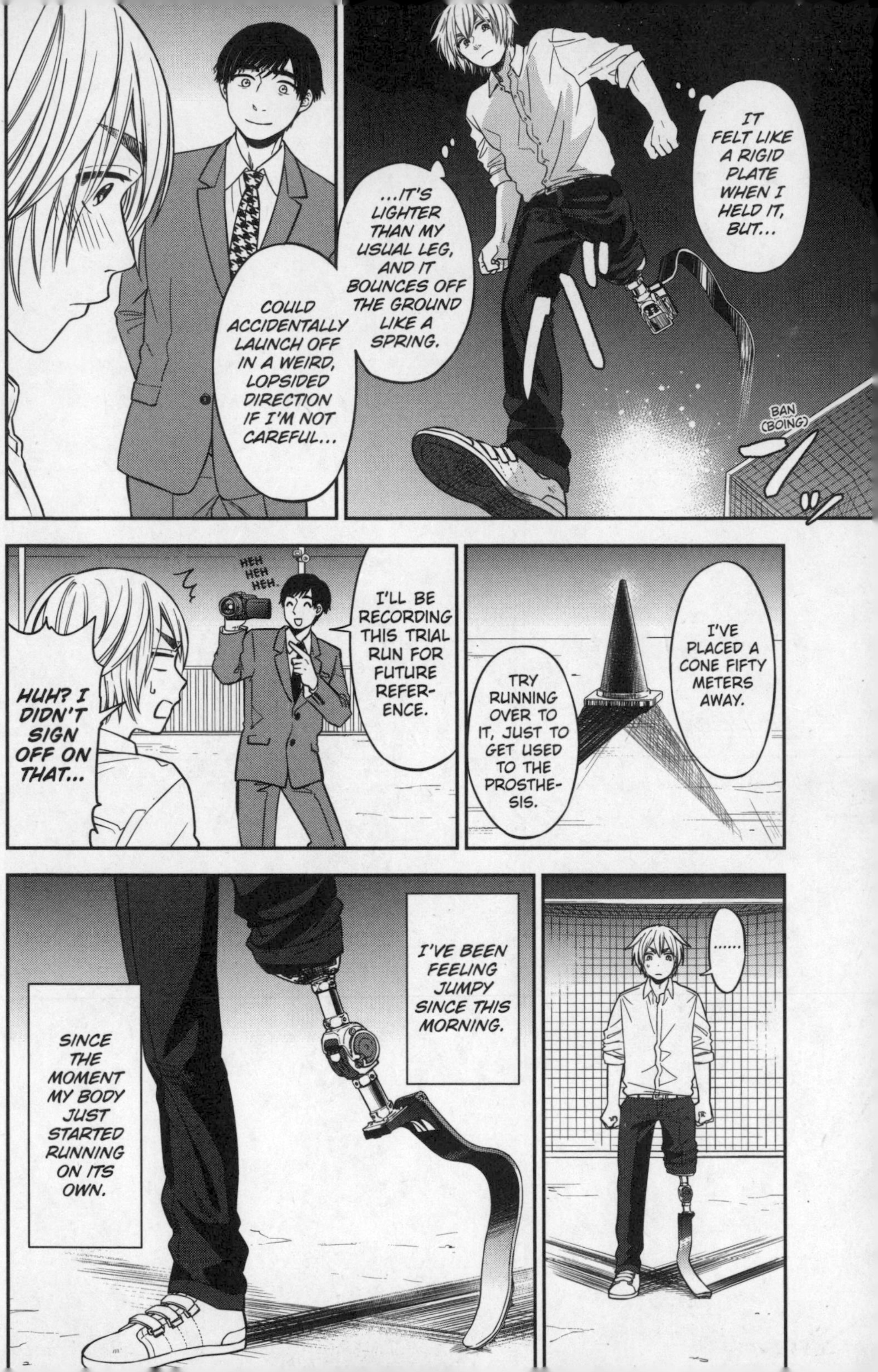
IT FELT LIKE A RIGID PLATE WHEN I HELD IT, BUT...
...IT'S LIGHTER THAN MY USUAL LEG, AND IT BOUNCES OFF THE GROUND LIKE A SPRING.
BAN (BOING)
COULD ACCIDENTALLY LAUNCH OFF IN A WEIRD, LOPSIDED DIRECTION IF I'M NOT CAREFUL...
I'VE PLACED A CONE FIFTY METERS AWAY.
TRY RUNNING OVER TO IT, JUST TO GET USED TO THE PROSTHE-SIS.
I'LL BE RECORDING THIS TRIAL RUN FOR FUTURE REFER-ENCE.
HEH HEH HEH.
HUH? I DIDN'T SIGN OFF ON THAT...
......
I'VE BEEN FEELING JUMPY SINCE THIS MORNING.
SINCE THE MOMENT MY BODY JUST STARTED RUNNING ON ITS OWN.

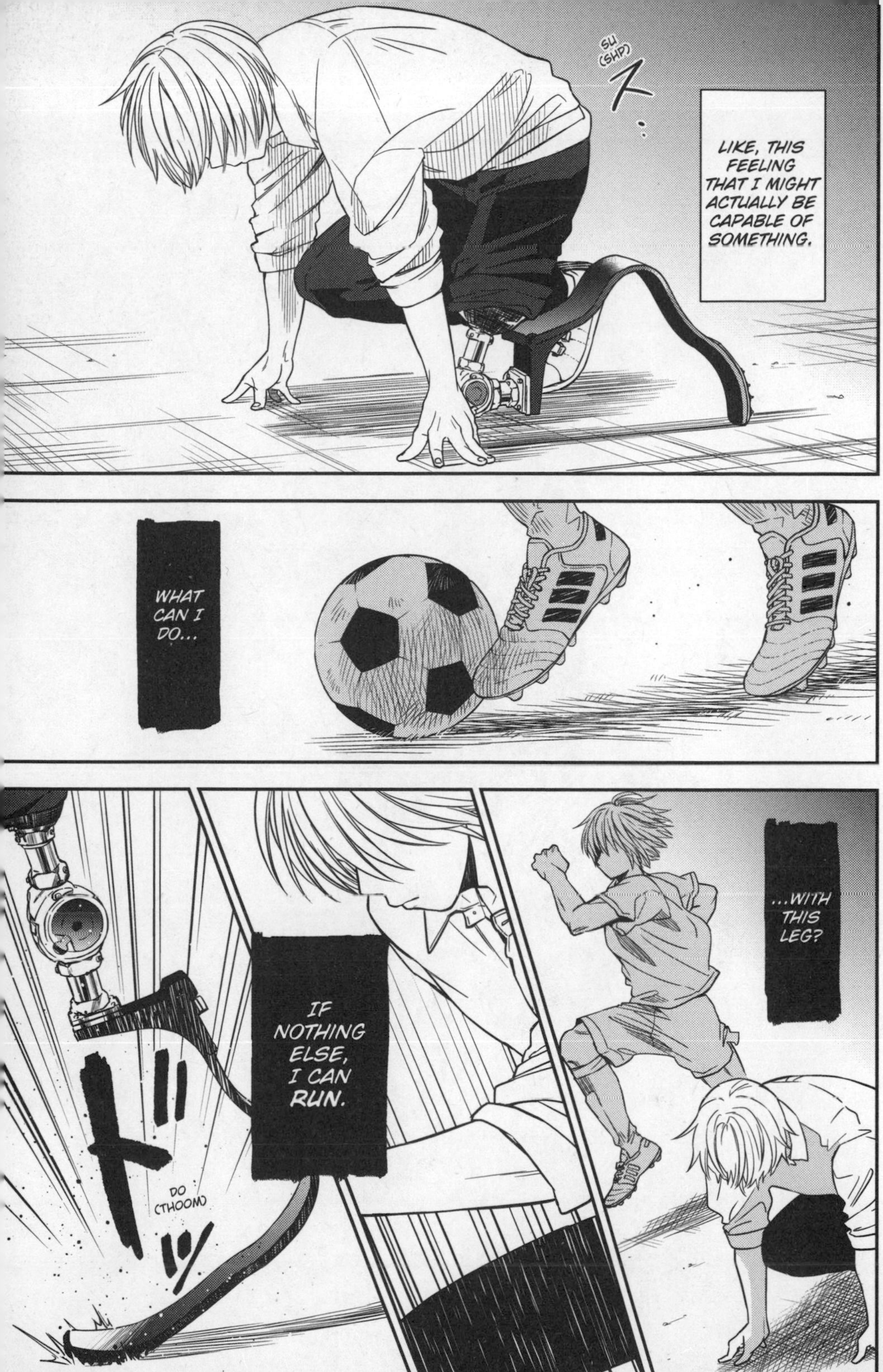
SU (SHP)
LIKE, THIS FEELING THAT I MIGHT ACTUALLY BE CAPABLE OF SOMETHING.
WHAT CAN I DO...
...WITH THIS LEG?
IF NOTHING ELSE, I CAN RUN.
DO (THOOM)

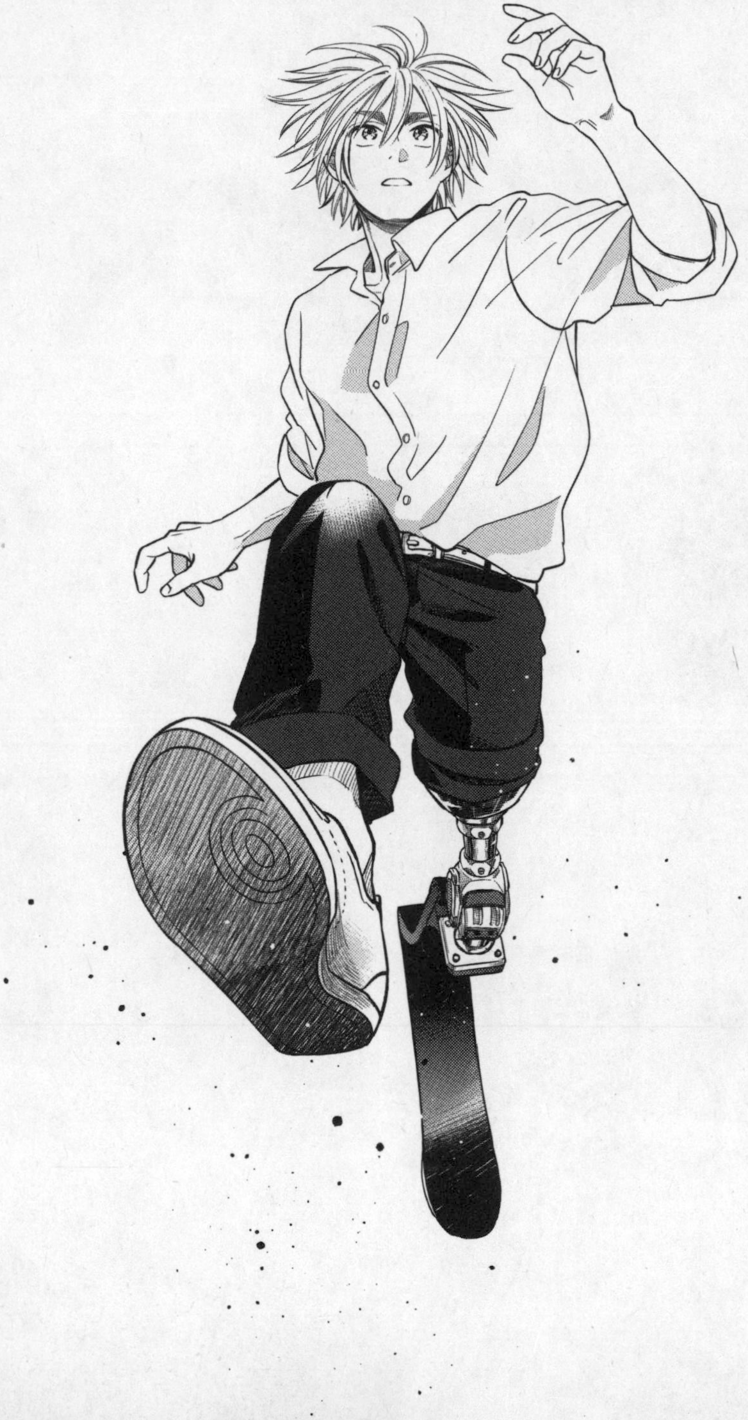

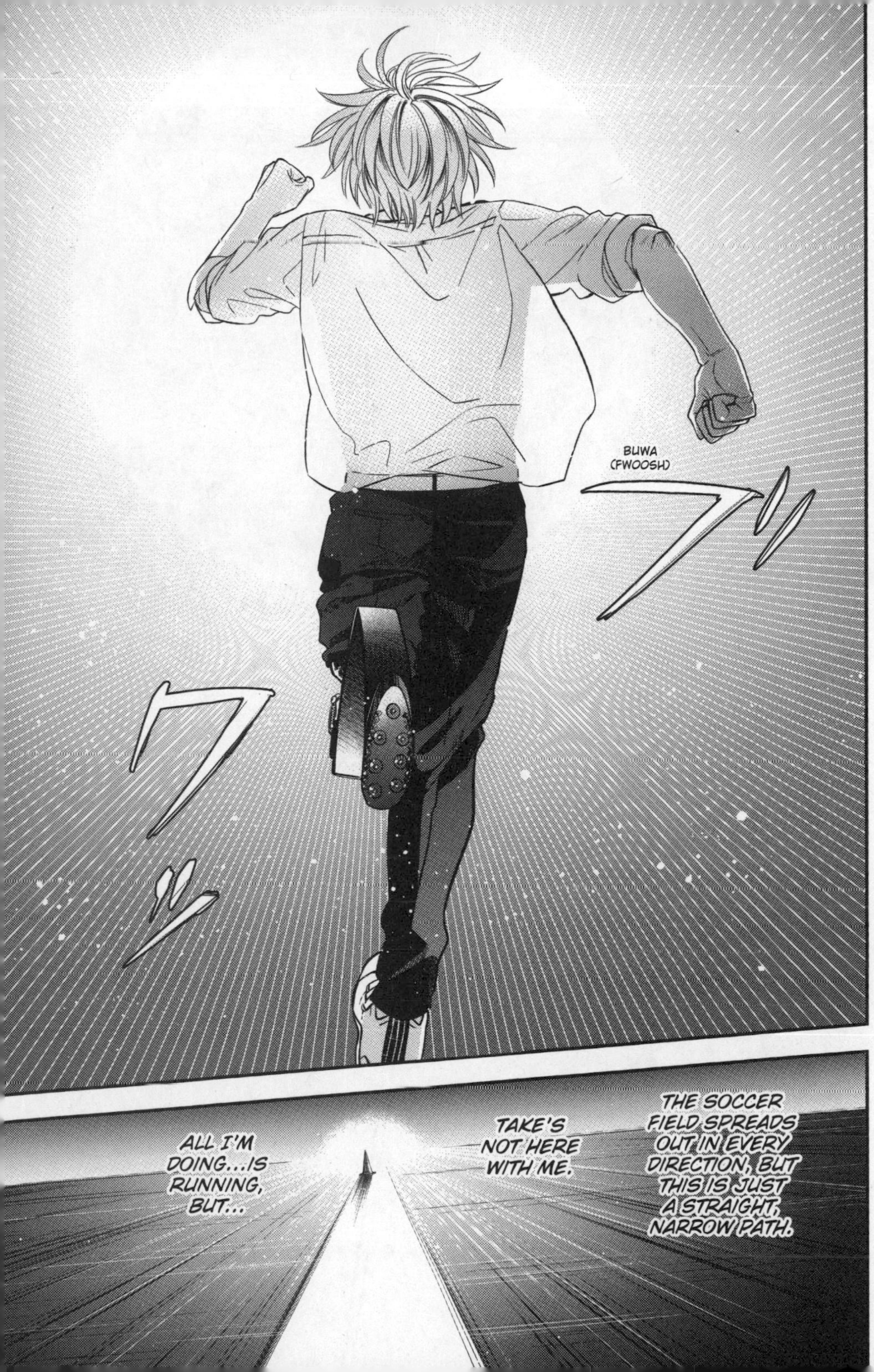
BUWA (FWOOSH)
THE SOCCER FIELD SPREADS OUT IN EVERY DIRECTION, BUT THIS IS JUST A STRAIGHT, NARROW PATH.
TAKE'S NOT HERE WITH ME.
ALL I'M DOING...IS RUNNING, BUT...

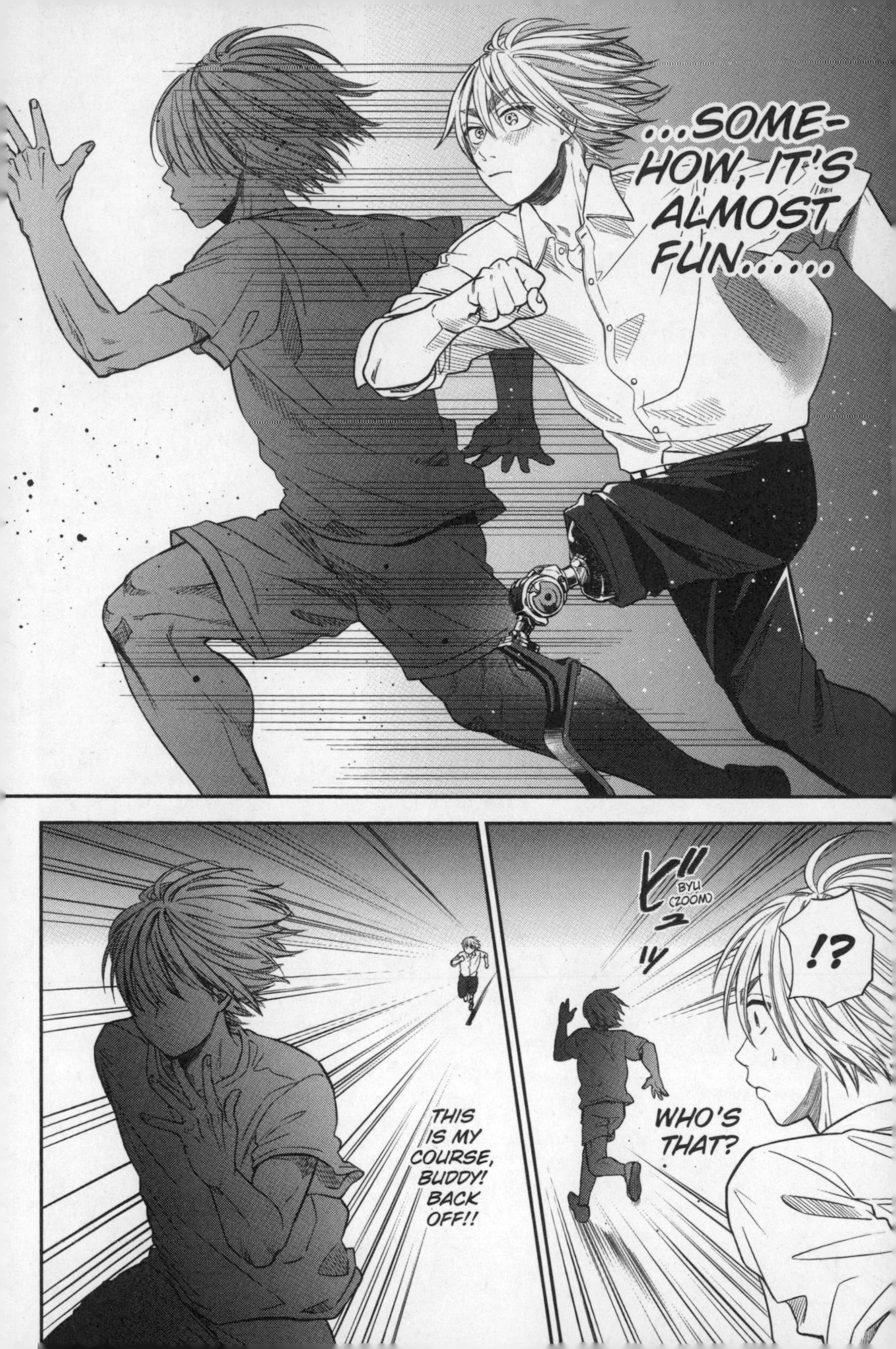
...SOME-HOW, IT'S ALMOST FUN......
!?
BYU (ZOOM)
WHO'S THAT?
THIS IS MY COURSE, BUDDY! BACK OFF!!

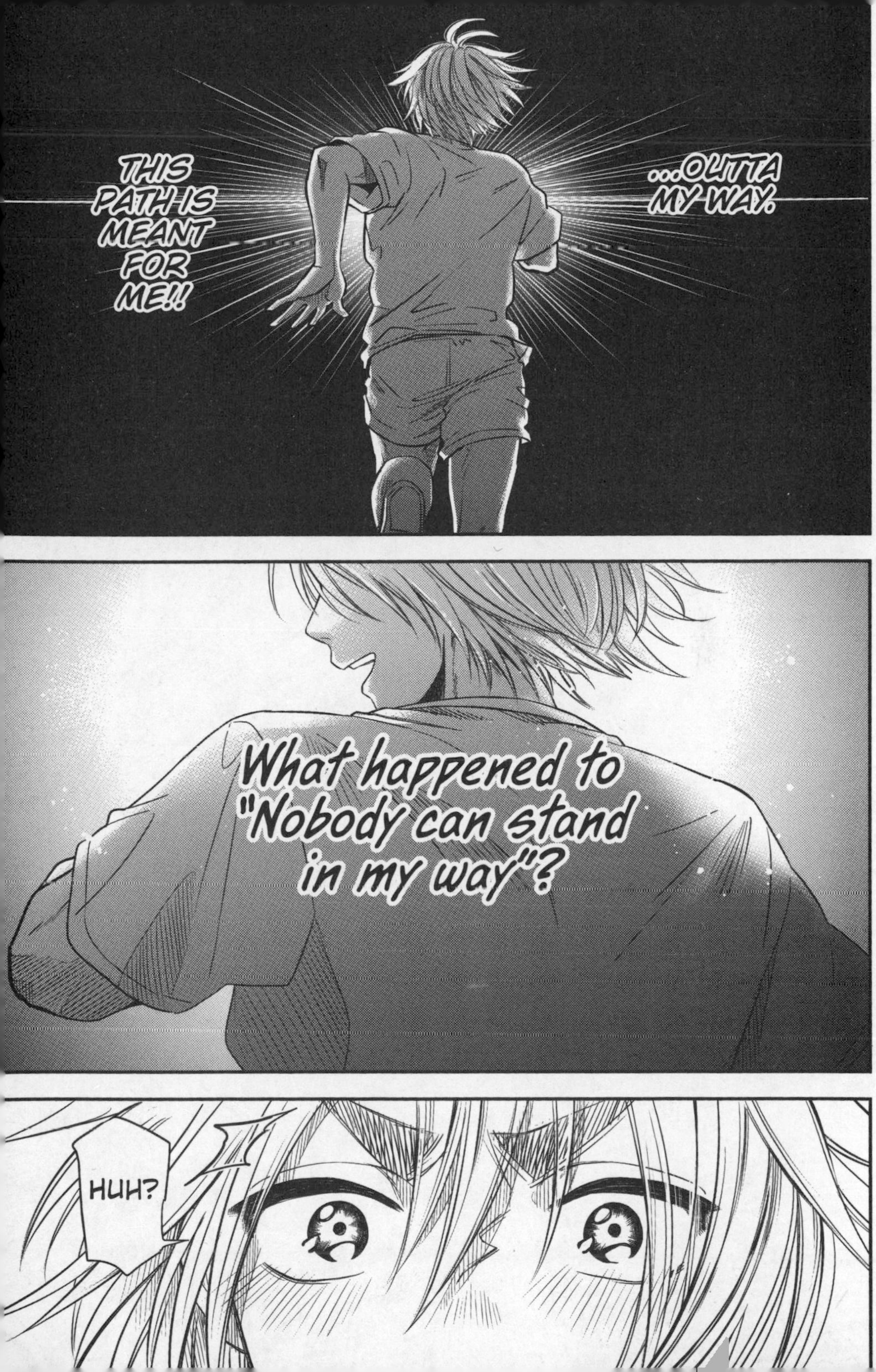
...OUTTA MY WAY.
THIS PATH IS MEANT FOR ME!!
What happened to "Nobody can stand in my way"?
HUH?

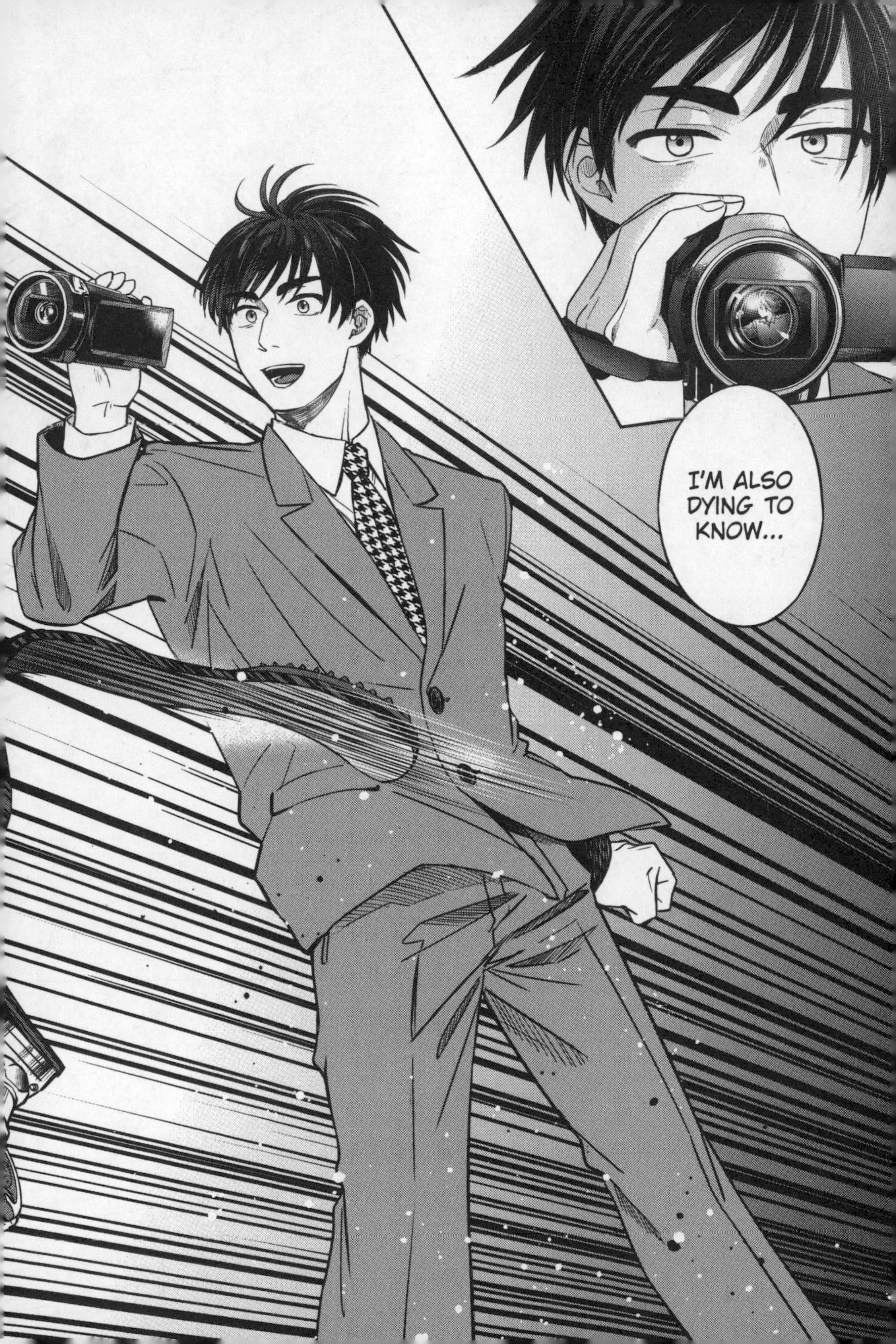
I'M ALSO DYING TO KNOW...

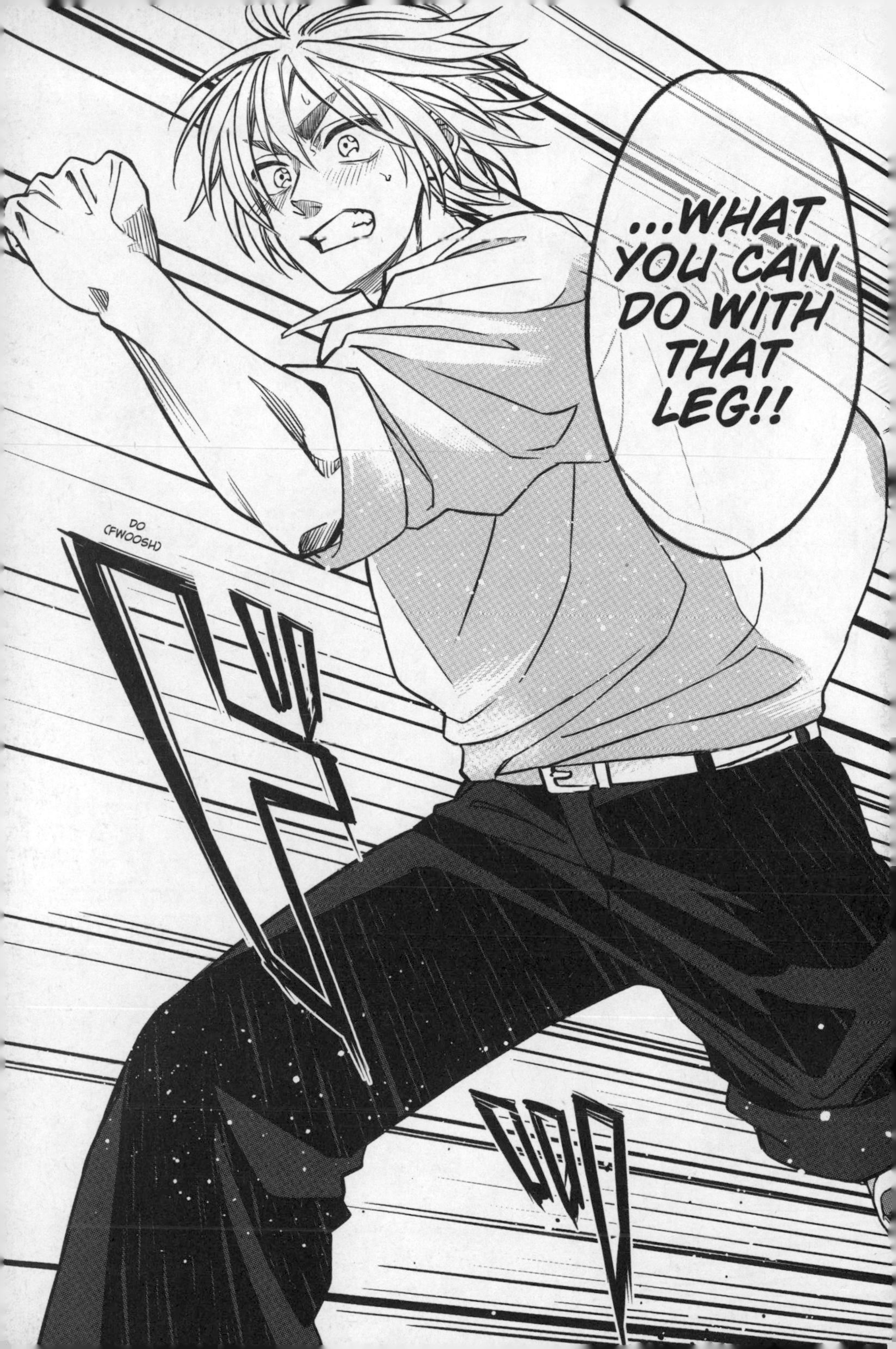
...WHAT YOU CAN DO WITH THAT LEG!!
DO (FWOOSH)

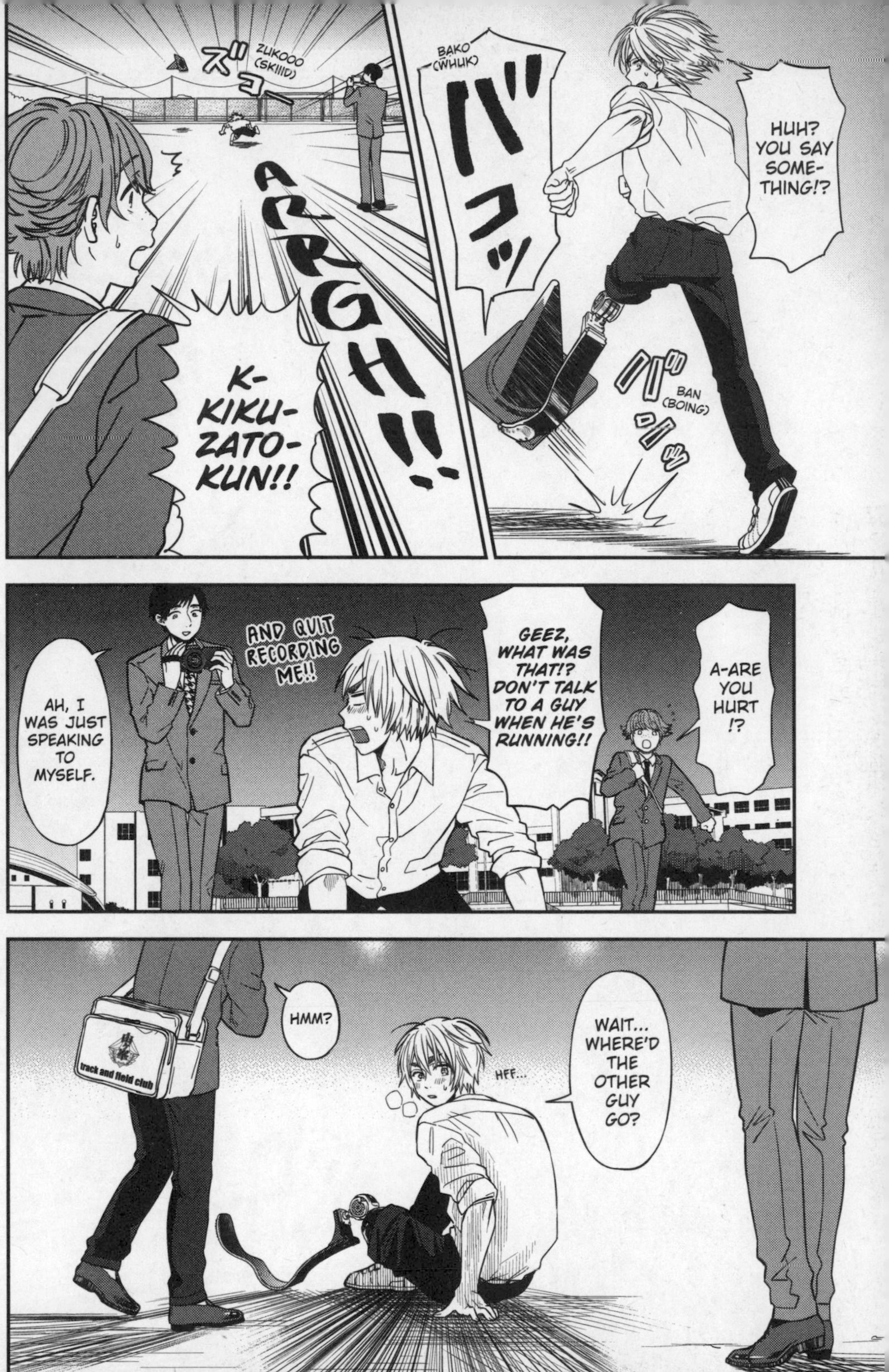

HUH? YOU SAY SOME-THING!?
BAKO (WHUK)
バコッ
BAN (BOING)
ZUKOOO (SKIIID)
ズコー
ARRGH!!
K-KIKU-ZATO-KUN!!
A-ARE YOU HURT!?
GEEZ, WHAT WAS THAT!? DON'T TALK TO A GUY WHEN HE'S RUNNING!!
AND QUIT RECORDING ME!!
AH, I WAS JUST SPEAKING TO MYSELF.
WAIT... WHERE'D THE OTHER GUY GO?
HFF...
HMM?
track and field club

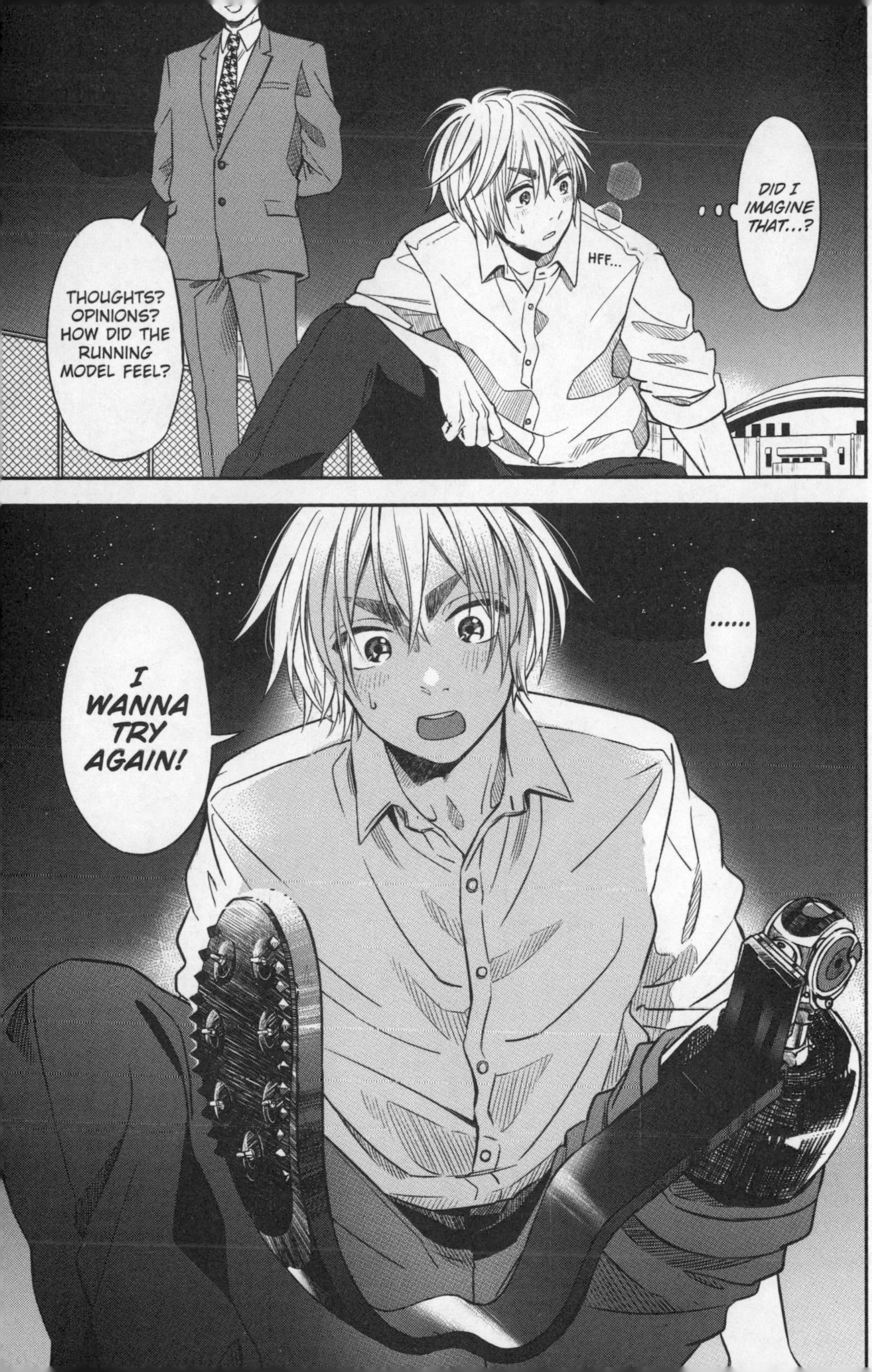
...DID I IMAGINE THAT...?
HFF...
THOUGHTS? OPINIONS? HOW DID THE RUNNING MODEL FEEL?
......
I WANNA TRY AGAIN!

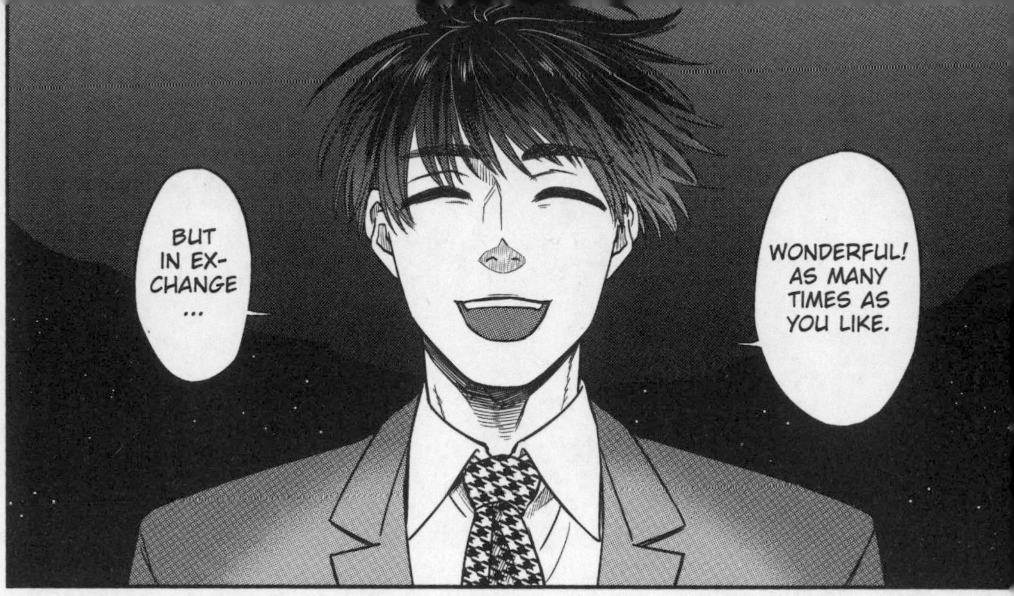
WONDERFUL! AS MANY TIMES AS YOU LIKE.
BUT IN EX-CHANGE ...
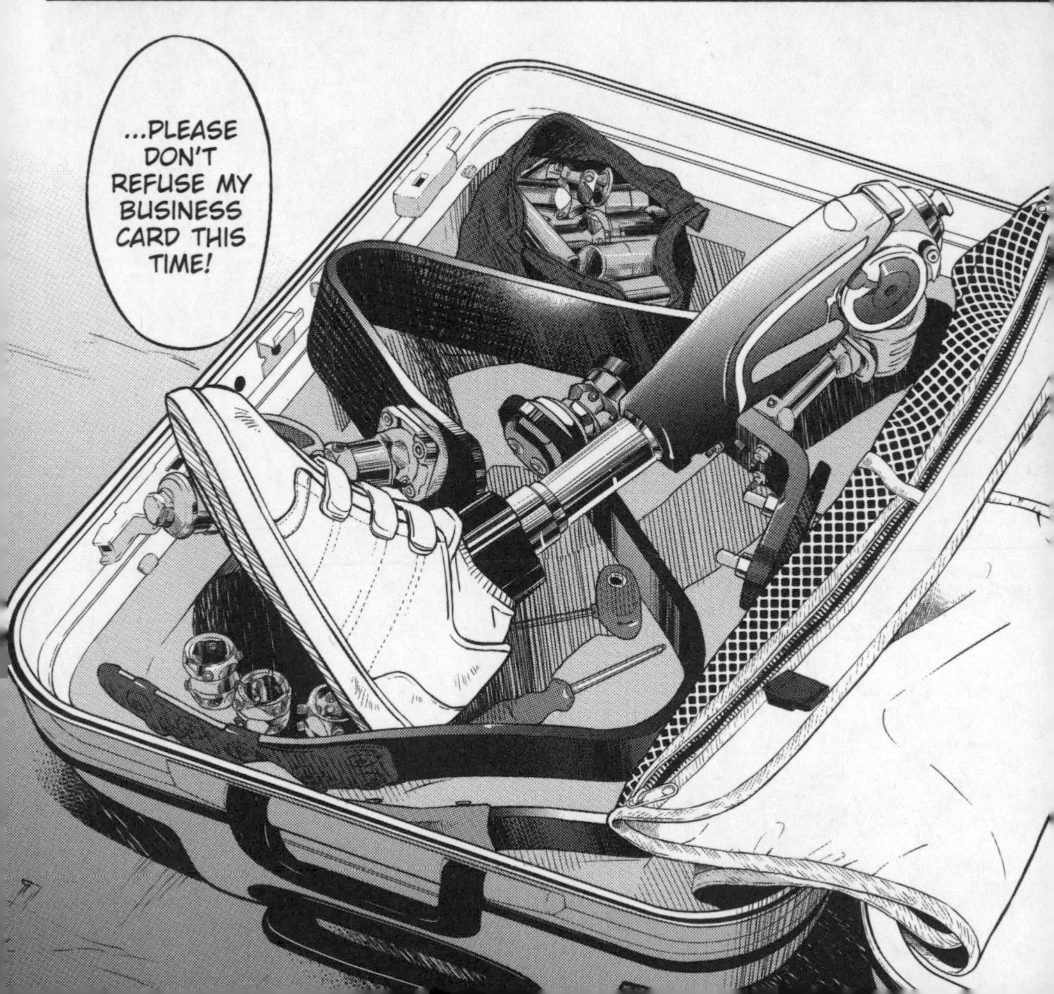
...PLEASE DON'T REFUSE MY BUSINESS CARD THIS TIME!

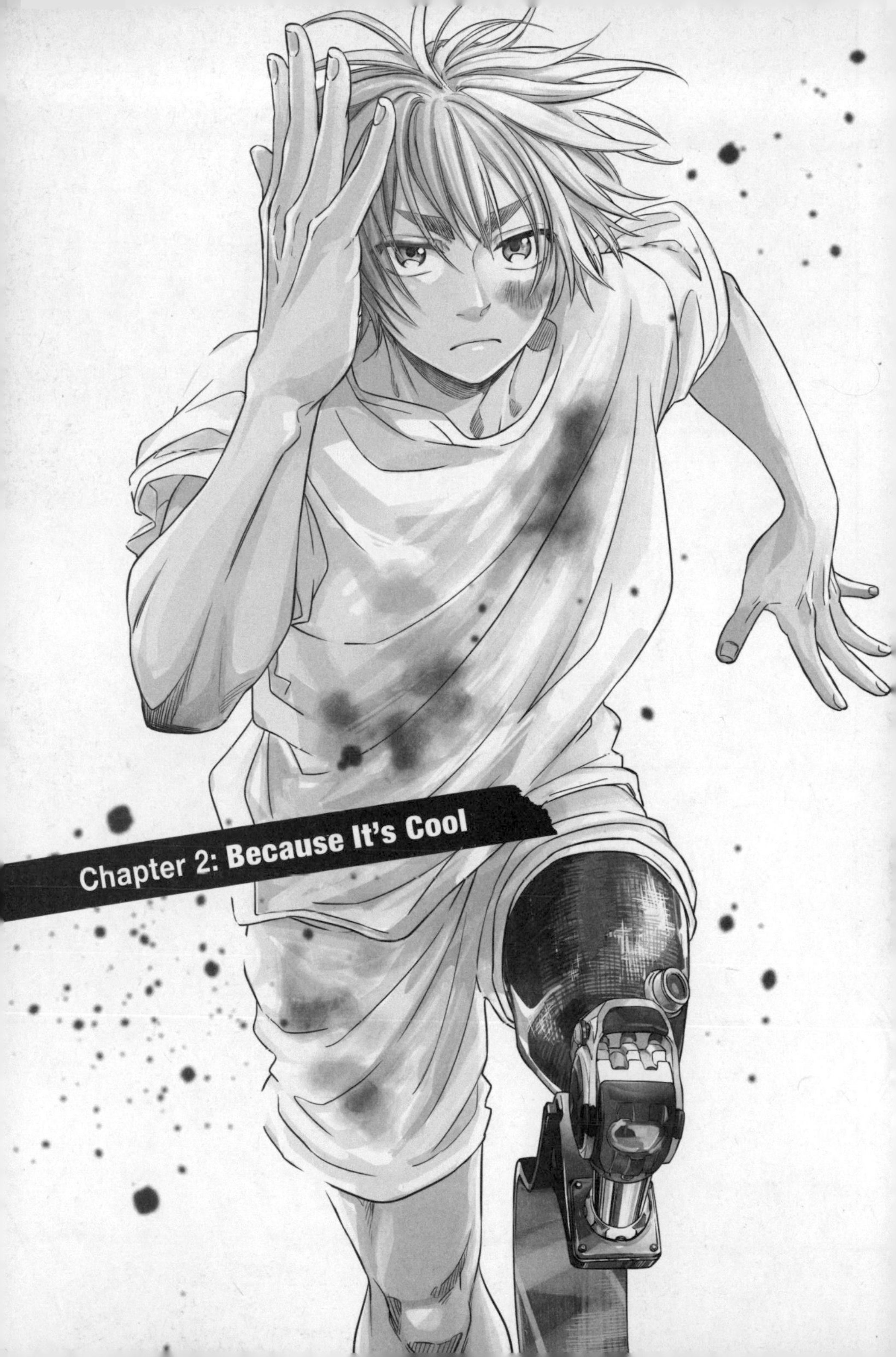
Chapter 2: Because It's Cool

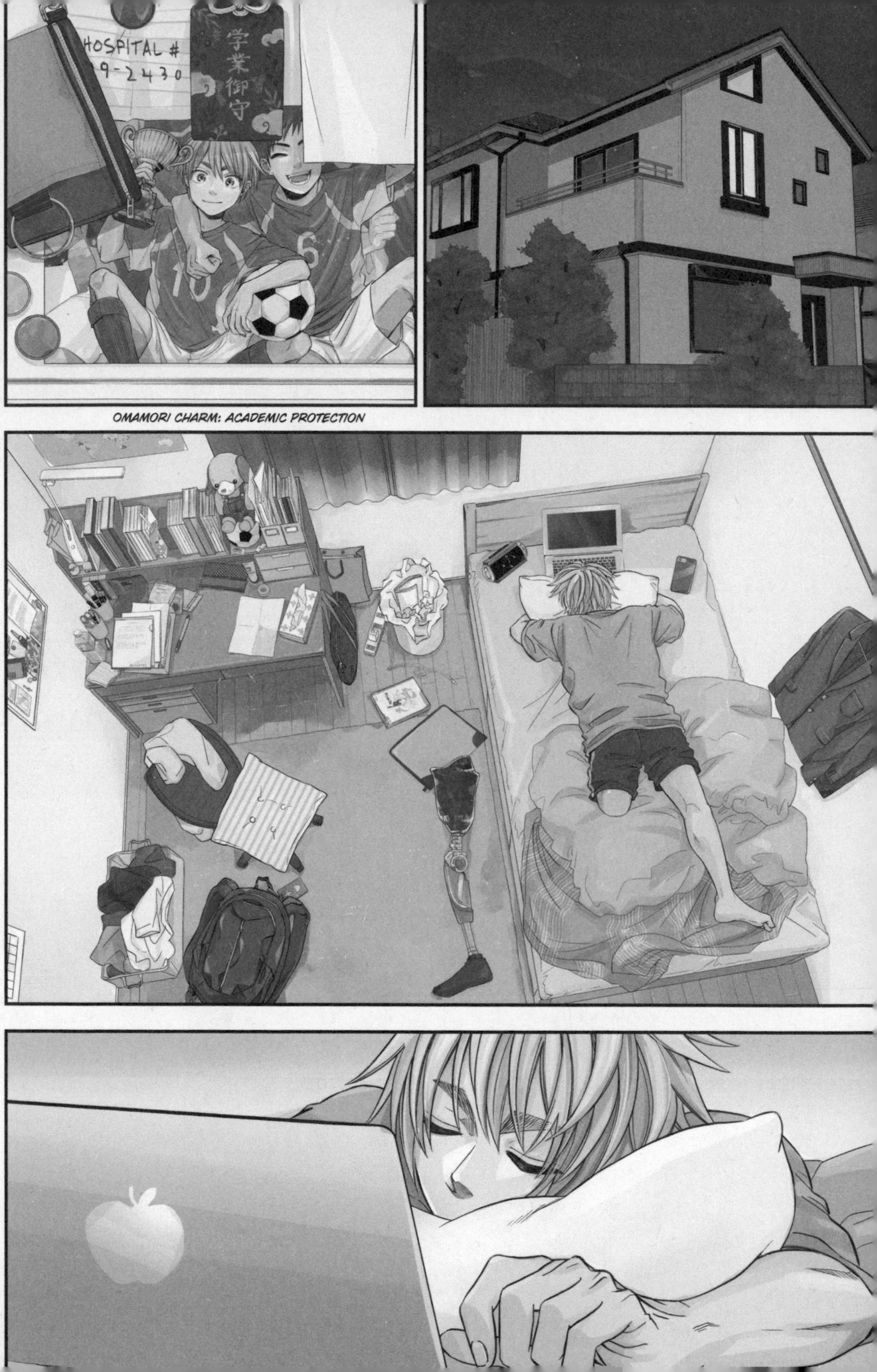
HOSPITAL #
9-2430
学業御守
OMAMORI CHARM: ACADEMIC PROTECTION

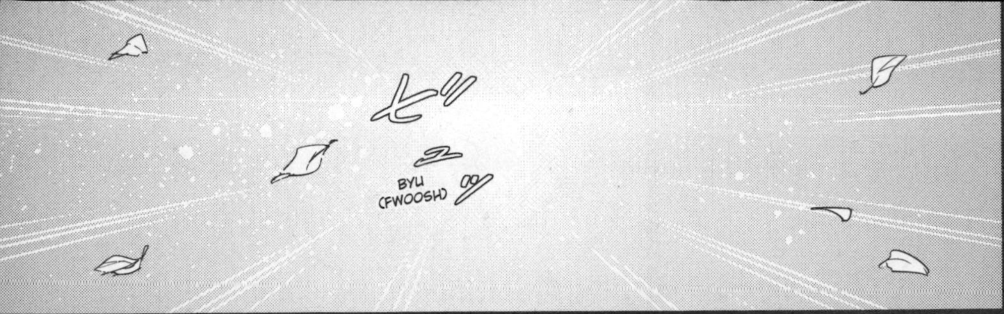
ヒュッ
BYU
(FWOOSH)
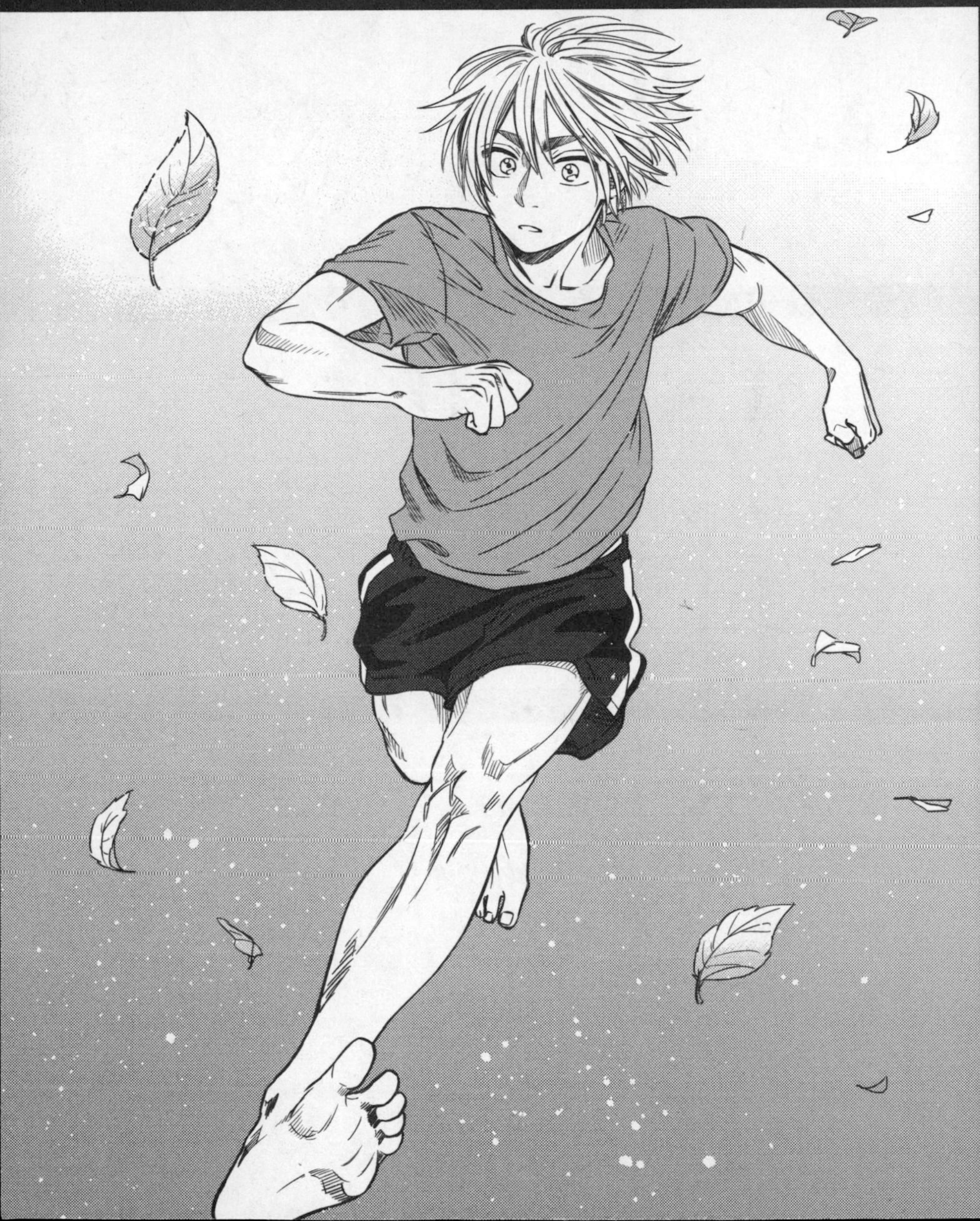

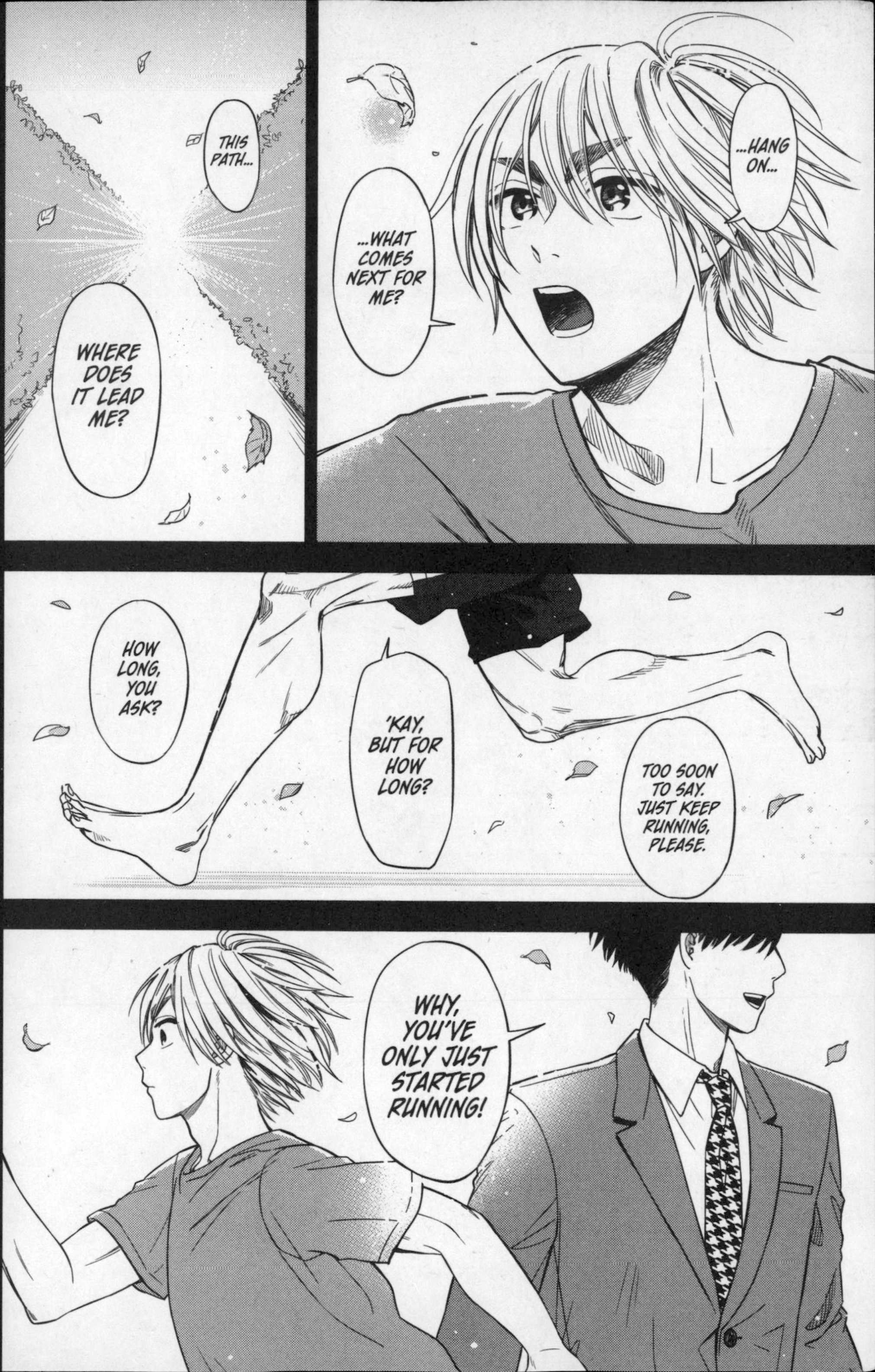
...HANG ON...
...WHAT COMES NEXT FOR ME?
THIS PATH...
WHERE DOES IT LEAD ME?
'KAY, BUT FOR HOW LONG?
HOW LONG, YOU ASK?
TOO SOON TO SAY. JUST KEEP RUNNING, PLEASE.
WHY, YOU'VE ONLY JUST STARTED RUNNING!

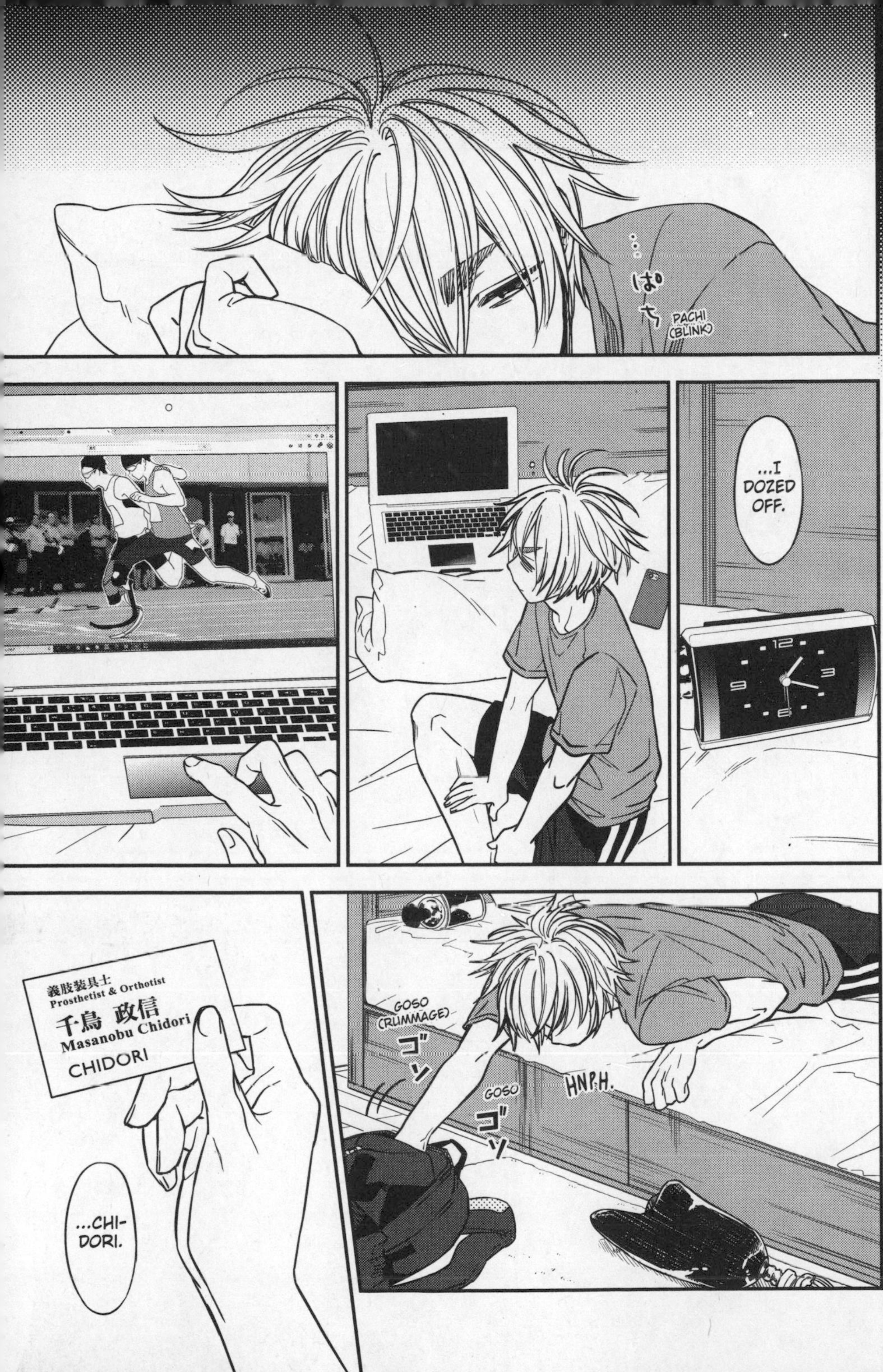
...
ぱち
PACHI (BLINK)
...I DOZED OFF.
GOSO (RUMMAGE)
ゴソ
GOSO
ゴソ
HNPH.
義肢装具士
Prosthetist & Orthotist
千鳥 政信
Masanobu Chidori
CHIDORI
...CHI-DORI.

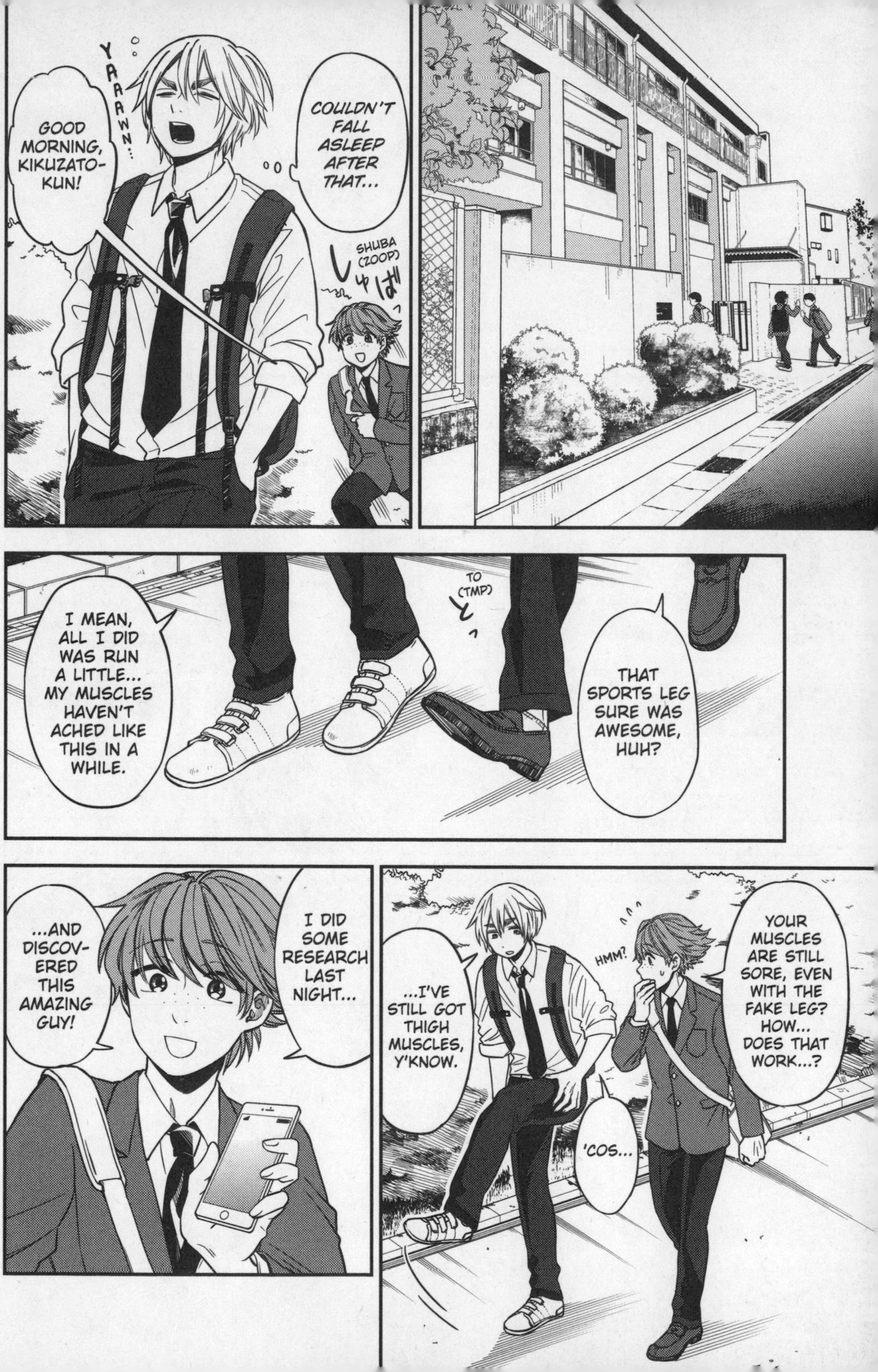
COULDN'T FALL ASLEEP AFTER THAT...
YAAAWN...
GOOD MORNING, KIKUZATO-KUN!
SHUBA (ZOOP)
THAT SPORTS LEG SURE WAS AWESOME, HUH?
TO (TMP)
I MEAN, ALL I DID WAS RUN A LITTLE... MY MUSCLES HAVEN'T ACHED LIKE THIS IN A WHILE.
YOUR MUSCLES ARE STILL SORE, EVEN WITH THE FAKE LEG? HOW... DOES THAT WORK...?
HMM?
'COS...
...I'VE STILL GOT THIGH MUSCLES, Y'KNOW.
I DID SOME RESEARCH LAST NIGHT...
...AND DISCOVER-ERED THIS AMAZING GUY!

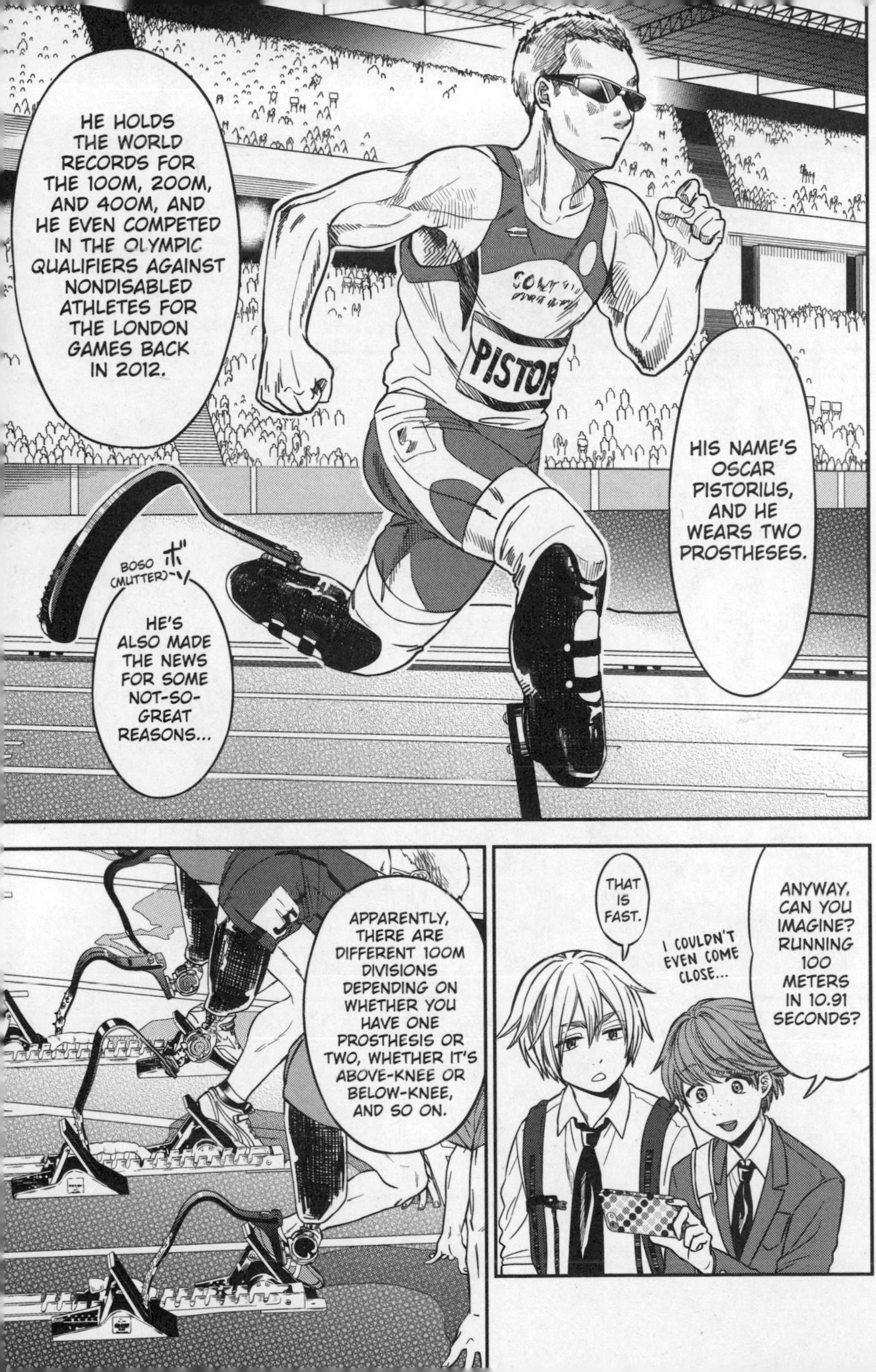
HIS NAME'S OSCAR PISTORIUS, AND HE WEARS TWO PROSTHESES.
HE HOLDS THE WORLD RECORDS FOR THE 100M, 200M, AND 400M, AND HE EVEN COMPETED IN THE OLYMPIC QUALIFIERS AGAINST NONDISABLED ATHLETES FOR THE LONDON GAMES BACK IN 2012.
PISTOR
ボ
BOSO (MUTTER)
HE'S ALSO MADE THE NEWS FOR SOME NOT-SO-GREAT REASONS...
ANYWAY, CAN YOU IMAGINE? RUNNING 100 METERS IN 10.91 SECONDS?
THAT IS FAST.
I COULDN'T EVEN COME CLOSE...
APPARENTLY, THERE ARE DIFFERENT 100M DIVISIONS DEPENDING ON WHETHER YOU HAVE ONE PROSTHESIS OR TWO, WHETHER IT'S ABOVE-KNEE OR BELOW-KNEE, AND SO ON.

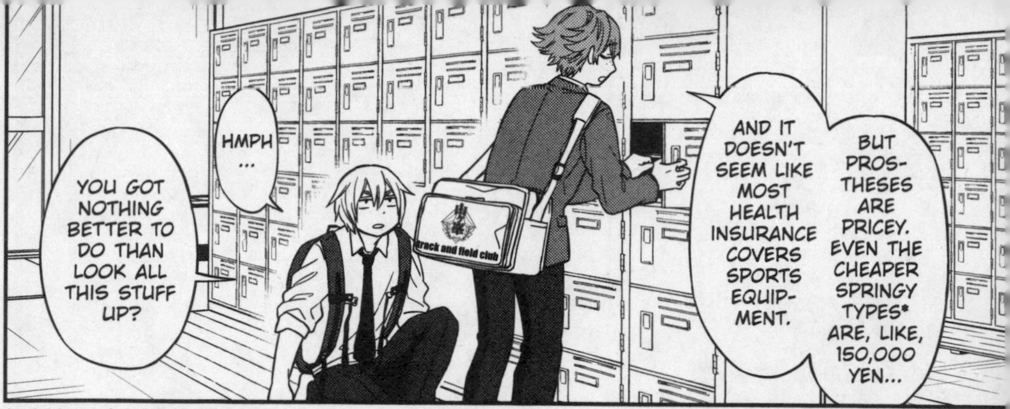
BUT PROSTHESES ARE PRICEY. EVEN THE CHEAPER SPRINGY TYPES* ARE, LIKE, 150,000 YEN...
AND IT DOESN'T SEEM LIKE MOST HEALTH INSURANCE COVERS SPORTS EQUIPMENT.
track and field club
HMPH...
YOU GOT NOTHING BETTER TO DO THAN LOOK ALL THIS STUFF UP?

*SPECIALLY SHAPED PROSTHETIC LEGS MADE FOR SPORTS. ALSO CALLED "BLADES."

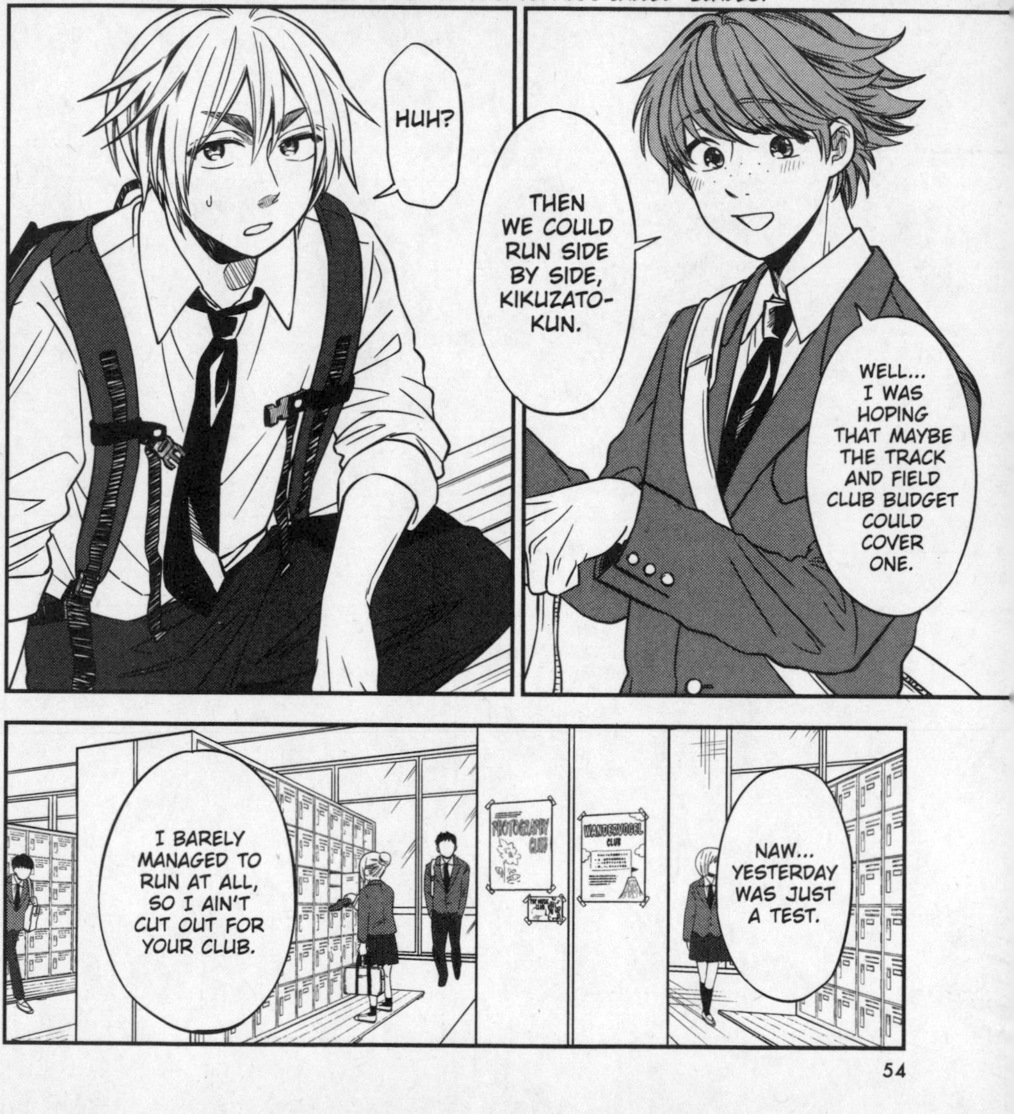
WELL... I WAS HOPING THAT MAYBE THE TRACK AND FIELD CLUB BUDGET COULD COVER ONE.
THEN WE COULD RUN SIDE BY SIDE, KIKUZATO-KUN.
HUH?
NAW... YESTERDAY WAS JUST A TEST.
WANDERVOGEL CLUB
PHOTOGRAPHY CLUB
I BARELY MANAGED TO RUN AT ALL, SO I AIN'T CUT OUT FOR YOUR CLUB.

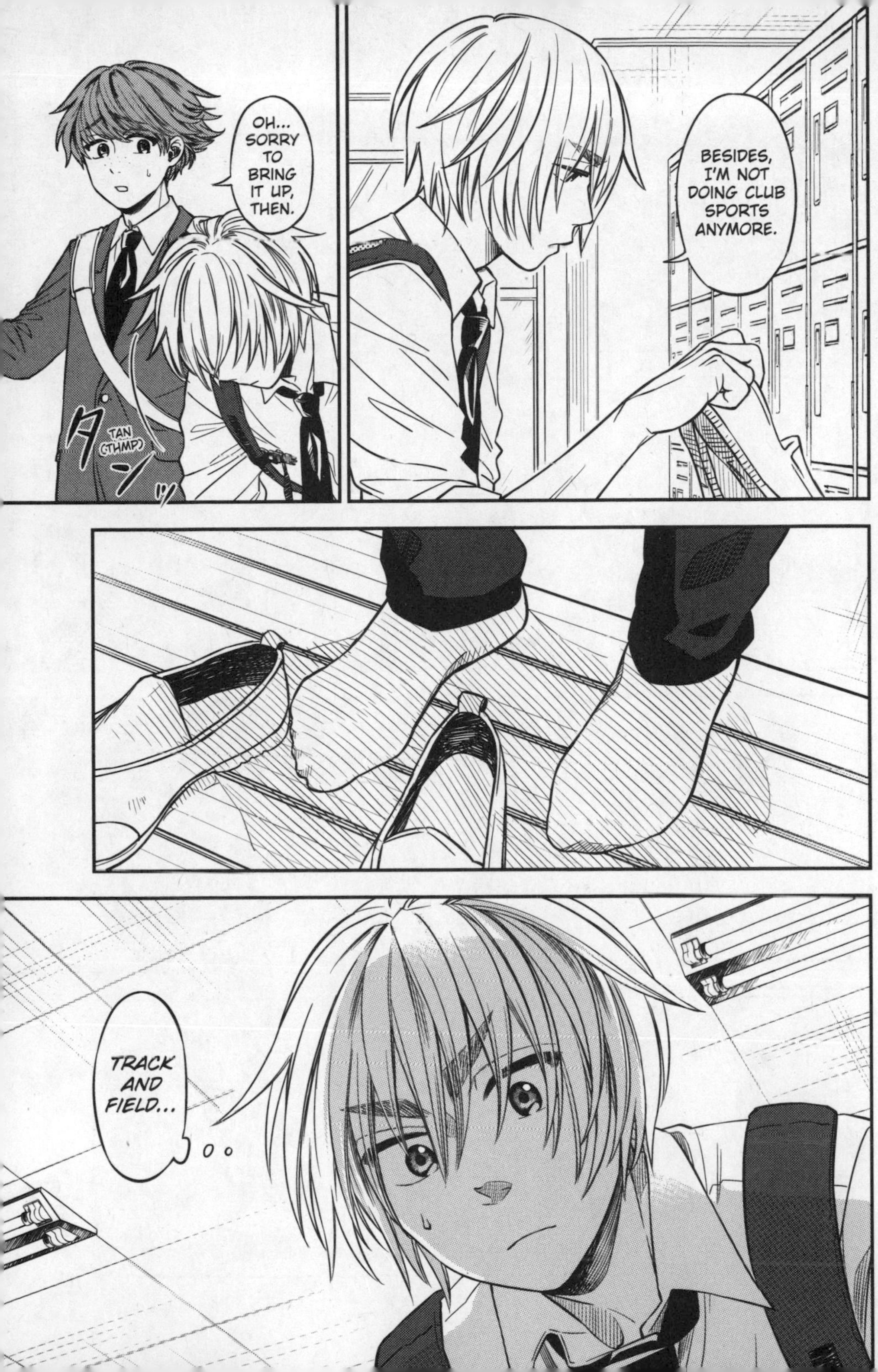
BESIDES, I'M NOT DOING CLUB SPORTS ANYMORE.
OH... SORRY TO BRING IT UP, THEN.
TAN (THMP)
TRACK AND FIELD...

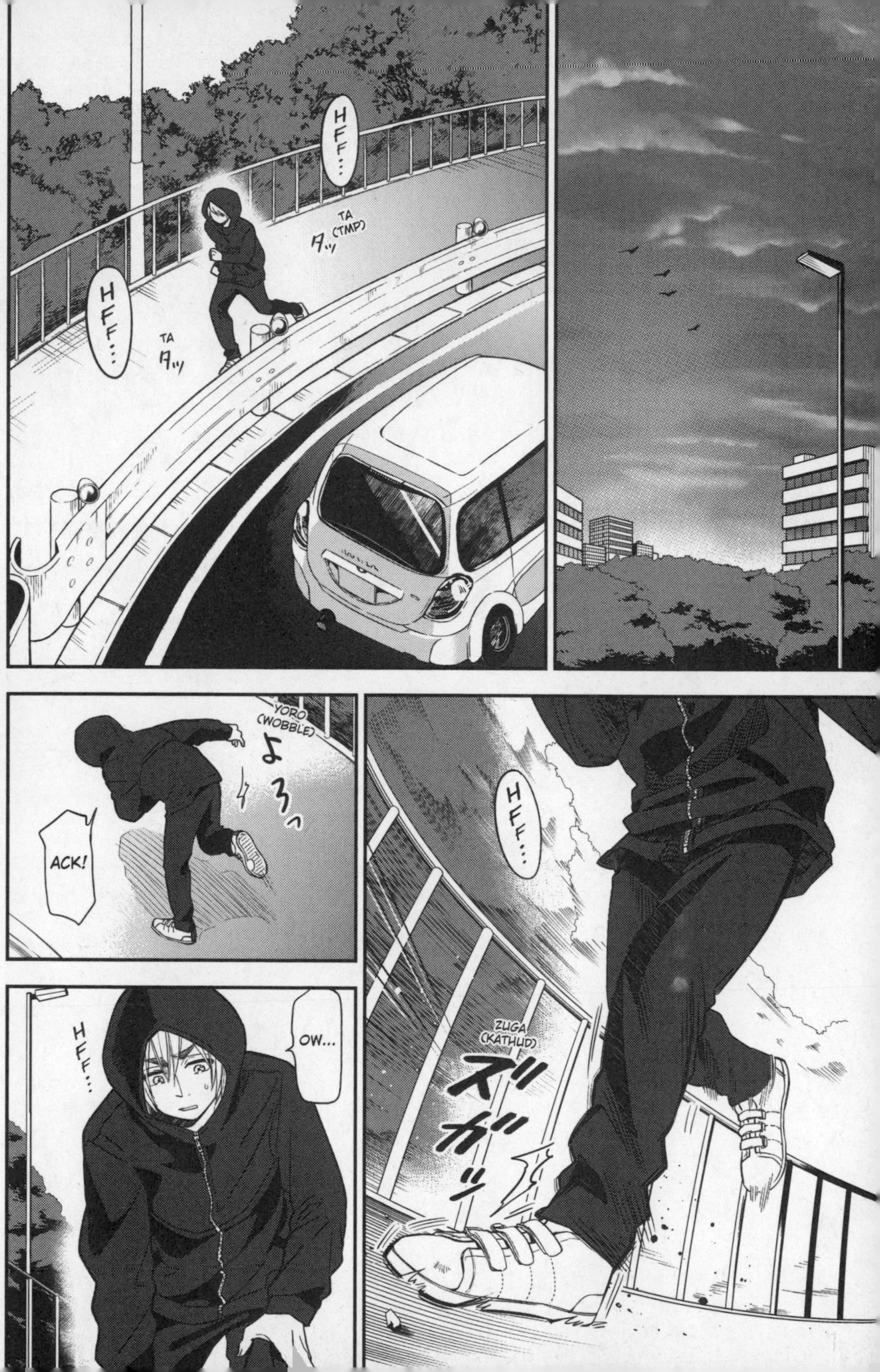
HFF...
TA (TMP)
タッ
HFF...
TA
タッ
HFF...
ZUGA (KATHUD)
ズガッ
YORO (WOBBLE)
よろ
ACK!
HFF...
OW...

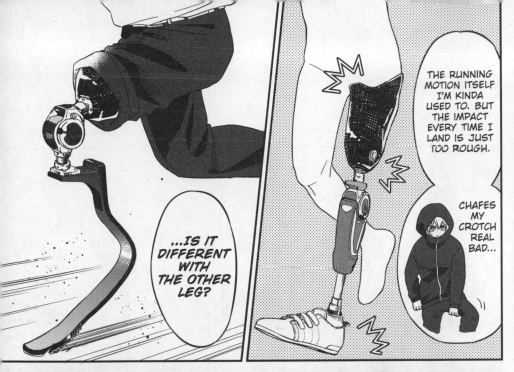

THE RUNNING MOTION ITSELF I'M KINDA USED TO. BUT THE IMPACT EVERY TIME I LAND IS JUST TOO ROUGH.

CHAFES MY CROTCH REAL BAD...

...IS IT DIFFERENT WITH THE OTHER LEG?

......

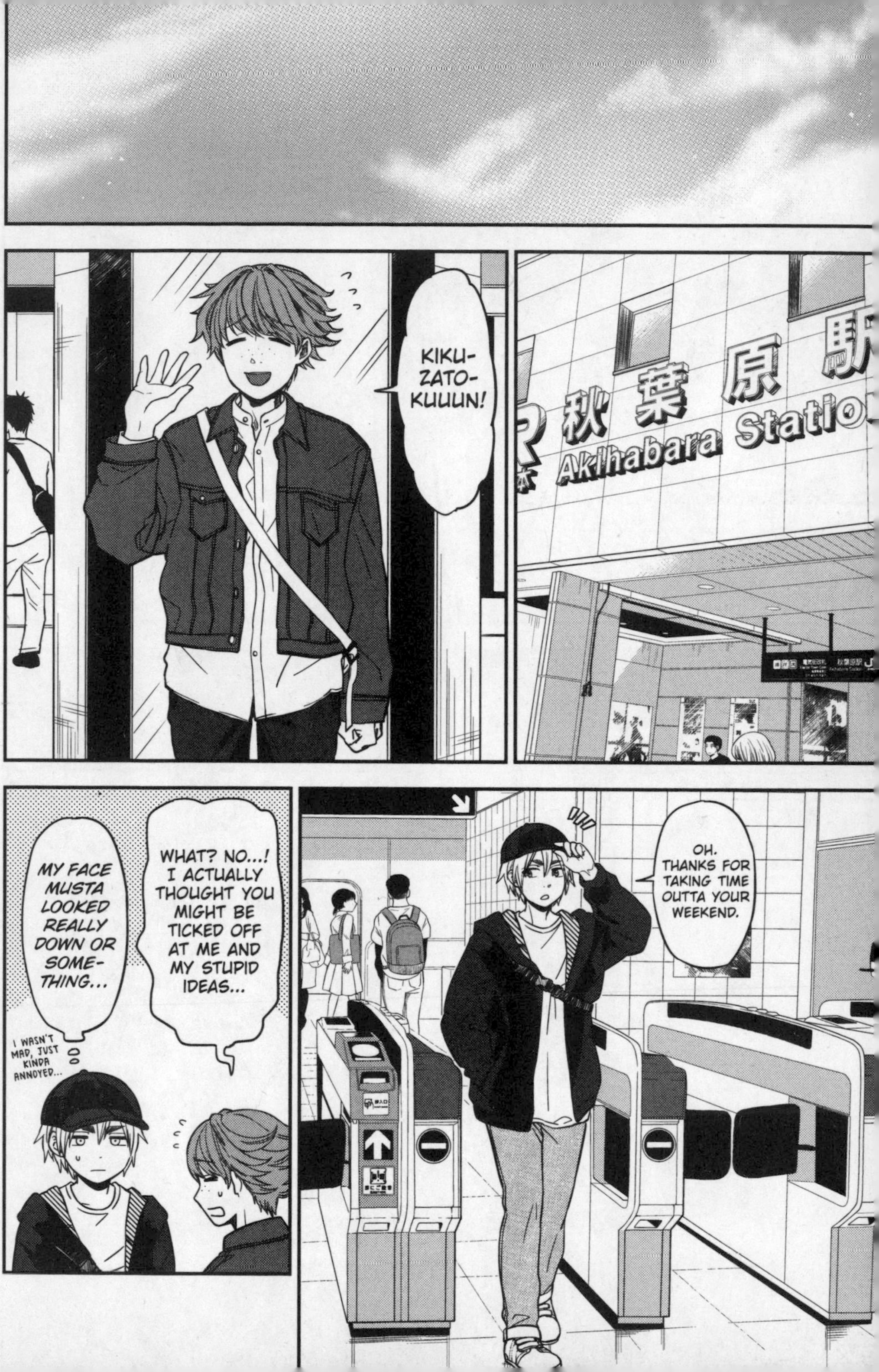
秋葉原駅
Akihabara Statio
KIKU-ZATO-KUUUN!
OH. THANKS FOR TAKING TIME OUTTA YOUR WEEKEND.
WHAT? NO...! I ACTUALLY THOUGHT YOU MIGHT BE TICKED OFF AT ME AND MY STUPID IDEAS...
MY FACE MUSTA LOOKED REALLY DOWN OR SOME-THING...
I WASN'T MAD, JUST KINDA ANNOYED...

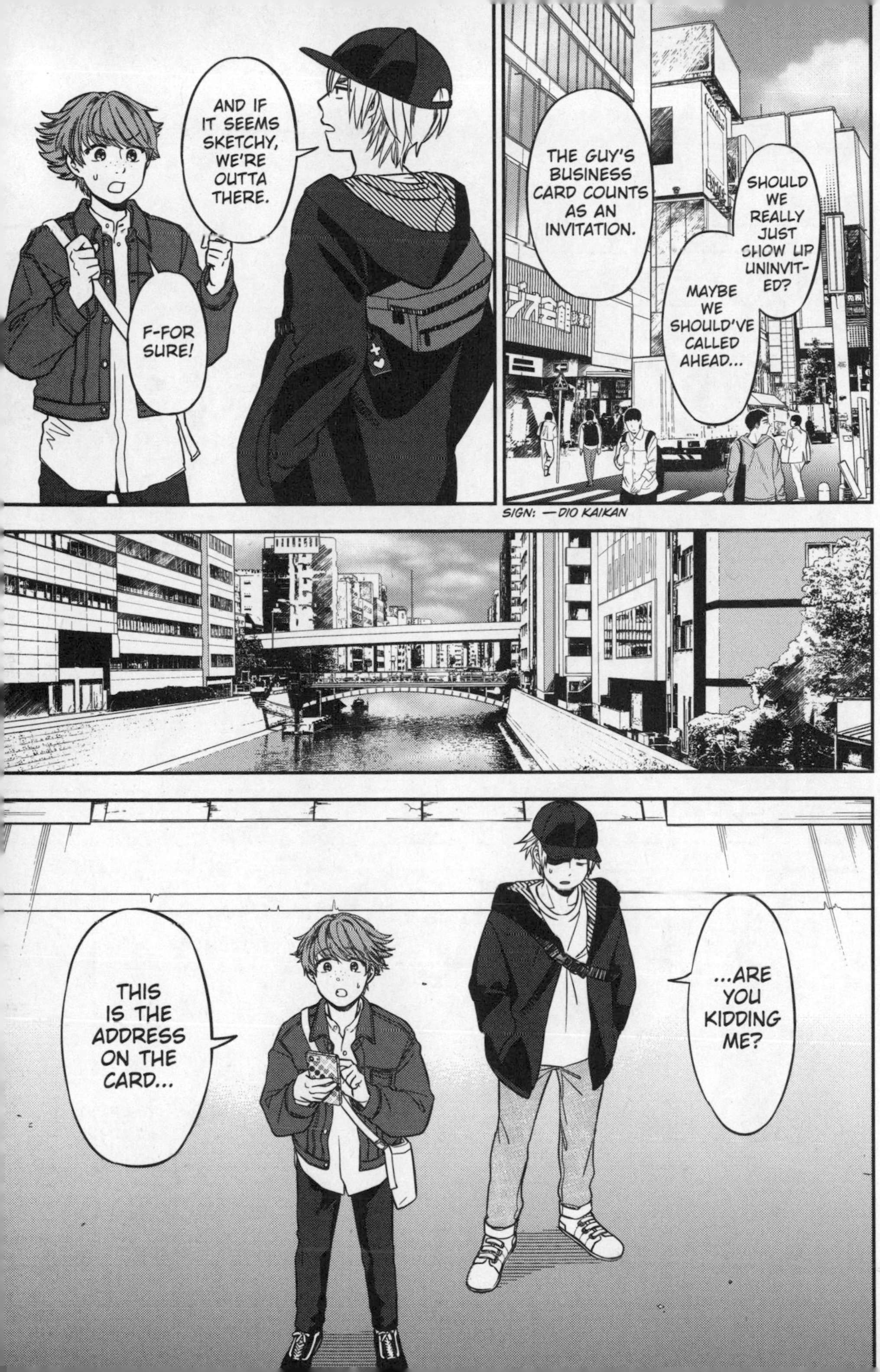
SHOULD WE REALLY JUST SHOW UP UNINVITED?
MAYBE WE SHOULD'VE CALLED AHEAD...
THE GUY'S BUSINESS CARD COUNTS AS AN INVITATION.
SIGN: —DIO KAIKAN
AND IF IT SEEMS SKETCHY, WE'RE OUTTA THERE.
F-FOR SURE!
THIS IS THE ADDRESS ON THE CARD...
...ARE YOU KIDDING ME?

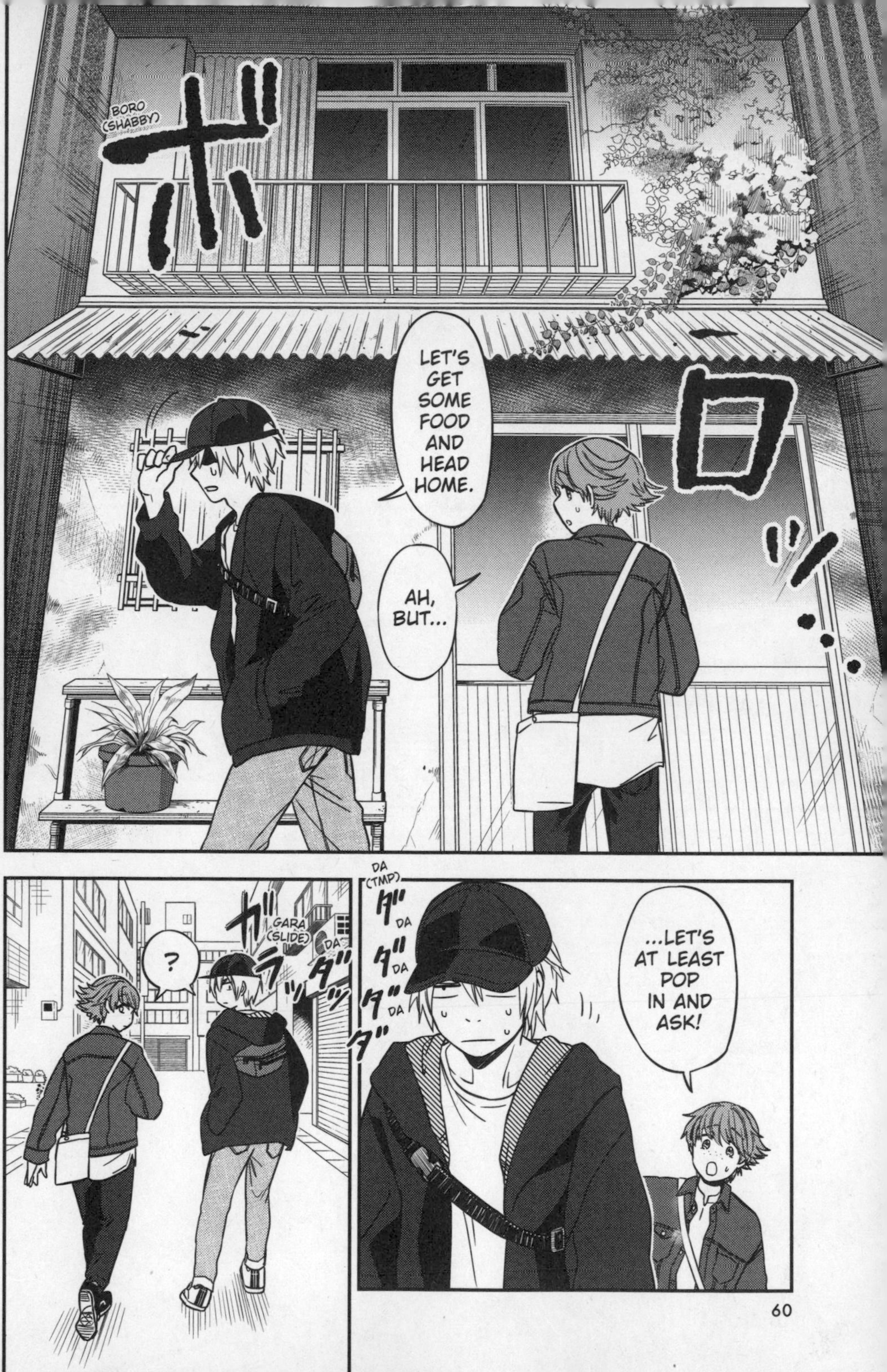
BORO (SHABBY)
LET'S GET SOME FOOD AND HEAD HOME.
AH, BUT...
DA (TMP)
DA
DA
DA
...LET'S AT LEAST POP IN AND ASK!
GARA (SLIDE)
DA
?

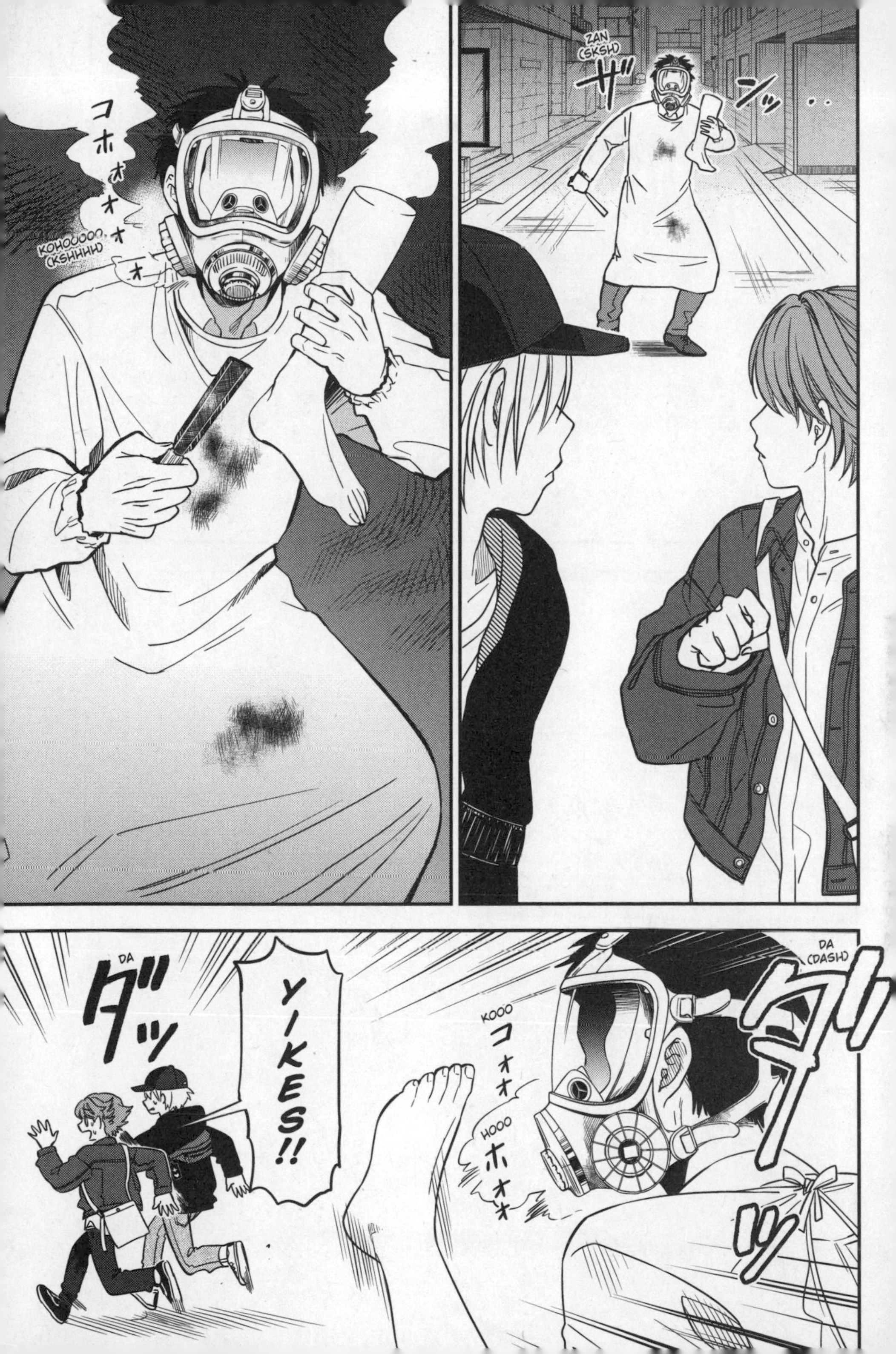

ZAN (SKSH)
ザ
ンッ
..
コホオオオオ
KOHOOOOO (KSHHHH)
DA (DASH)
ダッ
KOOO
コオオ
HOOO
ホオオ
YIKES!!
DA
ダッ

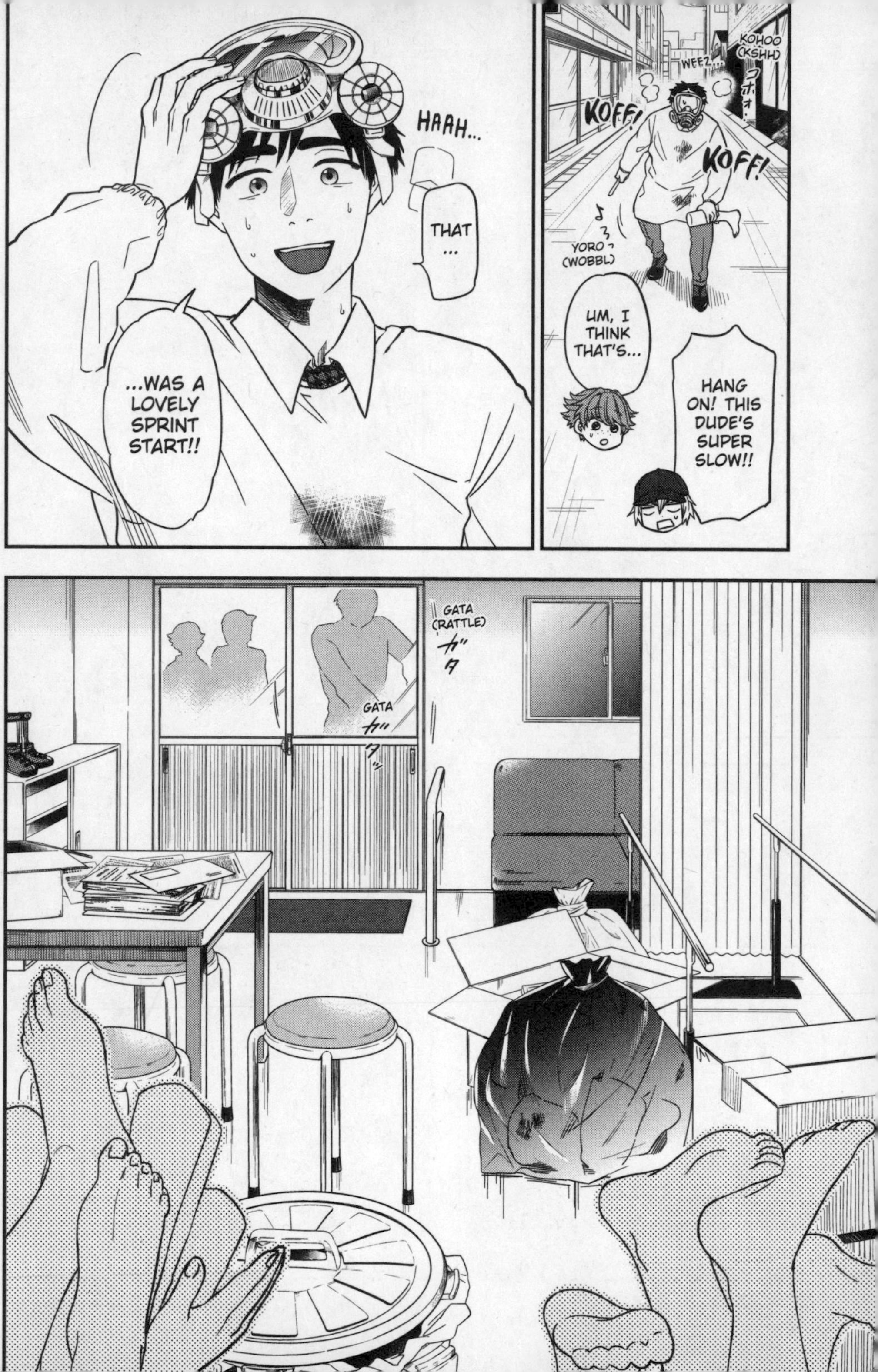
KOHOO (KSHH)
WEEZ...
KOFF!
KOFF!
YORO (WOBBL)
UM, I THINK THAT'S...
HANG ON! THIS DUDE'S SUPER SLOW!!
HAAH...
THAT...
...WAS A LOVELY SPRINT START!!
GATA (RATTLE)
ガタ
GATA
ガタッ

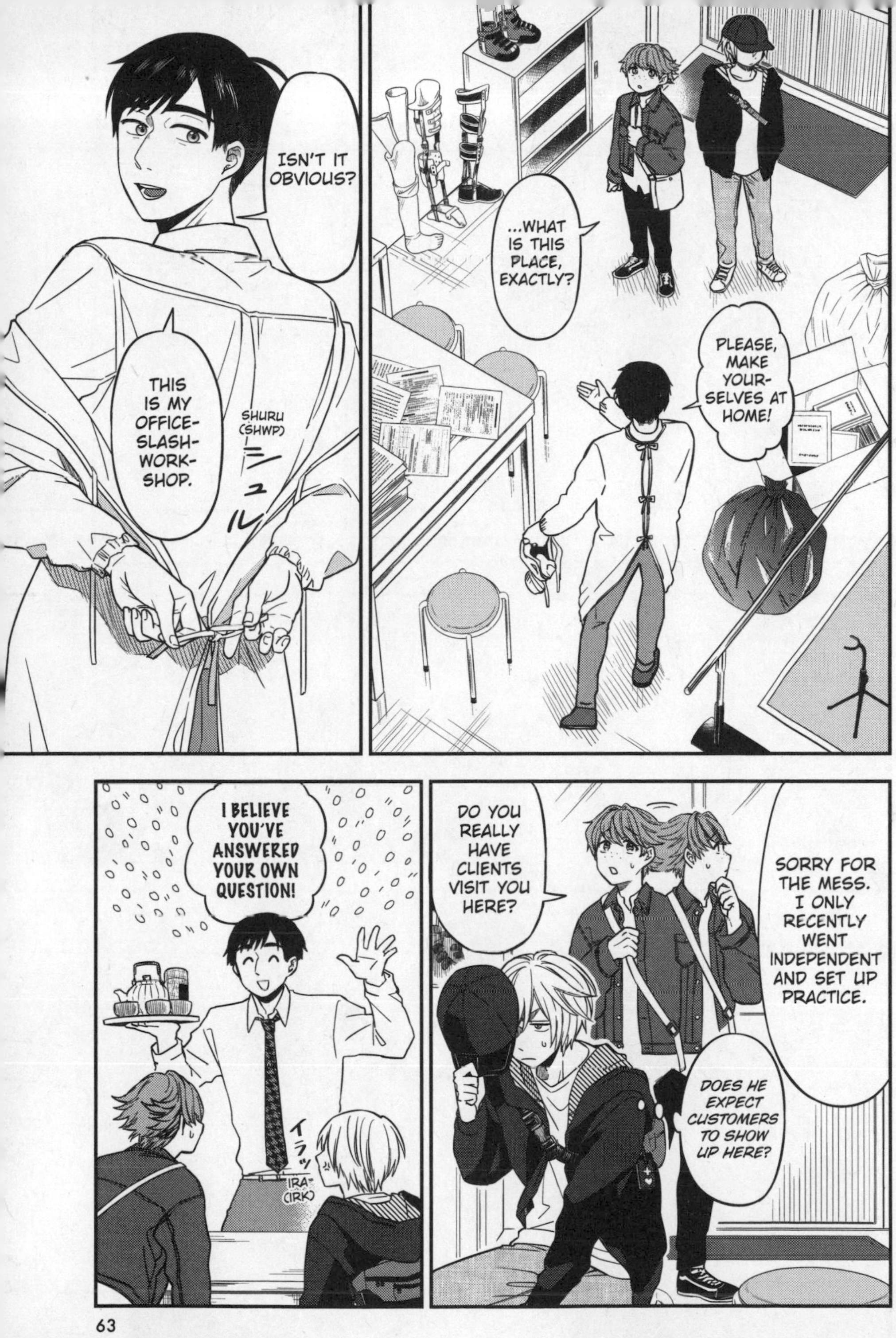
...WHAT IS THIS PLACE, EXACTLY?
PLEASE, MAKE YOURSELVES AT HOME!
ISN'T IT OBVIOUS?
THIS IS MY OFFICE-SLASH-WORKSHOP.
シュル
SHURU (SHWP)
SORRY FOR THE MESS. I ONLY RECENTLY WENT INDEPENDENT AND SET UP PRACTICE.
DO YOU REALLY HAVE CLIENTS VISIT YOU HERE?
DOES HE EXPECT CUSTOMERS TO SHOW UP HERE?
I BELIEVE YOU'VE ANSWERED YOUR OWN QUESTION!
イラッ
IRA (IRK)

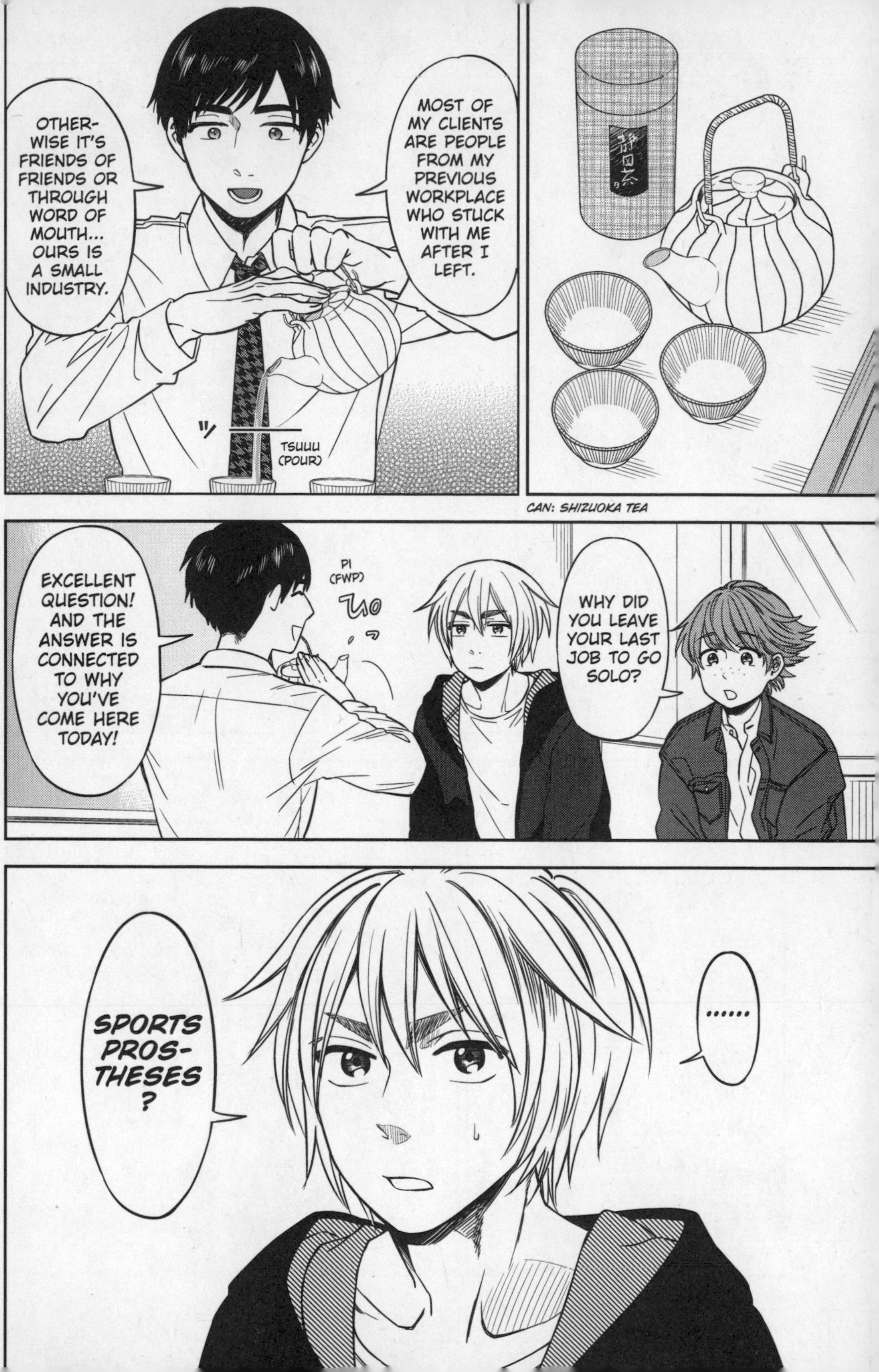
CAN: SHIZUOKA TEA
MOST OF MY CLIENTS ARE PEOPLE FROM MY PREVIOUS WORKPLACE WHO STUCK WITH ME AFTER I LEFT.
OTHER-WISE IT'S FRIENDS OF FRIENDS OR THROUGH WORD OF MOUTH... OURS IS A SMALL INDUSTRY.
TSUUU (POUR)
WHY DID YOU LEAVE YOUR LAST JOB TO GO SOLO?
PI (FWP)
EXCELLENT QUESTION! AND THE ANSWER IS CONNECTED TO WHY YOU'VE COME HERE TODAY!
......
SPORTS PROS-THESES?

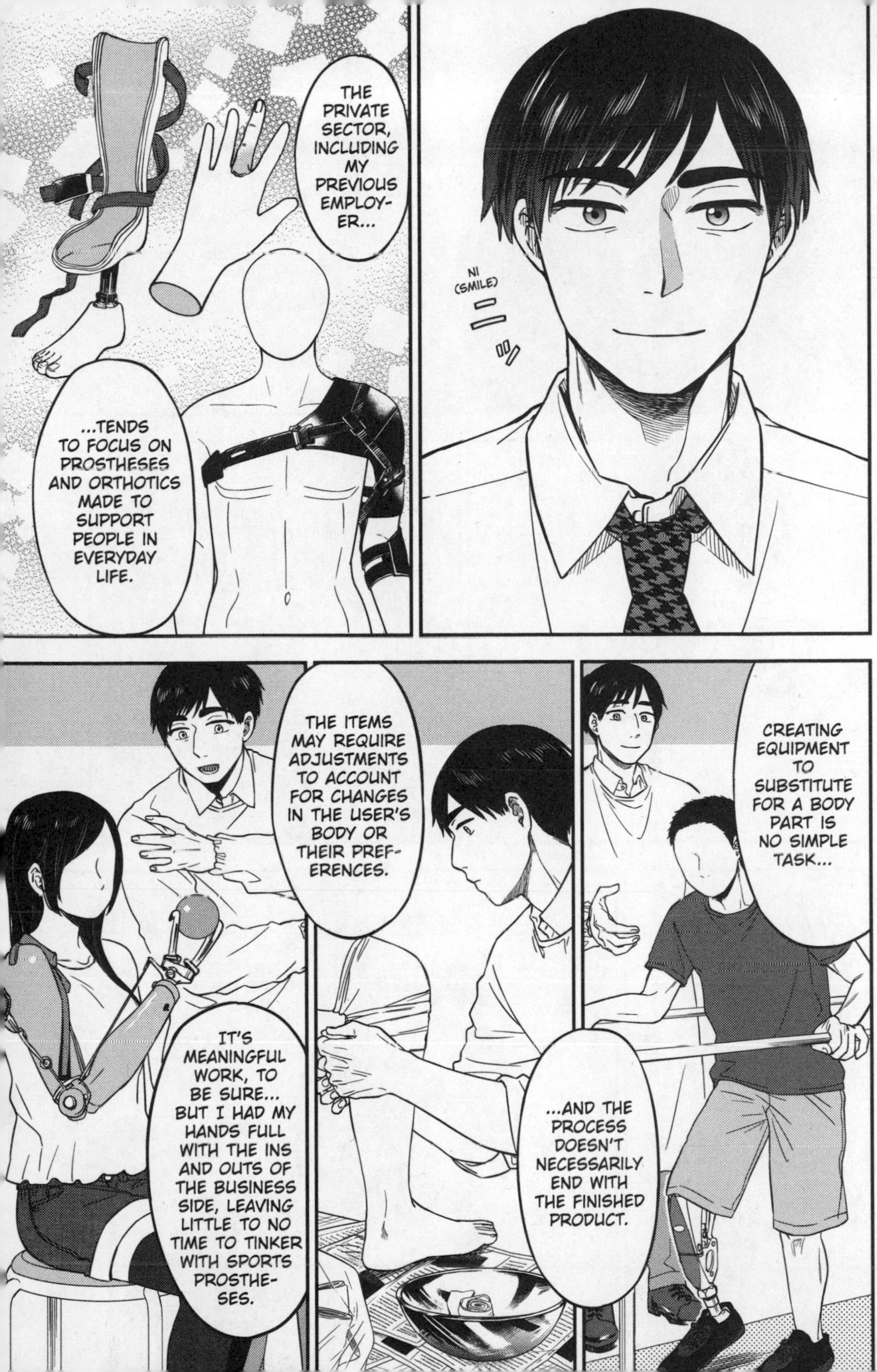
NI (SMILE)
THE PRIVATE SECTOR, INCLUDING MY PREVIOUS EMPLOYER...
...TENDS TO FOCUS ON PROSTHESES AND ORTHOTICS MADE TO SUPPORT PEOPLE IN EVERYDAY LIFE.
CREATING EQUIPMENT TO SUBSTITUTE FOR A BODY PART IS NO SIMPLE TASK...
...AND THE PROCESS DOESN'T NECESSARILY END WITH THE FINISHED PRODUCT.
THE ITEMS MAY REQUIRE ADJUSTMENTS TO ACCOUNT FOR CHANGES IN THE USER'S BODY OR THEIR PREFERENCES.
IT'S MEANINGFUL WORK, TO BE SURE... BUT I HAD MY HANDS FULL WITH THE INS AND OUTS OF THE BUSINESS SIDE, LEAVING LITTLE TO NO TIME TO TINKER WITH SPORTS PROSTHESES.

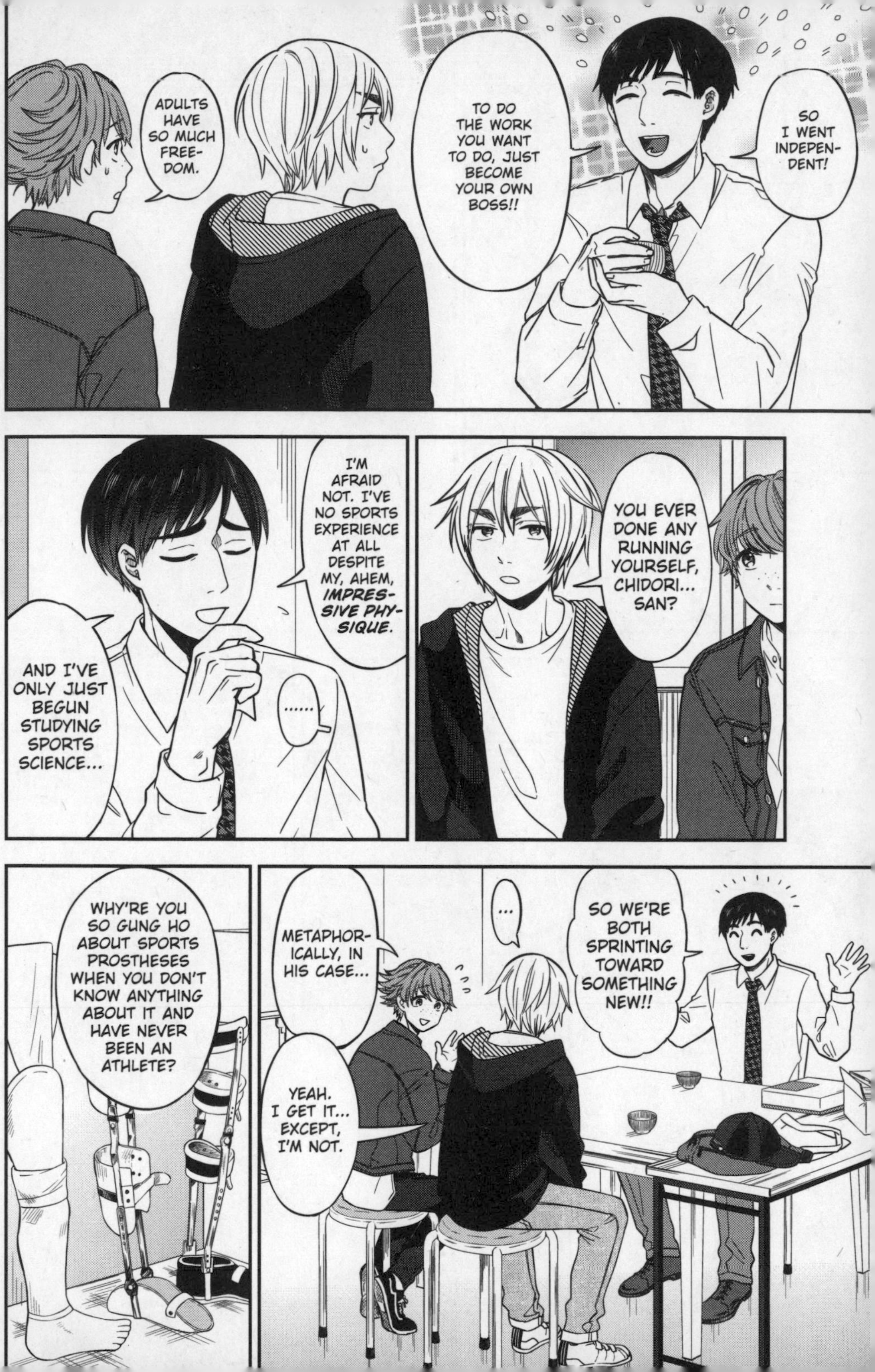
SO I WENT INDEPENDENT!
TO DO THE WORK YOU WANT TO DO, JUST BECOME YOUR OWN BOSS!!
ADULTS HAVE SO MUCH FREEDOM.
YOU EVER DONE ANY RUNNING YOURSELF, CHIDORI... SAN?
I'M AFRAID NOT. I'VE NO SPORTS EXPERIENCE AT ALL DESPITE MY, AHEM, *IMPRESSIVE PHYSIQUE*.
......
AND I'VE ONLY JUST BEGUN STUDYING SPORTS SCIENCE...
SO WE'RE BOTH SPRINTING TOWARD SOMETHING NEW!!
...
METAPHORICALLY, IN HIS CASE...
YEAH. I GET IT... EXCEPT, I'M NOT.
WHY'RE YOU SO GUNG HO ABOUT SPORTS PROSTHESES WHEN YOU DON'T KNOW ANYTHING ABOUT IT AND HAVE NEVER BEEN AN ATHLETE?

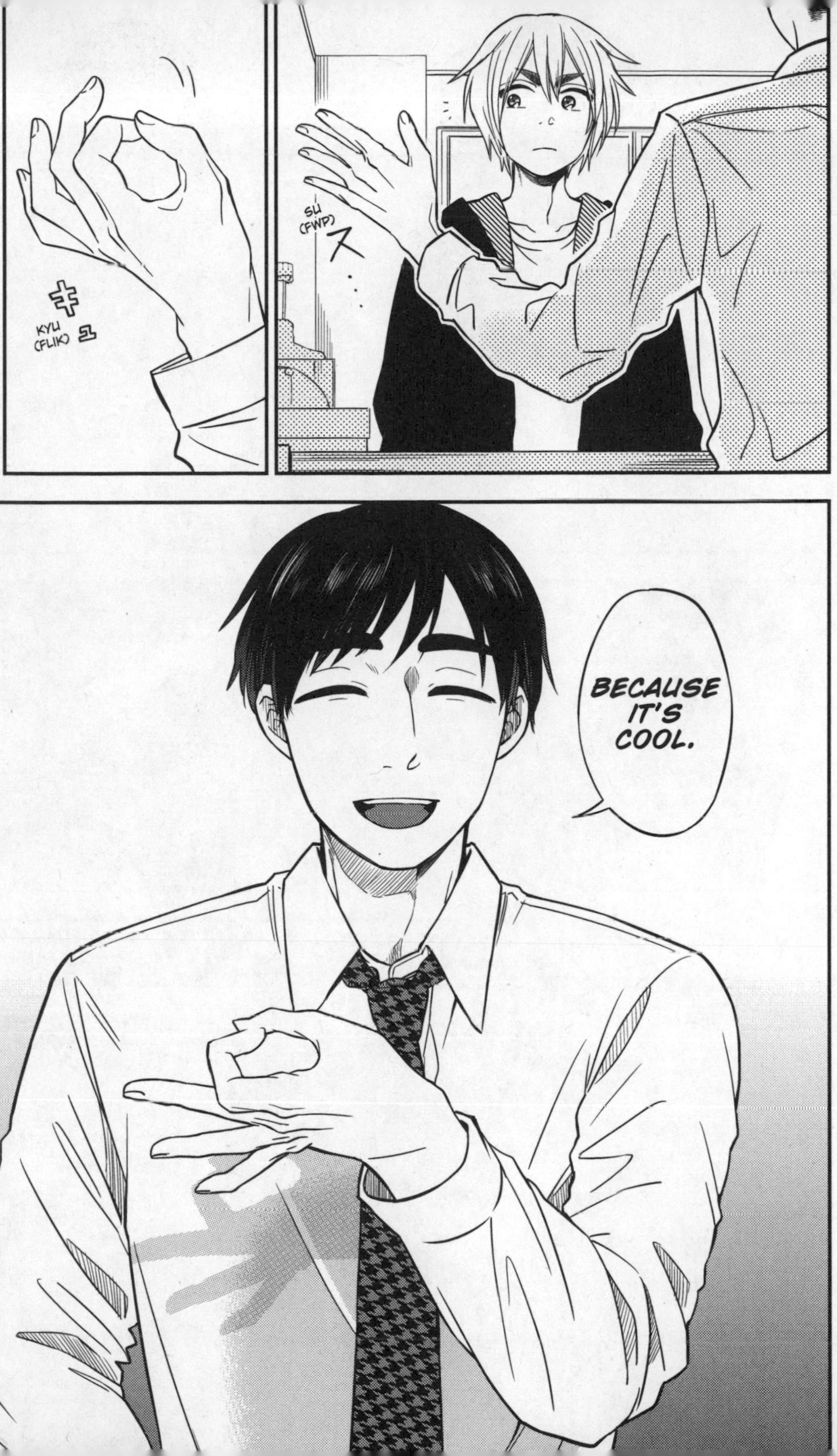
ス
SU (FWP)
キュ
KYU (FLIK)
BECAUSE IT'S COOL.

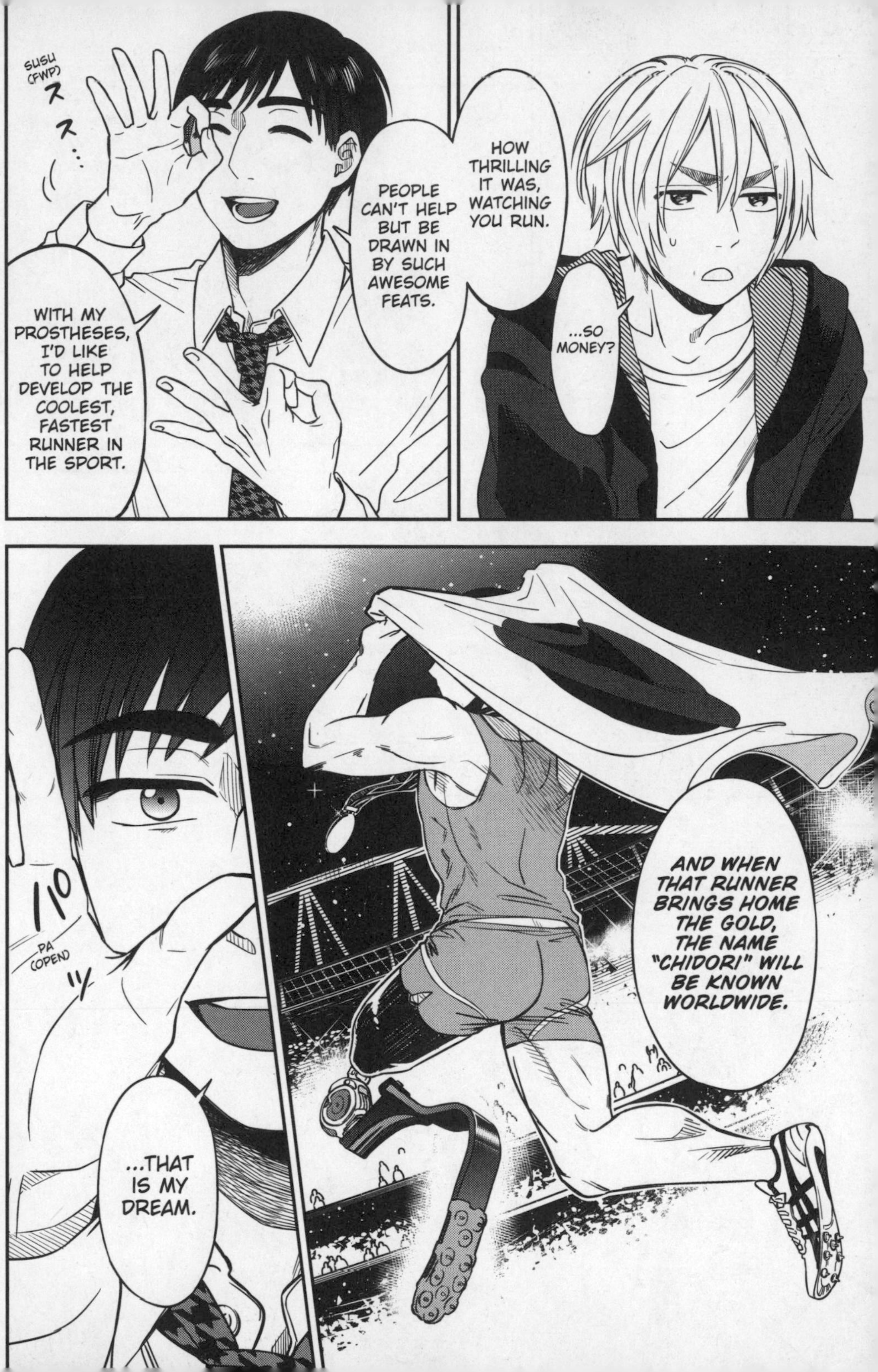
...SO MONEY?
HOW THRILLING IT WAS, WATCHING YOU RUN.
PEOPLE CAN'T HELP BUT BE DRAWN IN BY SUCH AWESOME FEATS.
SUSU (FWP) スス…
WITH MY PROSTHESES, I'D LIKE TO HELP DEVELOP THE COOLEST, FASTEST RUNNER IN THE SPORT.
AND WHEN THAT RUNNER BRINGS HOME THE GOLD, THE NAME "CHIDORI" WILL BE KNOWN WORLDWIDE.
PA (OPEN)
...THAT IS MY DREAM.

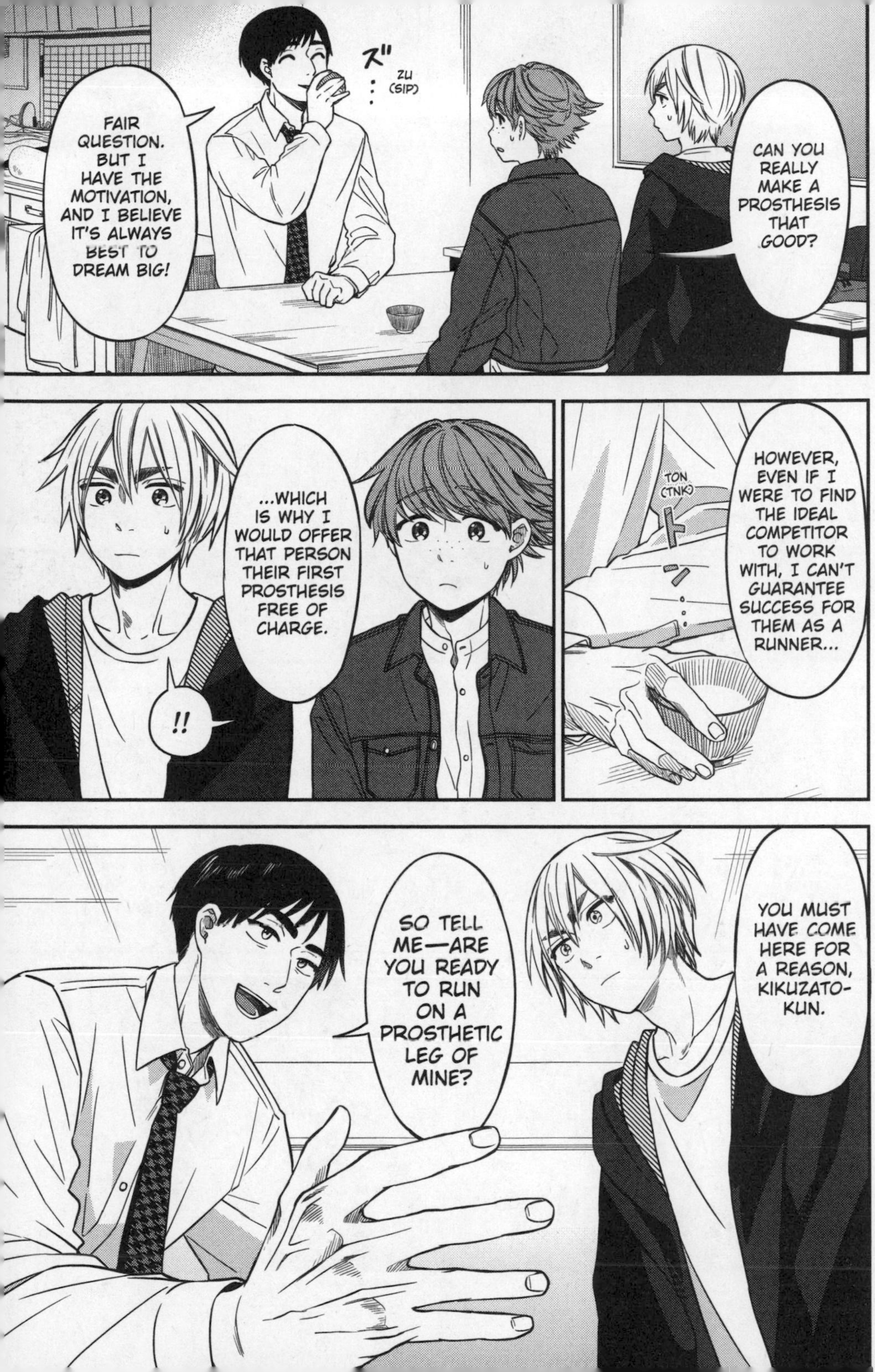
CAN YOU REALLY MAKE A PROSTHESIS THAT GOOD?
ズ
ZU (SIP)
FAIR QUESTION. BUT I HAVE THE MOTIVATION, AND I BELIEVE IT'S ALWAYS BEST TO DREAM BIG!
HOWEVER, EVEN IF I WERE TO FIND THE IDEAL COMPETITOR TO WORK WITH, I CAN'T GUARANTEE SUCCESS FOR THEM AS A RUNNER...
TON (TNK)
...WHICH IS WHY I WOULD OFFER THAT PERSON THEIR FIRST PROSTHESIS FREE OF CHARGE.
!!
YOU MUST HAVE COME HERE FOR A REASON, KIKUZATO-KUN.
SO TELL ME—ARE YOU READY TO RUN ON A PROSTHETIC LEG OF MINE?

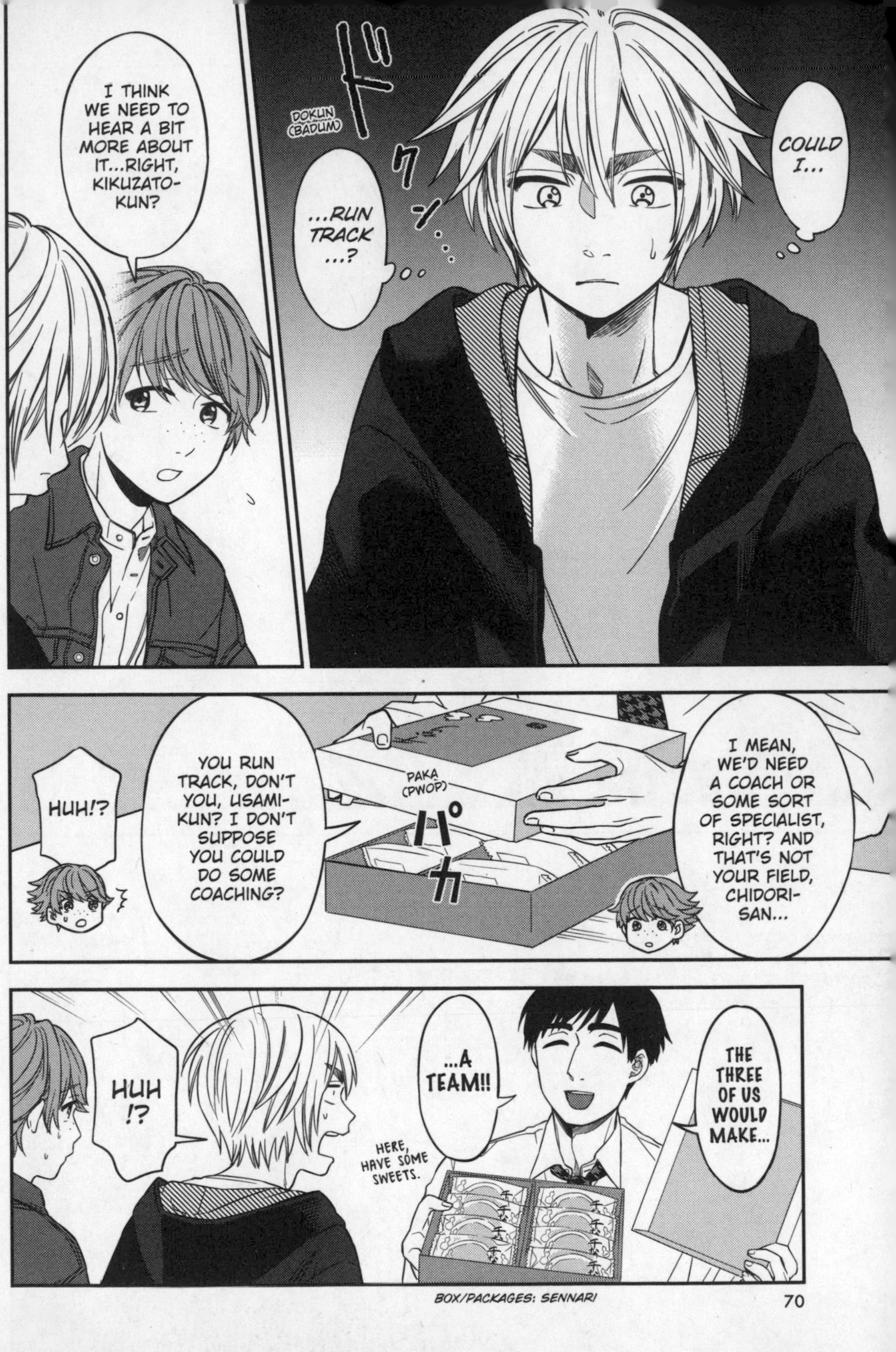
COULD I...
...RUN TRACK ...?
DOKUN (BADUM)
I THINK WE NEED TO HEAR A BIT MORE ABOUT IT...RIGHT, KIKUZATO-KUN?
I MEAN, WE'D NEED A COACH OR SOME SORT OF SPECIALIST, RIGHT? AND THAT'S NOT YOUR FIELD, CHIDORI-SAN...
PAKA (PWOP)
YOU RUN TRACK, DON'T YOU, USAMI-KUN? I DON'T SUPPOSE YOU COULD DO SOME COACHING?
HUH!?
THE THREE OF US WOULD MAKE...
...A TEAM!!
HERE, HAVE SOME SWEETS.
HUH !?

BOX/PACKAGES: SENNARI

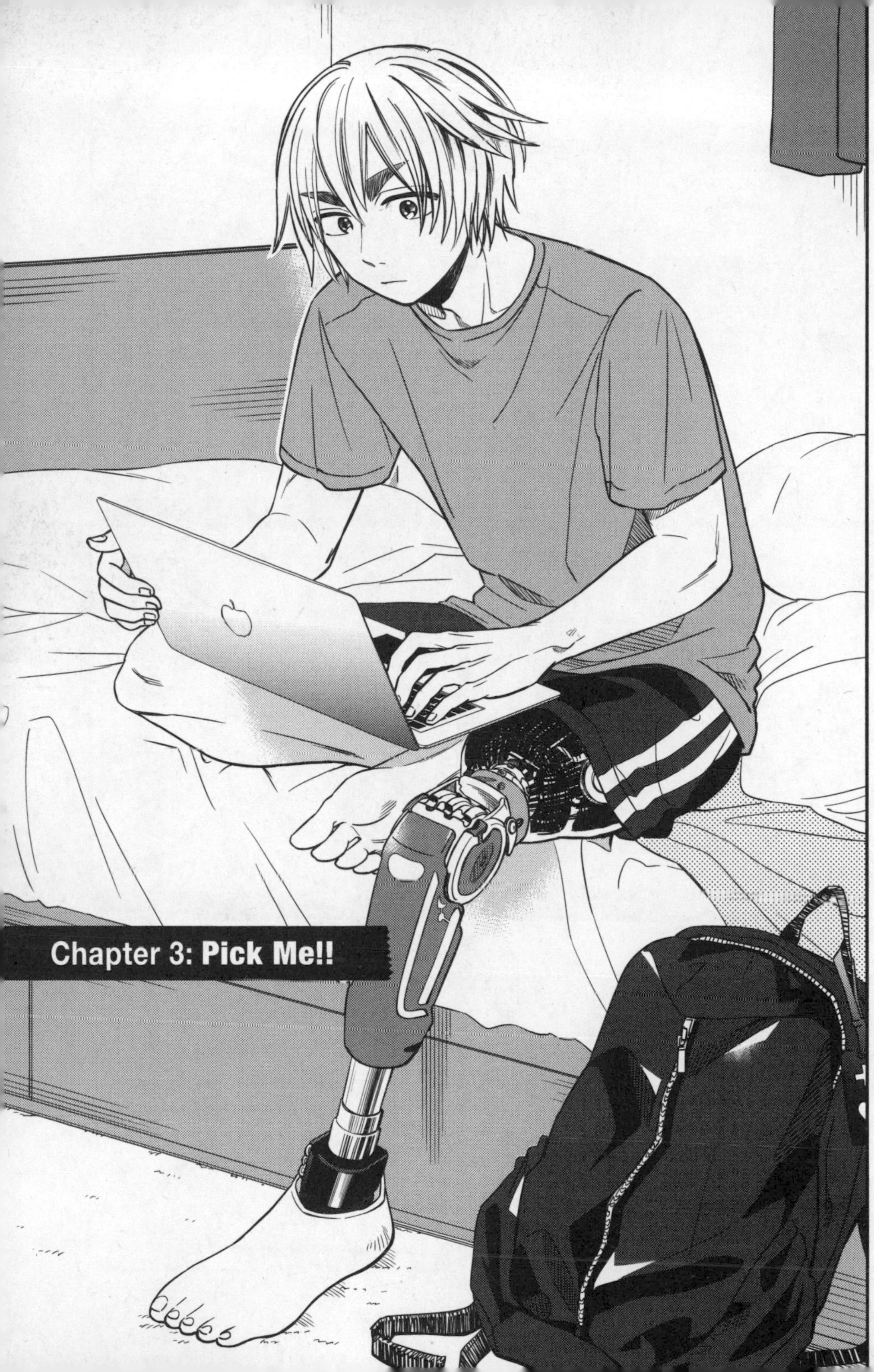
Chapter 3: Pick Me!!

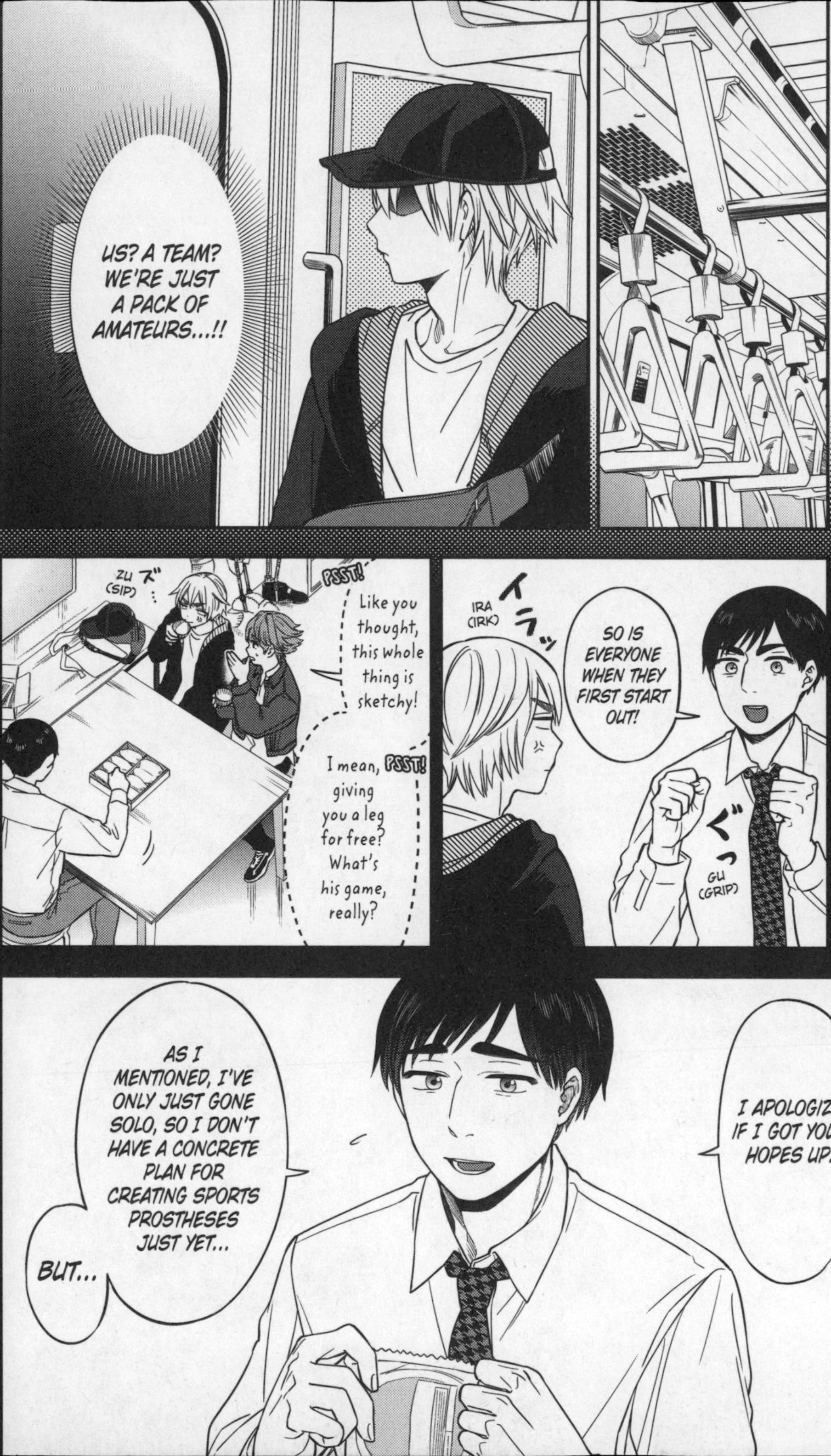
US? A TEAM? WE'RE JUST A PACK OF AMATEURS...!!
IRA (IRK) イラッ
SO IS EVERYONE WHEN THEY FIRST START OUT!
ぐっ GU (GRIP)
ZU ズ (SIP)
PSST!
Like you thought, this whole thing is sketchy!
I mean, PSST! giving you a leg for free? What's his game, really?
I APOLOGIZE IF I GOT YOUR HOPES UP.
AS I MENTIONED, I'VE ONLY JUST GONE SOLO, SO I DON'T HAVE A CONCRETE PLAN FOR CREATING SPORTS PROSTHESES JUST YET...
BUT...

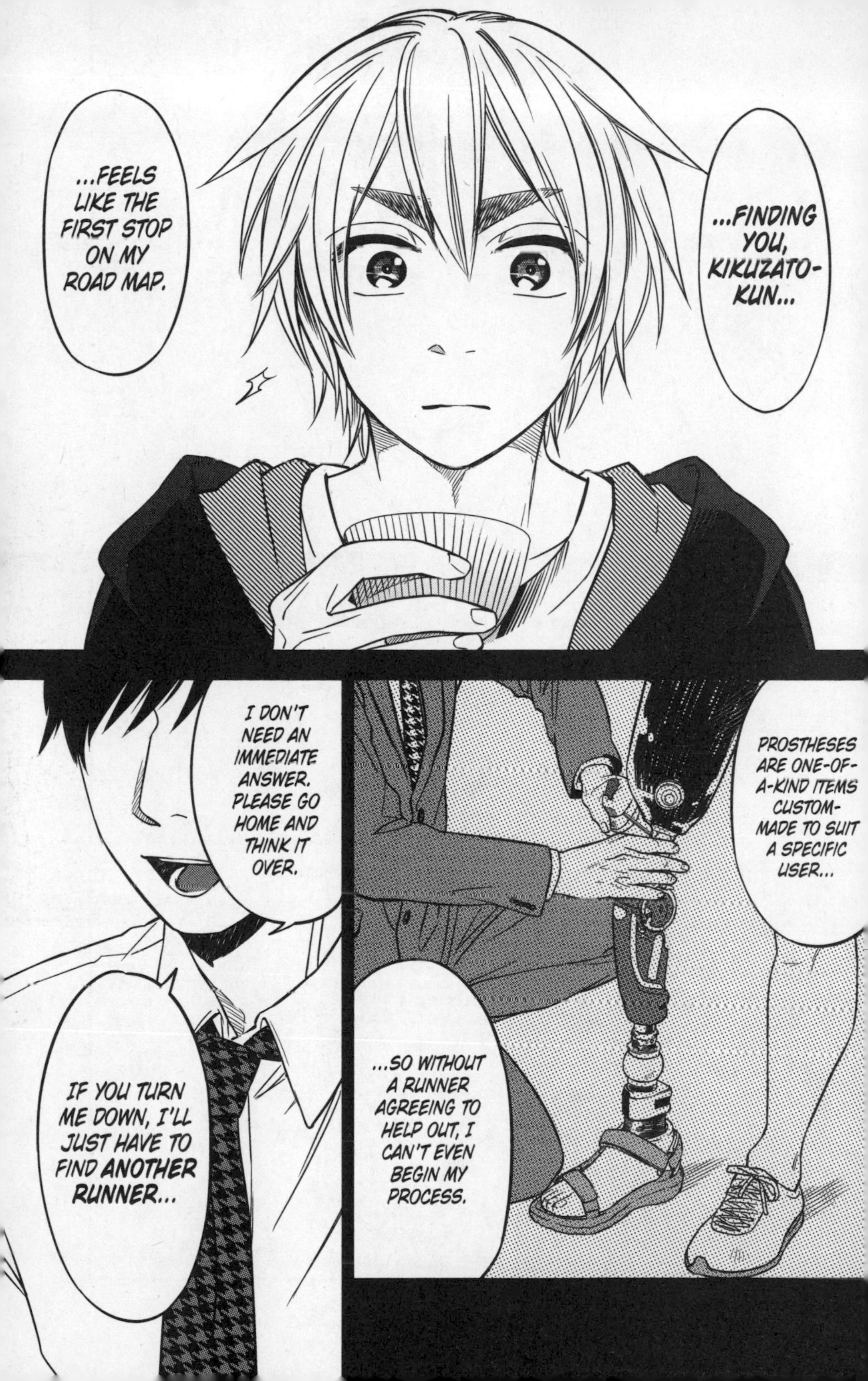
...FINDING YOU, KIKUZATO-KUN...
...FEELS LIKE THE FIRST STOP ON MY ROAD MAP.
PROSTHESES ARE ONE-OF-A-KIND ITEMS CUSTOM-MADE TO SUIT A SPECIFIC USER...
...SO WITHOUT A RUNNER AGREEING TO HELP OUT, I CAN'T EVEN BEGIN MY PROCESS.
I DON'T NEED AN IMMEDIATE ANSWER. PLEASE GO HOME AND THINK IT OVER.
IF YOU TURN ME DOWN, I'LL JUST HAVE TO FIND **ANOTHER RUNNER**...

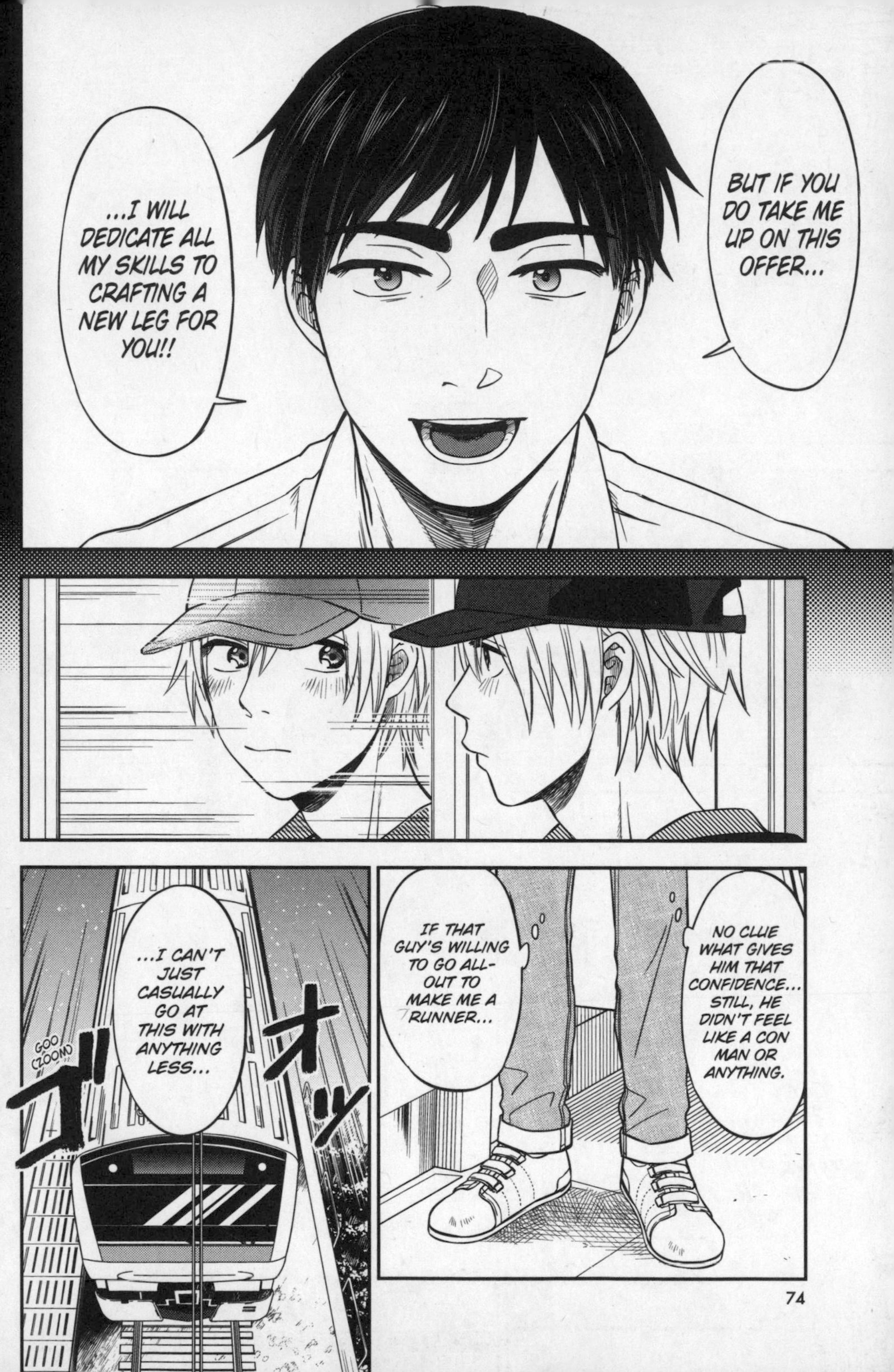
BUT IF YOU DO TAKE ME UP ON THIS OFFER...
...I WILL DEDICATE ALL MY SKILLS TO CRAFTING A NEW LEG FOR YOU!!
NO CLUE WHAT GIVES HIM THAT CONFIDENCE... STILL, HE DIDN'T FEEL LIKE A CON MAN OR ANYTHING.
IF THAT GUY'S WILLING TO GO ALL-OUT TO MAKE ME A RUNNER...
...I CAN'T JUST CASUALLY GO AT THIS WITH ANYTHING LESS...
GOO (ZOOM)

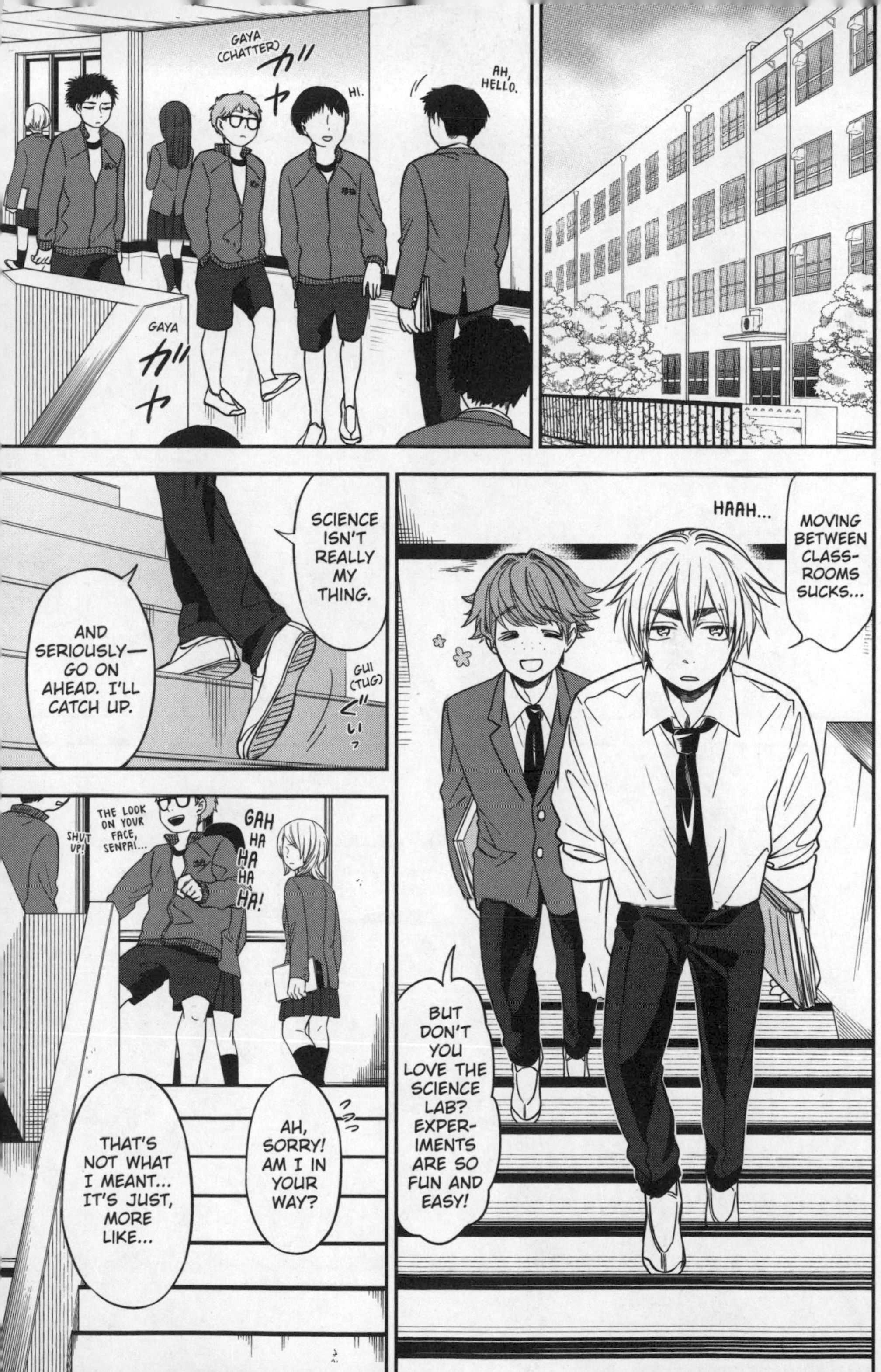
AH, HELLO.
HI.
GAYA (CHATTER)
GAYA
HAAH...
MOVING BETWEEN CLASS-ROOMS SUCKS...
BUT DON'T YOU LOVE THE SCIENCE LAB? EXPER-IMENTS ARE SO FUN AND EASY!
SCIENCE ISN'T REALLY MY THING.
AND SERIOUSLY— GO ON AHEAD. I'LL CATCH UP.
GUI (TUG)
GAH HA HA HA HA!
THE LOOK ON YOUR FACE, SENPAI...
SHUT UP!
AH, SORRY! AM I IN YOUR WAY?
THAT'S NOT WHAT I MEANT... IT'S JUST, MORE LIKE...

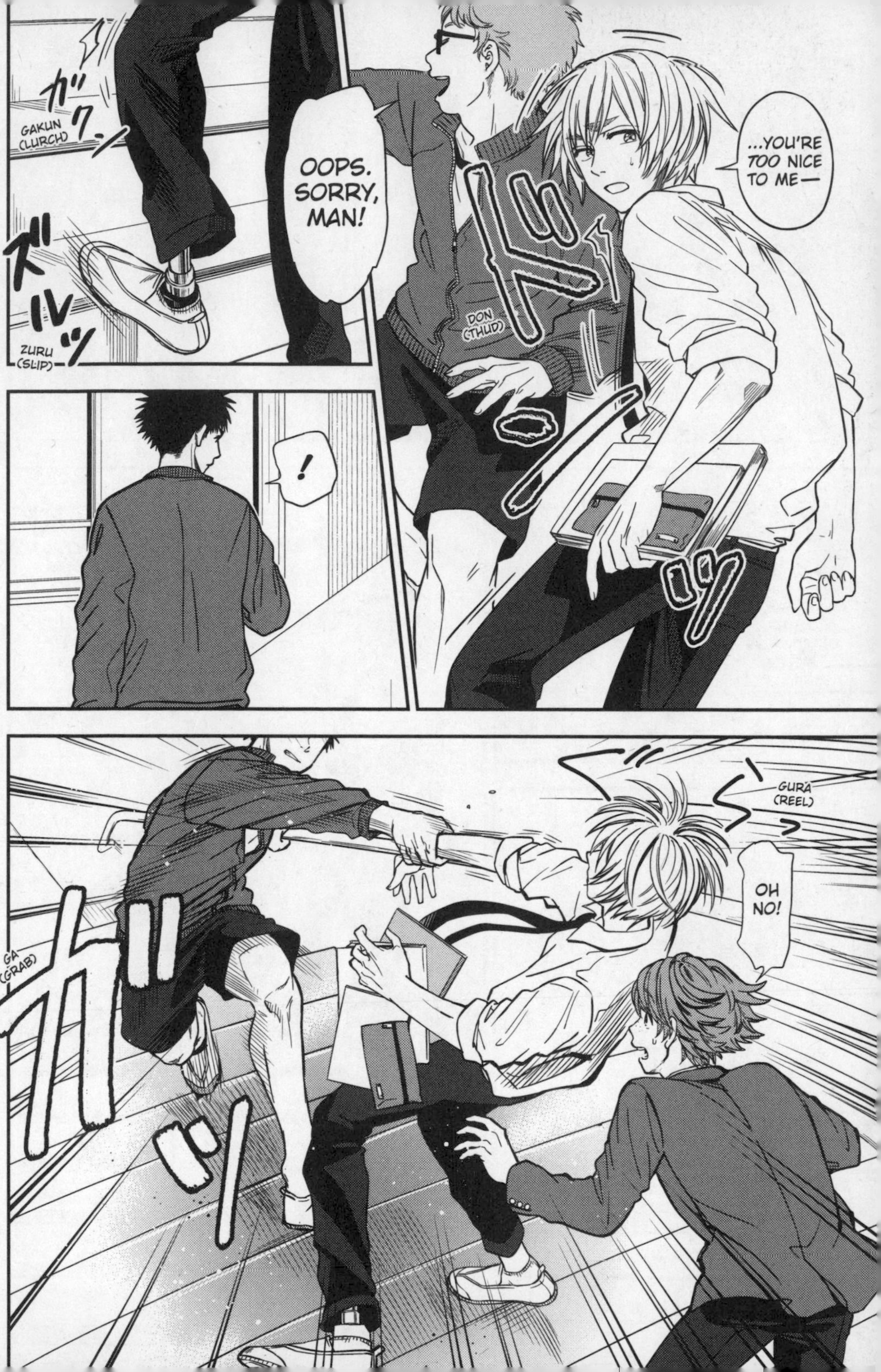
...YOU'RE *TOO* NICE TO ME—
OOPS. SORRY, MAN!
DON (THUD)
GAKUN (LURCH)
ZURU (SLIP)
!
GURA (REEL)
OH NO!
GA (GRAB)

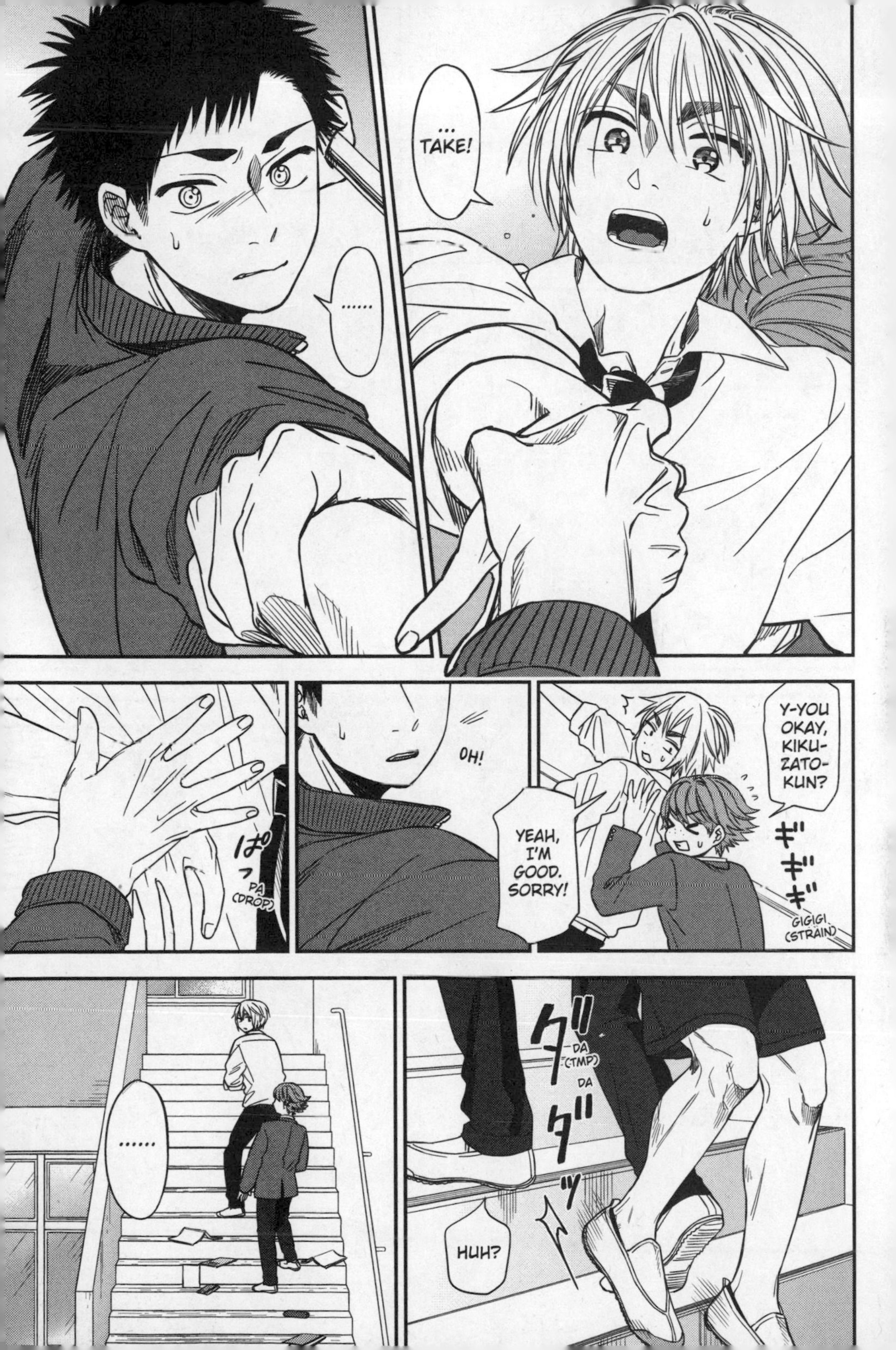
...TAKE!
......
Y-YOU OKAY, KIKU-ZATO-KUN?
YEAH, I'M GOOD. SORRY!
ギギギ
GIGIGI (STRAIN)
OH!
ぱっ
PA (DROP)
ダ
DA (TMP)
DA
ダッ
HUH?
......

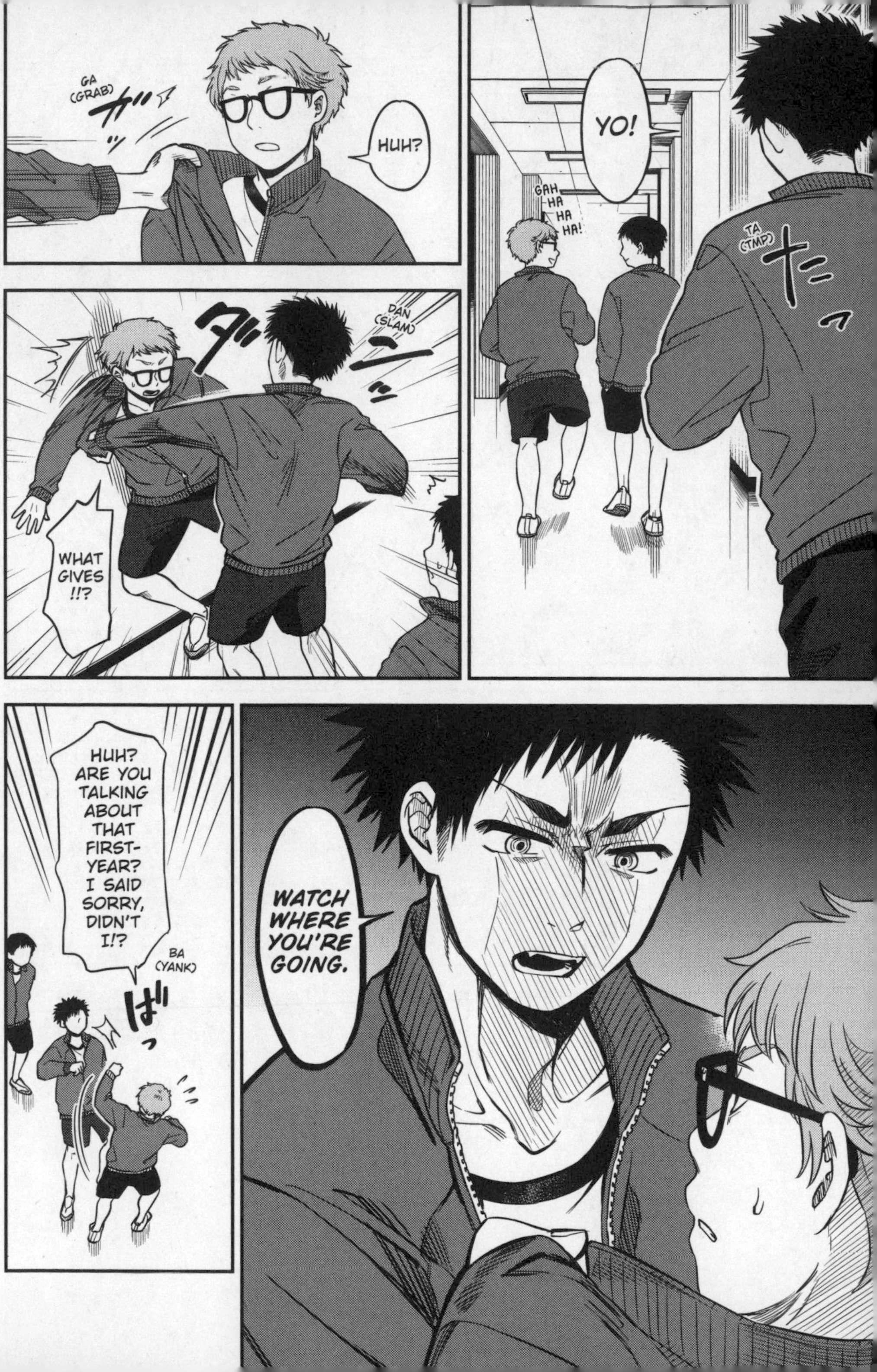

YO!
GAH HA HA HA!
TA (TMP)
GA (GRAB)
HUH?
DAN (SLAM)
WHAT GIVES !!?
WATCH WHERE YOU'RE GOING.
HUH? ARE YOU TALKING ABOUT THAT FIRST-YEAR? I SAID SORRY, DIDN'T I!?
BA (YANK)

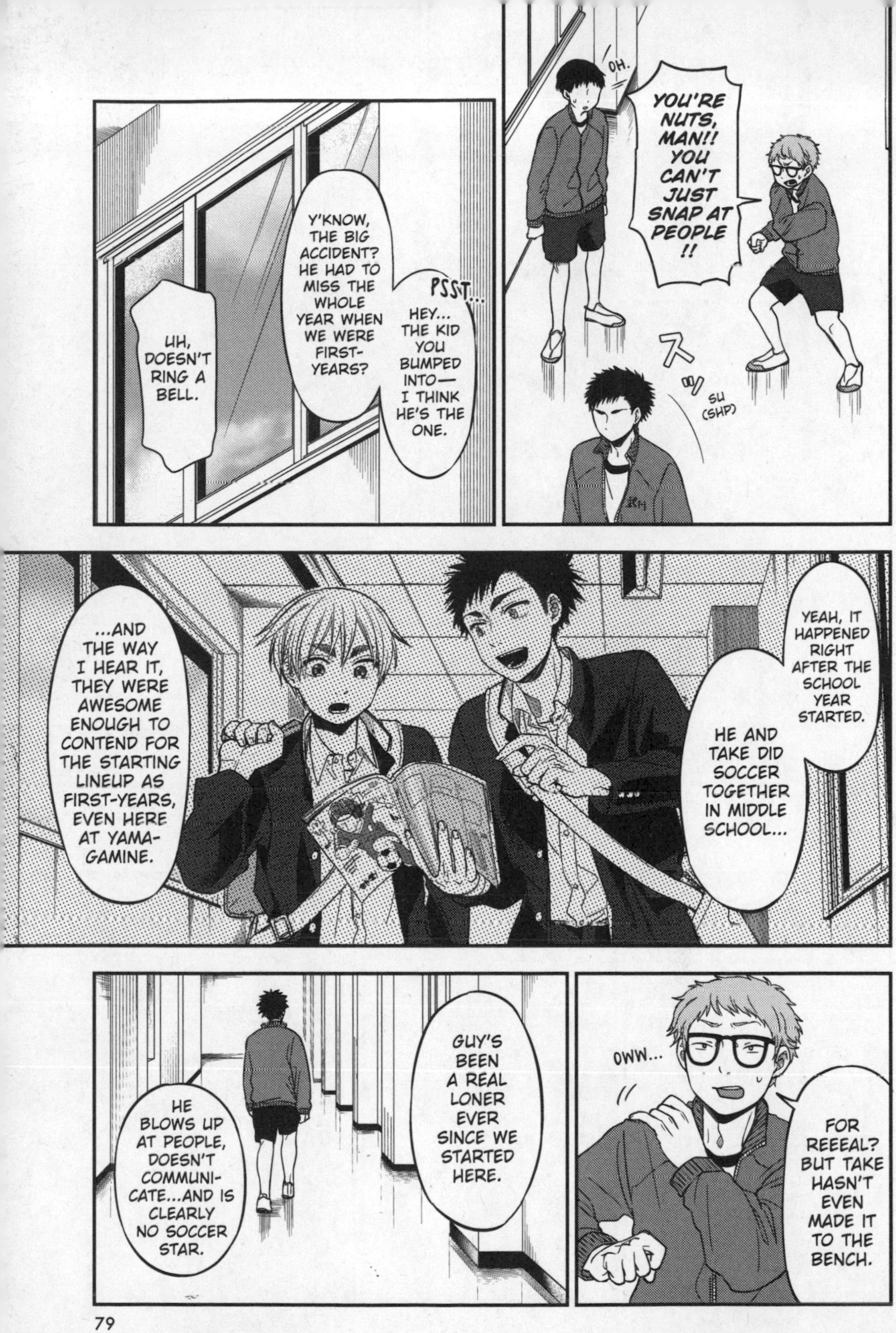
OH.
YOU'RE NUTS, MAN!! YOU CAN'T JUST SNAP AT PEOPLE!!
スッ
SU (SHP)
PSST...
HEY... THE KID YOU BUMPED INTO— I THINK HE'S THE ONE.
Y'KNOW, THE BIG ACCIDENT? HE HAD TO MISS THE WHOLE YEAR WHEN WE WERE FIRST-YEARS?
UH, DOESN'T RING A BELL.
YEAH, IT HAPPENED RIGHT AFTER THE SCHOOL YEAR STARTED.
HE AND TAKE DID SOCCER TOGETHER IN MIDDLE SCHOOL...
...AND THE WAY I HEAR IT, THEY WERE AWESOME ENOUGH TO CONTEND FOR THE STARTING LINEUP AS FIRST-YEARS, EVEN HERE AT YAMA-GAMINE.
OWW...
FOR REEEAL? BUT TAKE HASN'T EVEN MADE IT TO THE BENCH.
GUY'S BEEN A REAL LONER EVER SINCE WE STARTED HERE.
HE BLOWS UP AT PEOPLE, DOESN'T COMMUNI-CATE...AND IS CLEARLY NO SOCCER STAR.

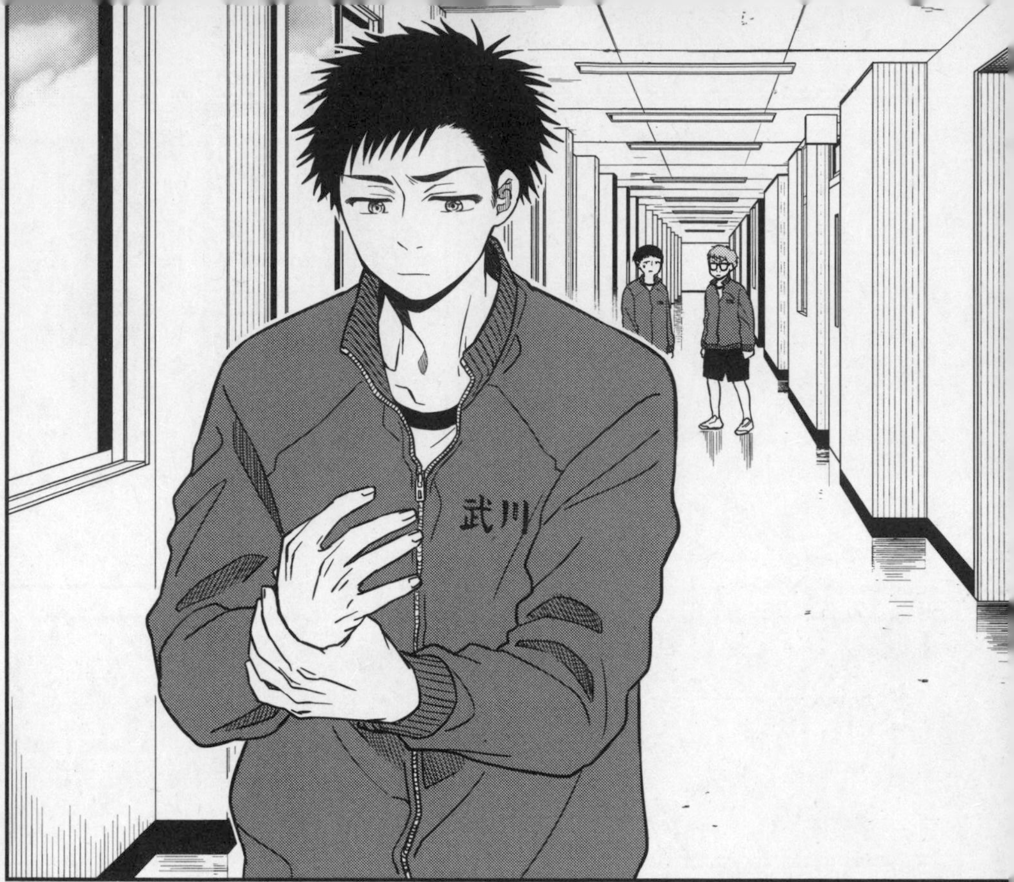
武川

JERSEY: TAKEKAWA

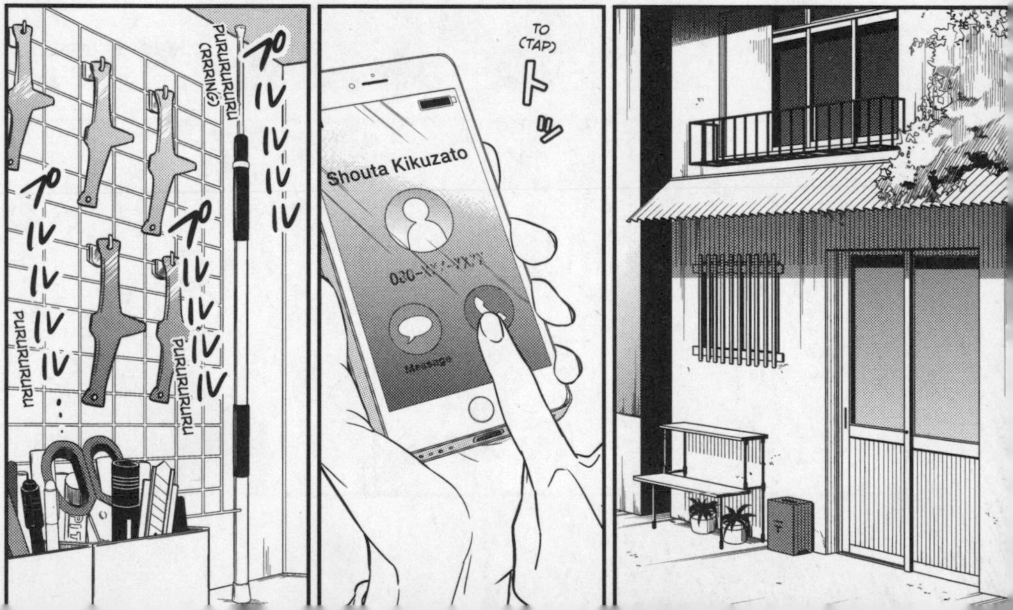
トッ
TO (TAP)
Shouta Kikuzato
プルルルル
PURURURURU (RRRING)
プルルルルル
PURURURURU
プルルルル…
PURURURURU

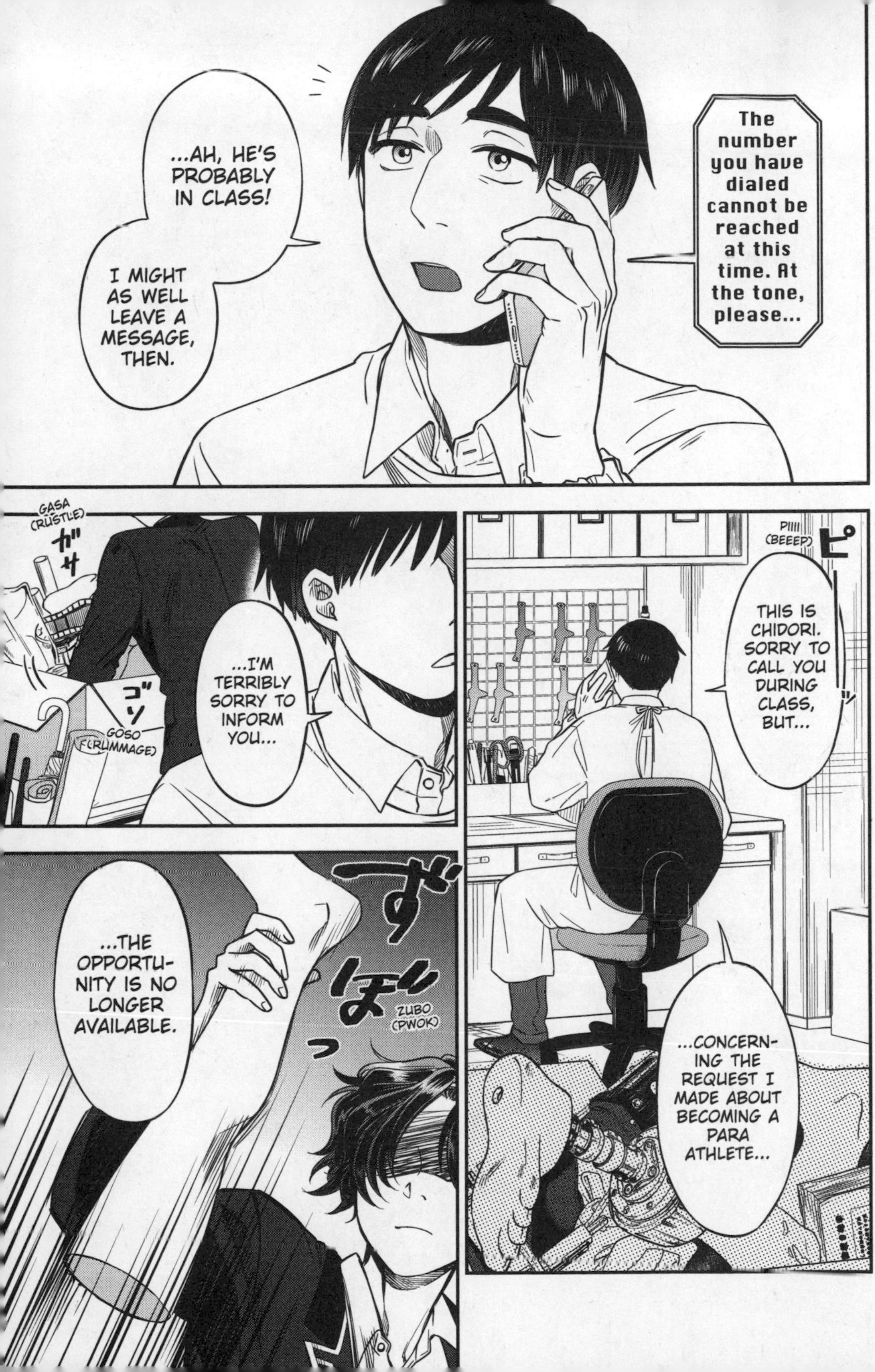
The number you have dialed cannot be reached at this time. At the tone, please...
...AH, HE'S PROBABLY IN CLASS!
I MIGHT AS WELL LEAVE A MESSAGE, THEN.
PIIII (BEEEP)
THIS IS CHIDORI. SORRY TO CALL YOU DURING CLASS, BUT...
...CONCERNING THE REQUEST I MADE ABOUT BECOMING A PARA ATHLETE...
GASA (RUSTLE)
...I'M TERRIBLY SORRY TO INFORM YOU...
GOSO (RUMMAGE)
...THE OPPORTUNITY IS NO LONGER AVAILABLE.
ZUBO (PWOK)

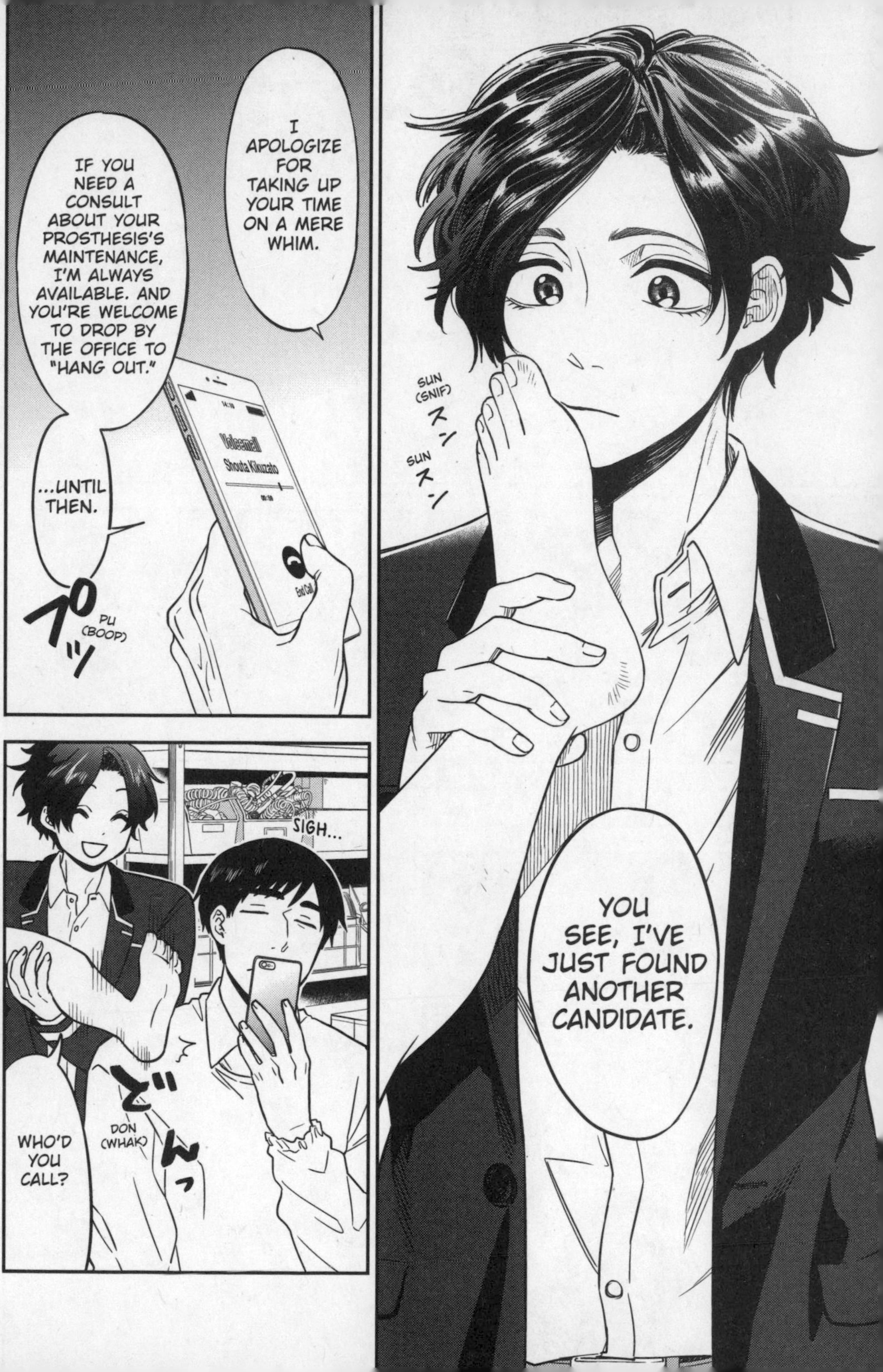
SUN (SNIF)
スン
SUN
スン
YOU SEE, I'VE JUST FOUND ANOTHER CANDIDATE.
I APOLOGIZE FOR TAKING UP YOUR TIME ON A MERE WHIM.
IF YOU NEED A CONSULT ABOUT YOUR PROSTHESIS'S MAINTENANCE, I'M ALWAYS AVAILABLE. AND YOU'RE WELCOME TO DROP BY THE OFFICE TO "HANG OUT."
Voicemail
Shouta Kikuzato
End Call
...UNTIL THEN.
プッ
PU (BOOP)
SIGH...
どんっ
DON (WHAK)
WHO'D YOU CALL?

AWW.

...IT'S A
SECRET.

...Until
then.

And
you're
welcome
to drop by
the office
to "hang
out."

...about
your
pros-
thesis's
mainte-
nance,
I'm
always
avail-
able.

THAT JERK... GETTING A GUY'S HOPES UP LIKE THAT...

ESPECIALLY IF HE HAD SOME BACKUP RUNNER IN MIND.

WHAT THE HECK? DAMN!

ど (DOSA (FWMP))さっ．

...SOCCER'S NOT IN THE CARDS FOR ME...AND NEITHER IS RUNNING.

IN THE END...

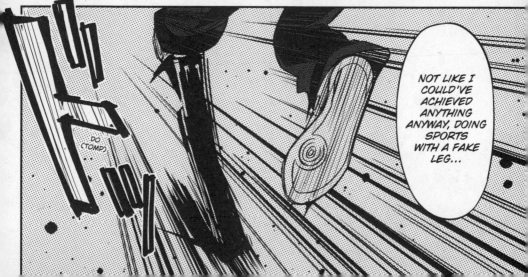

NOT LIKE I COULD'VE ACHIEVED ANYTHING ANYWAY, DOING SPORTS WITH A FAKE LEG...

ド (DO (TOMP))

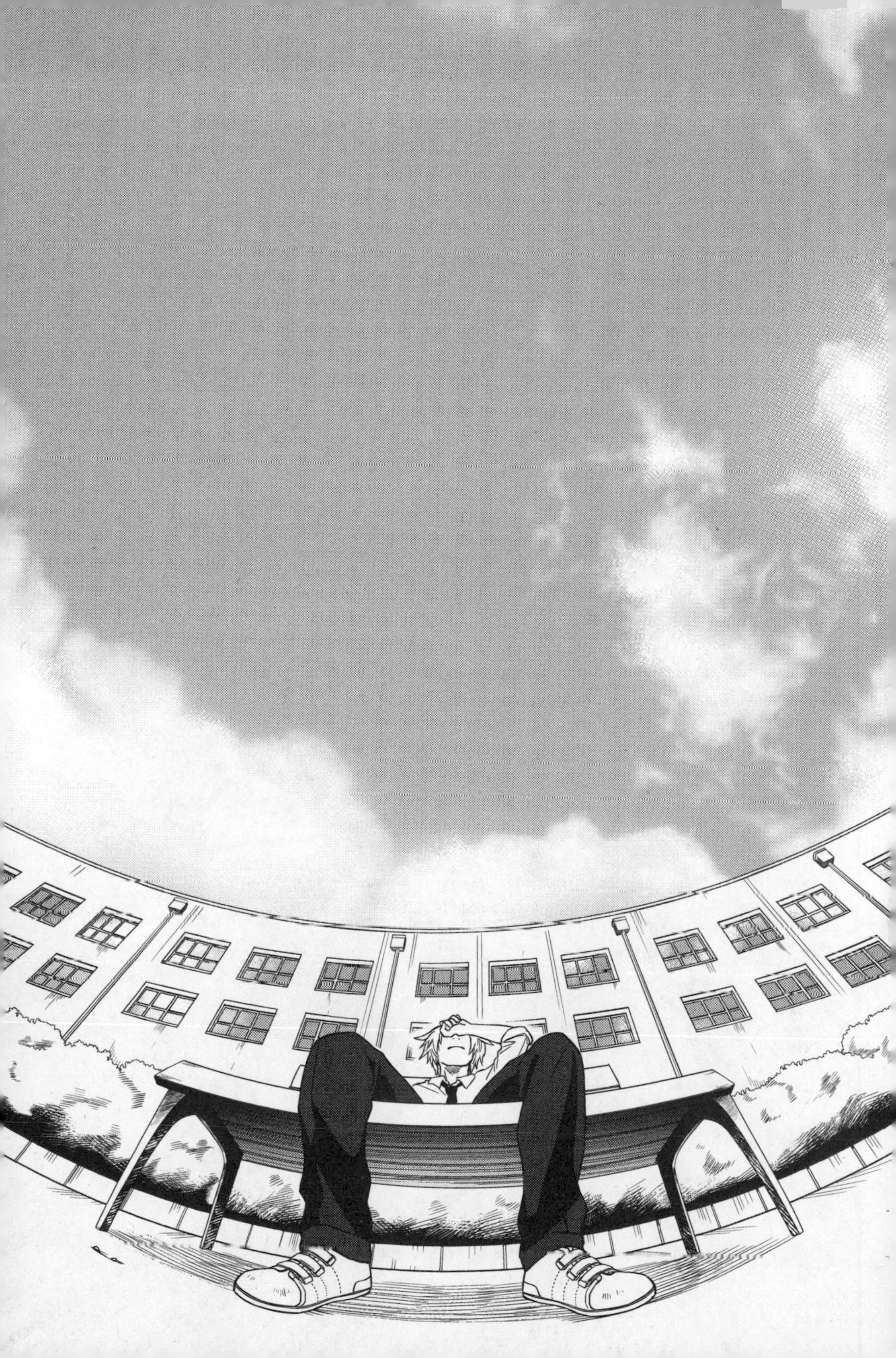

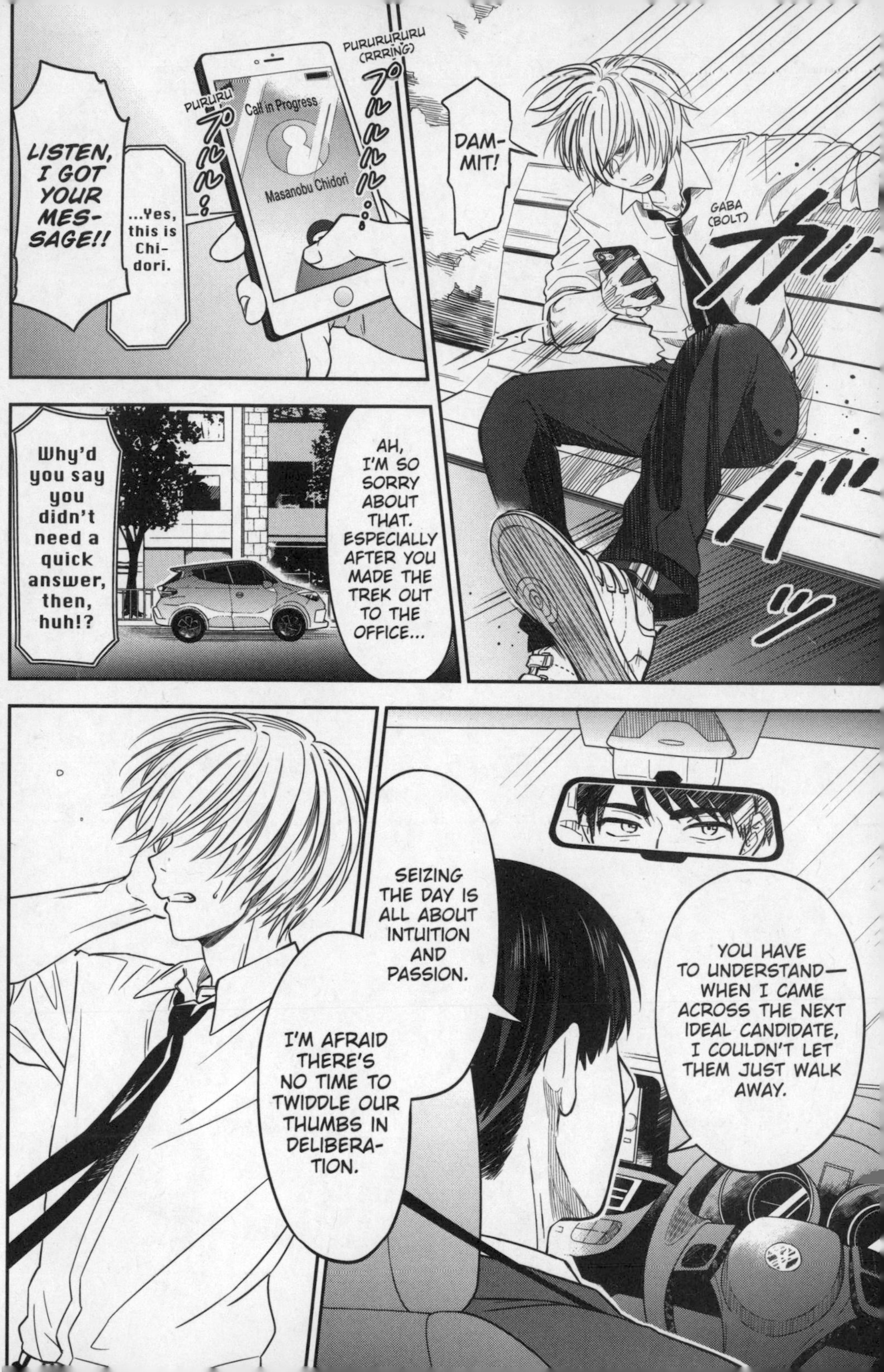
DAM-MIT!
GABA (BOLT)
PURURURURU (RRRING)
PURURU
Call in Progress
Masanobu Chidori
...Yes, this is Chi-dori.
LISTEN, I GOT YOUR MES-SAGE!!
AH, I'M SO SORRY ABOUT THAT. ESPECIALLY AFTER YOU MADE THE TREK OUT TO THE OFFICE...
Why'd you say you didn't need a quick answer, then, huh!?
YOU HAVE TO UNDERSTAND— WHEN I CAME ACROSS THE NEXT IDEAL CANDIDATE, I COULDN'T LET THEM JUST WALK AWAY.
SEIZING THE DAY IS ALL ABOUT INTUITION AND PASSION.
I'M AFRAID THERE'S NO TIME TO TWIDDLE OUR THUMBS IN DELIBERA-TION.

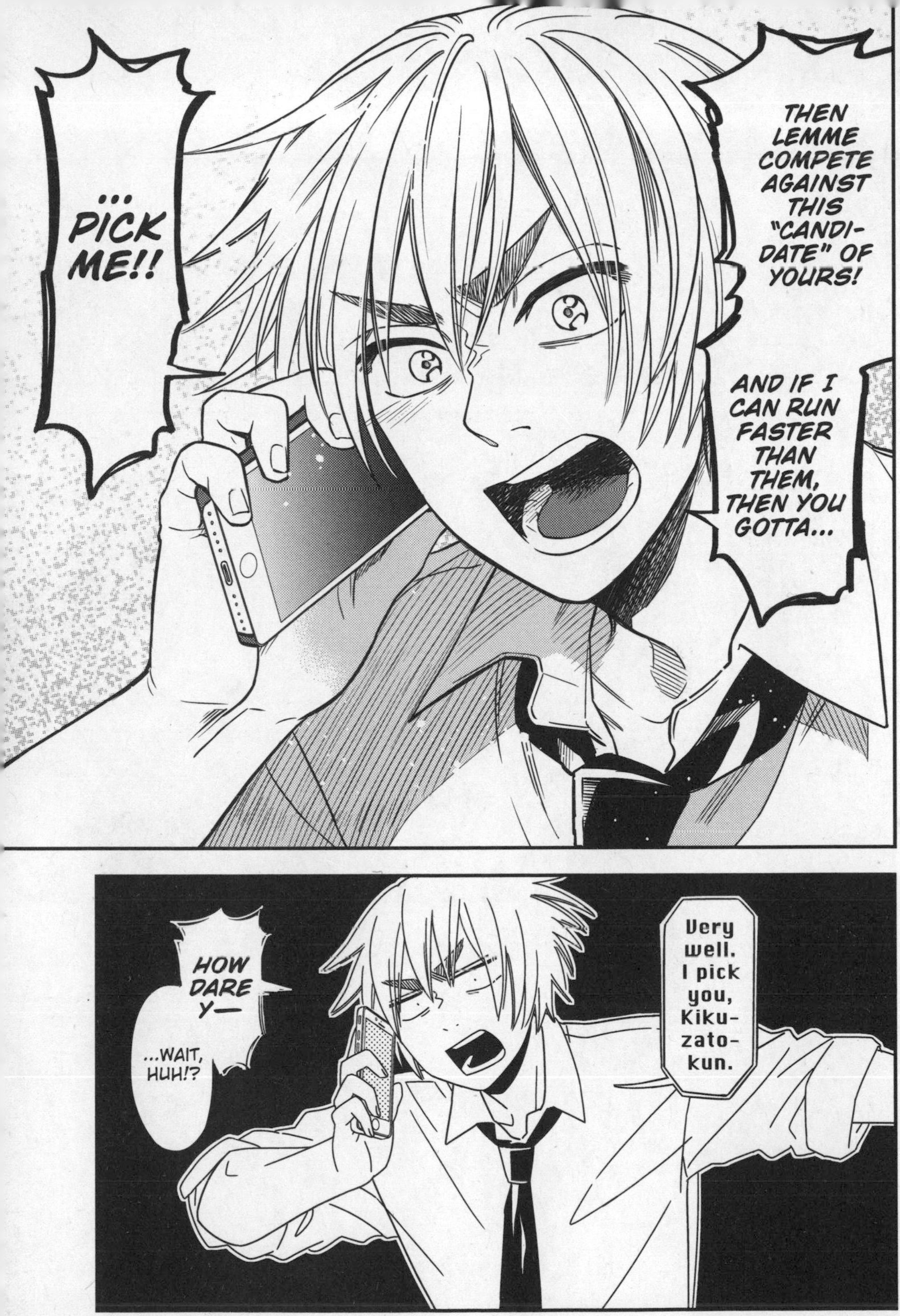
THEN LEMME COMPETE AGAINST THIS "CANDI-DATE" OF YOURS!
AND IF I CAN RUN FASTER THAN THEM, THEN YOU GOTTA...
...PICK ME!!
Very well. I pick you, Kiku-zato-kun.
HOW DARE Y—
...WAIT, HUH!?

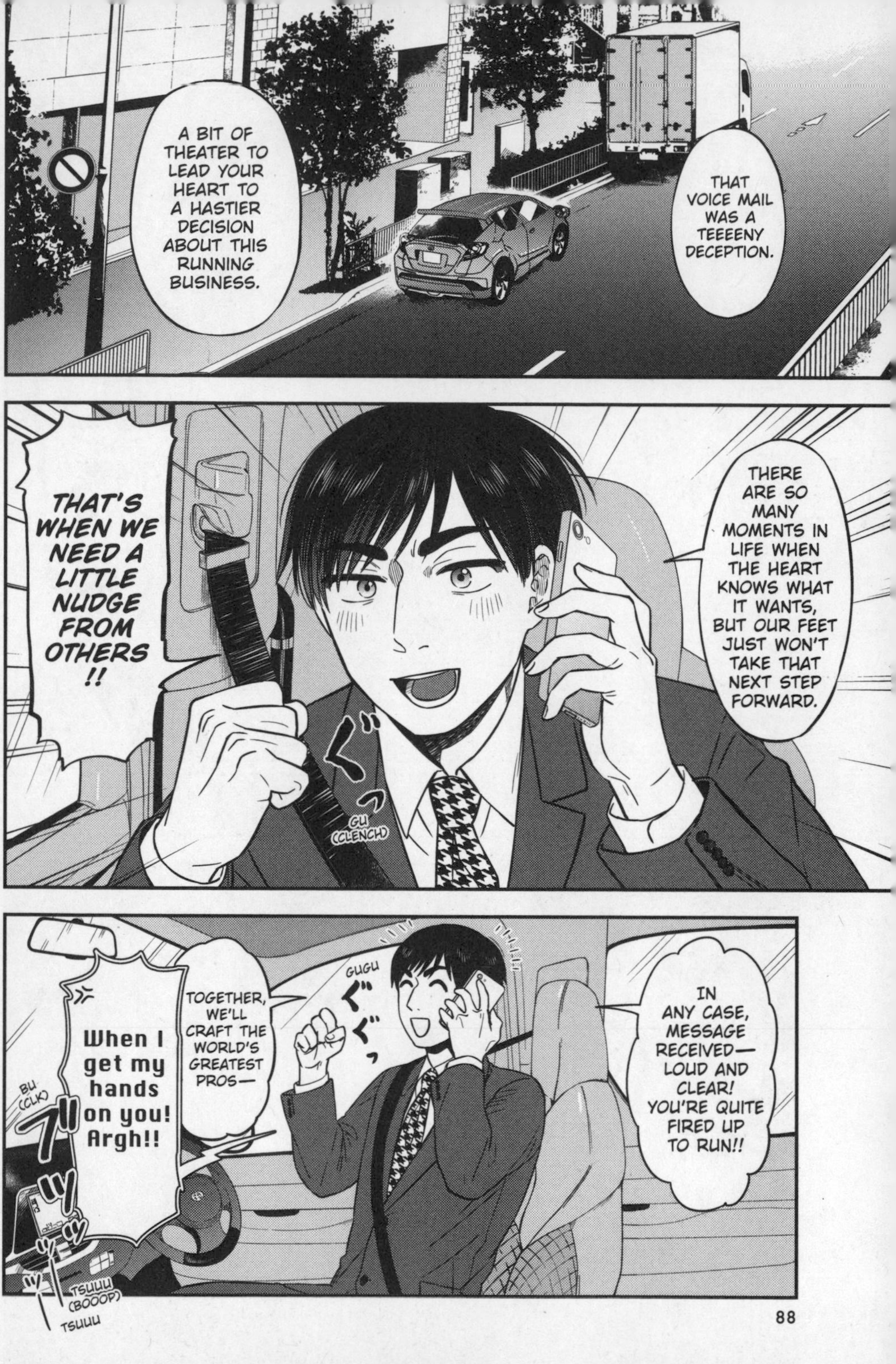
THAT VOICE MAIL WAS A TEEEENY DECEPTION.
A BIT OF THEATER TO LEAD YOUR HEART TO A HASTIER DECISION ABOUT THIS RUNNING BUSINESS.
THERE ARE SO MANY MOMENTS IN LIFE WHEN THE HEART KNOWS WHAT IT WANTS, BUT OUR FEET JUST WON'T TAKE THAT NEXT STEP FORWARD.
THAT'S WHEN WE NEED A LITTLE NUDGE FROM OTHERS!!
GU (CLENCH)
IN ANY CASE, MESSAGE RECEIVED—LOUD AND CLEAR! YOU'RE QUITE FIRED UP TO RUN!!
GUGU
TOGETHER, WE'LL CRAFT THE WORLD'S GREATEST PROS—
When I get my hands on you! Argh!!
BU (CLK)
TSUUU (BOOOP)
TSUUU

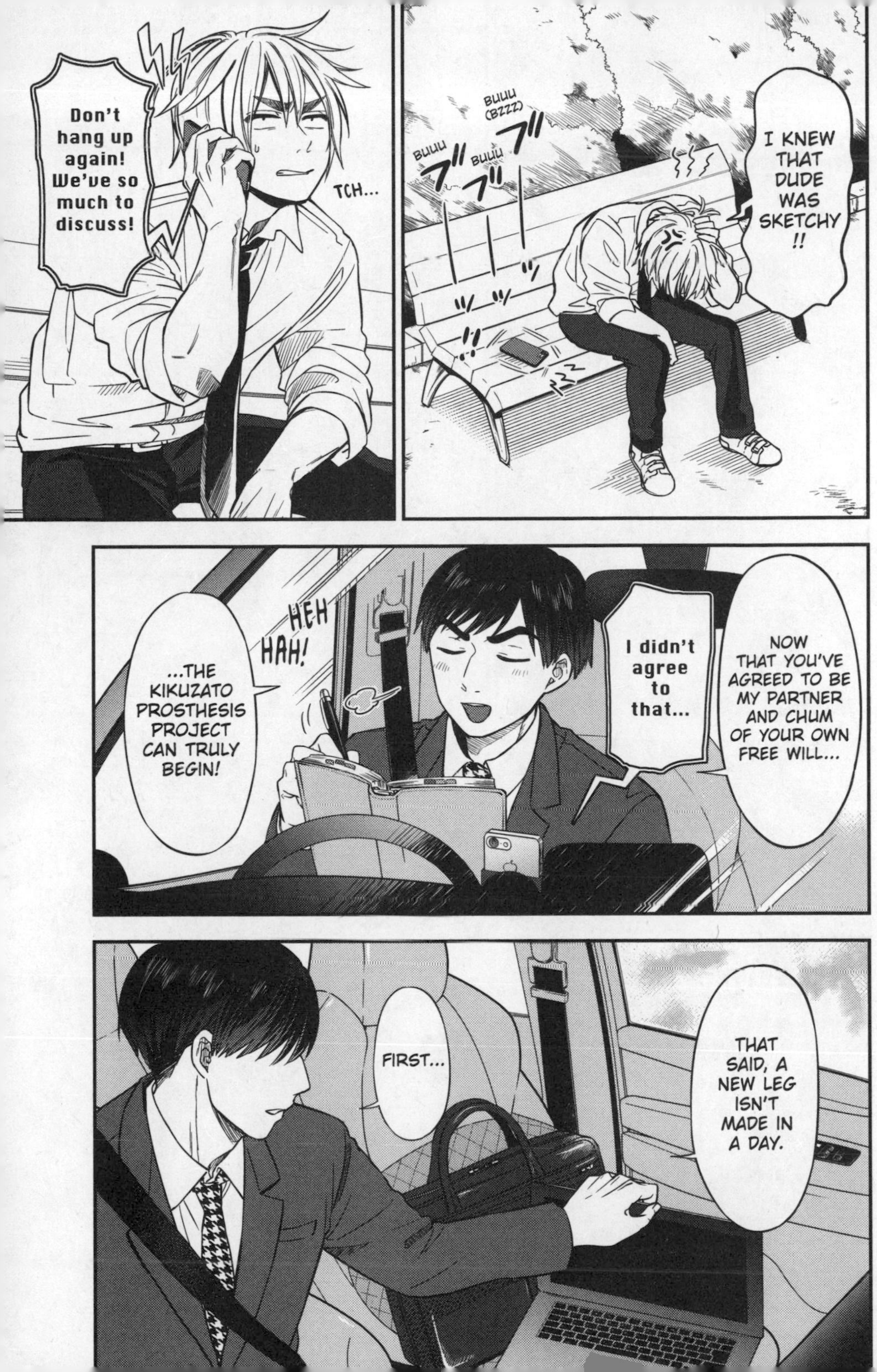
I KNEW THAT DUDE WAS SKETCHY!!
BUUU (BZZZ)
BUUU
BUUU
Don't hang up again! We've so much to discuss!
TCH...
NOW THAT YOU'VE AGREED TO BE MY PARTNER AND CHUM OF YOUR OWN FREE WILL...
I didn't agree to that...
...THE KIKUZATO PROSTHESIS PROJECT CAN TRULY BEGIN!
HEH HAH!
THAT SAID, A NEW LEG ISN'T MADE IN A DAY.
FIRST...

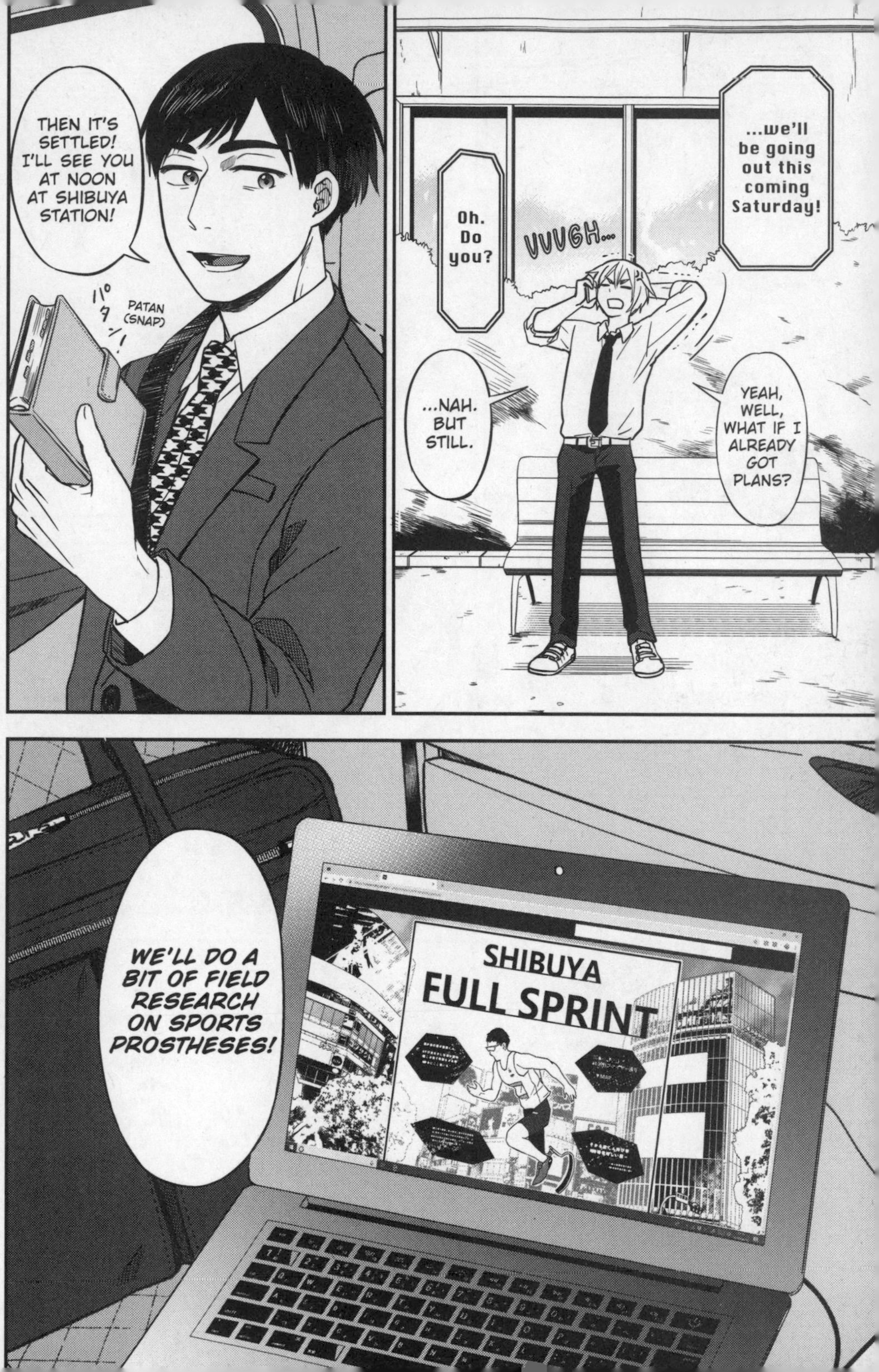
...we'll be going out this coming Saturday!
Oh. Do you?
VUUGH...
YEAH, WELL, WHAT IF I ALREADY GOT PLANS?
...NAH. BUT STILL.
THEN IT'S SETTLED! I'LL SEE YOU AT NOON AT SHIBUYA STATION!
PATAN (SNAP)
WE'LL DO A BIT OF FIELD RESEARCH ON SPORTS PROSTHESES!
SHIBUYA FULL SPRINT

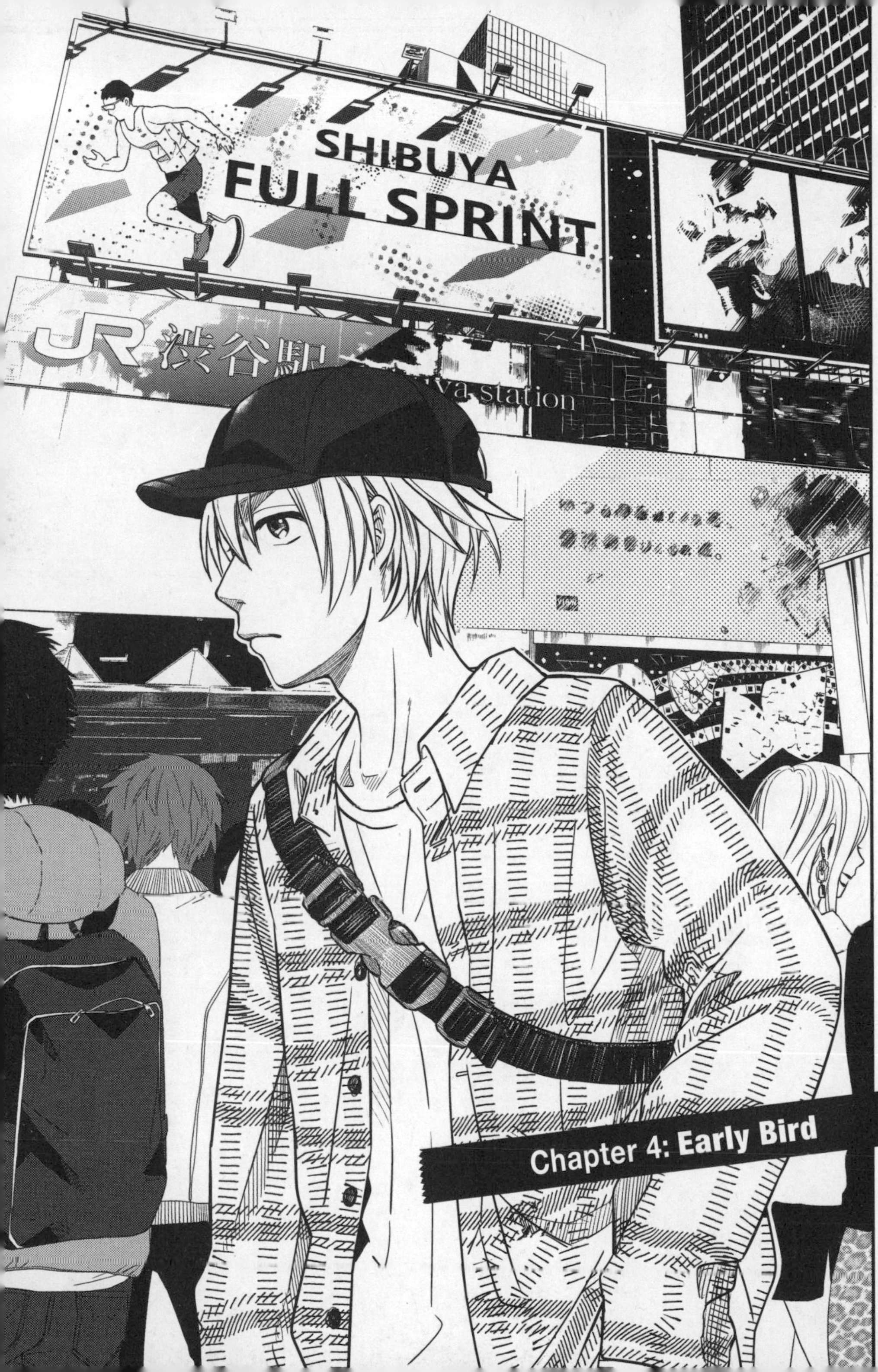
SHIBUYA
FULL SPRINT
Chapter 4: Early Bird

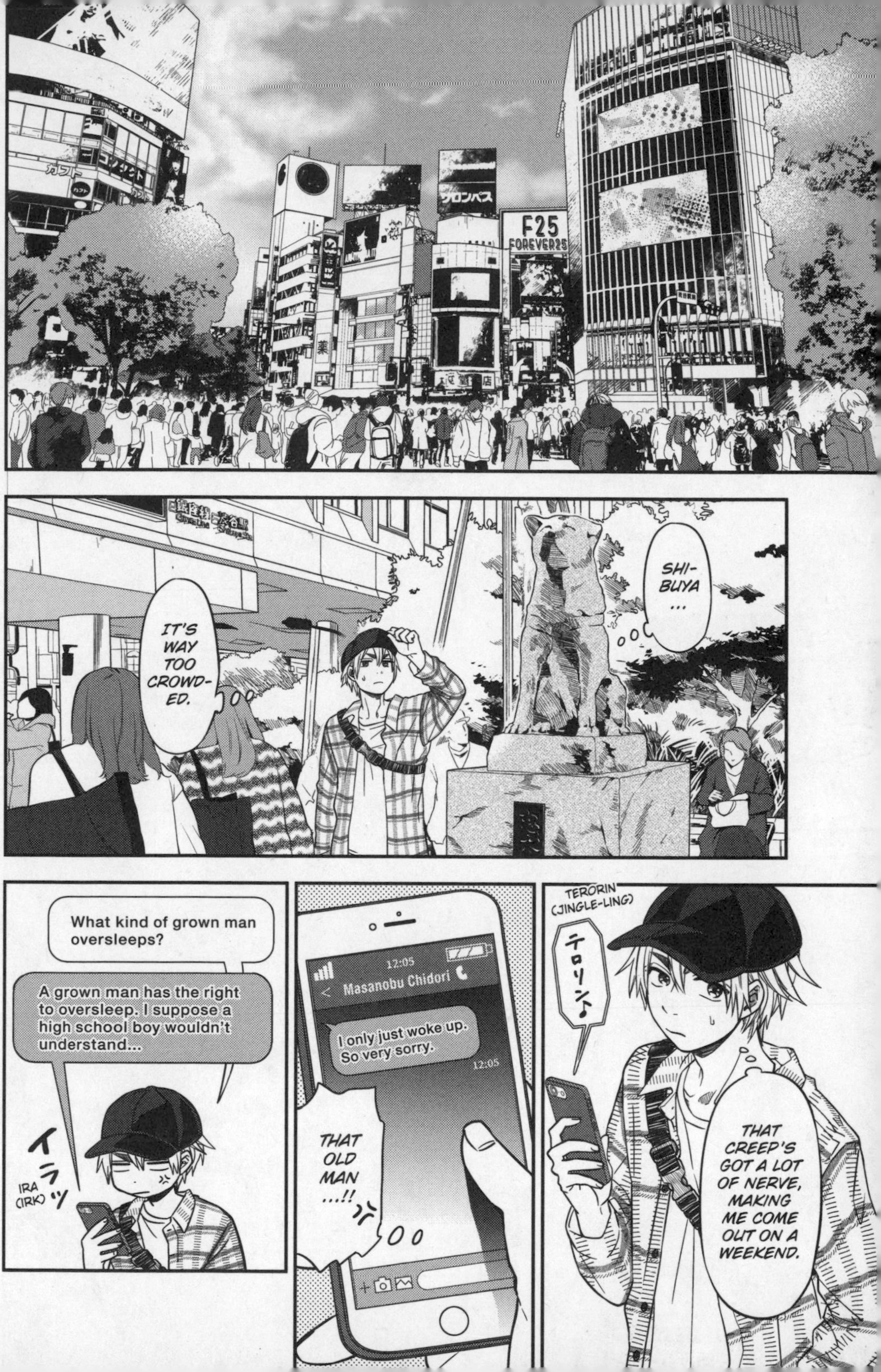
F25
FOREVER25
SHI-BUYA...
IT'S WAY TOO CROWDED.
TERORIN (JINGLE-LING)
テロリン♪
THAT CREEP'S GOT A LOT OF NERVE, MAKING ME COME OUT ON A WEEKEND.
12:05
Masanobu Chidori
I only just woke up. So very sorry.
12:05
THAT OLD MAN ...!!
What kind of grown man oversleeps?
A grown man has the right to oversleep. I suppose a high school boy wouldn't understand...
イラッ
IRA (IRK)

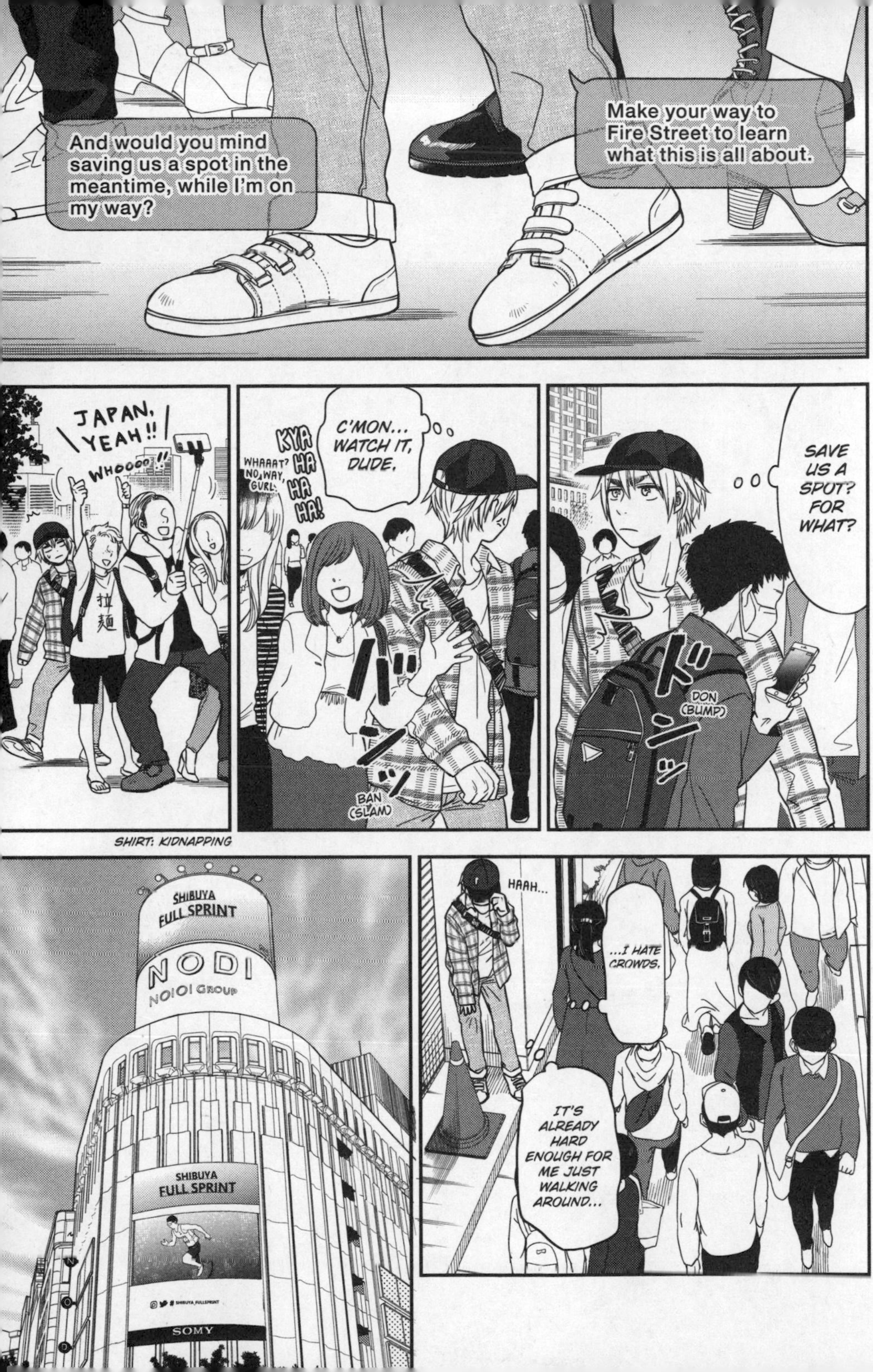

Make your way to Fire Street to learn what this is all about.
And would you mind saving us a spot in the meantime, while I'm on my way?
SAVE US A SPOT? FOR WHAT?
DON (BUMP)
C'MON... WATCH IT, DUDE.
KYA HA HA HA!
WHAAAT? NO WAY, GURL!
BAN (SLAM)
JAPAN, YEAH!!
WHOOOO!!
拉麺
SHIRT: KIDNAPPING
HAAH...
...I HATE CROWDS.
IT'S ALREADY HARD ENOUGH FOR ME JUST WALKING AROUND...
SHIBUYA FULL SPRINT
NODI
NOIOI Group
SHIBUYA FULL SPRINT
SHIBUYA_FULLSPRINT
SOMY

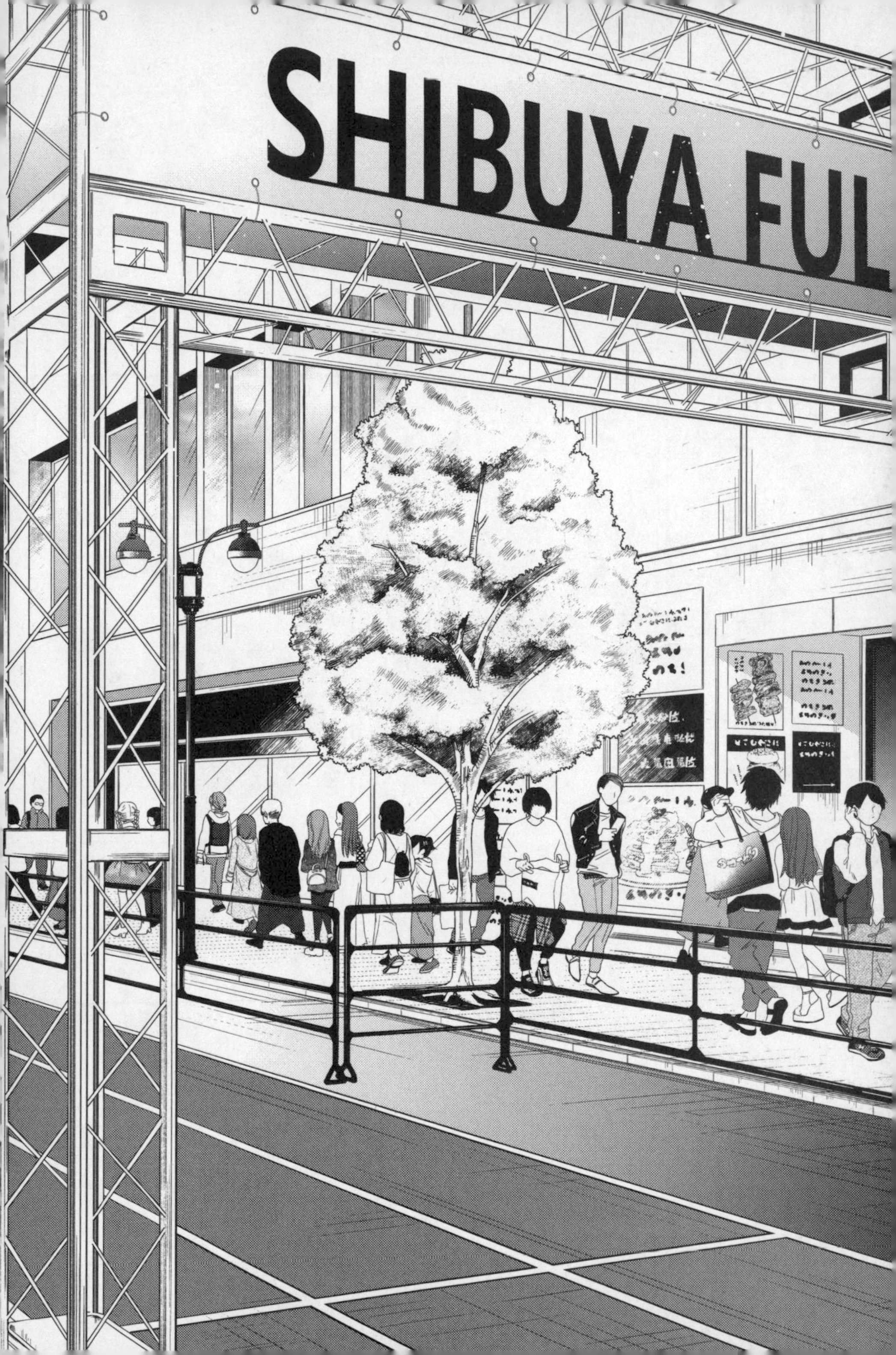
SHIBUYA FUL

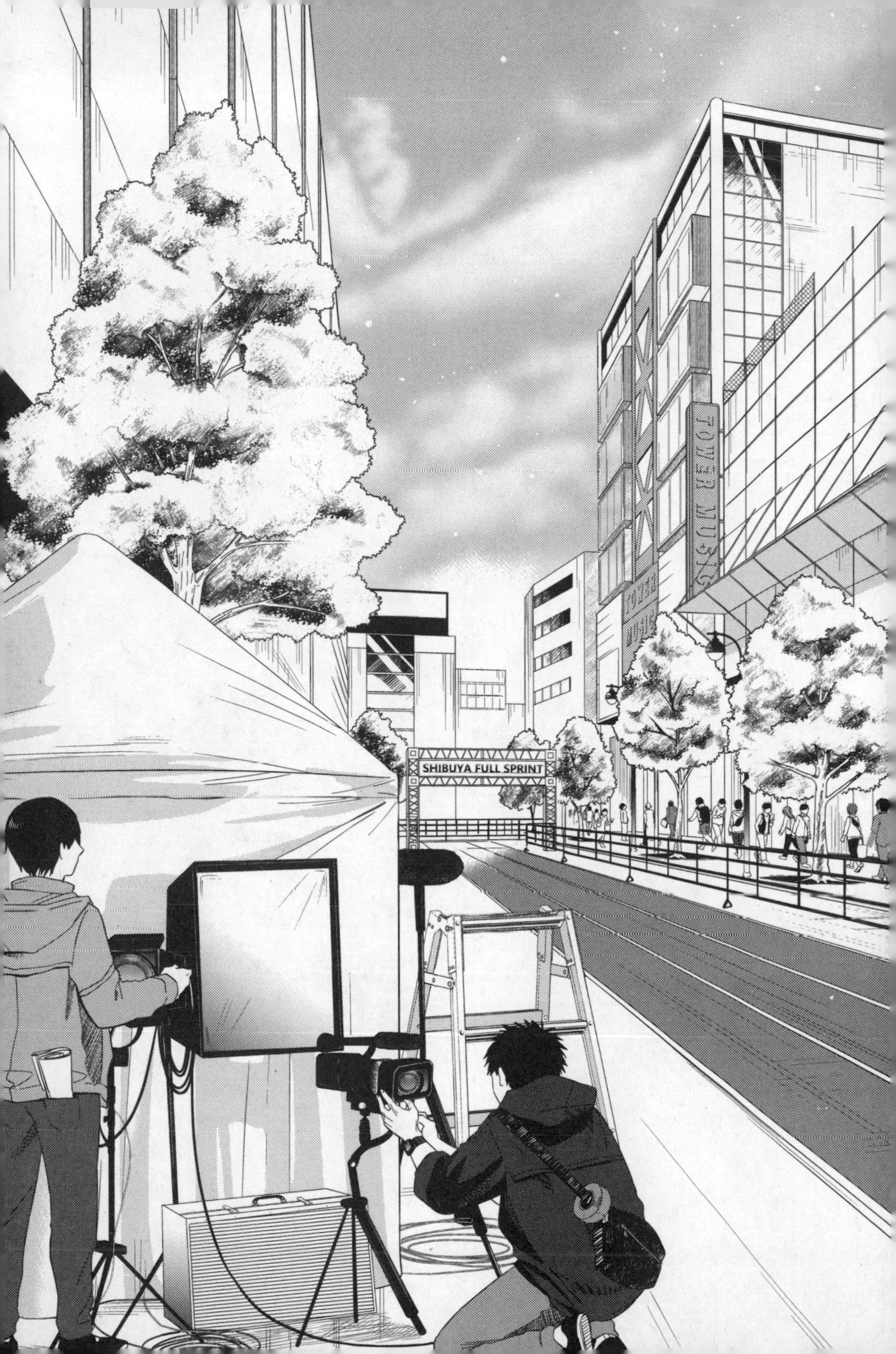
TOWER MUSIC
SHIBUYA FULL SPRINT

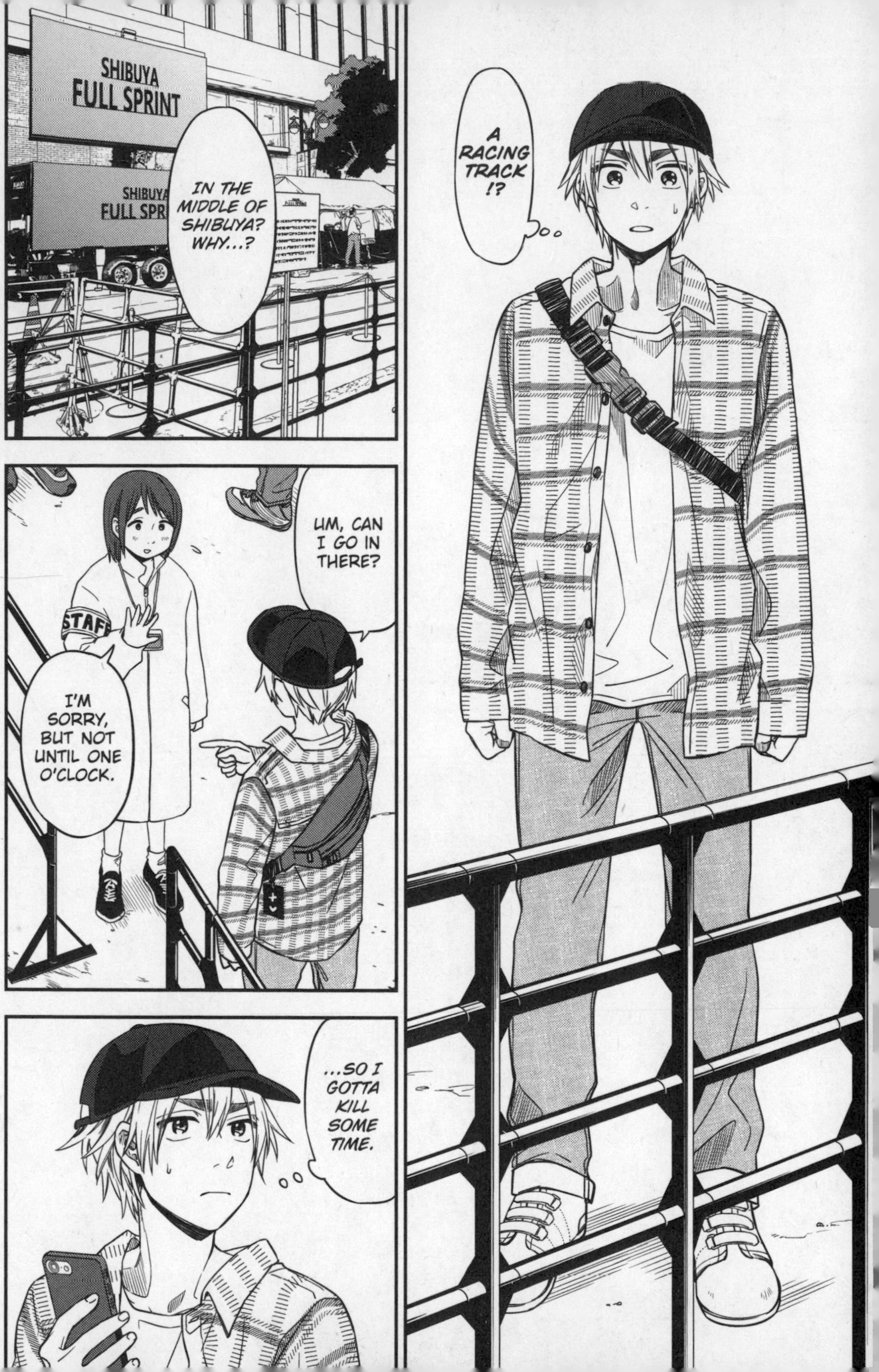
A RACING TRACK!?
SHIBUYA FULL SPRINT
SHIBUYA FULL SPR
IN THE MIDDLE OF SHIBUYA? WHY...?
UM, CAN I GO IN THERE?
STAFF
I'M SORRY, BUT NOT UNTIL ONE O'CLOCK.
...SO I GOTTA KILL SOME TIME.

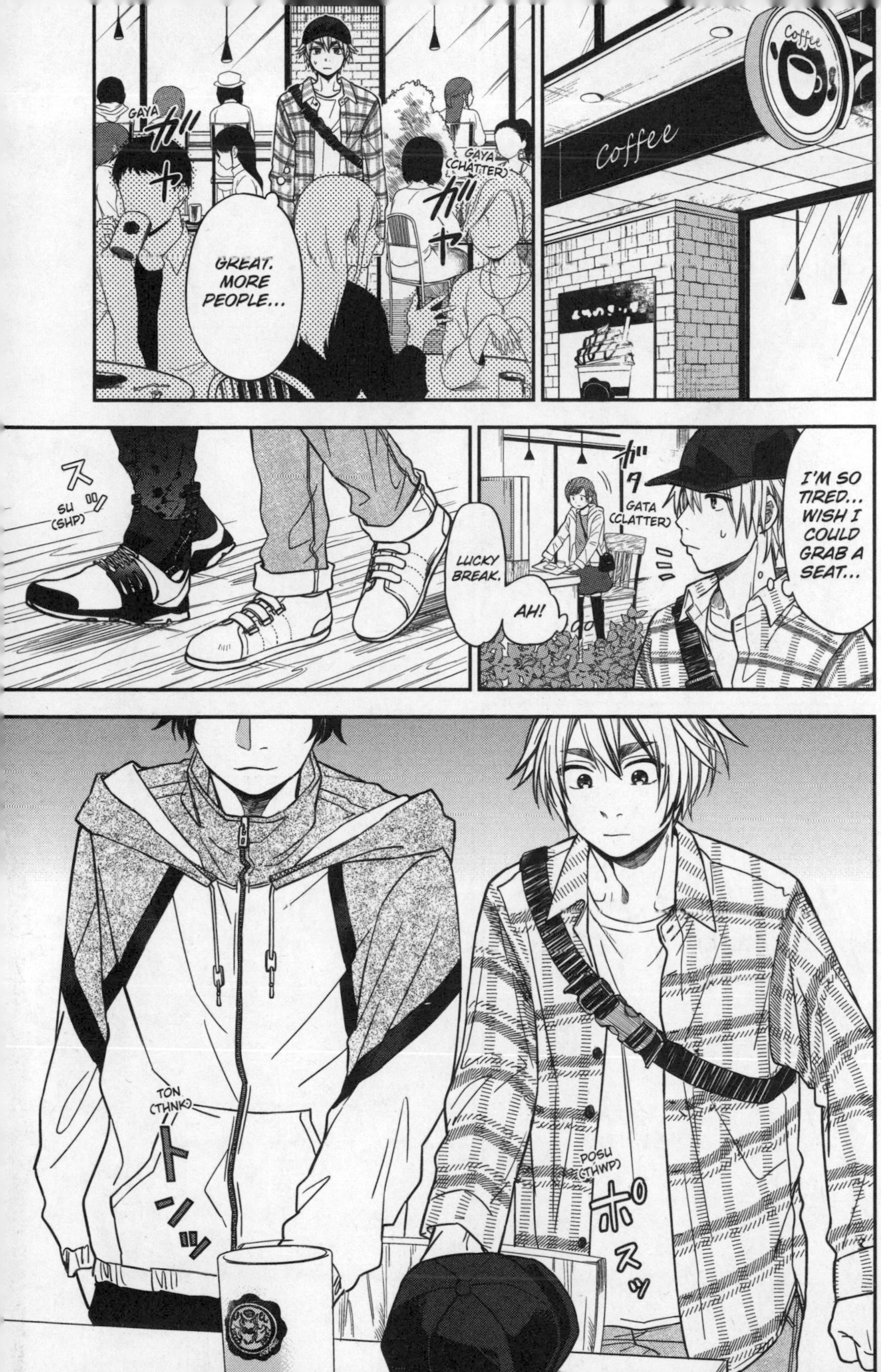
Coffee
Coffee
GAYA
GAYA (CHATTER)
GREAT. MORE PEOPLE...
I'M SO TIRED... WISH I COULD GRAB A SEAT...
GATA (CLATTER)
AH!
LUCKY BREAK.
SU (SHP)
POSU (THWP)
TON (THNK)

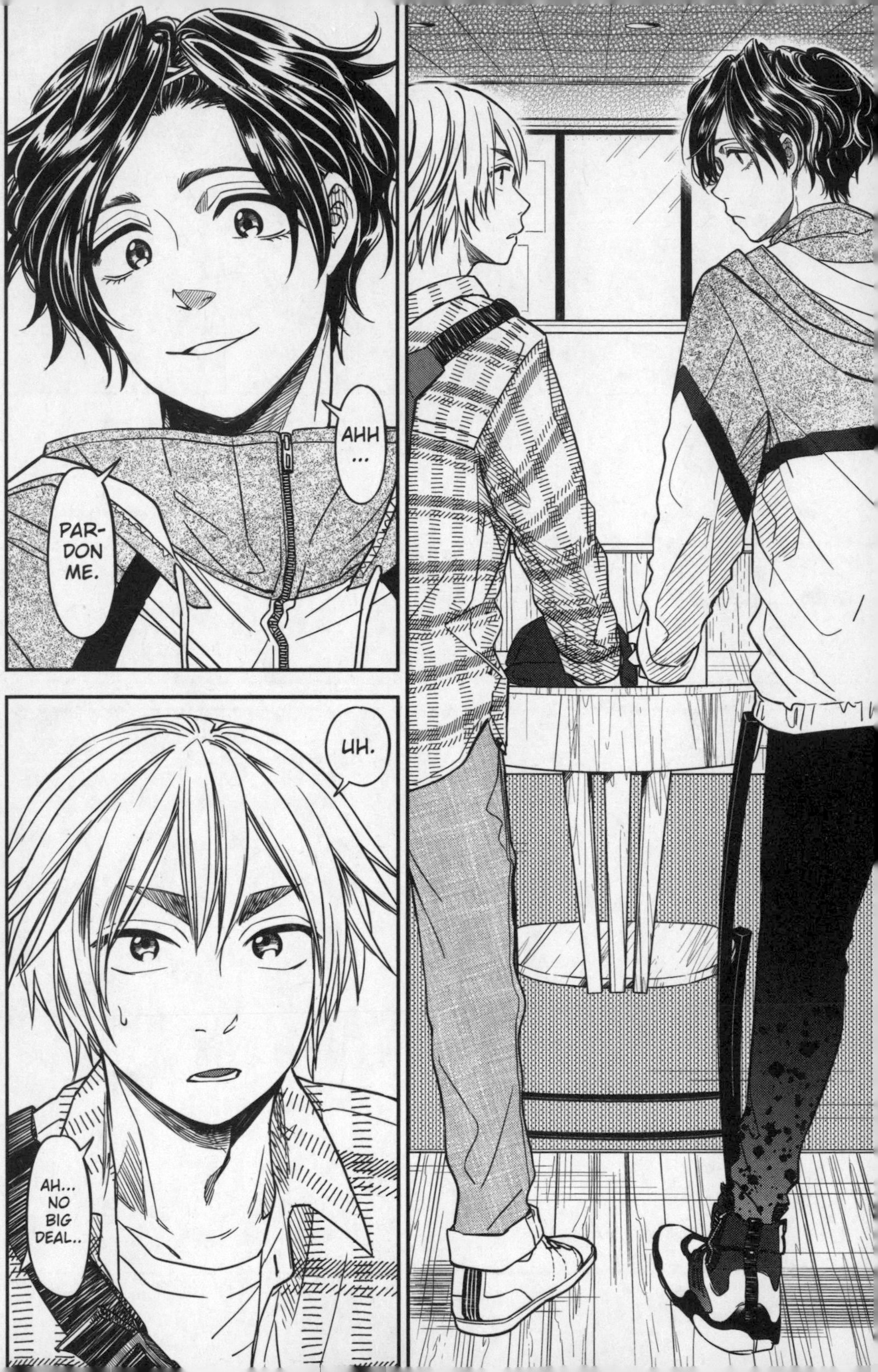
AHH...
PARDON ME.
UH.
AH... NO BIG DEAL..

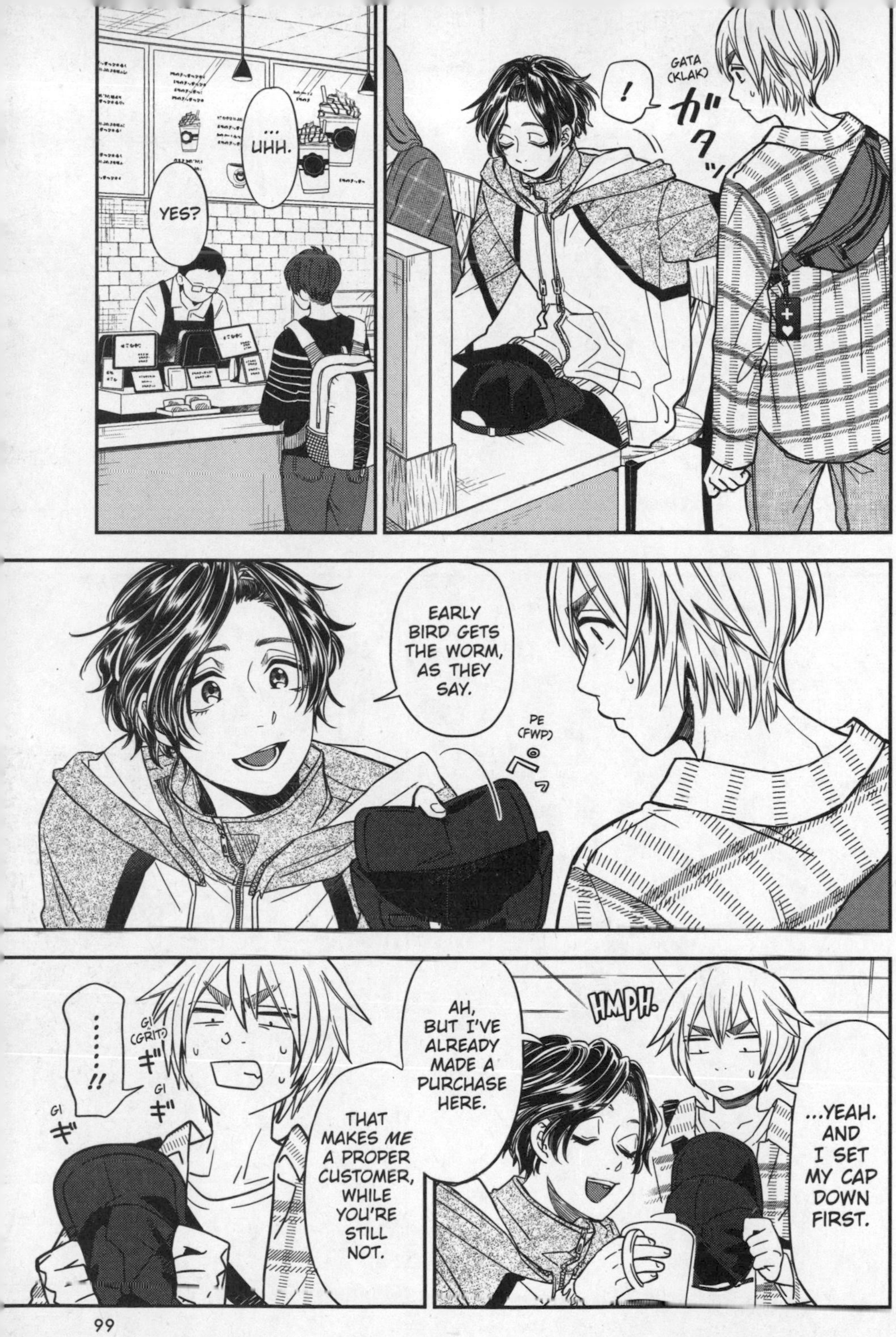
!
GATA (KLAK)
ガタッ
...UHH.
YES?
EARLY BIRD GETS THE WORM, AS THEY SAY.
PE (FWP)
ぺっ
HMPH.
...YEAH. AND I SET MY CAP DOWN FIRST.
AH, BUT I'VE ALREADY MADE A PURCHASE HERE.
THAT MAKES *ME* A PROPER CUSTOMER, WHILE YOU'RE STILL NOT.
GI (GRIT)
ギ
GI
ギ
GI
ギ
......!!

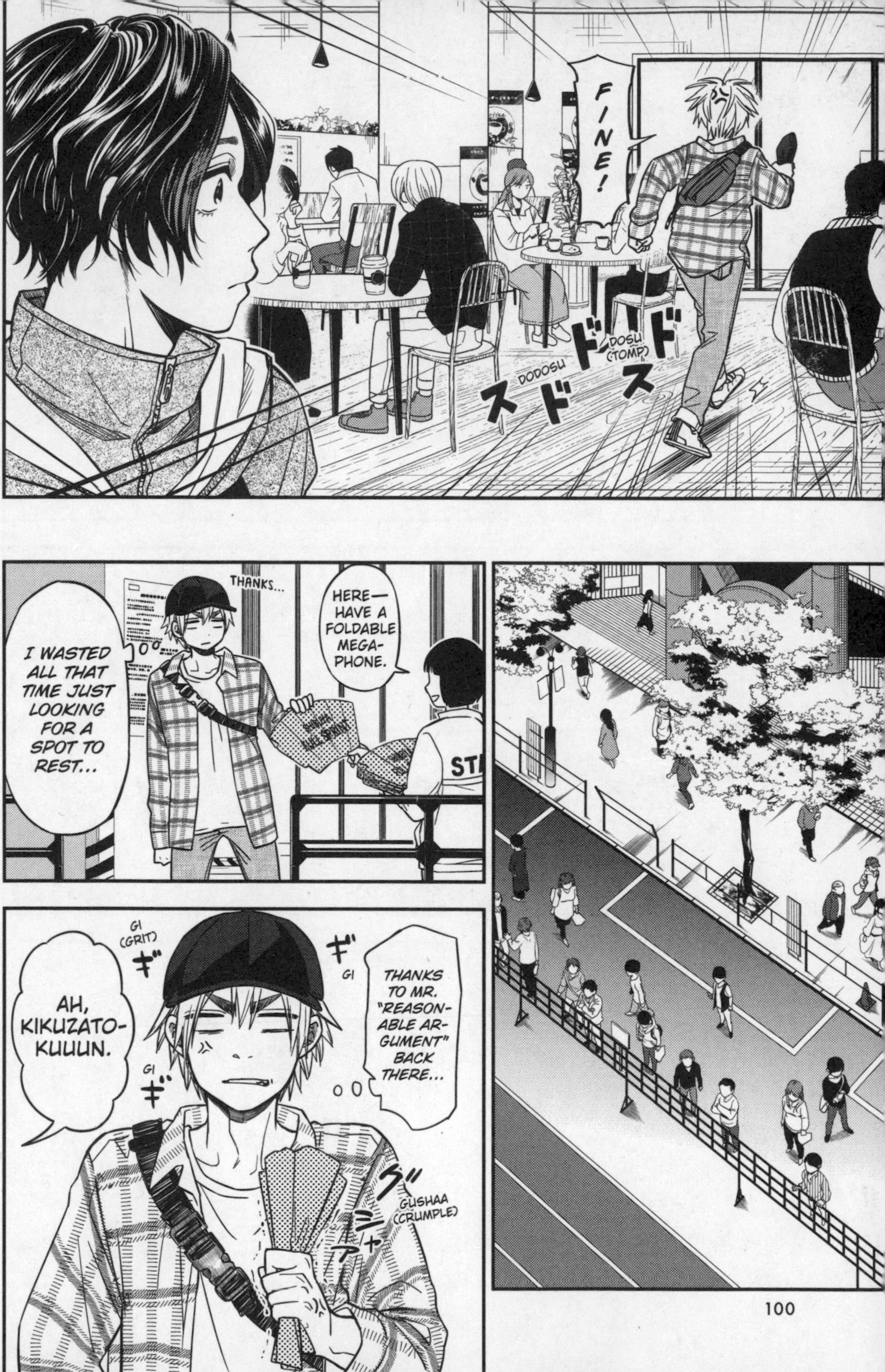
FINE!
ドド DOSU (TOMP)
スドス DODOSU
HERE— HAVE A FOLDABLE MEGA-PHONE.
THANKS...
I WASTED ALL THAT TIME JUST LOOKING FOR A SPOT TO REST...
ギ GI
THANKS TO MR. "REASON-ABLE AR-GUMENT" BACK THERE...
GI (GRIT) ギ
AH, KIKUZATO-KUUUN.
GI ギ
グシャア GUSHAA (CRUMPLE)

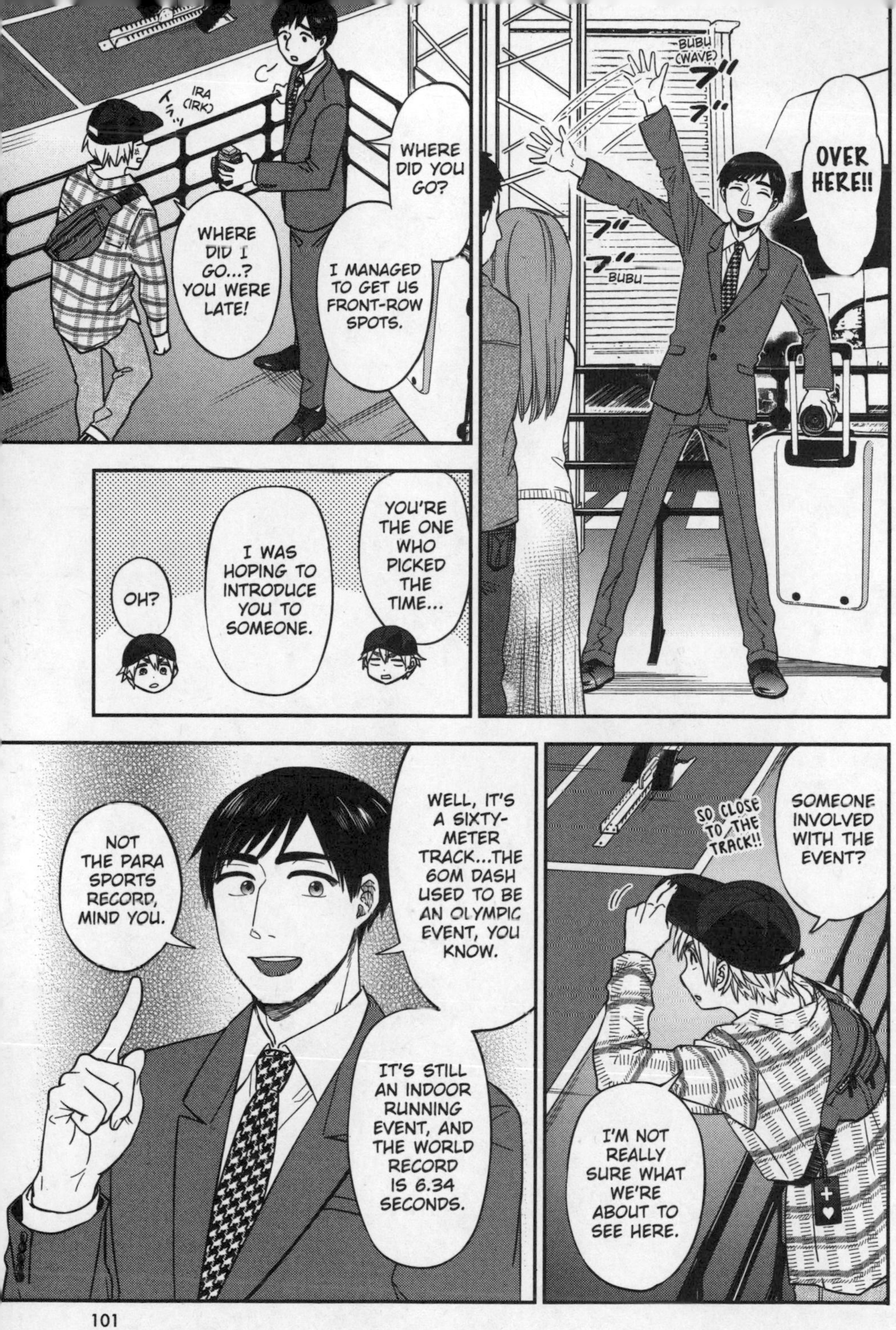
BUBU (WAVE)
OVER HERE!!
BUBU
WHERE DID YOU GO?
I MANAGED TO GET US FRONT-ROW SPOTS.
WHERE DID I GO...? YOU WERE LATE!
IRA (IRK)
YOU'RE THE ONE WHO PICKED THE TIME...
I WAS HOPING TO INTRODUCE YOU TO SOMEONE.
OH?
SOMEONE INVOLVED WITH THE EVENT?
SO CLOSE TO THE TRACK!!
I'M NOT REALLY SURE WHAT WE'RE ABOUT TO SEE HERE.
WELL, IT'S A SIXTY-METER TRACK...THE 60M DASH USED TO BE AN OLYMPIC EVENT, YOU KNOW.
IT'S STILL AN INDOOR RUNNING EVENT, AND THE WORLD RECORD IS 6.34 SECONDS.
NOT THE PARA SPORTS RECORD, MIND YOU.

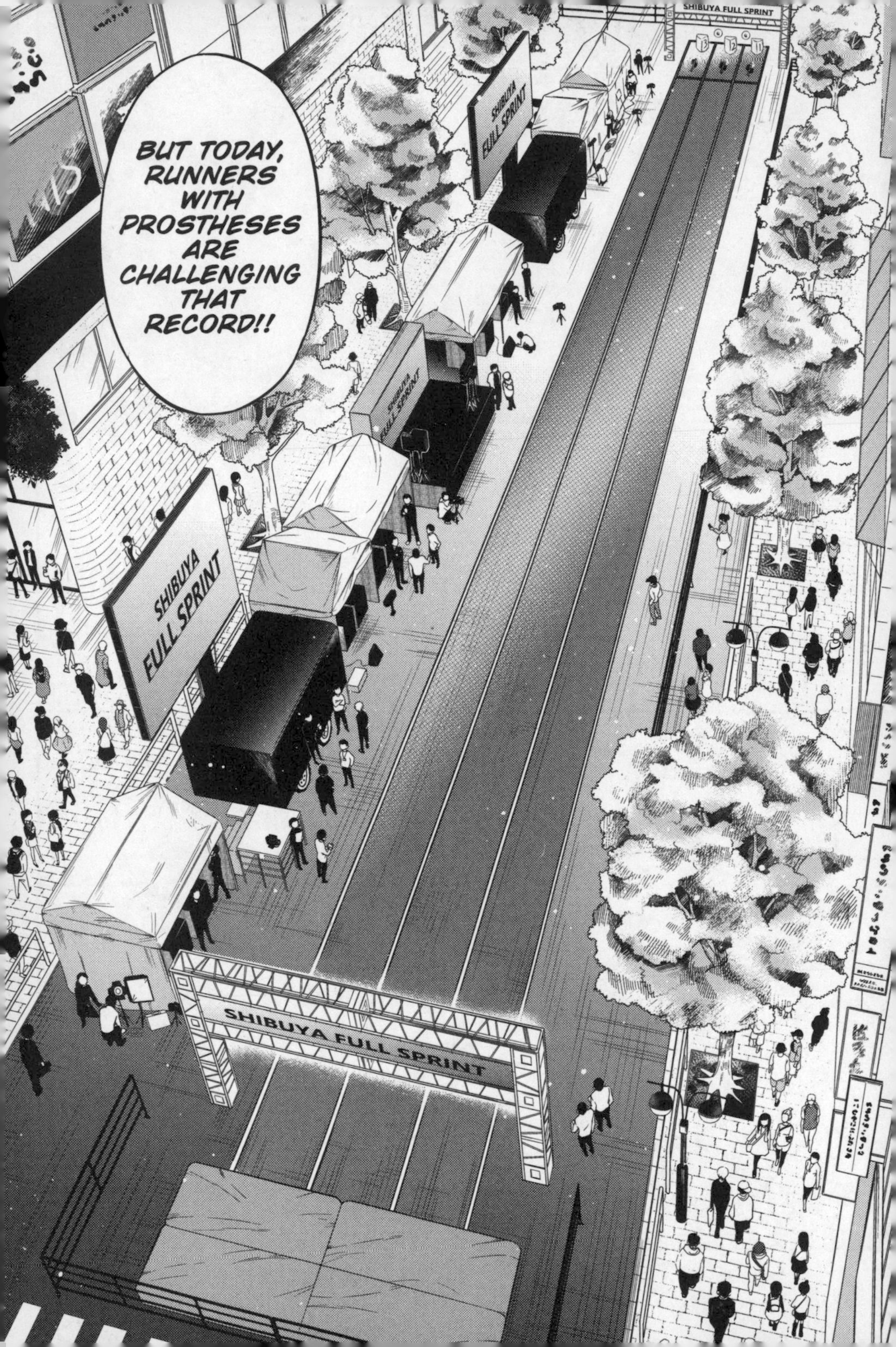
BUT TODAY, RUNNERS WITH PROSTHESES ARE CHALLENGING THAT RECORD!!
SHIBUYA FULL SPRINT
SHIBUYA FULL SPRINT
SHIBUYA FULL SPRINT
SHIBUYA FULL SPRINT
SHIBUYA FULL SPRINT

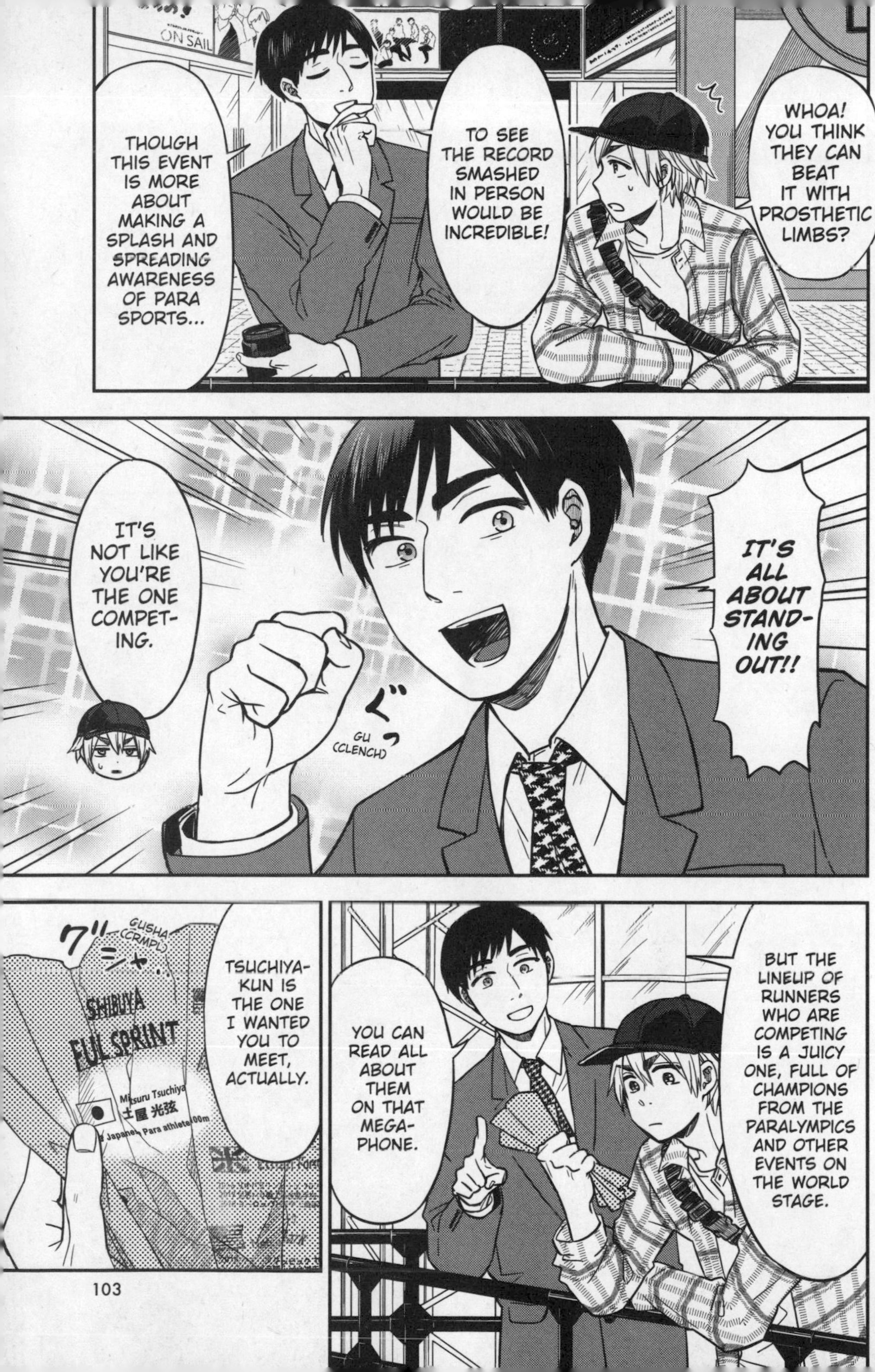
ON SAIL
WHOA! YOU THINK THEY CAN BEAT IT WITH PROSTHETIC LIMBS?
TO SEE THE RECORD SMASHED IN PERSON WOULD BE INCREDIBLE!
THOUGH THIS EVENT IS MORE ABOUT MAKING A SPLASH AND SPREADING AWARENESS OF PARA SPORTS...
IT'S ALL ABOUT STANDING OUT!!
GU (CLENCH)
IT'S NOT LIKE YOU'RE THE ONE COMPETING.
BUT THE LINEUP OF RUNNERS WHO ARE COMPETING IS A JUICY ONE, FULL OF CHAMPIONS FROM THE PARALYMPICS AND OTHER EVENTS ON THE WORLD STAGE.
YOU CAN READ ALL ABOUT THEM ON THAT MEGAPHONE.
TSUCHIYA-KUN IS THE ONE I WANTED YOU TO MEET, ACTUALLY.
GUSHA (CRMPL)
SHIBUYA FUL SPRINT
Mitsuru Tsuchiya
土屋 光弦

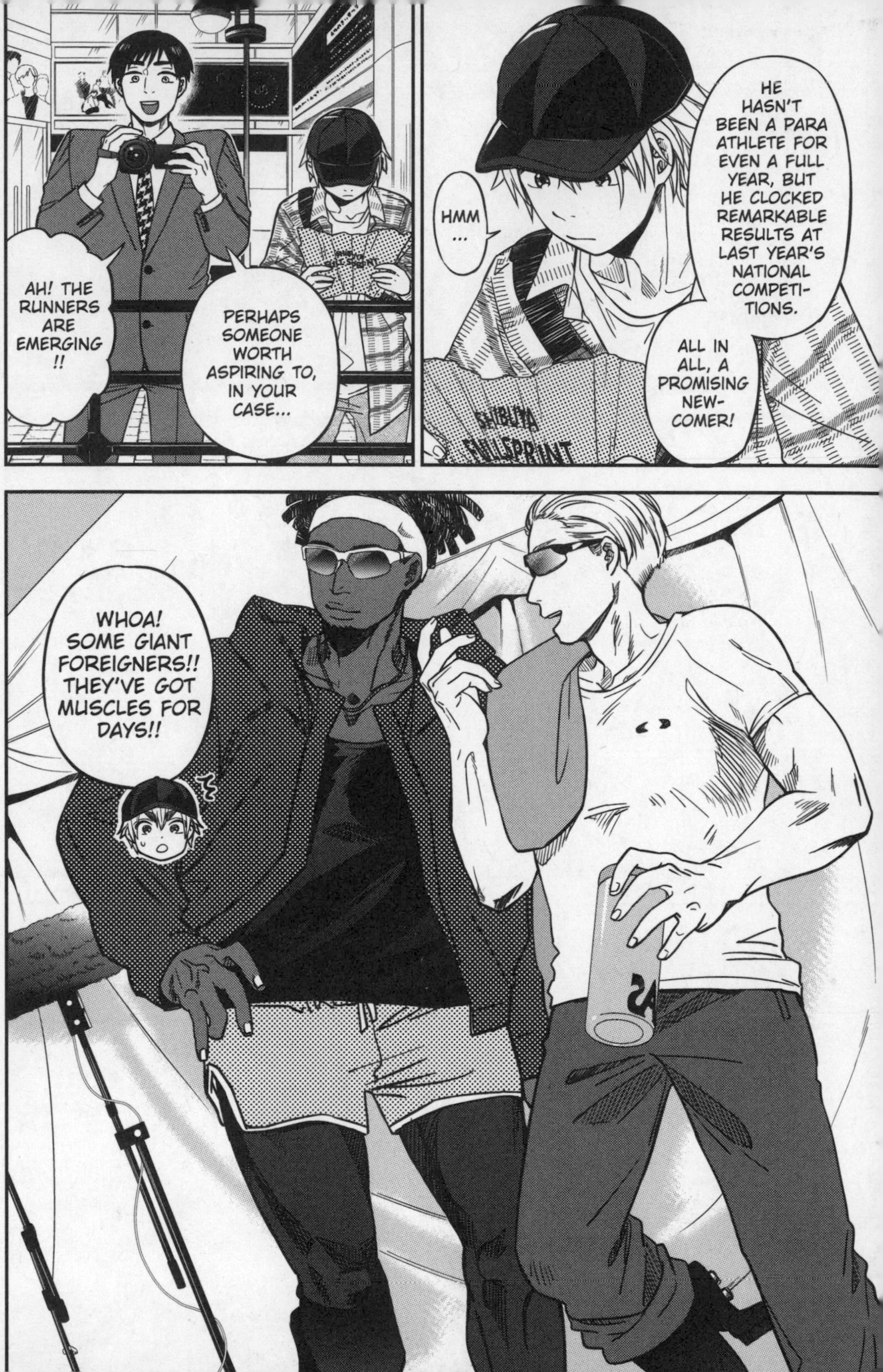
HE HASN'T BEEN A PARA ATHLETE FOR EVEN A FULL YEAR, BUT HE CLOCKED REMARKABLE RESULTS AT LAST YEAR'S NATIONAL COMPETI-TIONS.
HMM ...
ALL IN ALL, A PROMISING NEW-COMER!
PERHAPS SOMEONE WORTH ASPIRING TO, IN YOUR CASE...
AH! THE RUNNERS ARE EMERGING !!
WHOA! SOME GIANT FOREIGNERS!! THEY'VE GOT MUSCLES FOR DAYS!!

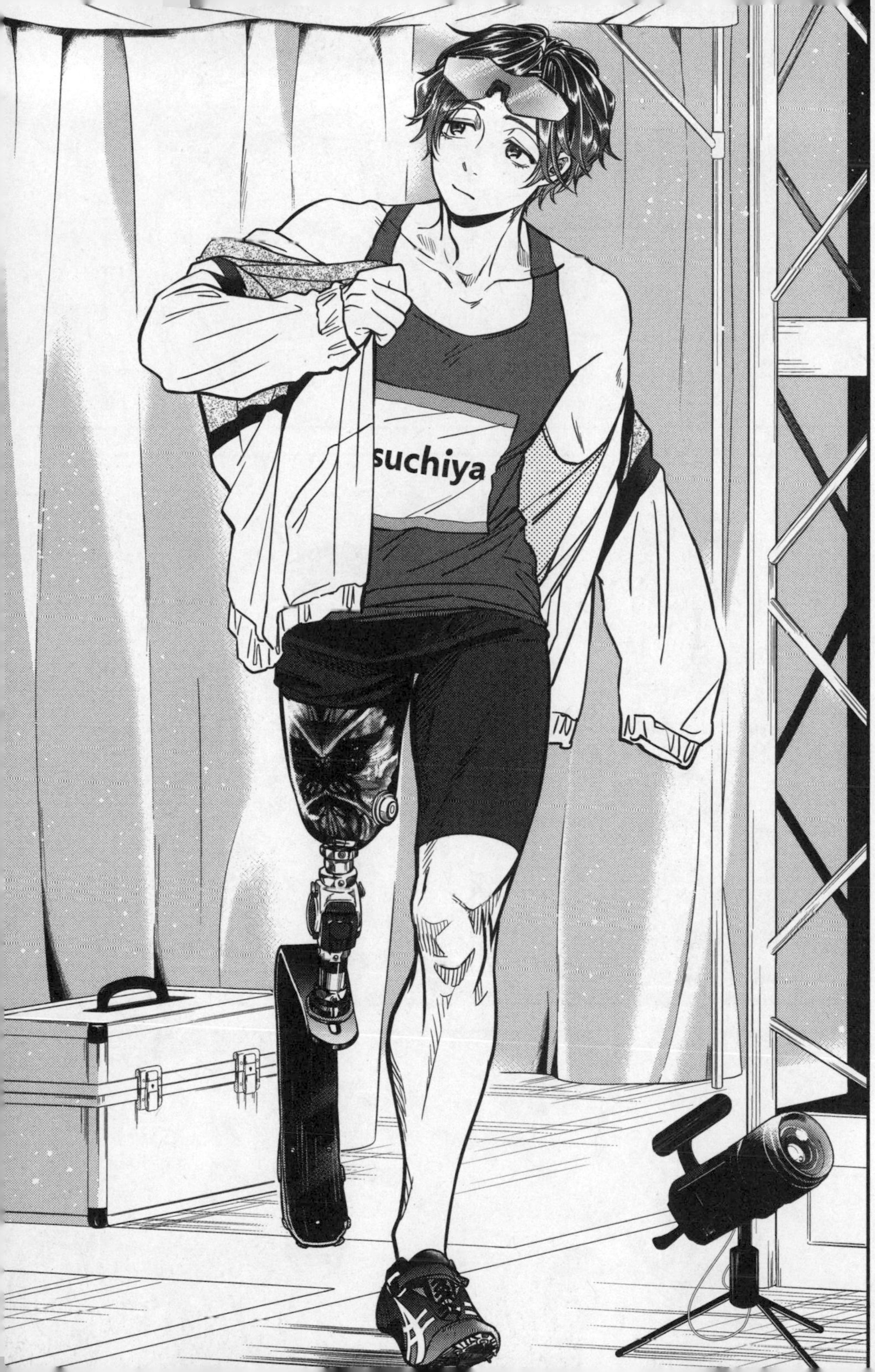
suchiya

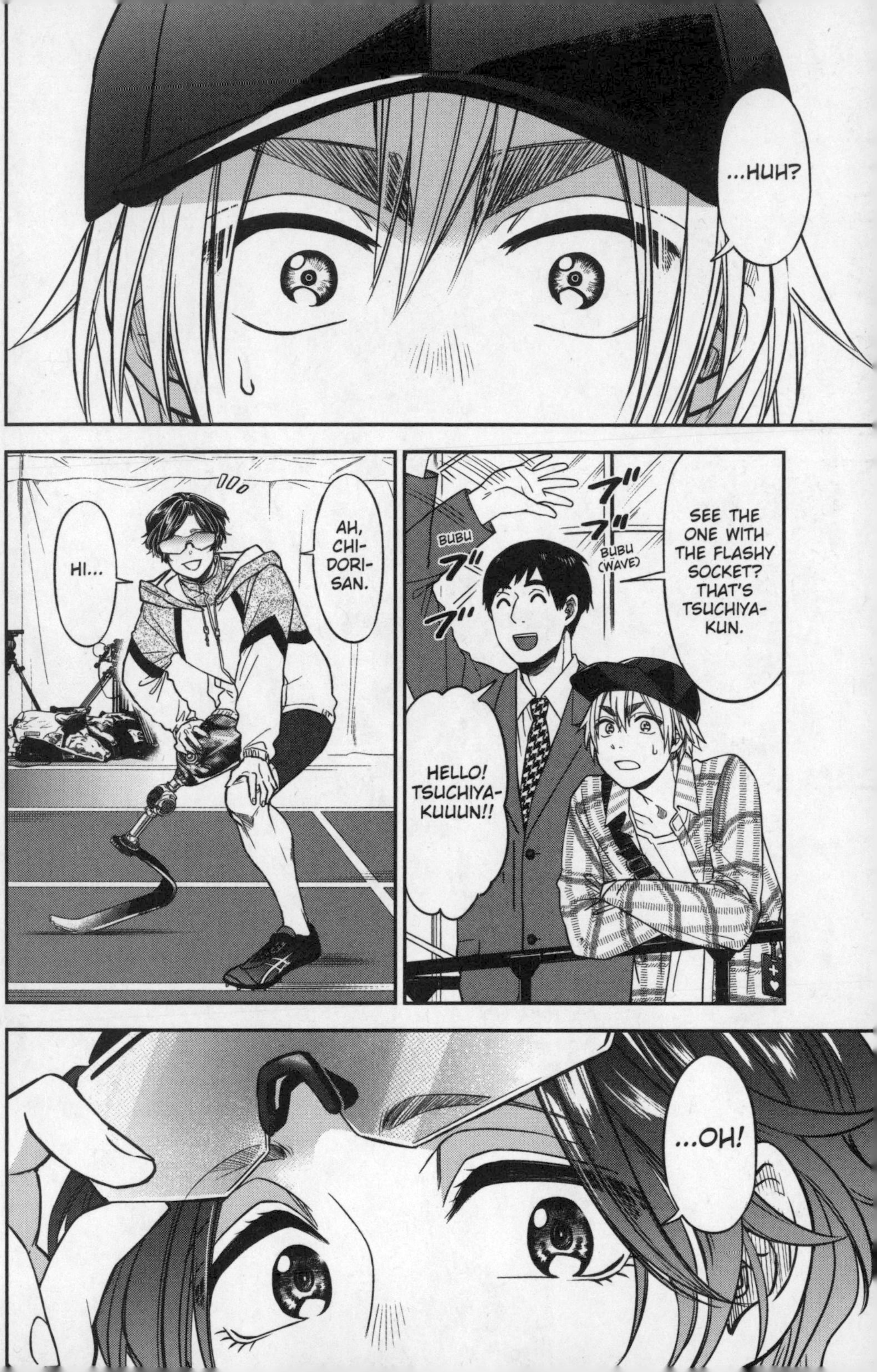
...HUH?
SEE THE ONE WITH THE FLASHY SOCKET? THAT'S TSUCHIYA-KUN.
BUBU (WAVE)
BUBU
HELLO! TSUCHIYA-KUUUN!!
AH, CHIDORI-SAN.
HI...
...OH!

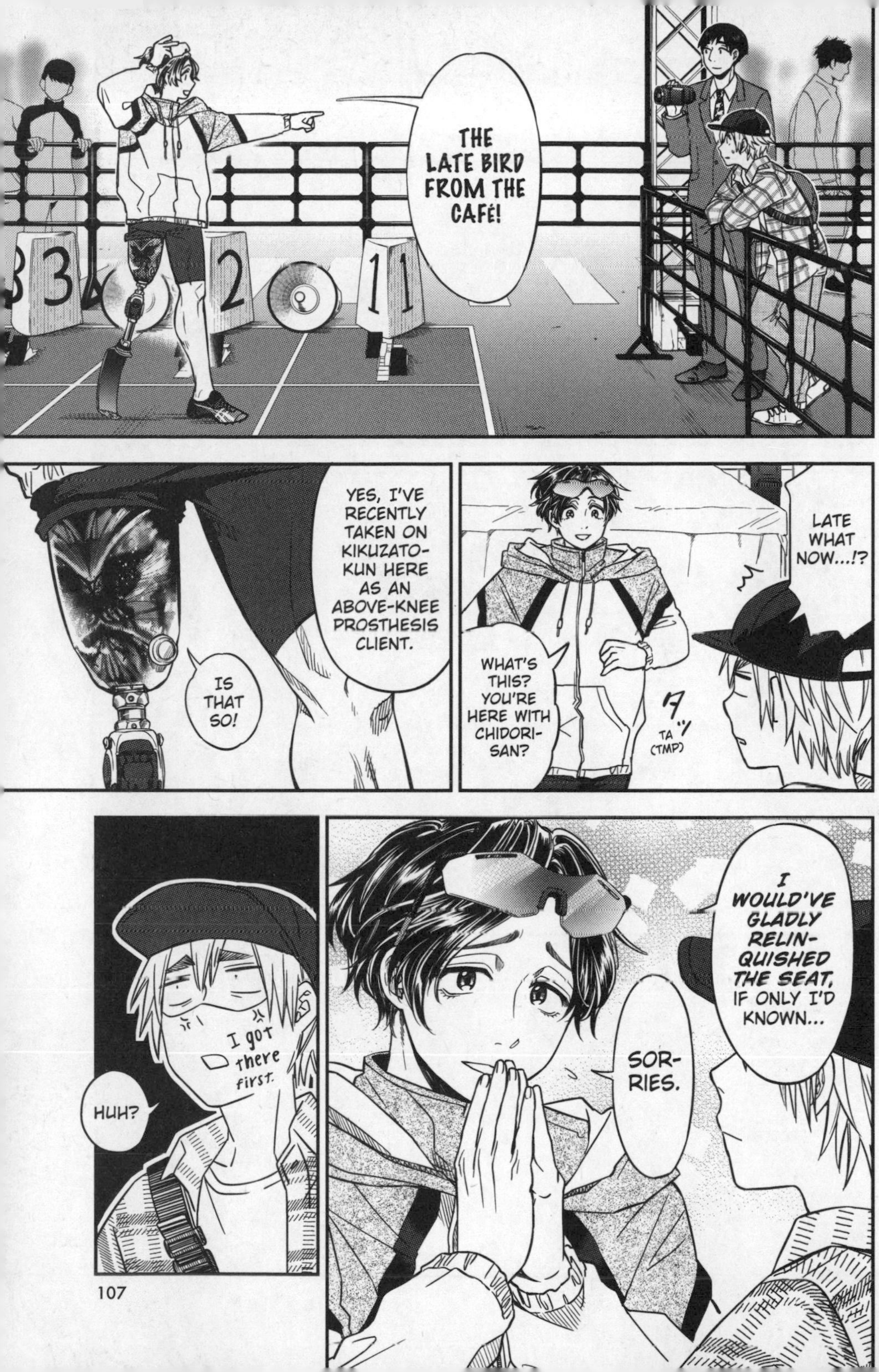
THE LATE BIRD FROM THE CAFÉ!
LATE WHAT NOW...!?
WHAT'S THIS? YOU'RE HERE WITH CHIDORI-SAN?
TA (TMP)
YES, I'VE RECENTLY TAKEN ON KIKUZATO-KUN HERE AS AN ABOVE-KNEE PROSTHESIS CLIENT.
IS THAT SO!
I WOULD'VE GLADLY RELINQUISHED THE SEAT, IF ONLY I'D KNOWN...
SORRIES.
I got there first.
HUH?

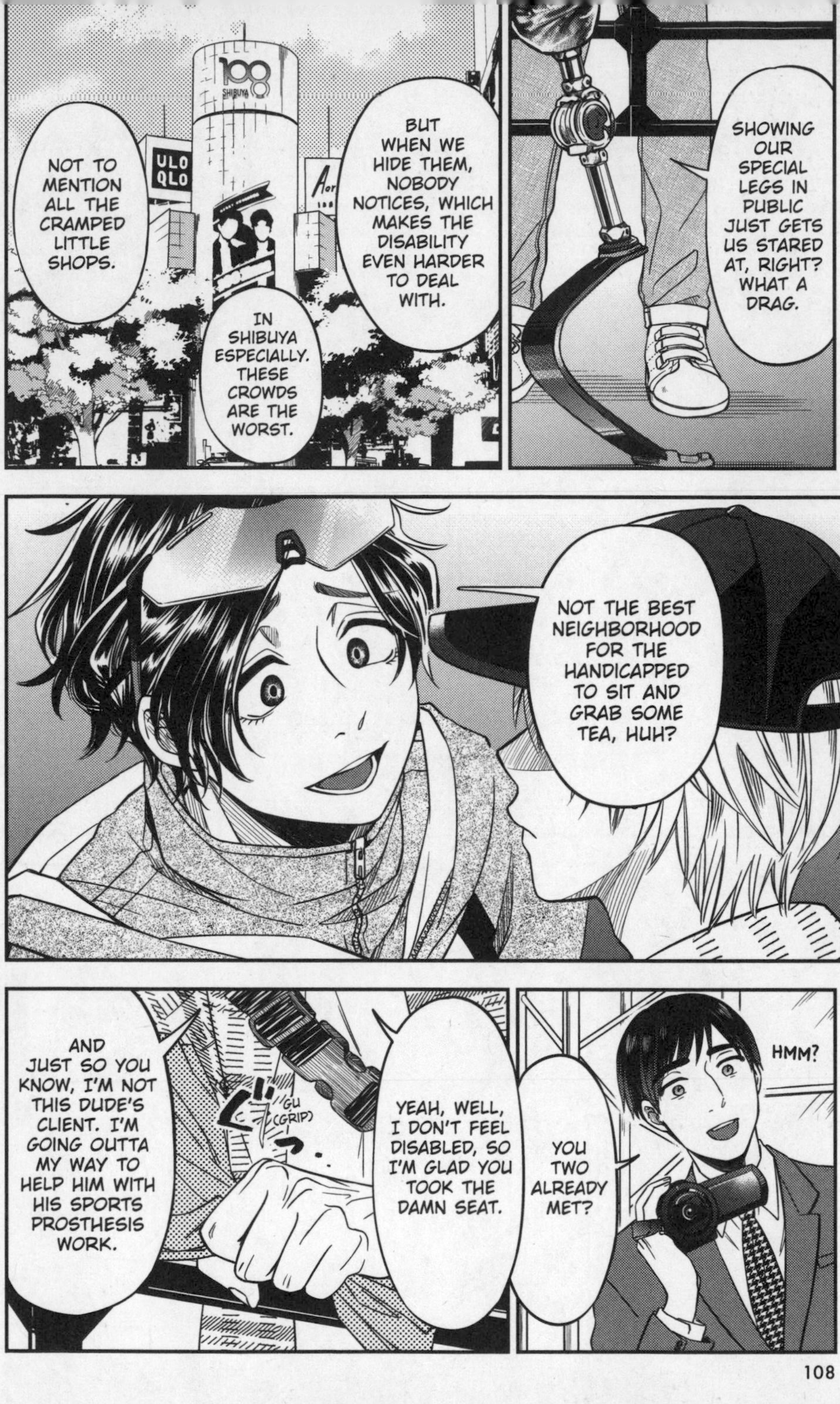
SHOWING OUR SPECIAL LEGS IN PUBLIC JUST GETS US STARED AT, RIGHT? WHAT A DRAG.
BUT WHEN WE HIDE THEM, NOBODY NOTICES, WHICH MAKES THE DISABILITY EVEN HARDER TO DEAL WITH.
IN SHIBUYA ESPECIALLY. THESE CROWDS ARE THE WORST.
NOT TO MENTION ALL THE CRAMPED LITTLE SHOPS.
NOT THE BEST NEIGHBORHOOD FOR THE HANDICAPPED TO SIT AND GRAB SOME TEA, HUH?
HMM?
YOU TWO ALREADY MET?
YEAH, WELL, I DON'T FEEL DISABLED, SO I'M GLAD YOU TOOK THE DAMN SEAT.
GU (GRIP)
AND JUST SO YOU KNOW, I'M NOT THIS DUDE'S CLIENT. I'M GOING OUTTA MY WAY TO HELP HIM WITH HIS SPORTS PROSTHESIS WORK.

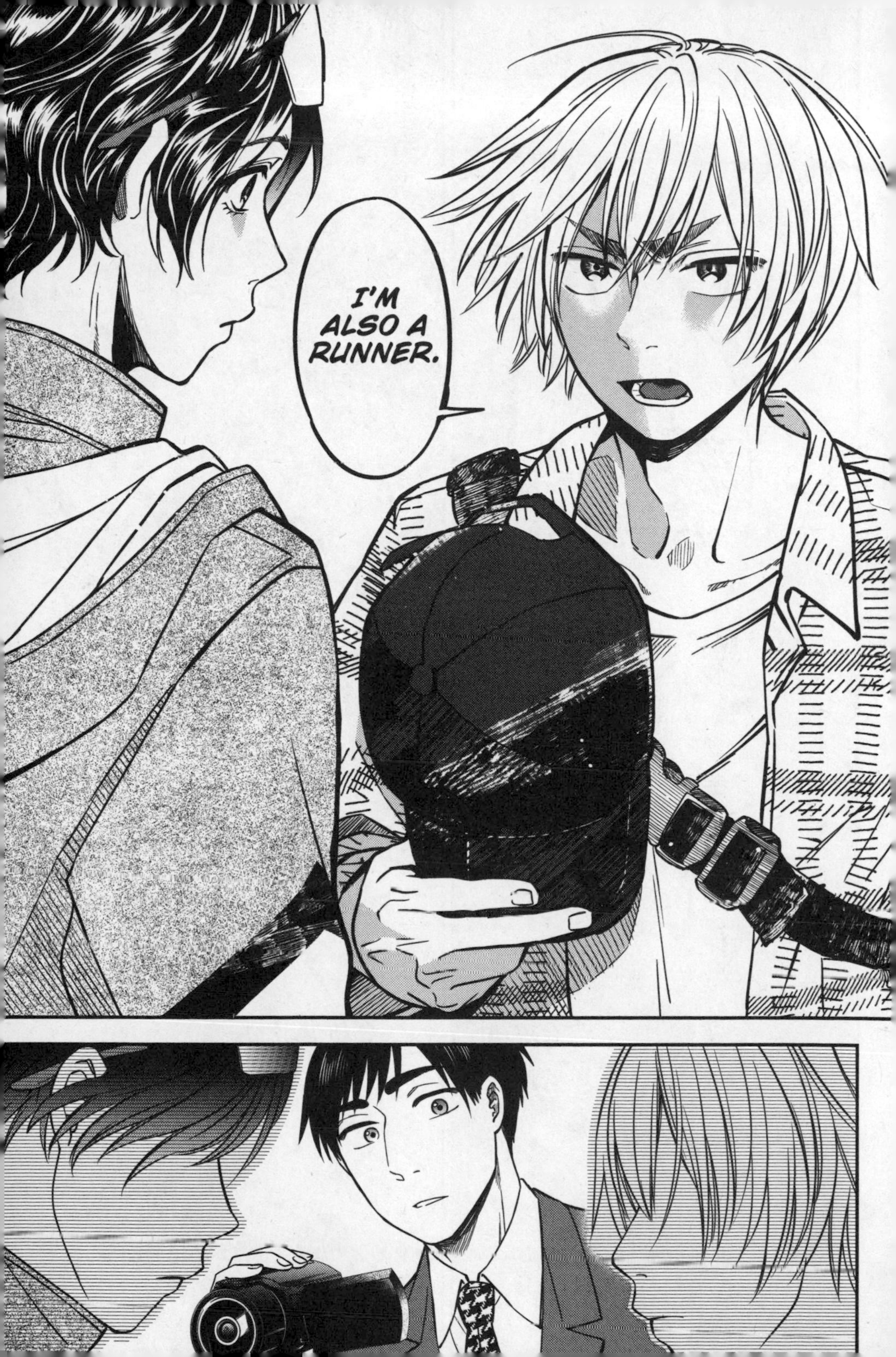
I'M ALSO A RUNNER.

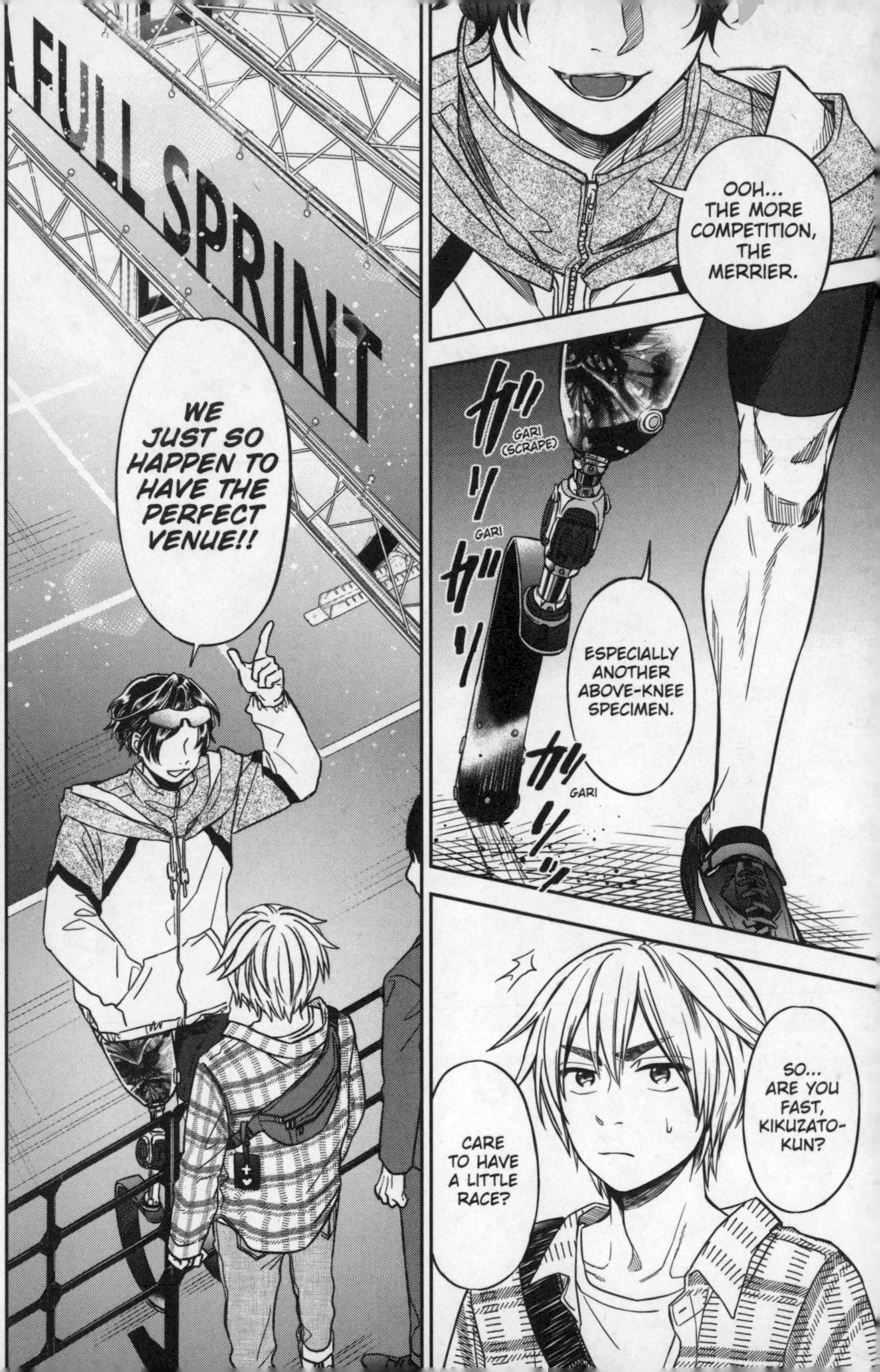
OOH... THE MORE COMPETITION, THE MERRIER.
ESPECIALLY ANOTHER ABOVE-KNEE SPECIMEN.
GARI (SCRAPE)
GARI
GARI
SO... ARE YOU FAST, KIKUZATO-KUN?
CARE TO HAVE A LITTLE RACE?
A FULL SPRINT
WE JUST SO HAPPEN TO HAVE THE PERFECT VENUE!!

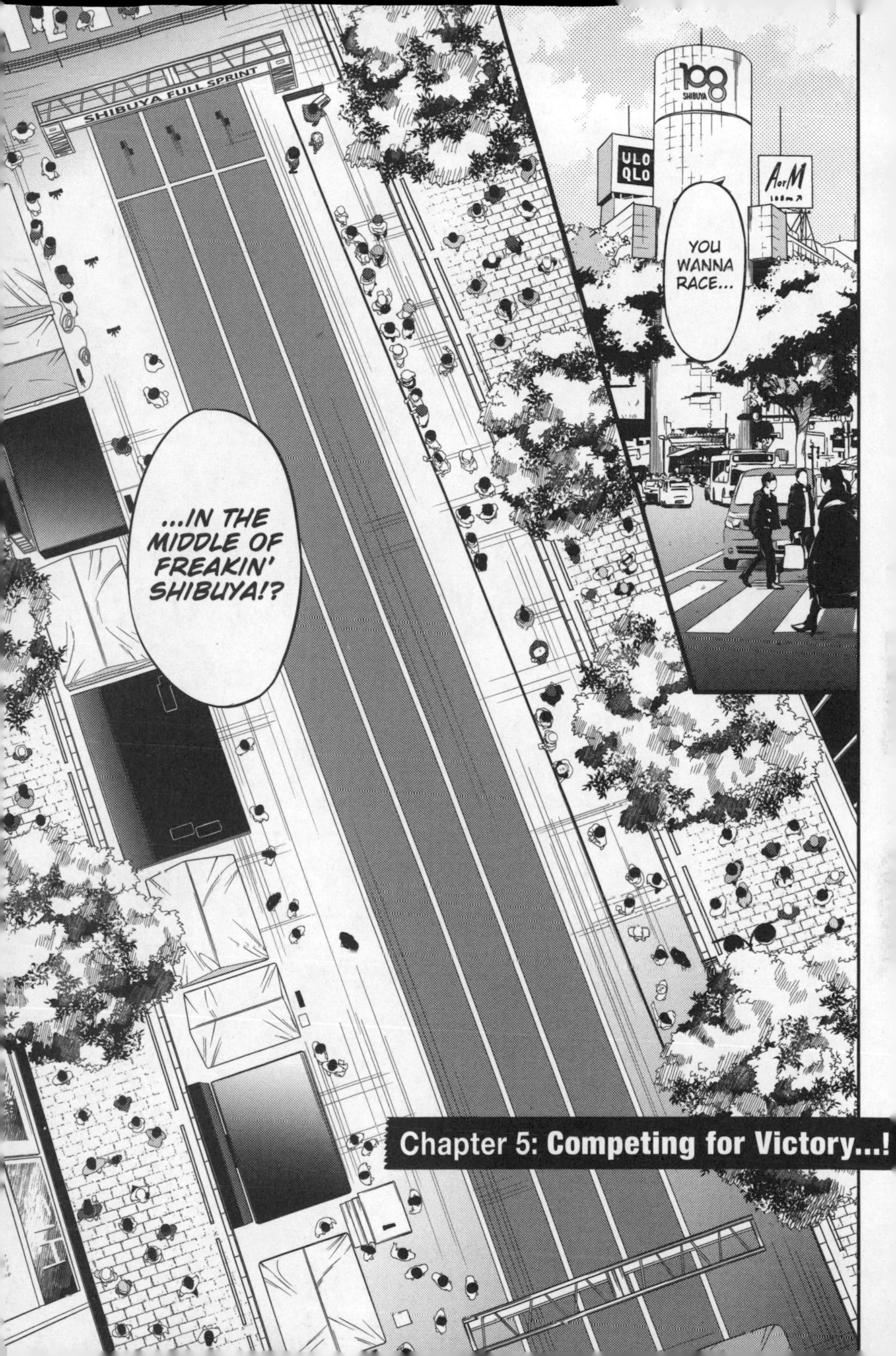

109 SHIBUYA
ULO QLO
AorM
YOU WANNA RACE...
SHIBUYA FULL SPRINT
...IN THE MIDDLE OF FREAKIN' SHIBUYA!?

Chapter 5: Competing for Victory...!

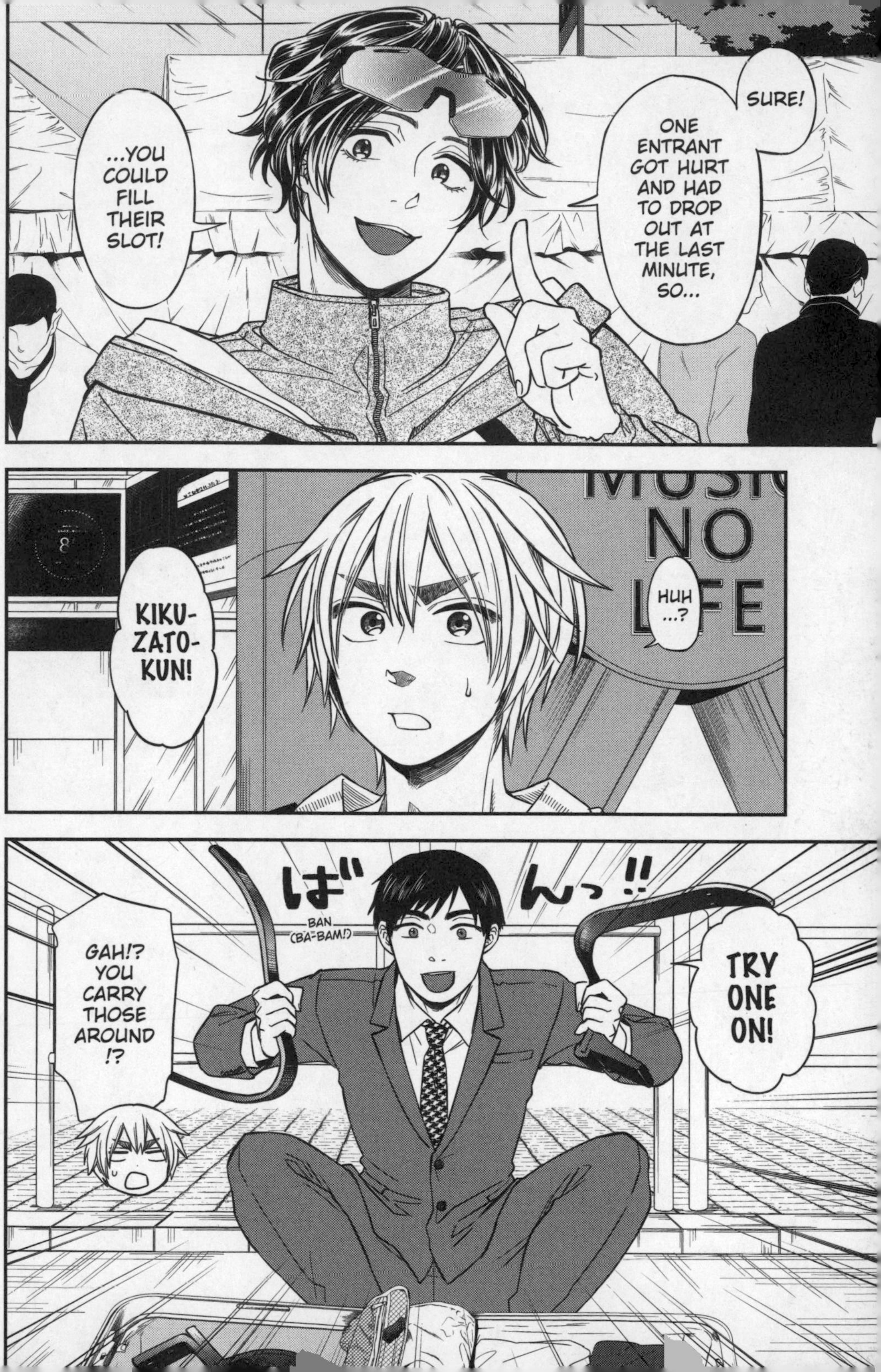
SURE!
ONE ENTRANT GOT HURT AND HAD TO DROP OUT AT THE LAST MINUTE, SO...
...YOU COULD FILL THEIR SLOT!
MUSIC NO LIFE
HUH ...?
KIKU-ZATO-KUN!
ばんっ!!
BAN (BA-BAM!)
TRY ONE ON!
GAH!? YOU CARRY THOSE AROUND !?

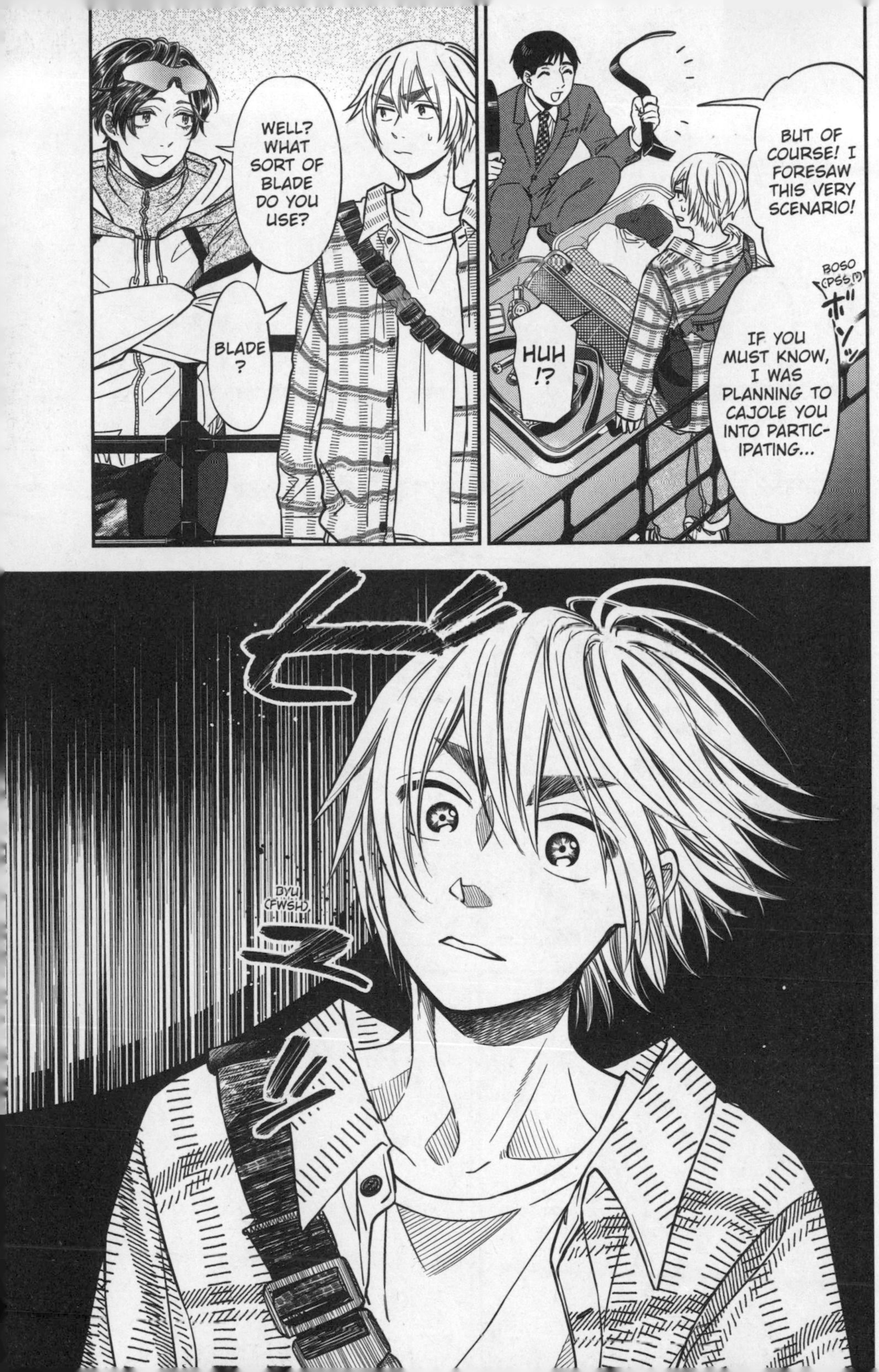
BUT OF COURSE! I FORESAW THIS VERY SCENARIO!
BOSO (PSS!)
ボソッ
IF YOU MUST KNOW, I WAS PLANNING TO CAJOLE YOU INTO PARTIC-IPATING...
HUH!?
WELL? WHAT SORT OF BLADE DO YOU USE?
BLADE?
BYU (FWSH)

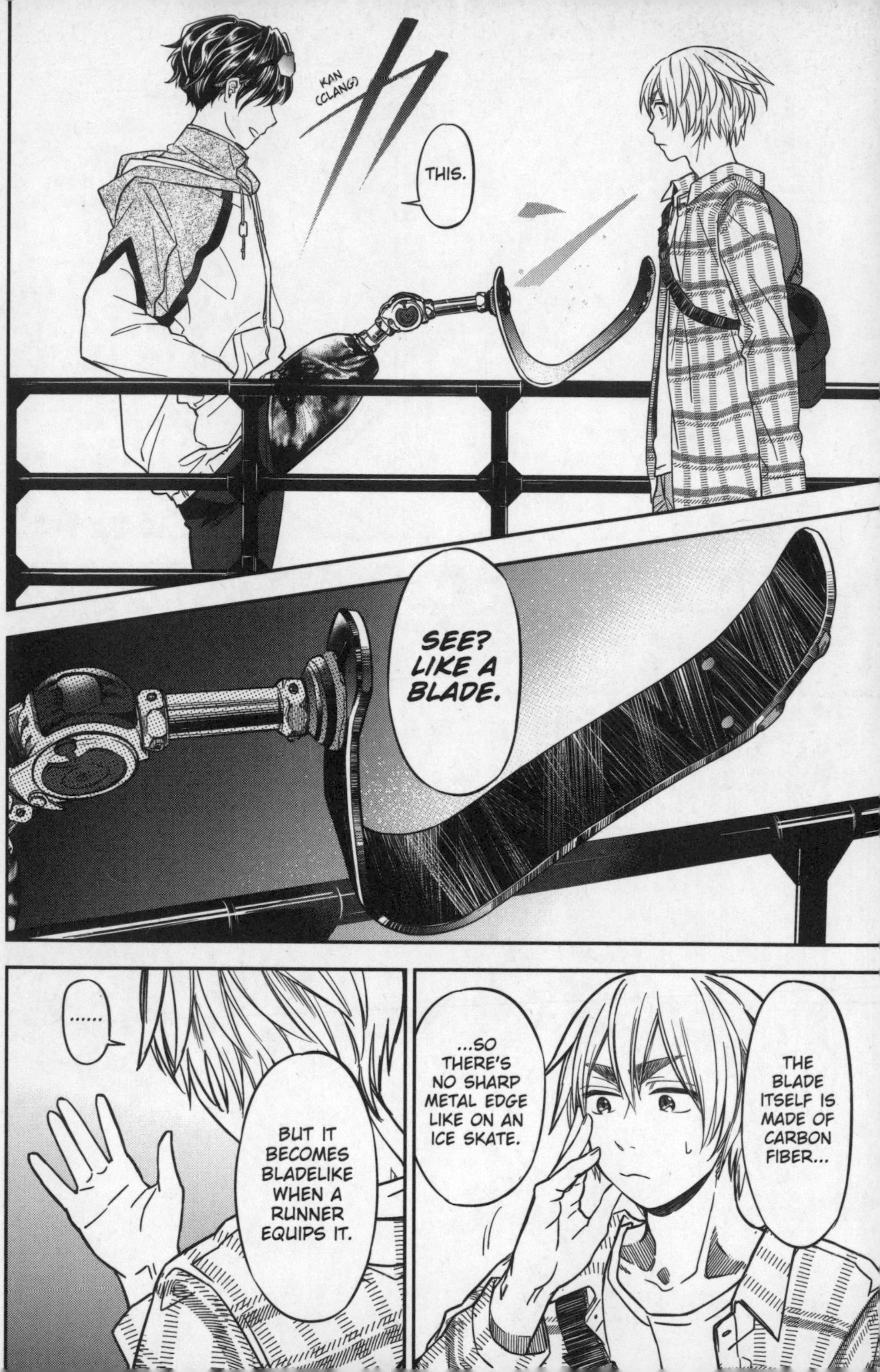
KAN (CLANG)
THIS.
SEE? LIKE A BLADE.
THE BLADE ITSELF IS MADE OF CARBON FIBER...
...SO THERE'S NO SHARP METAL EDGE LIKE ON AN ICE SKATE.
......
BUT IT BECOMES BLADELIKE WHEN A RUNNER EQUIPS IT.

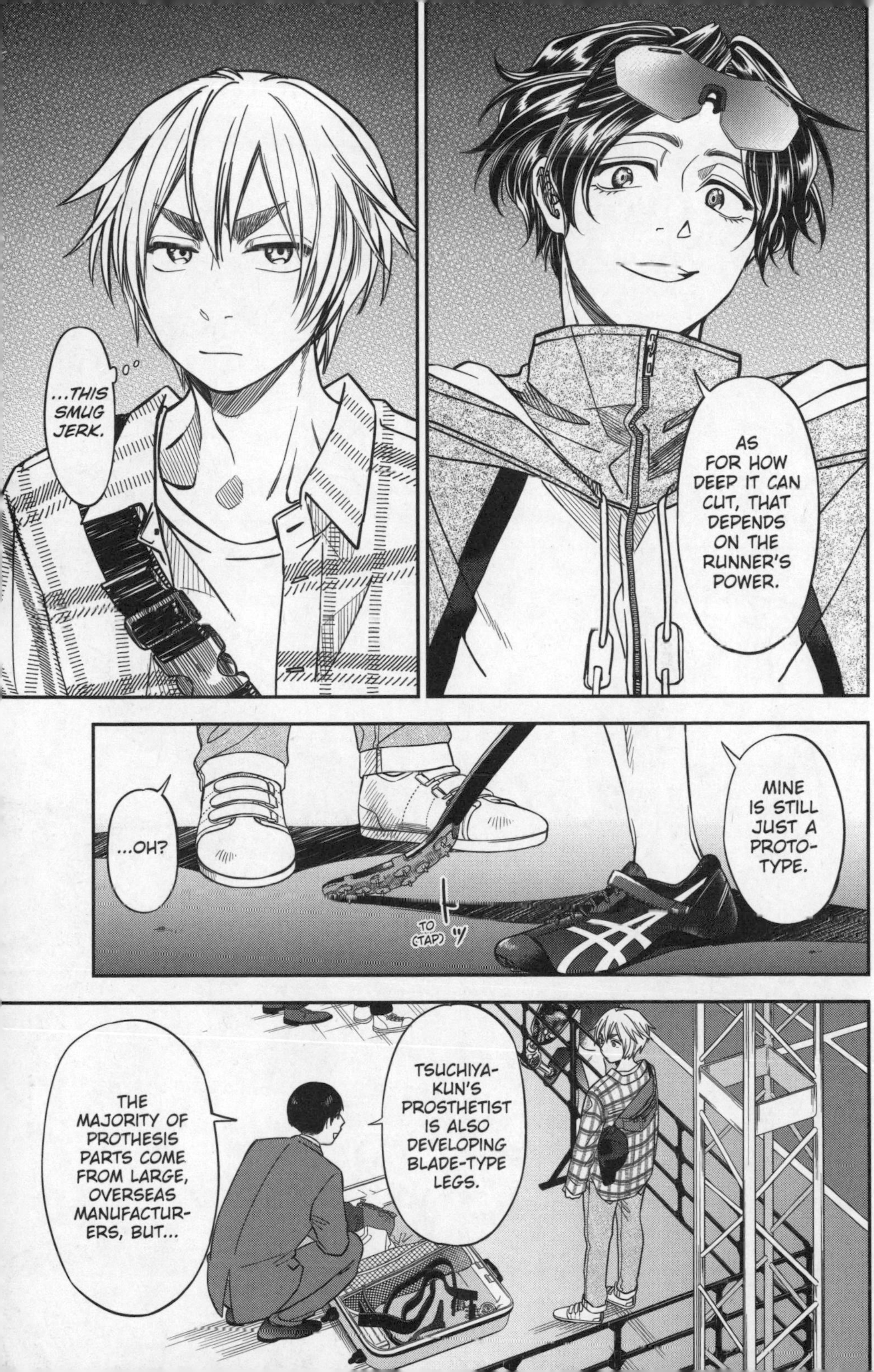
AS FOR HOW DEEP IT CAN CUT, THAT DEPENDS ON THE RUNNER'S POWER.
...THIS SMUG JERK.
MINE IS STILL JUST A PROTO-TYPE.
TO (TAP)
...OH?
TSUCHIYA-KUN'S PROSTHETIST IS ALSO DEVELOPING BLADE-TYPE LEGS.
THE MAJORITY OF PROTHESIS PARTS COME FROM LARGE, OVERSEAS MANUFACTUR-ERS, BUT...

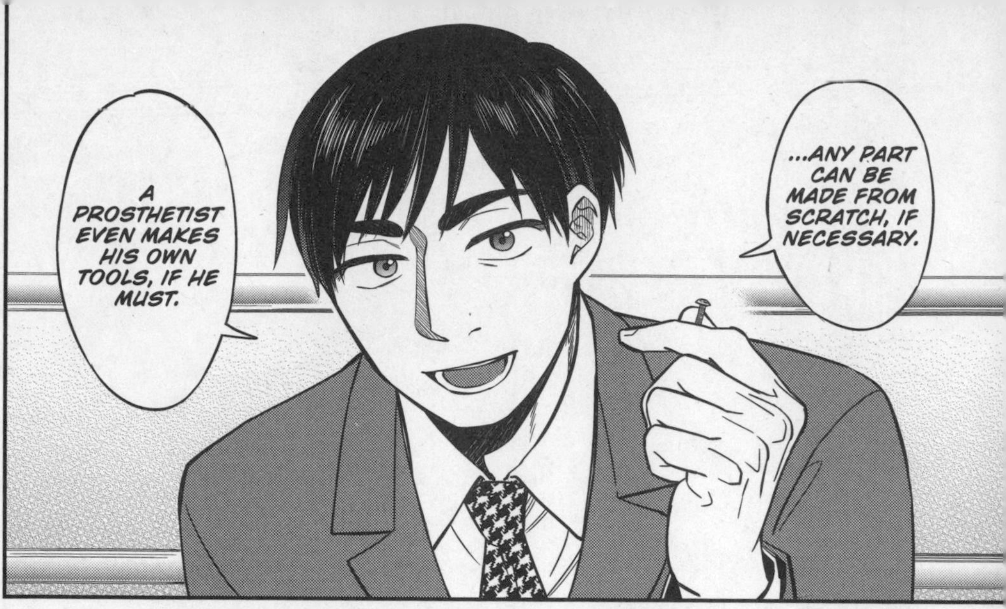
...ANY PART CAN BE MADE FROM SCRATCH, IF NECESSARY.
A PROSTHETIST EVEN MAKES HIS OWN TOOLS, IF HE MUST.

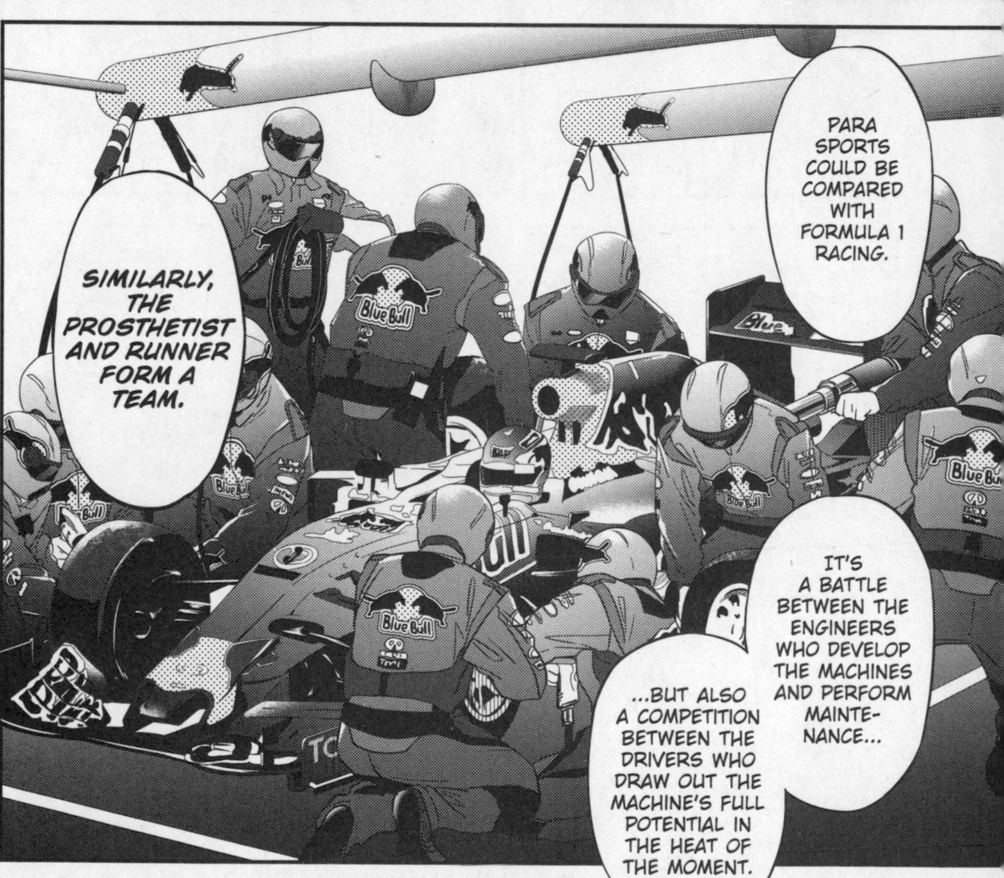
PARA SPORTS COULD BE COMPARED WITH FORMULA 1 RACING.
IT'S A BATTLE BETWEEN THE ENGINEERS WHO DEVELOP THE MACHINES AND PERFORM MAINTE-NANCE...
...BUT ALSO A COMPETITION BETWEEN THE DRIVERS WHO DRAW OUT THE MACHINE'S FULL POTENTIAL IN THE HEAT OF THE MOMENT.
SIMILARLY, THE PROSTHETIST AND RUNNER FORM A TEAM.
Blue Bull

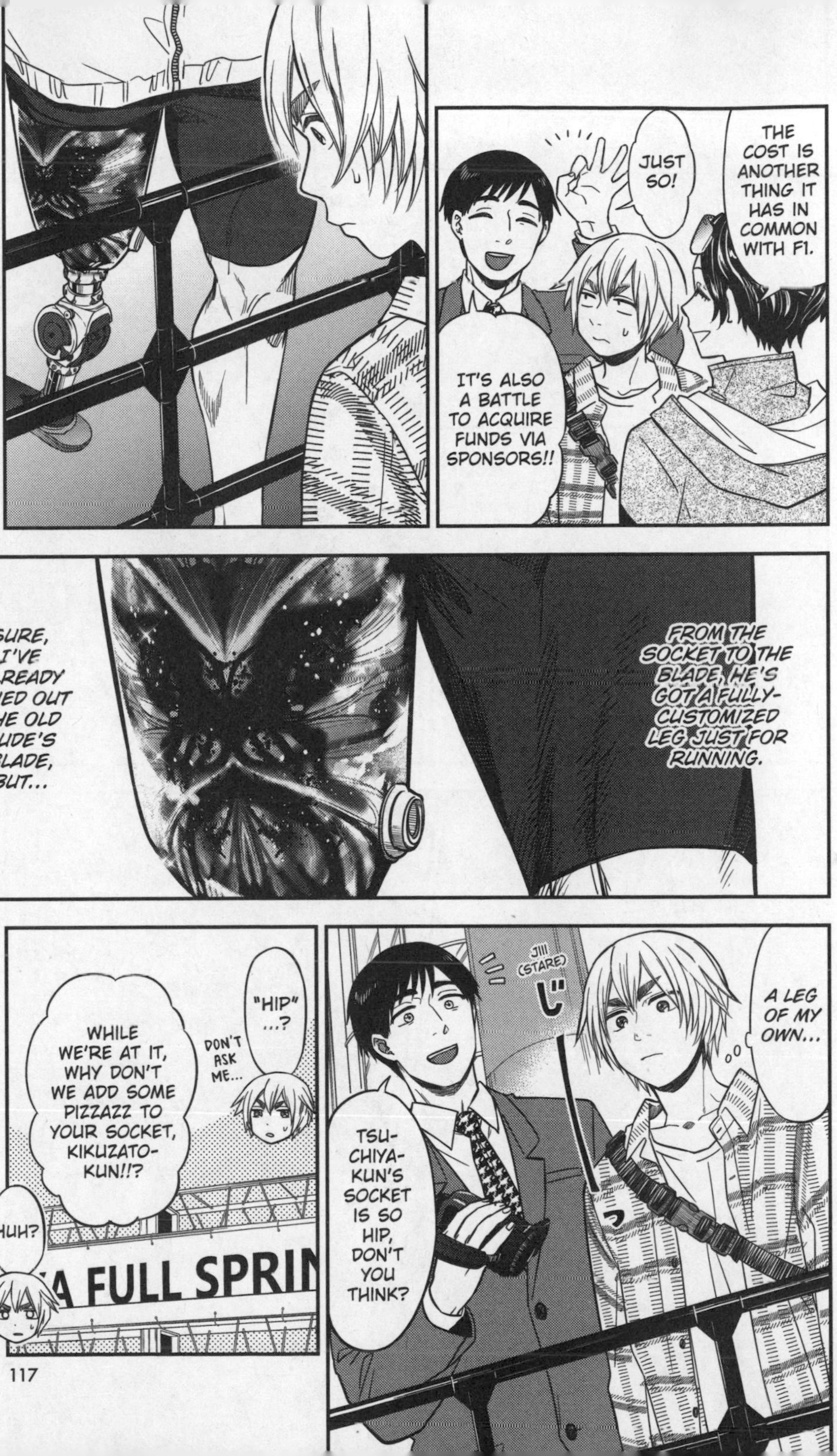
THE COST IS ANOTHER THING IT HAS IN COMMON WITH F1.
JUST SO!
IT'S ALSO A BATTLE TO ACQUIRE FUNDS VIA SPONSORS!!
FROM THE SOCKET TO THE BLADE, HE'S GOT A FULLY-CUSTOMIZED LEG JUST FOR RUNNING.
SURE, I'VE ALREADY TRIED OUT THE OLD DUDE'S BLADE, BUT...
A LEG OF MY OWN...
JIII (STARE)
じ
TSU-CHIYA-KUN'S SOCKET IS SO HIP, DON'T YOU THINK?
"HIP" ...?
DON'T ASK ME...
WHILE WE'RE AT IT, WHY DON'T WE ADD SOME PIZZAZZ TO YOUR SOCKET, KIKUZATO-KUN!!?
HUH?
A FULL SPRIN

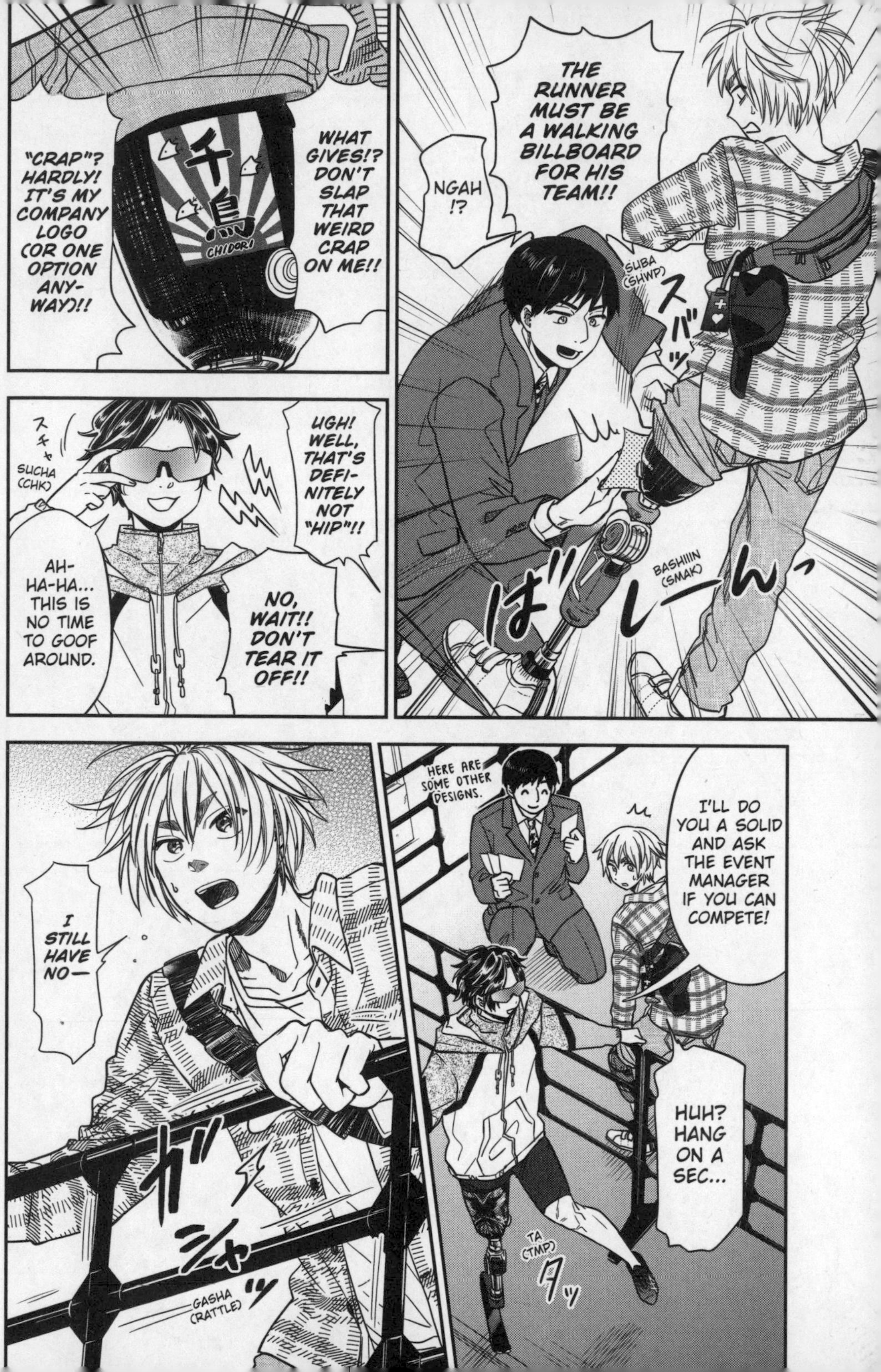
THE RUNNER MUST BE A WALKING BILLBOARD FOR HIS TEAM!!
NGAH!?
SUBA (SHWP)
BASHIIIN (SMAK)
WHAT GIVES!? DON'T SLAP THAT WEIRD CRAP ON ME!!
CHIDORI
"CRAP"? HARDLY! IT'S MY COMPANY LOGO (OR ONE OPTION ANYWAY)!!
UGH! WELL, THAT'S DEFINITELY NOT "HIP"!!
SUCHA (CHK)
NO, WAIT!! DON'T TEAR IT OFF!!
AH-HA-HA... THIS IS NO TIME TO GOOF AROUND.
I'LL DO YOU A SOLID AND ASK THE EVENT MANAGER IF YOU CAN COMPETE!
HERE ARE SOME OTHER DESIGNS.
HUH? HANG ON A SEC...
TA (TMP)
I STILL HAVE NO—
GASHA (RATTLE)

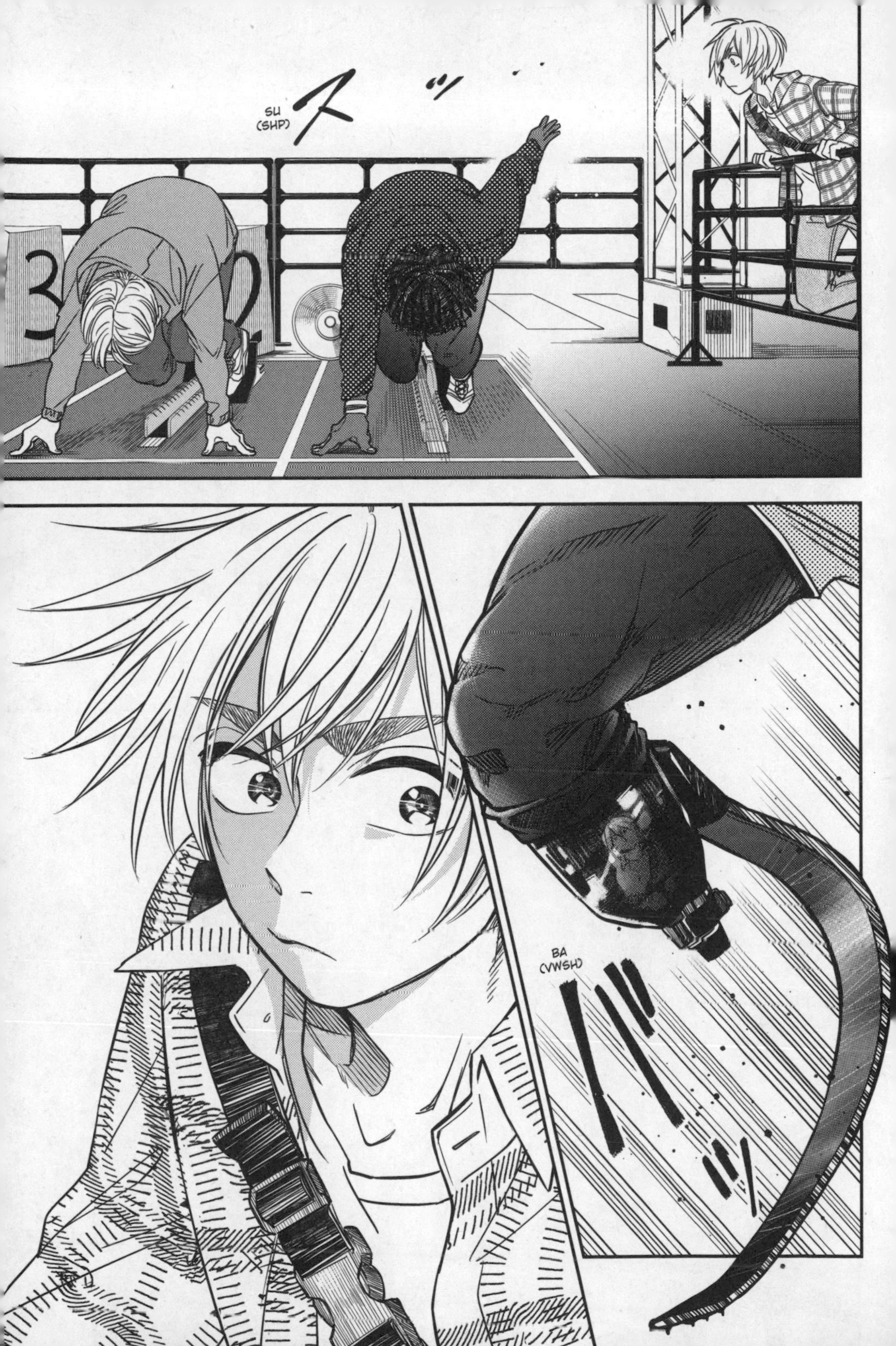
SU (SHP)
BA (VWSH)

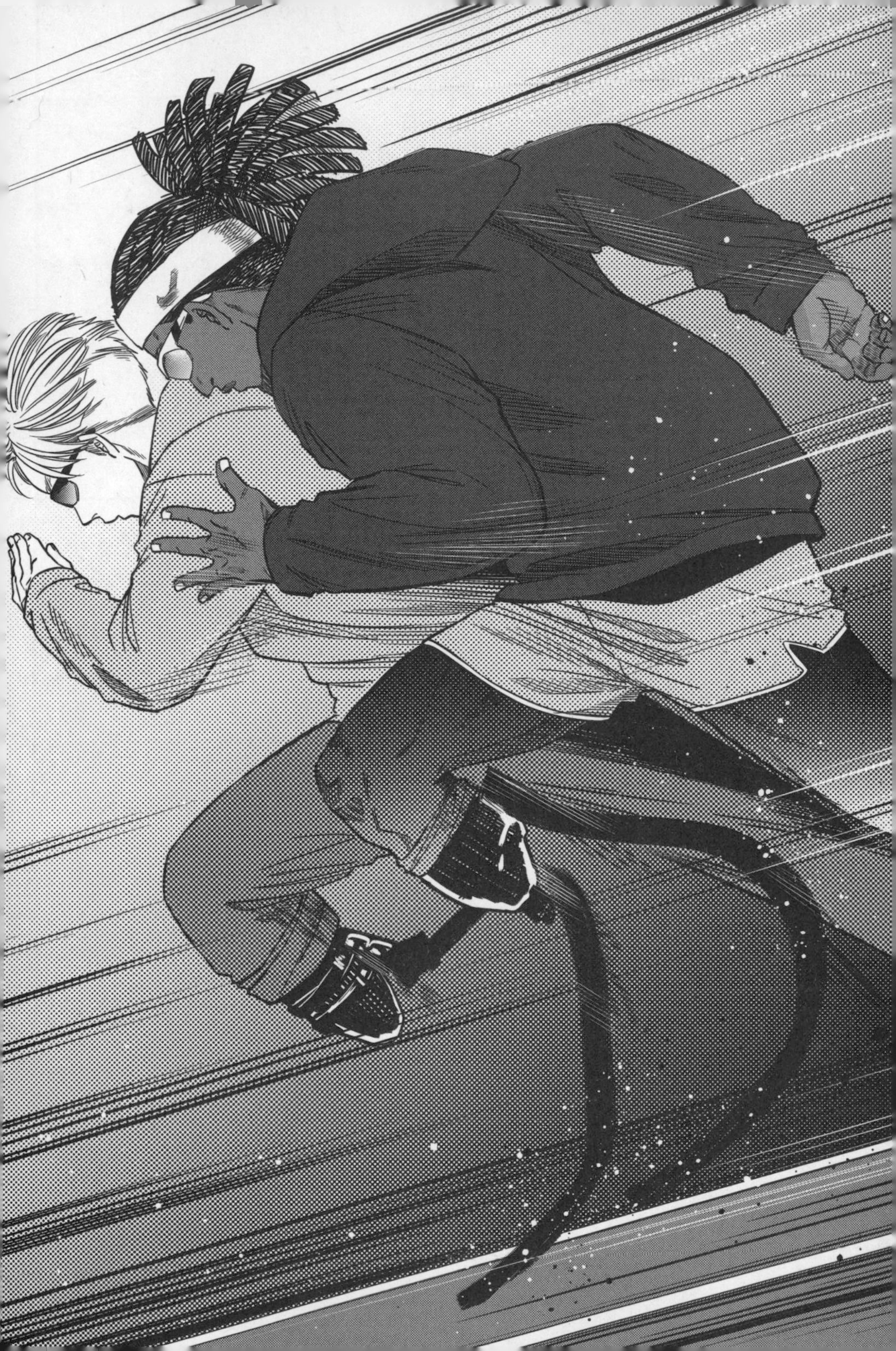

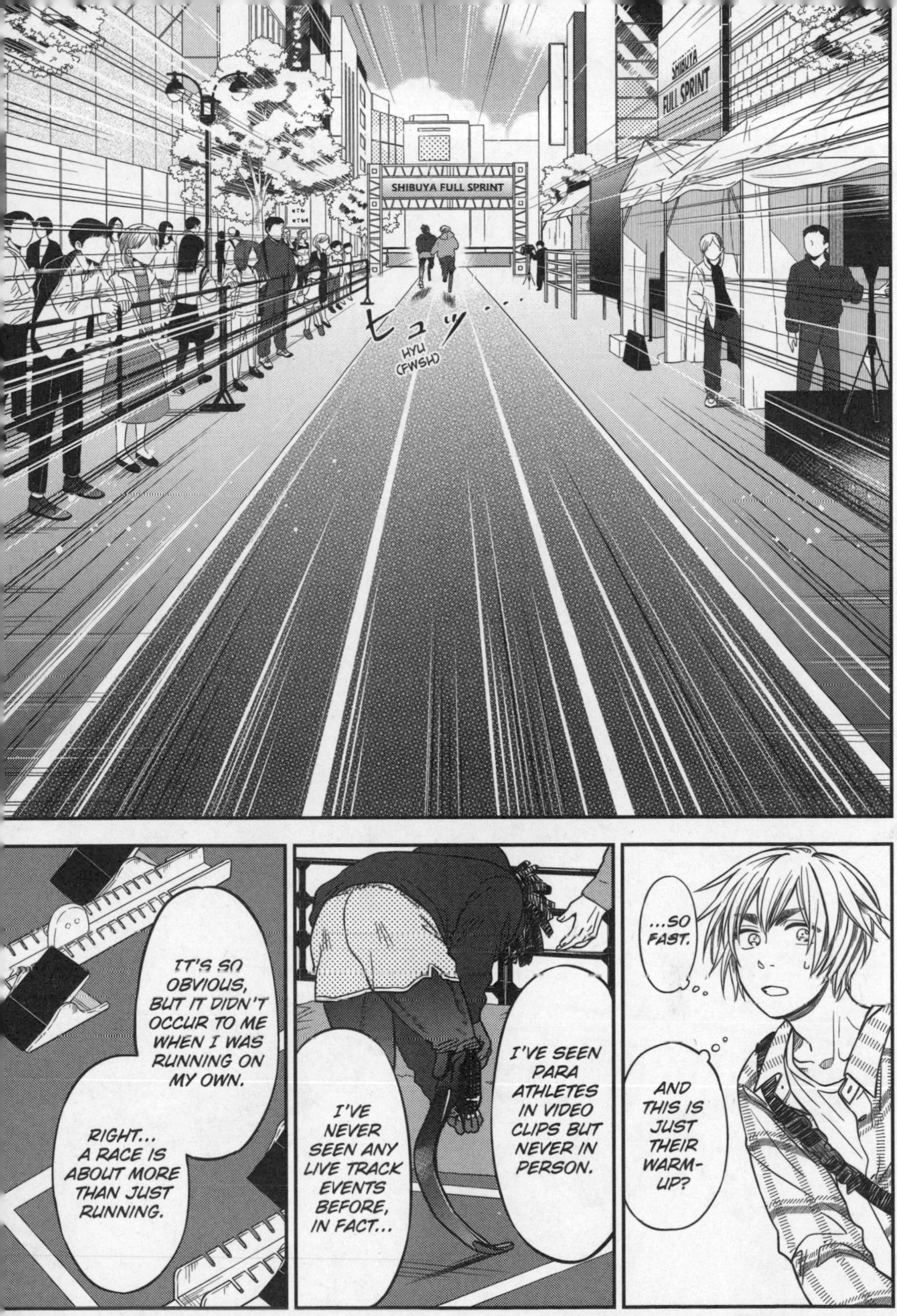
SHIBUYA FULL SPRINT
SHIBUYA FULL SPRINT
ヒュッ…
HYU (FWSH)
...SO FAST.
AND THIS IS JUST THEIR WARM-UP?
I'VE SEEN PARA ATHLETES IN VIDEO CLIPS BUT NEVER IN PERSON.
I'VE NEVER SEEN ANY LIVE TRACK EVENTS BEFORE, IN FACT...
IT'S SO OBVIOUS, BUT IT DIDN'T OCCUR TO ME WHEN I WAS RUNNING ON MY OWN.
RIGHT... A RACE IS ABOUT MORE THAN JUST RUNNING.

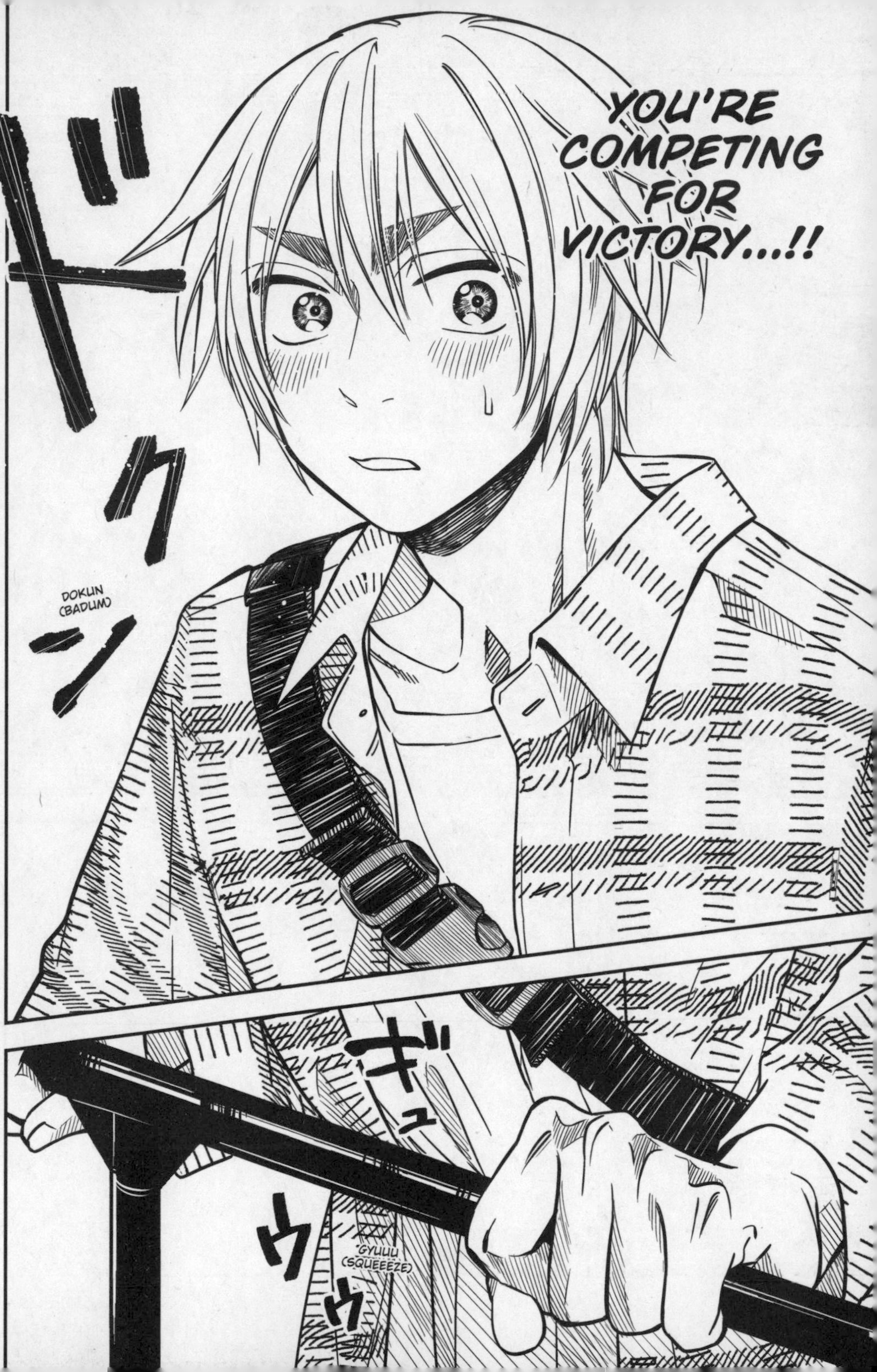
YOU'RE COMPETING FOR VICTORY...!!
ドクン
DOKUN (BADUM)
ギュウウ
GYUUU (SQUEEEZE)

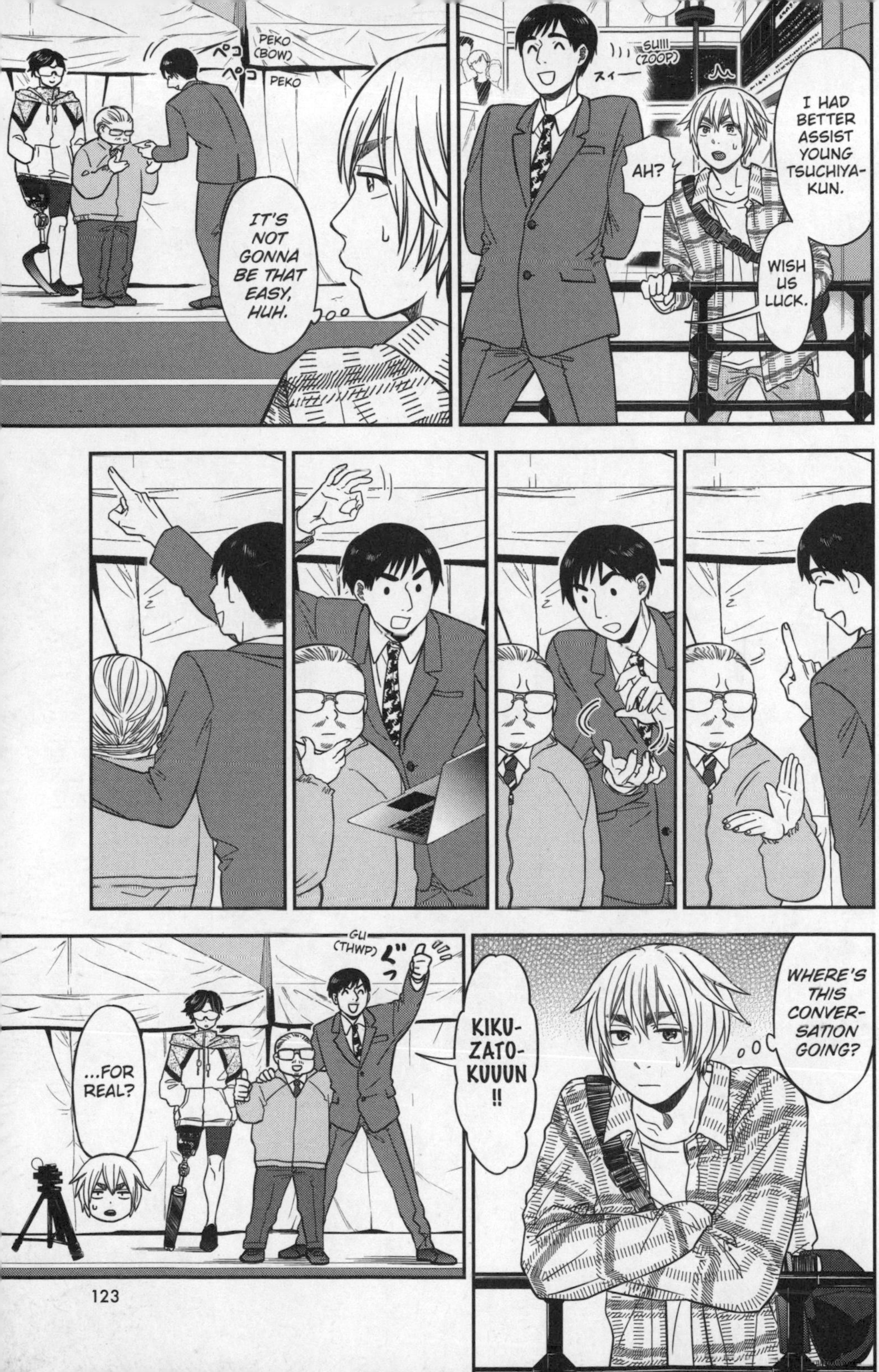
I HAD BETTER ASSIST YOUNG TSUCHIYA-KUN.
SUIII (ZOOP)
スィー
AH?
WISH US LUCK.
ペコ
PEKO (BOW)
ペコ
PEKO
IT'S NOT GONNA BE THAT EASY, HUH.
WHERE'S THIS CONVERSATION GOING?
KIKUZATO-KUUUN!!
GU (THWP)
ぐっ
...FOR REAL?

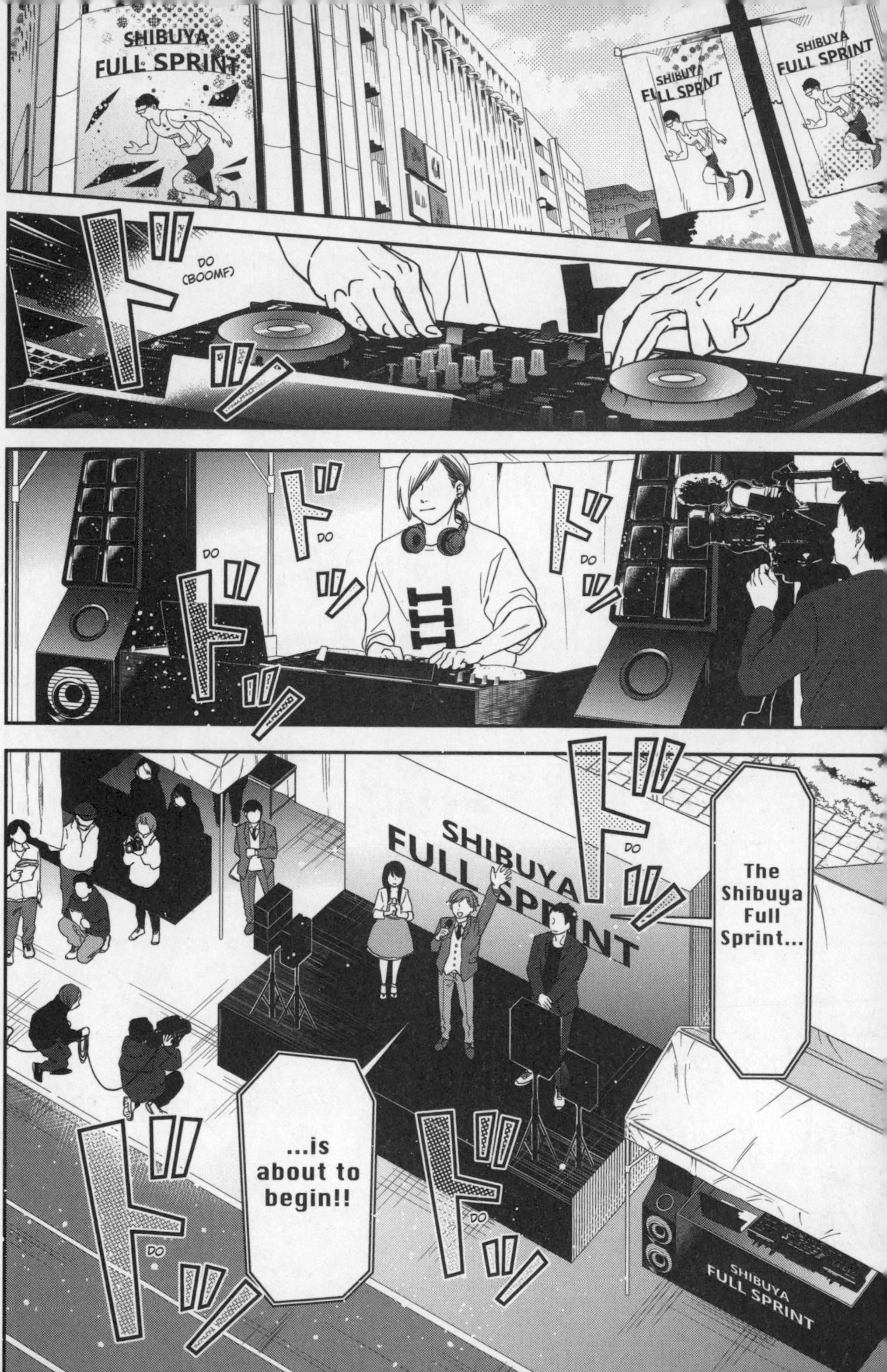
SHIBUYA FULL SPRINT
SHIBUYA FULL SPRINT
SHIBUYA FULL SPRINT
DO (BOOMF)
DO
DO
DO
SHIBUYA FULL SPRINT
DO
The Shibuya Full Sprint...
...is about to begin!!
DO
DO
SHIBUYA FULL SPRINT

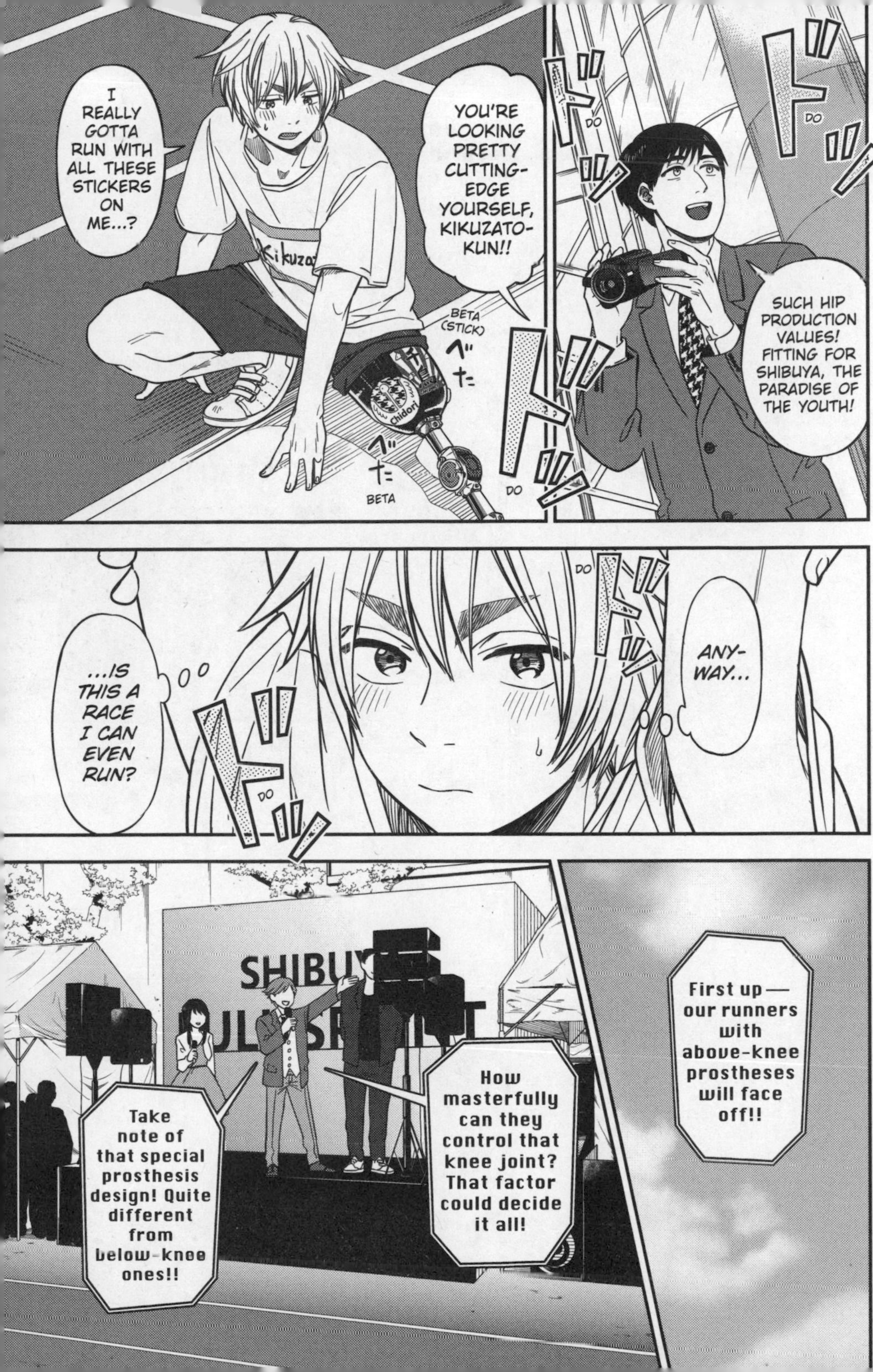
DO
DO
SUCH HIP PRODUCTION VALUES! FITTING FOR SHIBUYA, THE PARADISE OF THE YOUTH!
DO
YOU'RE LOOKING PRETTY CUTTING-EDGE YOURSELF, KIKUZATO-KUN!!
I REALLY GOTTA RUN WITH ALL THESE STICKERS ON ME...?
BETA (STICK)
BETA
DO
ANY-WAY...
...IS THIS A RACE I CAN EVEN RUN?
DO
First up — our runners with above-knee prostheses will face off!!
How masterfully can they control that knee joint? That factor could decide it all!
Take note of that special prosthesis design! Quite different from below-knee ones!!

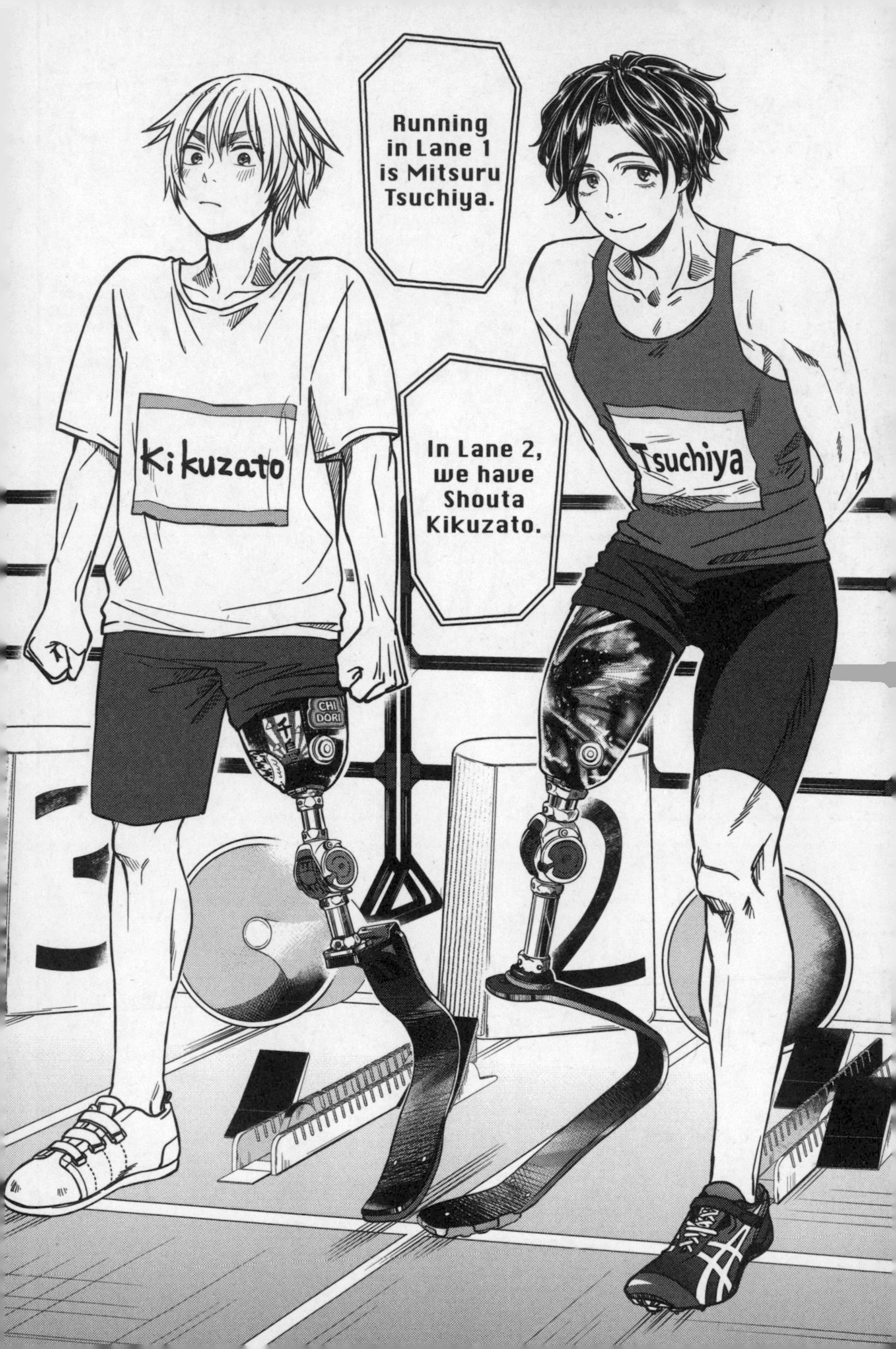
Running in Lane 1 is Mitsuru Tsuchiya.
Tsuchiya
In Lane 2, we have Shouta Kikuzato.
Kikuzato
CHI DORI

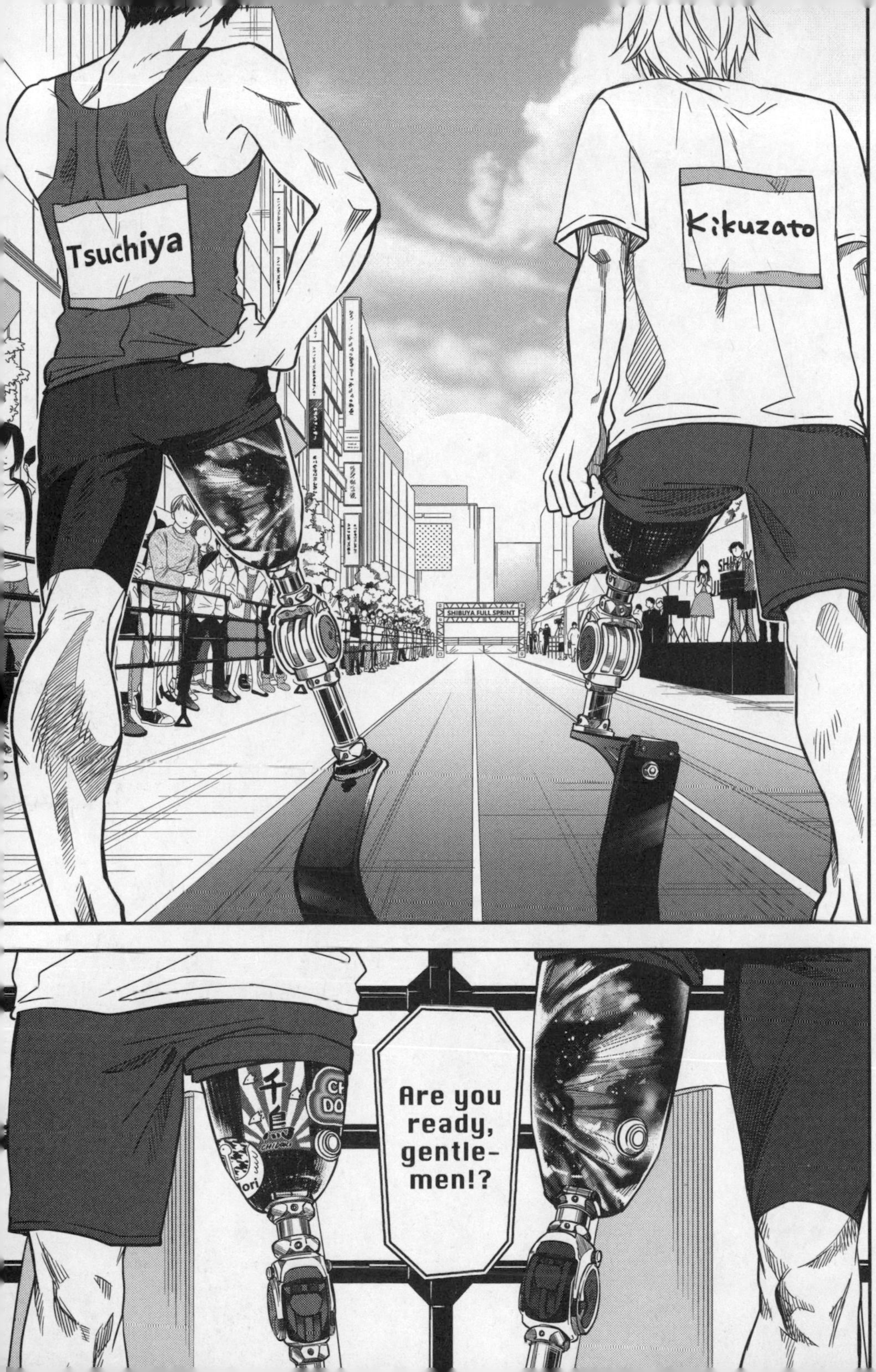
Kikuzato
Tsuchiya
SHIBUYA FULL SPRINT
Are you ready, gentle-men!?

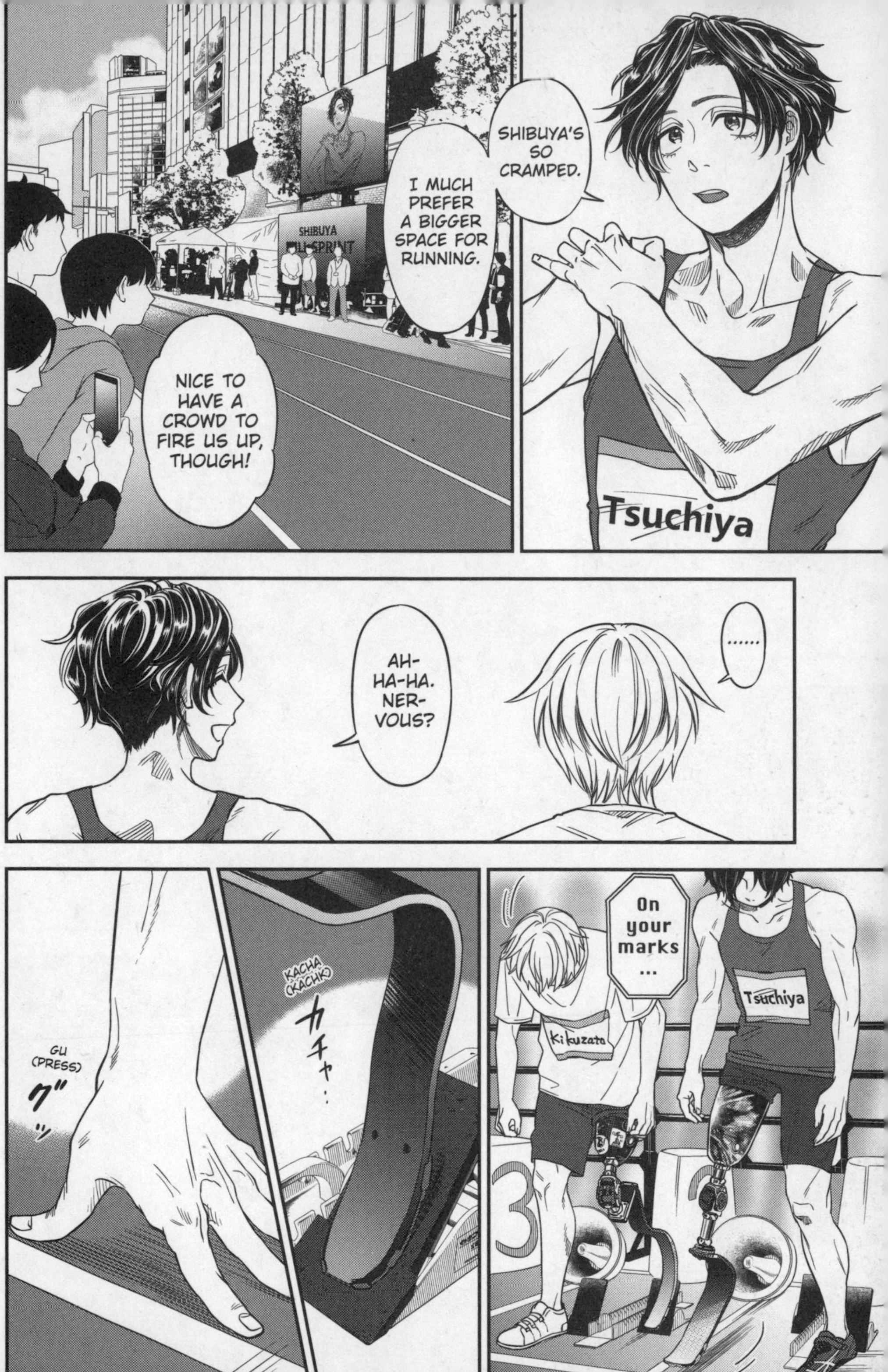
SHIBUYA'S SO CRAMPED.
I MUCH PREFER A BIGGER SPACE FOR RUNNING.
Tsuchiya
NICE TO HAVE A CROWD TO FIRE US UP, THOUGH!
......
AH-HA-HA. NER-VOUS?
On your marks ...
Tsuchiya
Kikuzato
KACHA (KACHK)
カチャ・・
GU (PRESS)
グッ

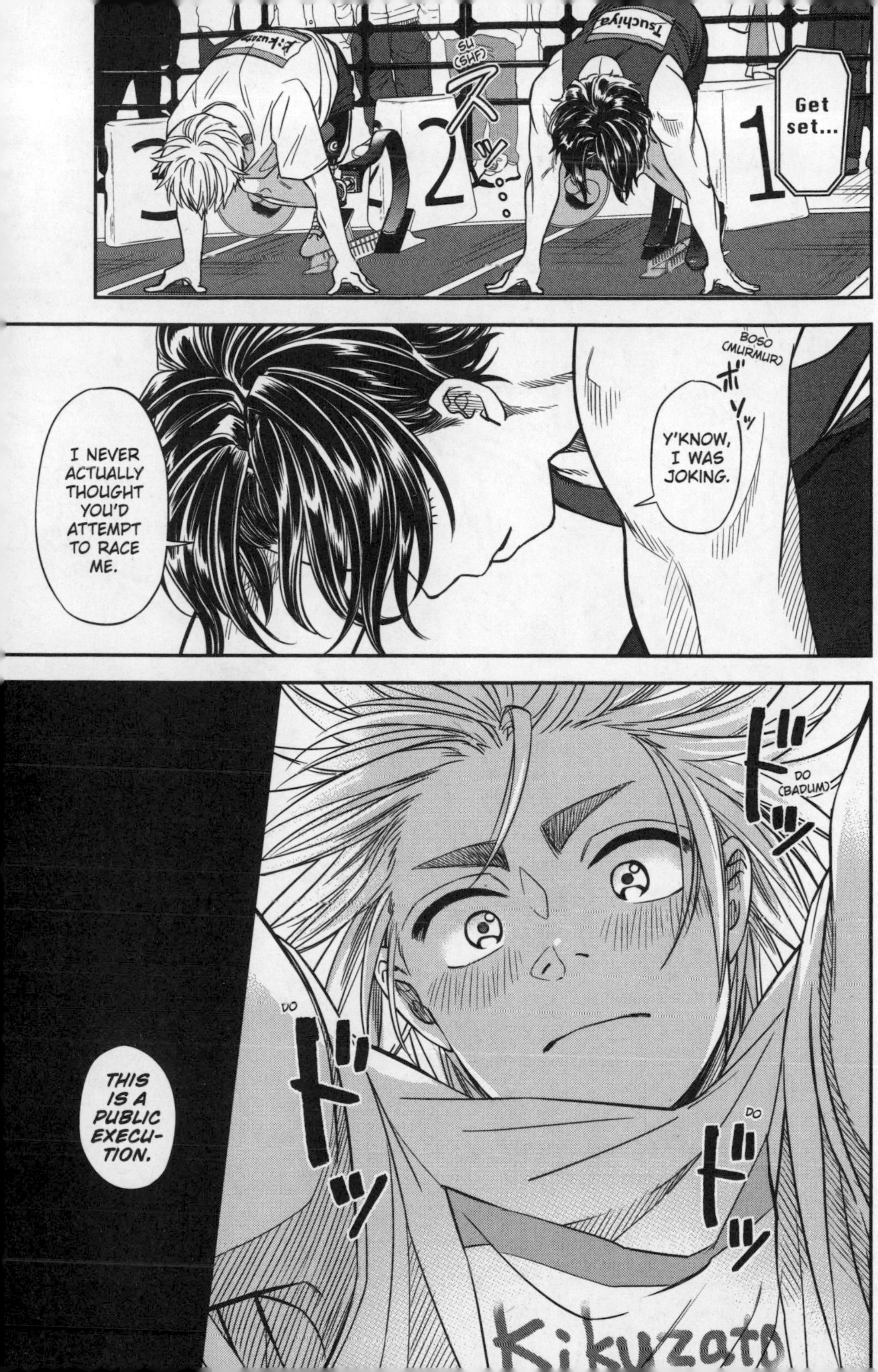
Get set...
SU (SHF)
Tsuchiya
BOSO (MURMUR)
Y'KNOW, I WAS JOKING.
I NEVER ACTUALLY THOUGHT YOU'D ATTEMPT TO RACE ME.
DO (BADUM)
DO
DO
THIS IS A PUBLIC EXECUTION.
Kikuzato

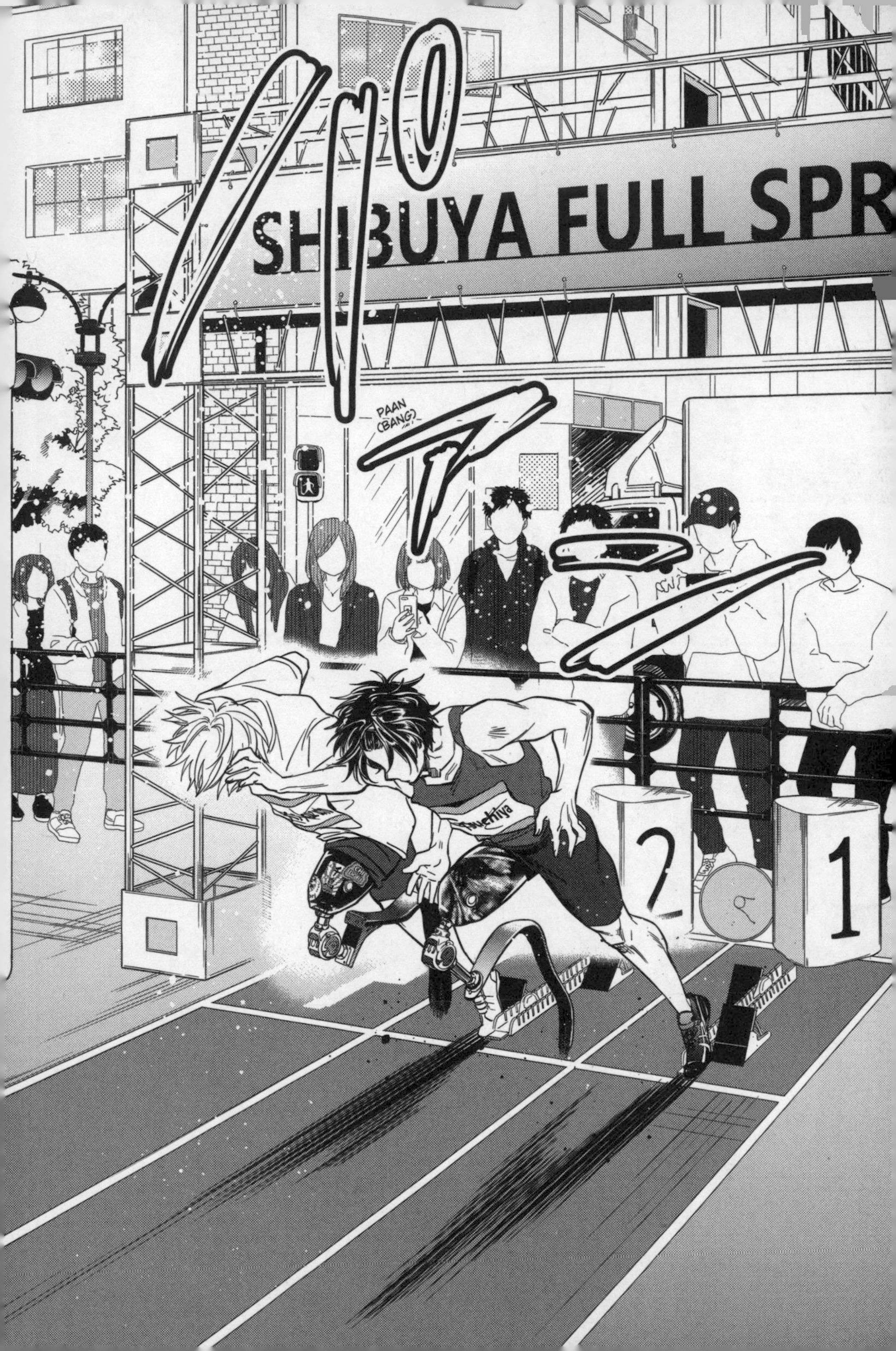
SHIBUYA FULL SPR
PAAN (BANG)
2
1

Chapter 6: A Leg of My Own

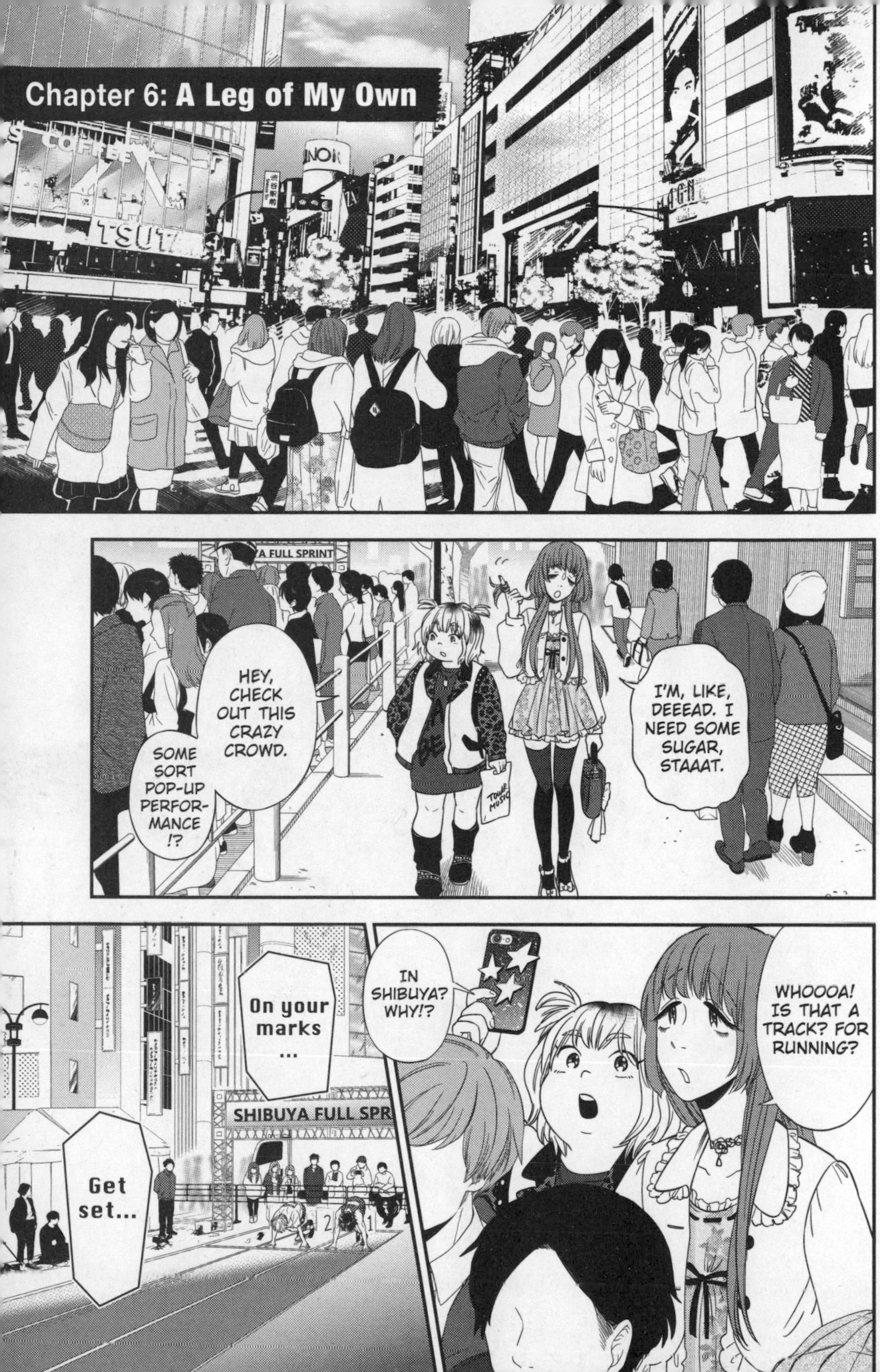
I'M, LIKE, DEEEAD. I NEED SOME SUGAR, STAAAT.
HEY, CHECK OUT THIS CRAZY CROWD.
SOME SORT POP-UP PERFORMANCE!?
WHOOOA! IS THAT A TRACK? FOR RUNNING?
IN SHIBUYA? WHY!?
On your marks...
SHIBUYA FULL SPR
Get set...

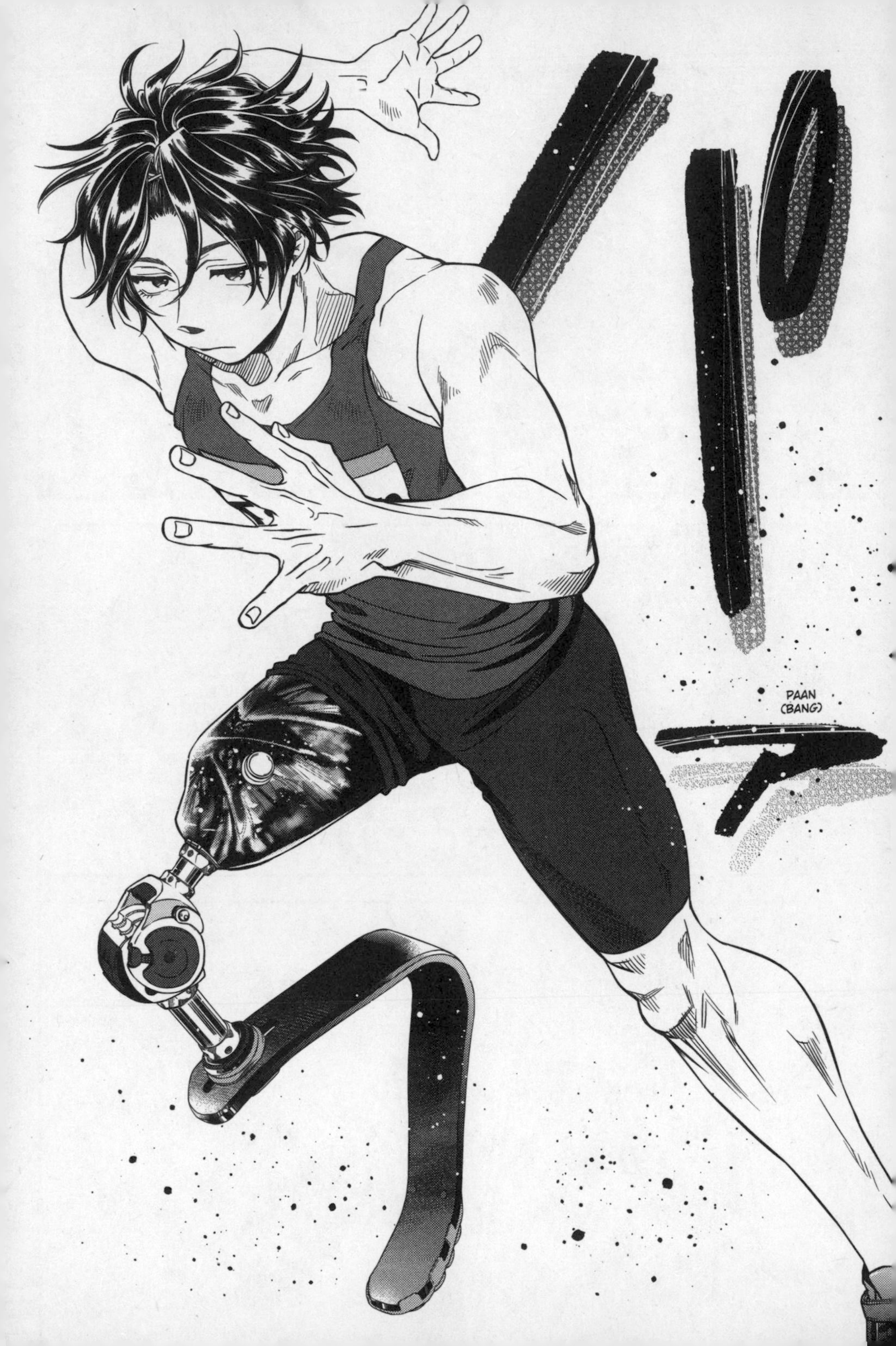

PAAN
(BANG)

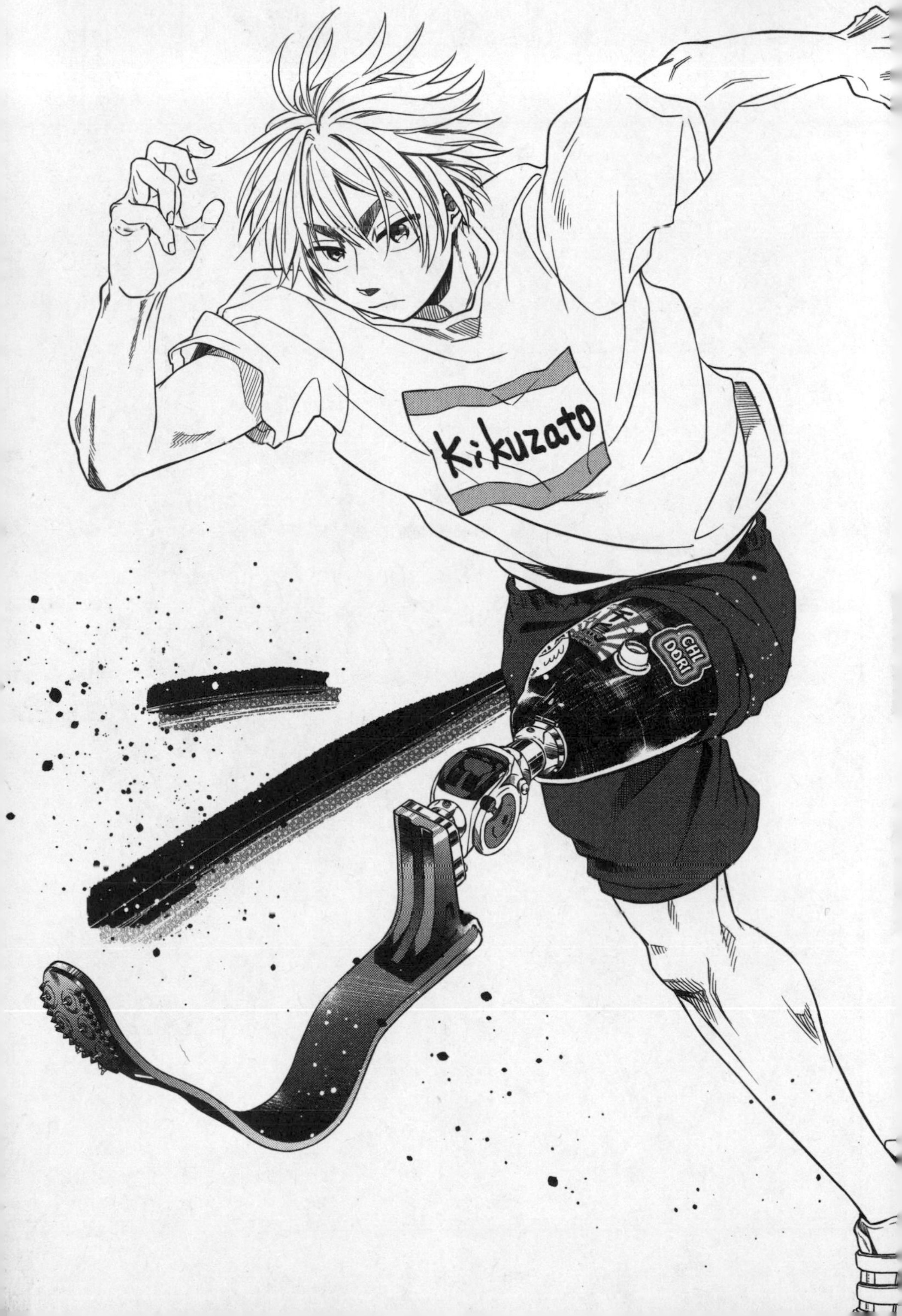
Kikuzato
CHI
DORI

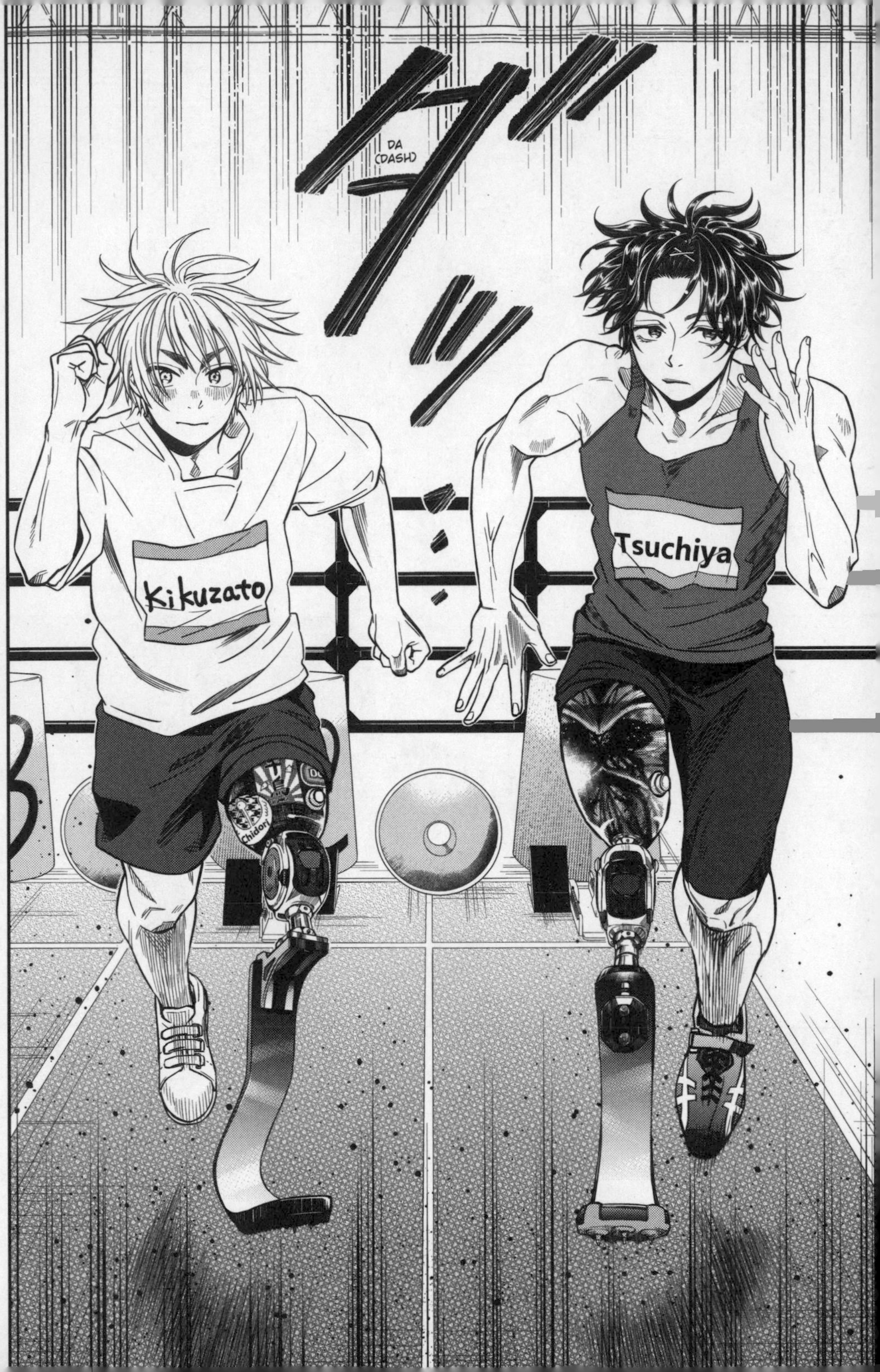
DA (DASH)
Kikuzato
Tsuchiya
Chidori

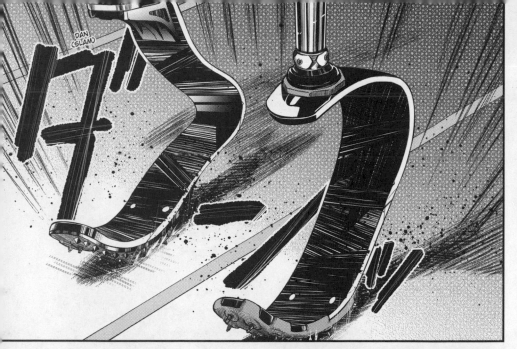

DAN
(SLAM)

ZUA
(ZOOM)

SO YOU CAN PLAY A GAME OF *TAG*, IF NOTHING ELSE.

135

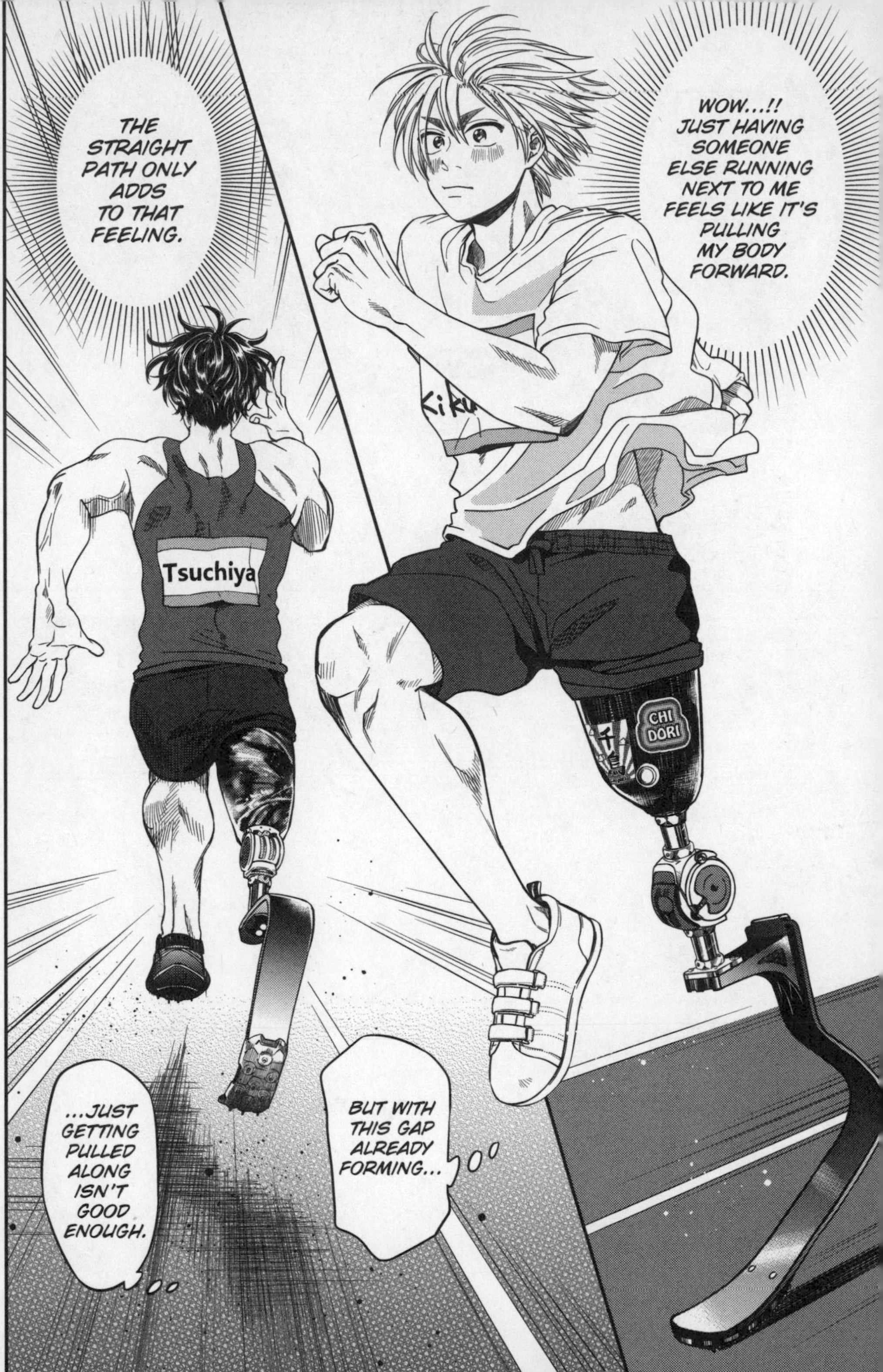
WOW...!! JUST HAVING SOMEONE ELSE RUNNING NEXT TO ME FEELS LIKE IT'S PULLING MY BODY FORWARD.
THE STRAIGHT PATH ONLY ADDS TO THAT FEELING.
Tsuchiya
CHI DORI
BUT WITH THIS GAP ALREADY FORMING...
...JUST GETTING PULLED ALONG ISN'T GOOD ENOUGH.

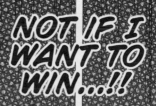

NOT IF I
WANT TO
WIN...!!

CRAP...
MY
SOCKET'S
COMING
LOOSE.

ZURI
(SHFF)

CHI
DORI

C'MON,
JUST ONE
MORE
STEP...

OR
THREE
!!

OR
TWO...

ZURU
(SLIP)

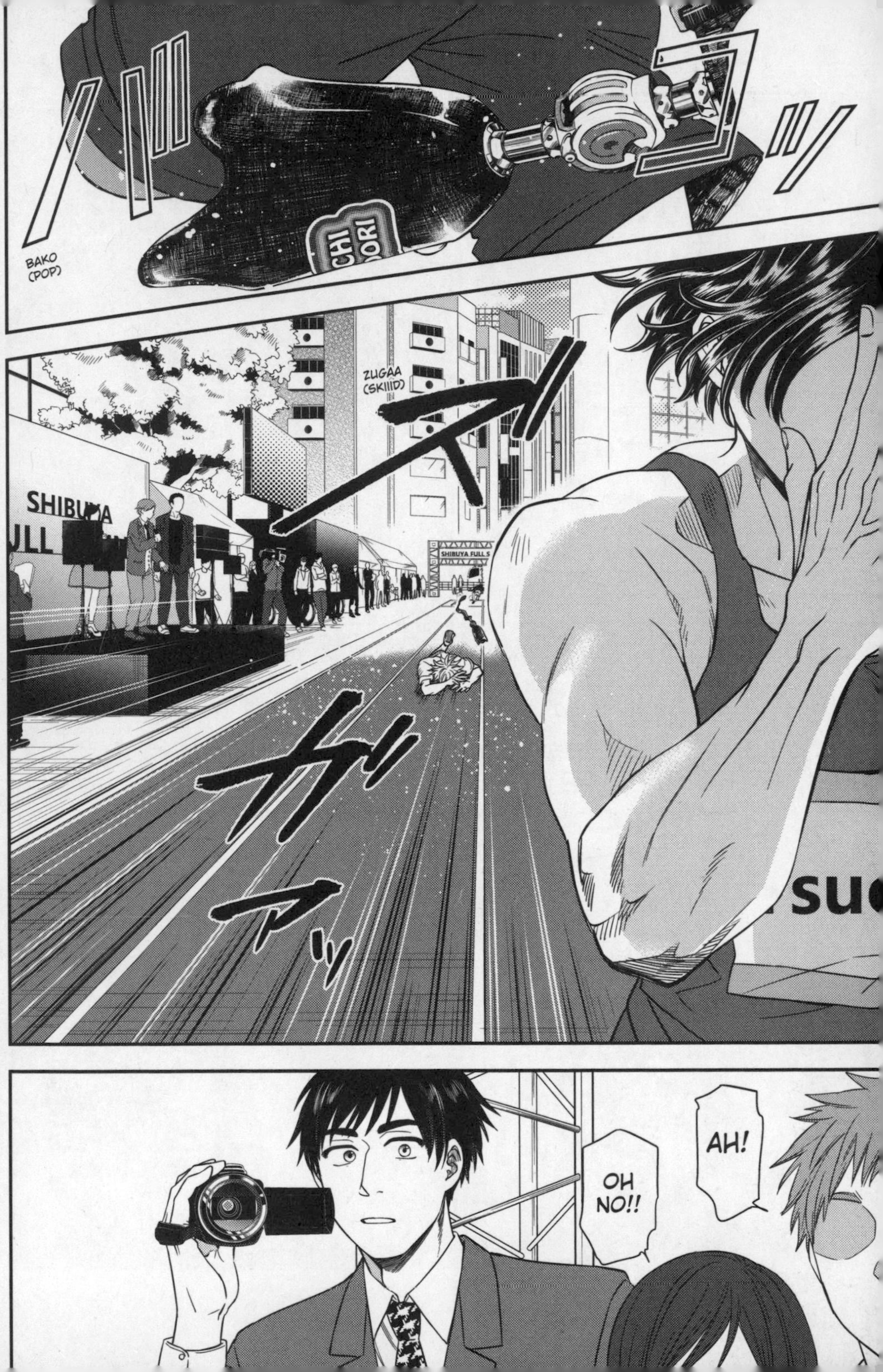

CHI DORI
BAKO (POP)
ZUGAA (SKIIID)
SHIBUYA
AH!
OH NO!!

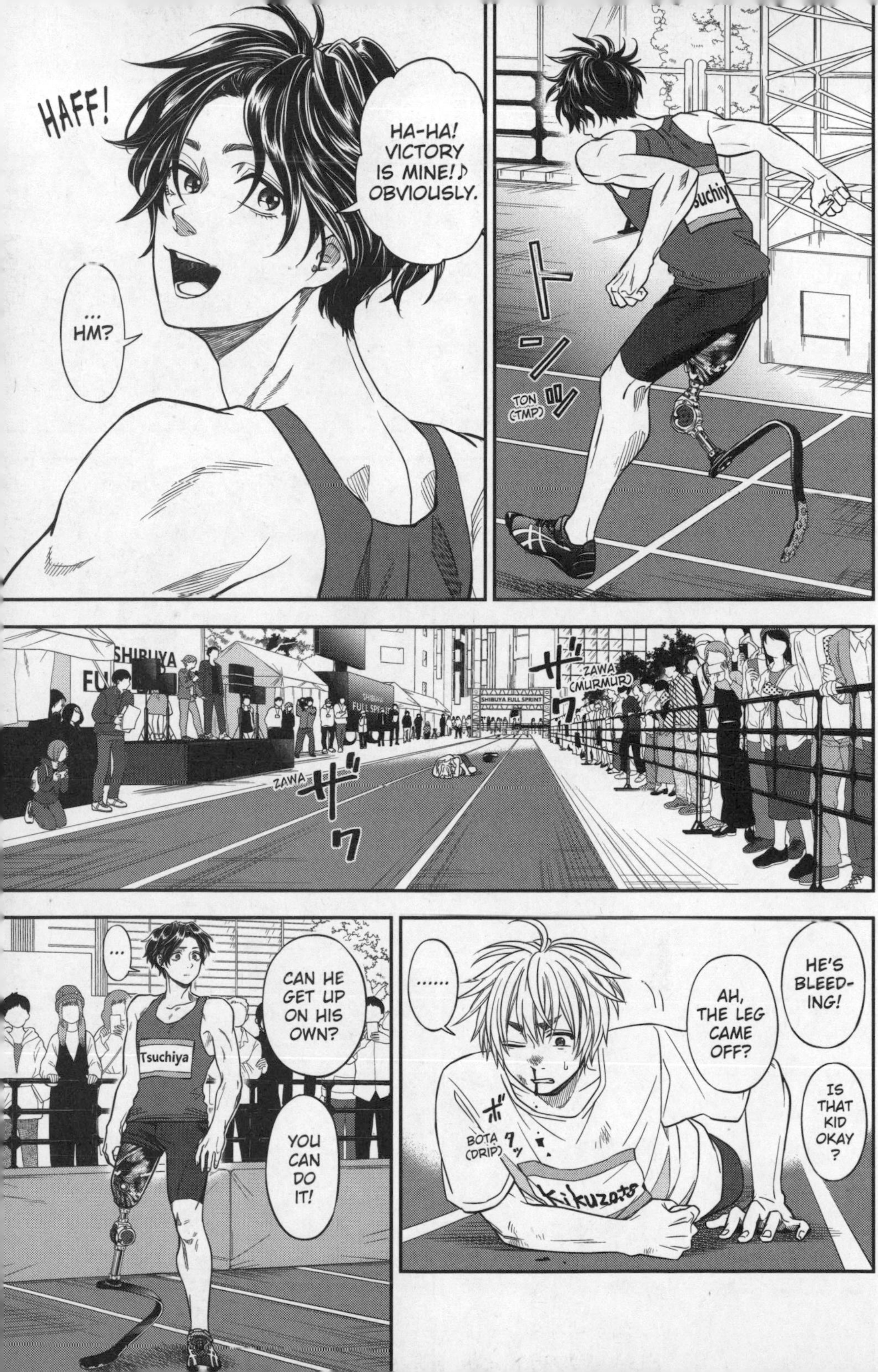

TON (TMP)
Suchiy
HA-HA! VICTORY IS MINE!♪ OBVIOUSLY.
HAFF!
... HM?
ZAWA (MURMUR)
SHIBUYA FULL SPRINT
SHIBUYA
ZAWA
HE'S BLEEDING!
AH, THE LEG CAME OFF?
......
IS THAT KID OKAY?
BOTA (DRIP)
Kikuzato
CAN HE GET UP ON HIS OWN?
...
YOU CAN DO IT!
Tsuchiya

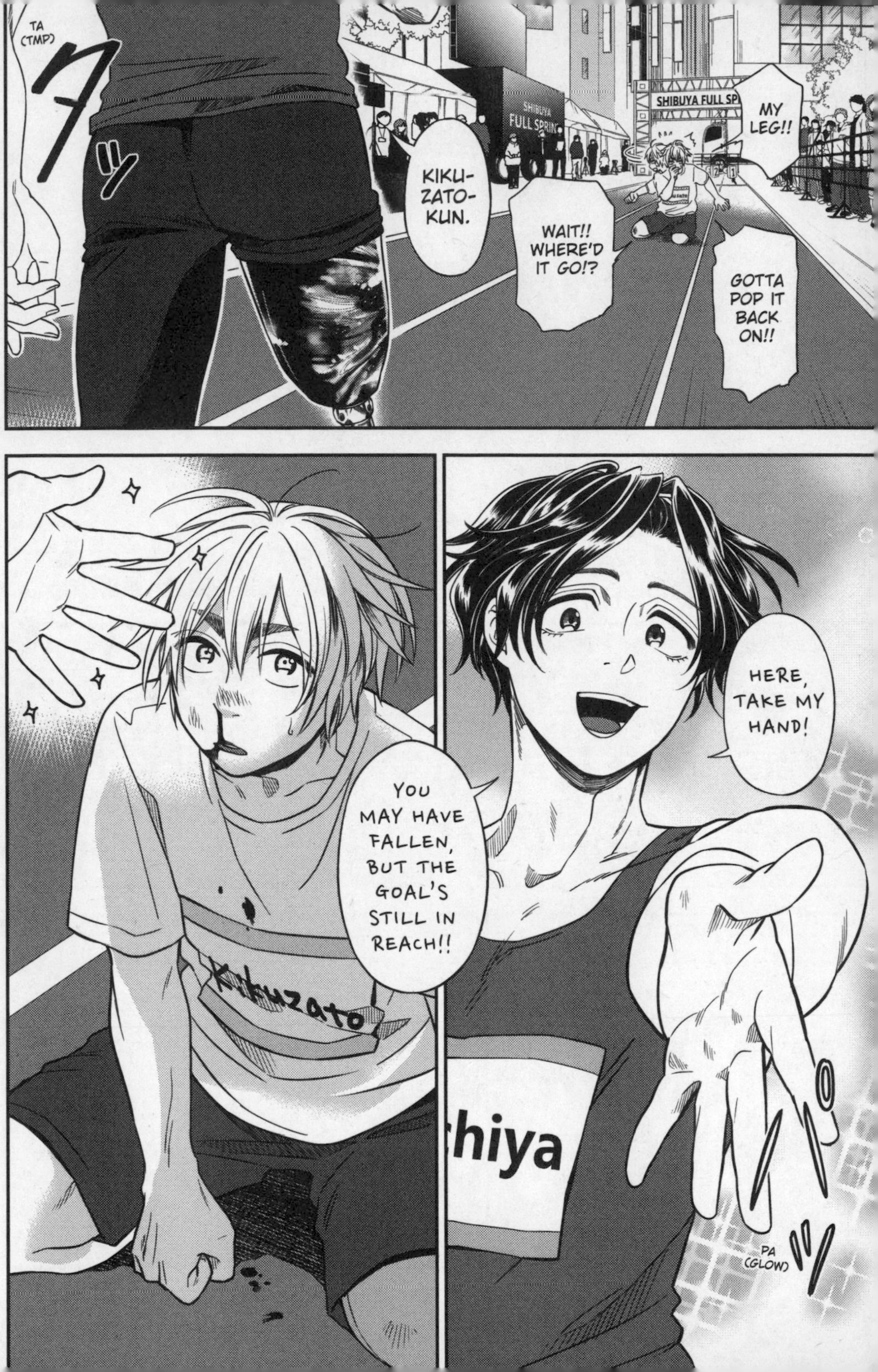
MY LEG!!
GOTTA POP IT BACK ON!!
WAIT!! WHERE'D IT GO!?
KIKUZATO-KUN.
TA (TMP)
HERE, TAKE MY HAND!
YOU MAY HAVE FALLEN, BUT THE GOAL'S STILL IN REACH!!
PA (GLOW)
Kikuzato

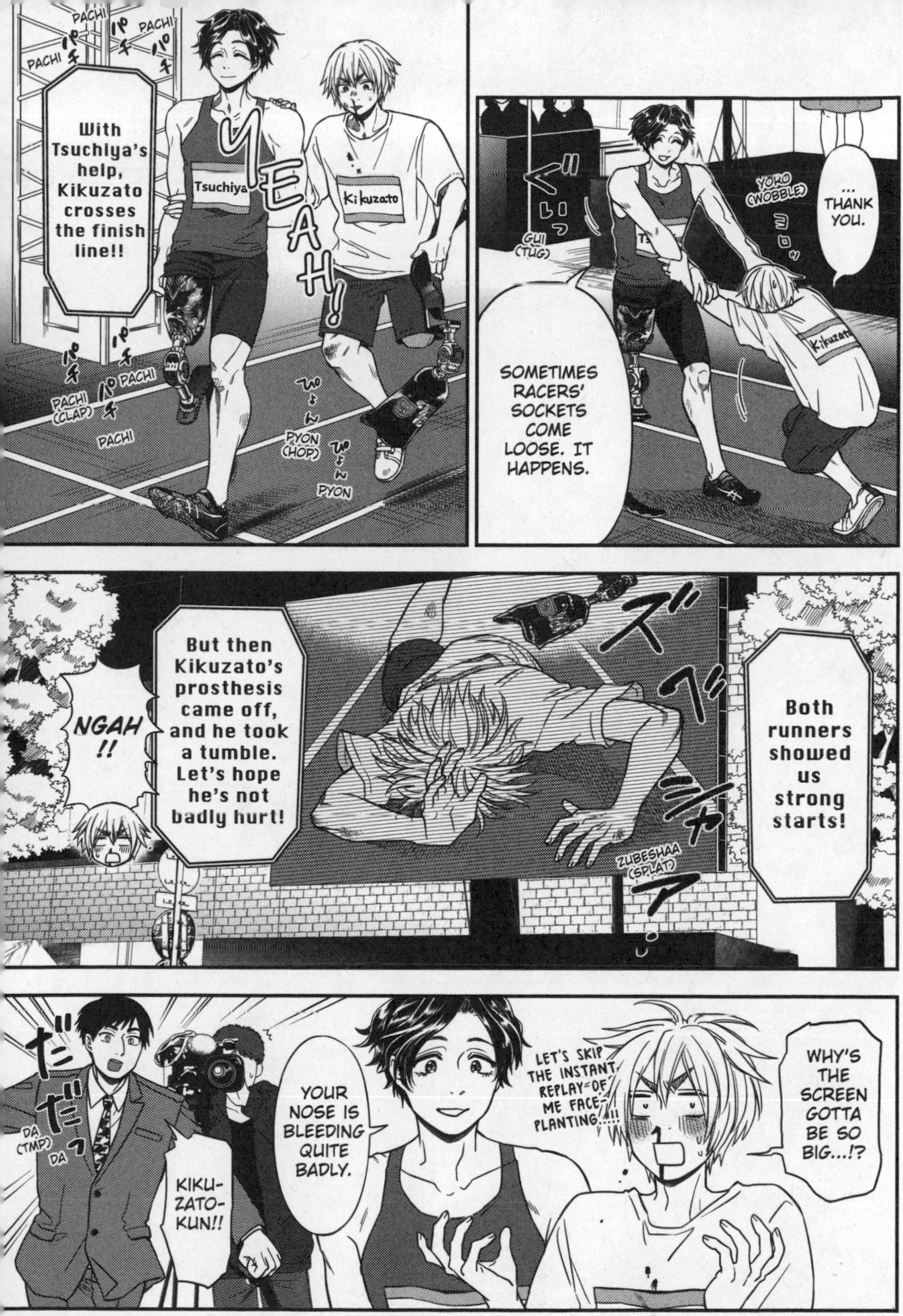
YOKO (WOBBLE)
...THANK YOU.
GUI (TUG)
SOMETIMES RACERS' SOCKETS COME LOOSE. IT HAPPENS.
PACHI
PACHI
PACHI
YEAH!
With Tsuchiya's help, Kikuzato crosses the finish line!!
Tsuchiya
Kikuzato
PACHI (CLAP)
PACHI
PACHI
PYON (HOP)
PYON
Both runners showed us strong starts!
ZUBESHAA (SPLAT)
But then Kikuzato's prosthesis came off, and he took a tumble. Let's hope he's not badly hurt!
NGAH!!
WHY'S THE SCREEN GOTTA BE SO BIG...!?
LET'S SKIP THE INSTANT REPLAY OF ME FACE-PLANTING...!!!
YOUR NOSE IS BLEEDING QUITE BADLY.
KIKU-ZATO-KUN!!
DA (TMP) DA

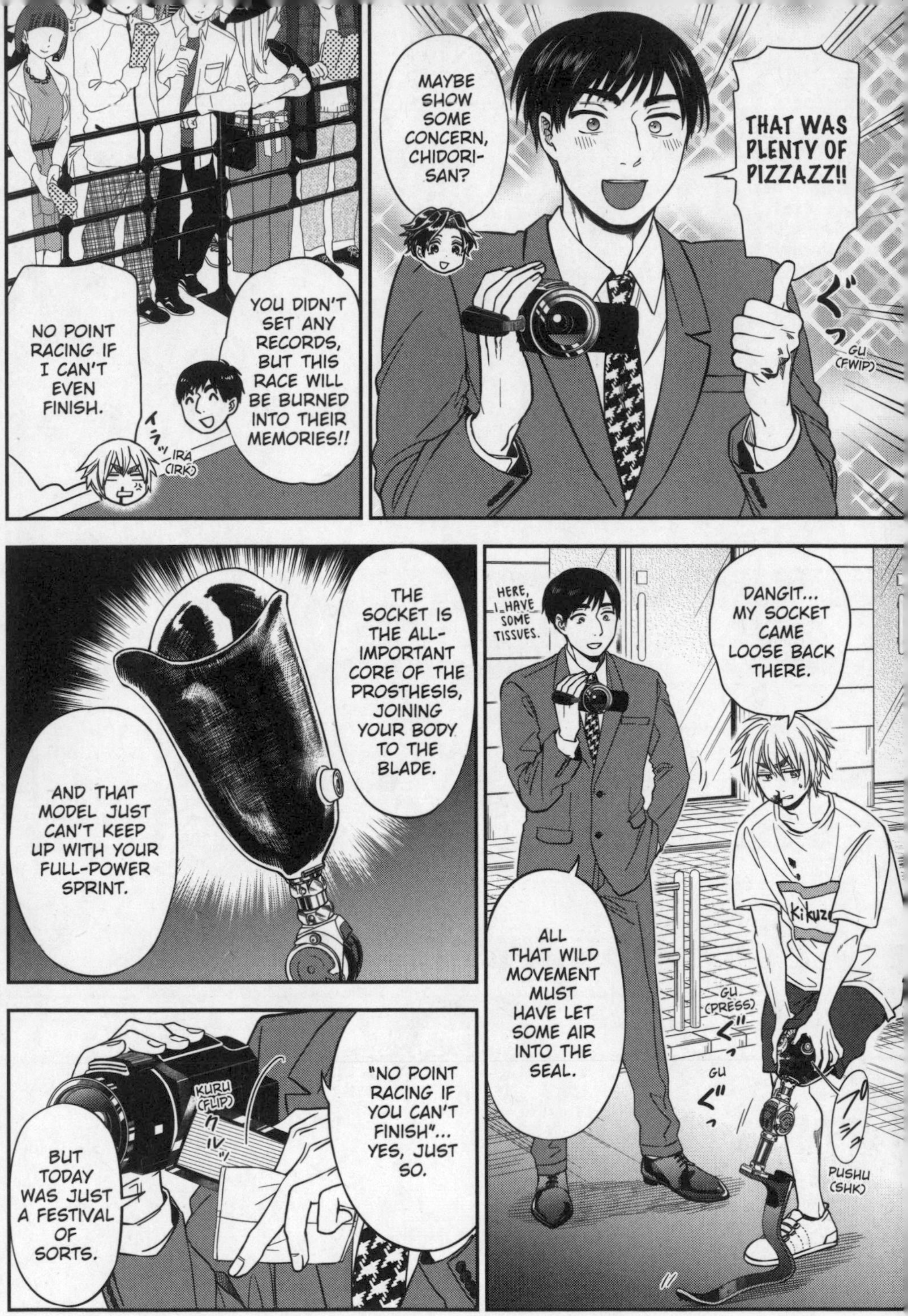

THAT WAS PLENTY OF PIZZAZZ!!
MAYBE SHOW SOME CONCERN, CHIDORI-SAN?
GU (FWIP)
YOU DIDN'T SET ANY RECORDS, BUT THIS RACE WILL BE BURNED INTO THEIR MEMORIES!!
IRA (IRK)
NO POINT RACING IF I CAN'T EVEN FINISH.
DANGIT... MY SOCKET CAME LOOSE BACK THERE.
HERE, I HAVE SOME TISSUES.
ALL THAT WILD MOVEMENT MUST HAVE LET SOME AIR INTO THE SEAL.
Kikuz
GU (PRESS)
GU
PUSHU (SHK)
THE SOCKET IS THE ALL-IMPORTANT CORE OF THE PROSTHESIS, JOINING YOUR BODY TO THE BLADE.
AND THAT MODEL JUST CAN'T KEEP UP WITH YOUR FULL-POWER SPRINT.
"NO POINT RACING IF YOU CAN'T FINISH"... YES, JUST SO.
KURU (FLIP)
BUT TODAY WAS JUST A FESTIVAL OF SORTS.

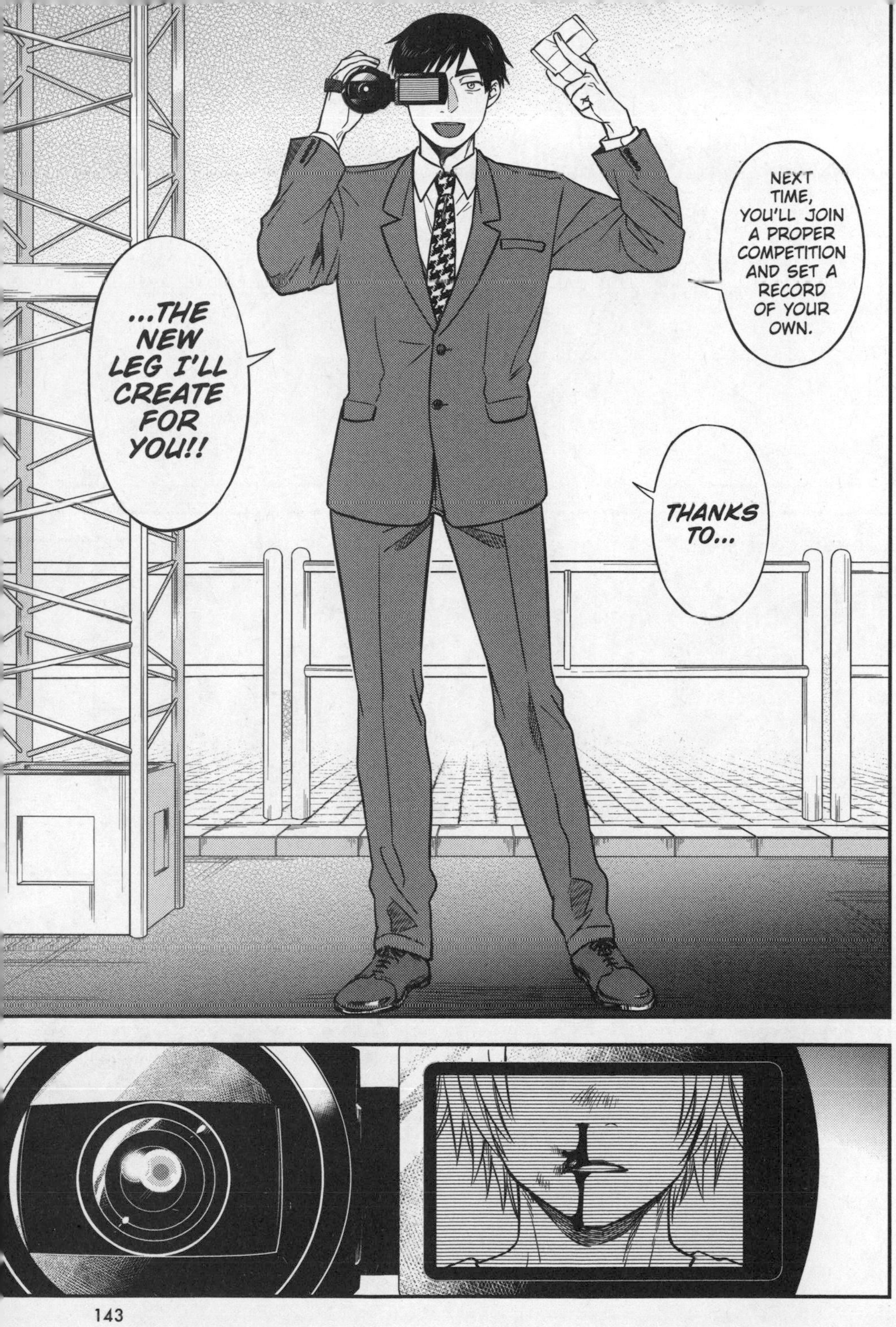
NEXT TIME, YOU'LL JOIN A PROPER COMPETITION AND SET A RECORD OF YOUR OWN.
THANKS TO...
...THE NEW LEG I'LL CREATE FOR YOU!!

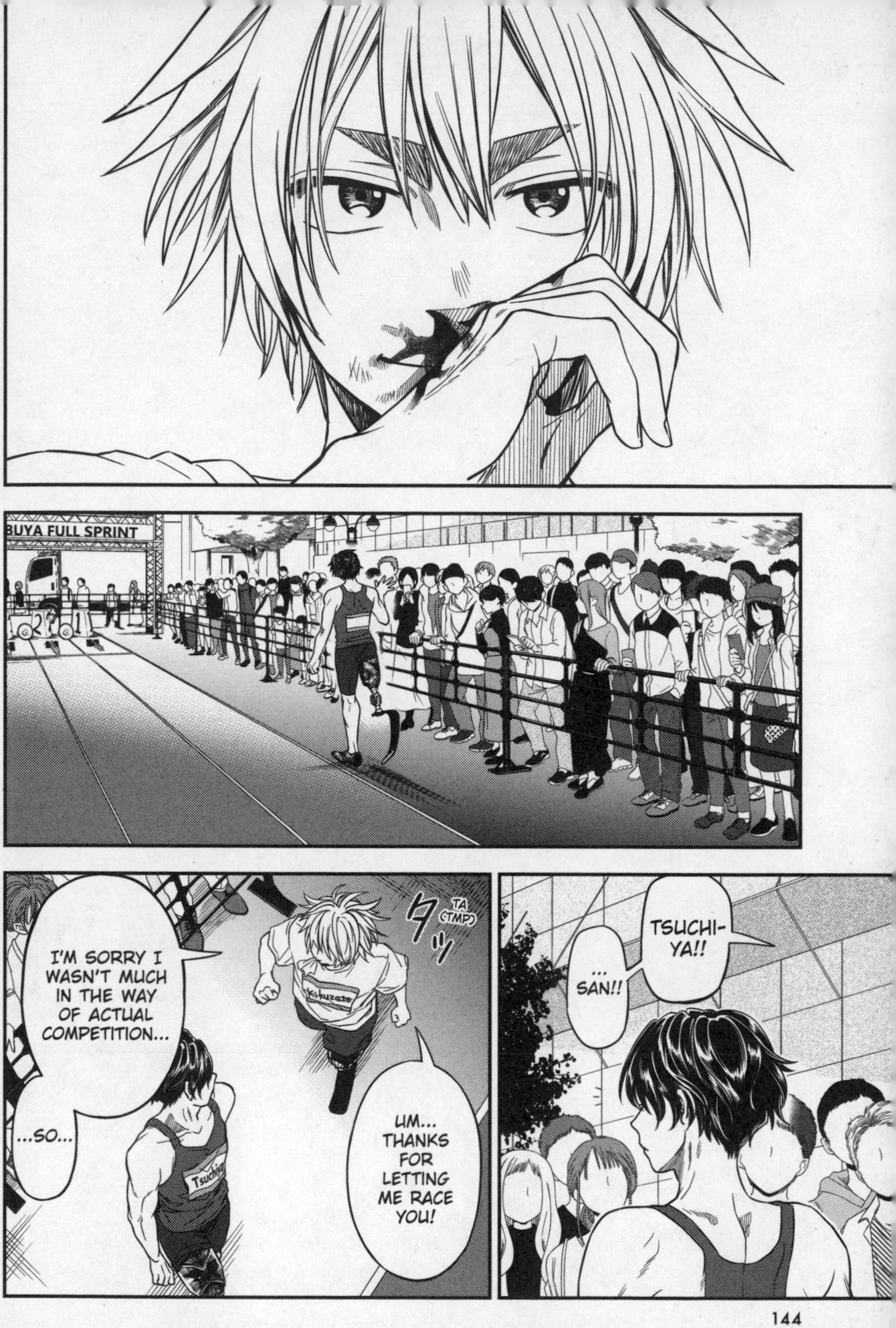

BUYA FULL SPRINT
TSUCHI-YA!!
... SAN!!
TA (TMP)
UM... THANKS FOR LETTING ME RACE YOU!
I'M SORRY I WASN'T MUCH IN THE WAY OF ACTUAL COMPETITION...
...SO...
Tsuchiya

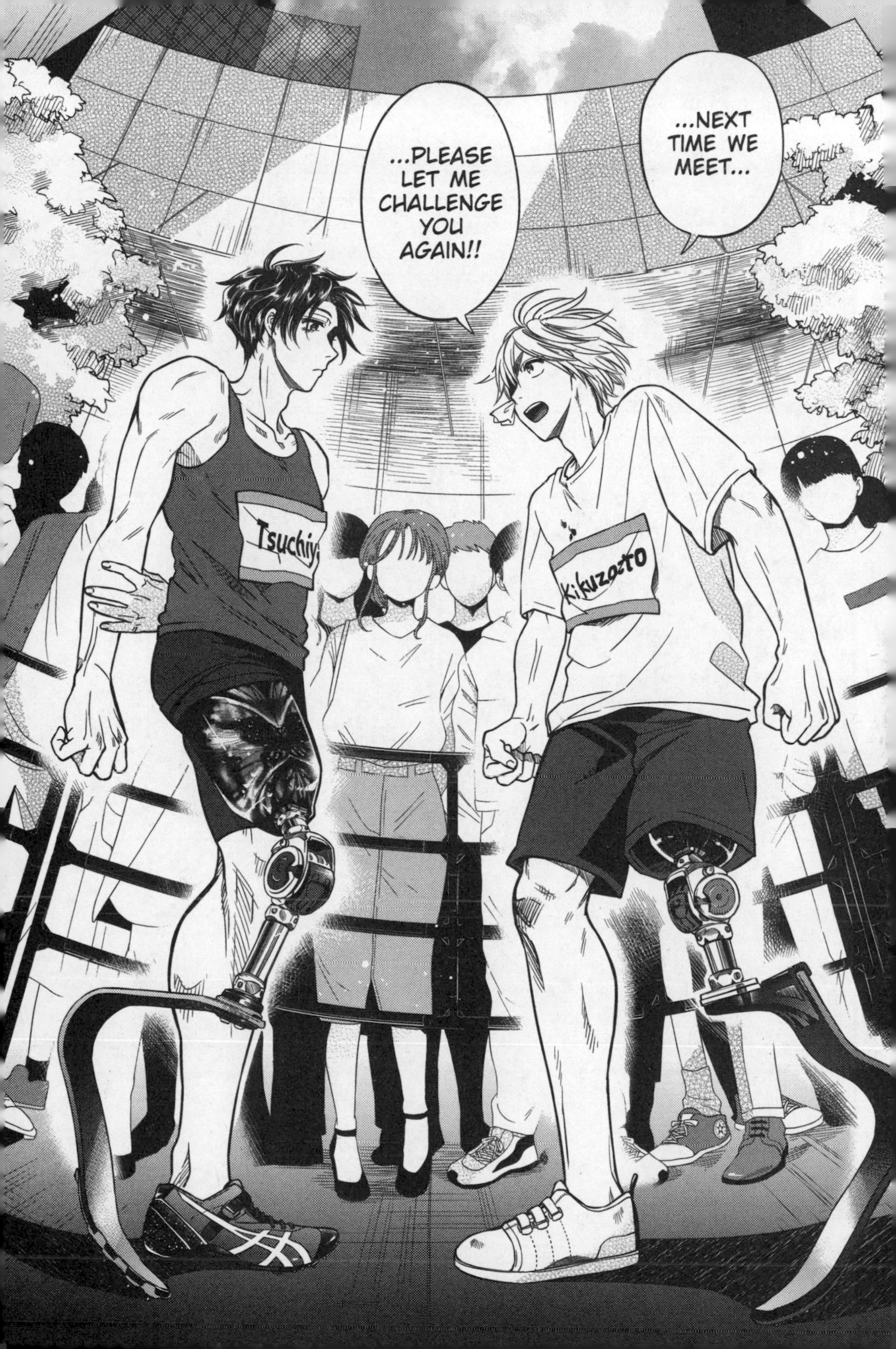
...NEXT TIME WE MEET...
...PLEASE LET ME CHALLENGE YOU AGAIN!!
Kikuzato
Tsuchiy

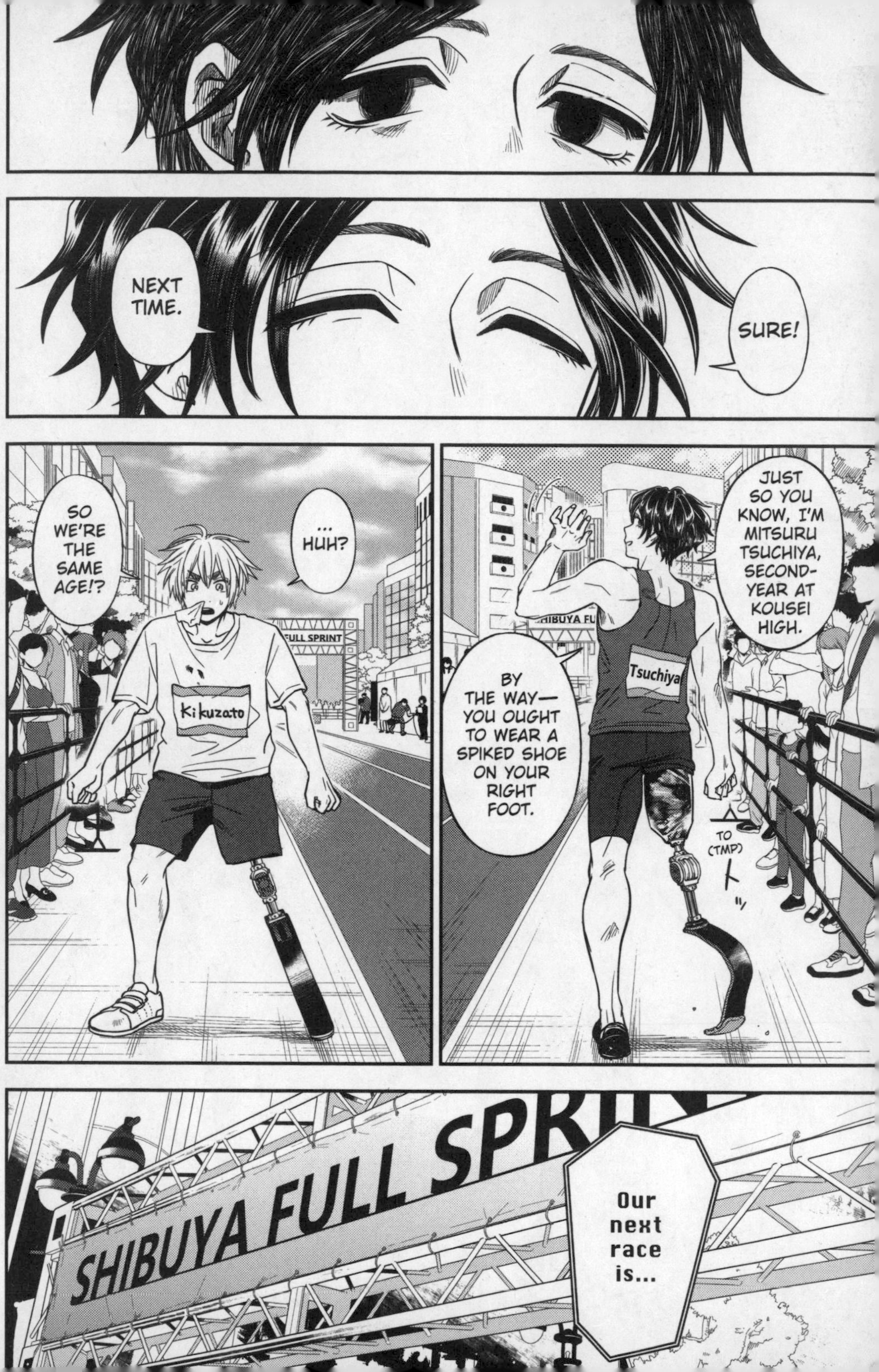
NEXT TIME.
SURE!
JUST SO YOU KNOW, I'M MITSURU TSUCHIYA, SECOND-YEAR AT KOUSEI HIGH.
SHIBUYA FU
Tsuchiya
BY THE WAY— YOU OUGHT TO WEAR A SPIKED SHOE ON YOUR RIGHT FOOT.
TO (TMP)
... HUH?
SO WE'RE THE SAME AGE!?
FULL SPRINT
Kikuzato
SHIBUYA FULL SPRIN
Our next race is...

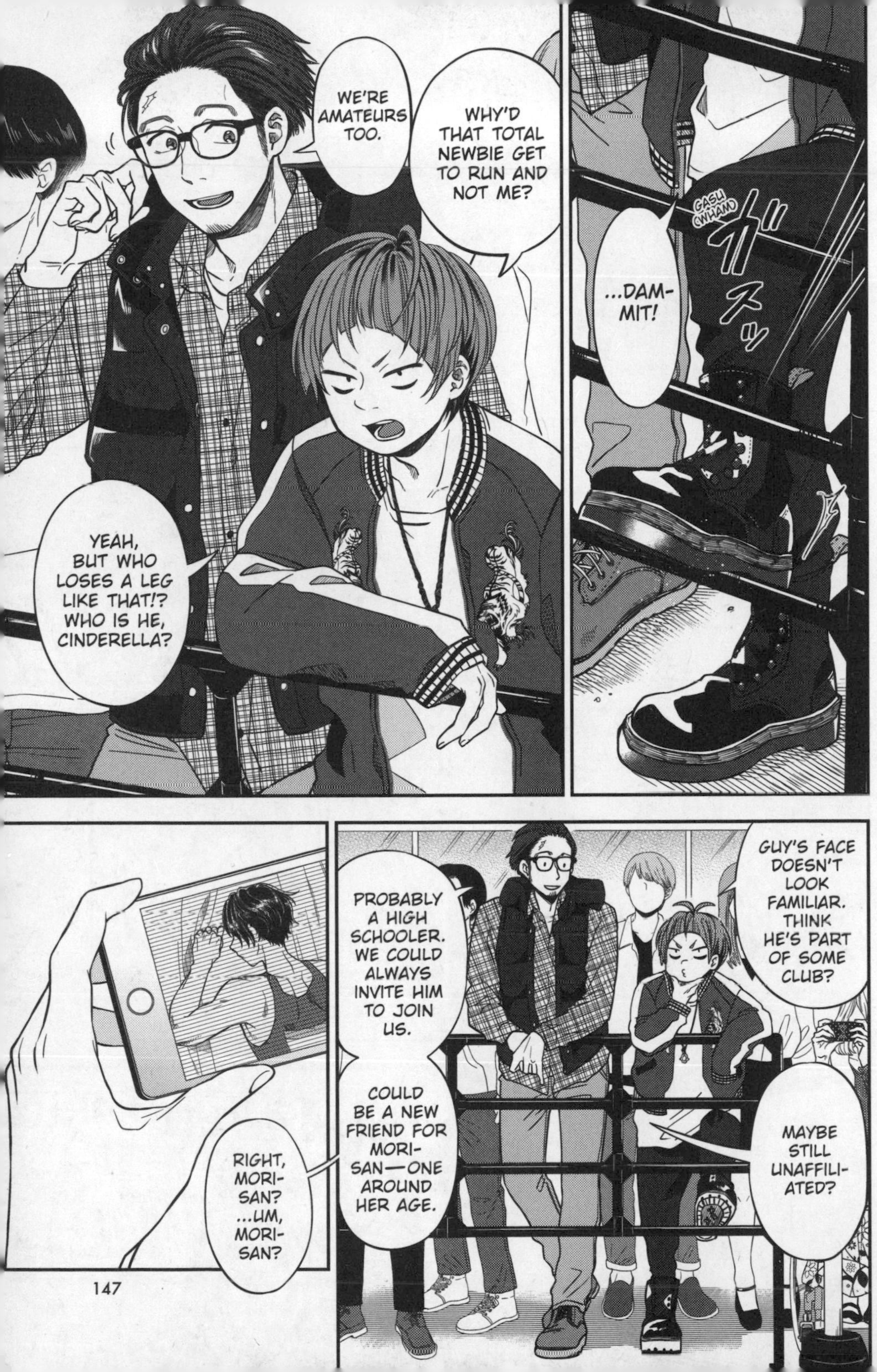
GASU (WHAM)
...DAM-MIT!
WHY'D THAT TOTAL NEWBIE GET TO RUN AND NOT ME?
WE'RE AMATEURS TOO.
YEAH, BUT WHO LOSES A LEG LIKE THAT!? WHO IS HE, CINDERELLA?
GUY'S FACE DOESN'T LOOK FAMILIAR. THINK HE'S PART OF SOME CLUB?
PROBABLY A HIGH SCHOOLER. WE COULD ALWAYS INVITE HIM TO JOIN US.
MAYBE STILL UNAFFILI-ATED?
COULD BE A NEW FRIEND FOR MORI-SAN—ONE AROUND HER AGE.
RIGHT, MORI-SAN? ...UM, MORI-SAN?

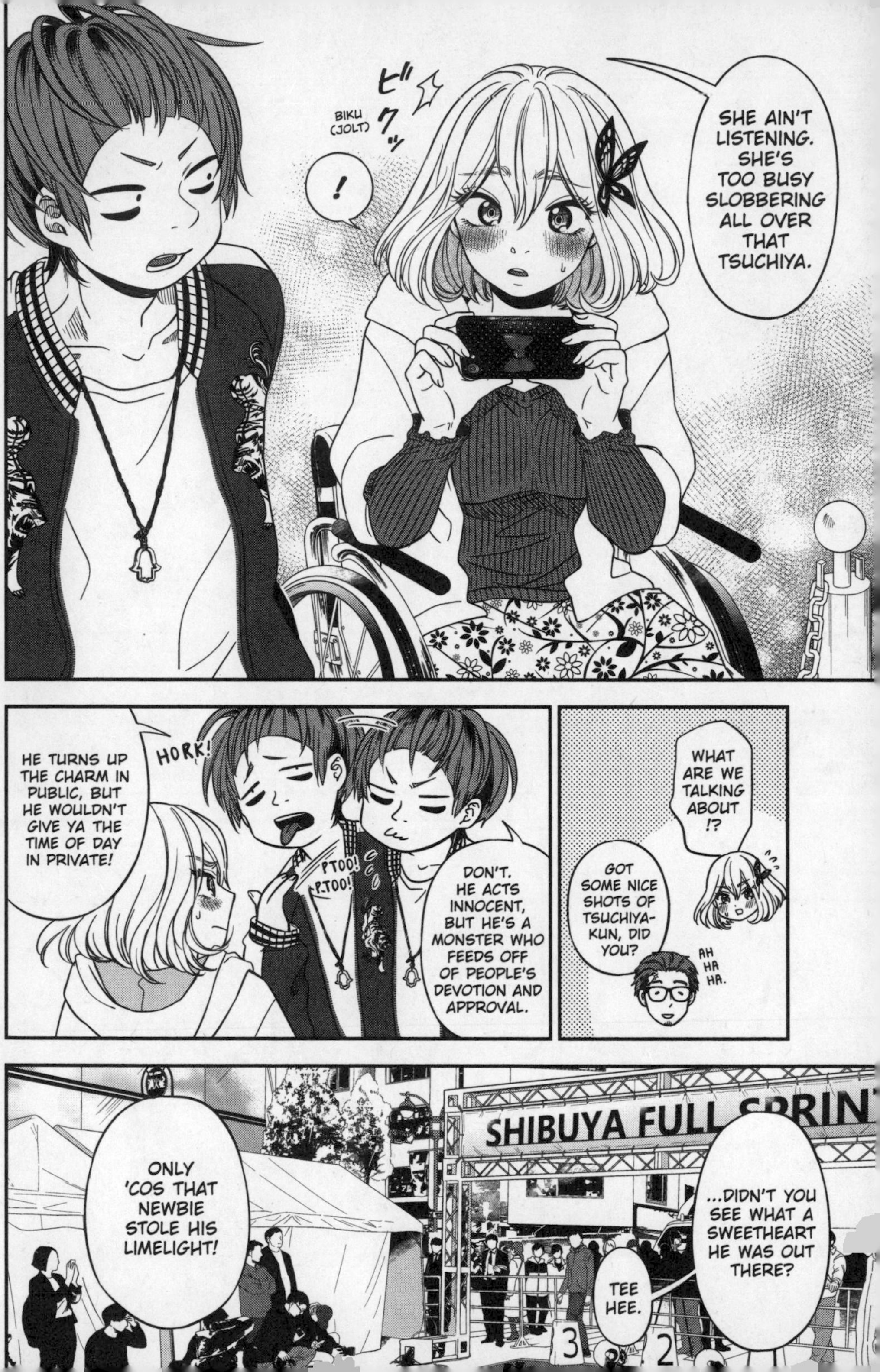

SHE AIN'T LISTENING. SHE'S TOO BUSY SLOBBERING ALL OVER THAT TSUCHIYA.
ビクッ
BIKU (JOLT)
!
WHAT ARE WE TALKING ABOUT !?
GOT SOME NICE SHOTS OF TSUCHIYA-KUN, DID YOU?
AH HA HA.
HORK!
HE TURNS UP THE CHARM IN PUBLIC, BUT HE WOULDN'T GIVE YA THE TIME OF DAY IN PRIVATE!
P.TOO! P.TOO!
DON'T. HE ACTS INNOCENT, BUT HE'S A MONSTER WHO FEEDS OFF OF PEOPLE'S DEVOTION AND APPROVAL.
SHIBUYA FULL SPRIN
...DIDN'T YOU SEE WHAT A SWEETHEART HE WAS OUT THERE?
TEE HEE.
ONLY 'COS THAT NEWBIE STOLE HIS LIMELIGHT!
3
2

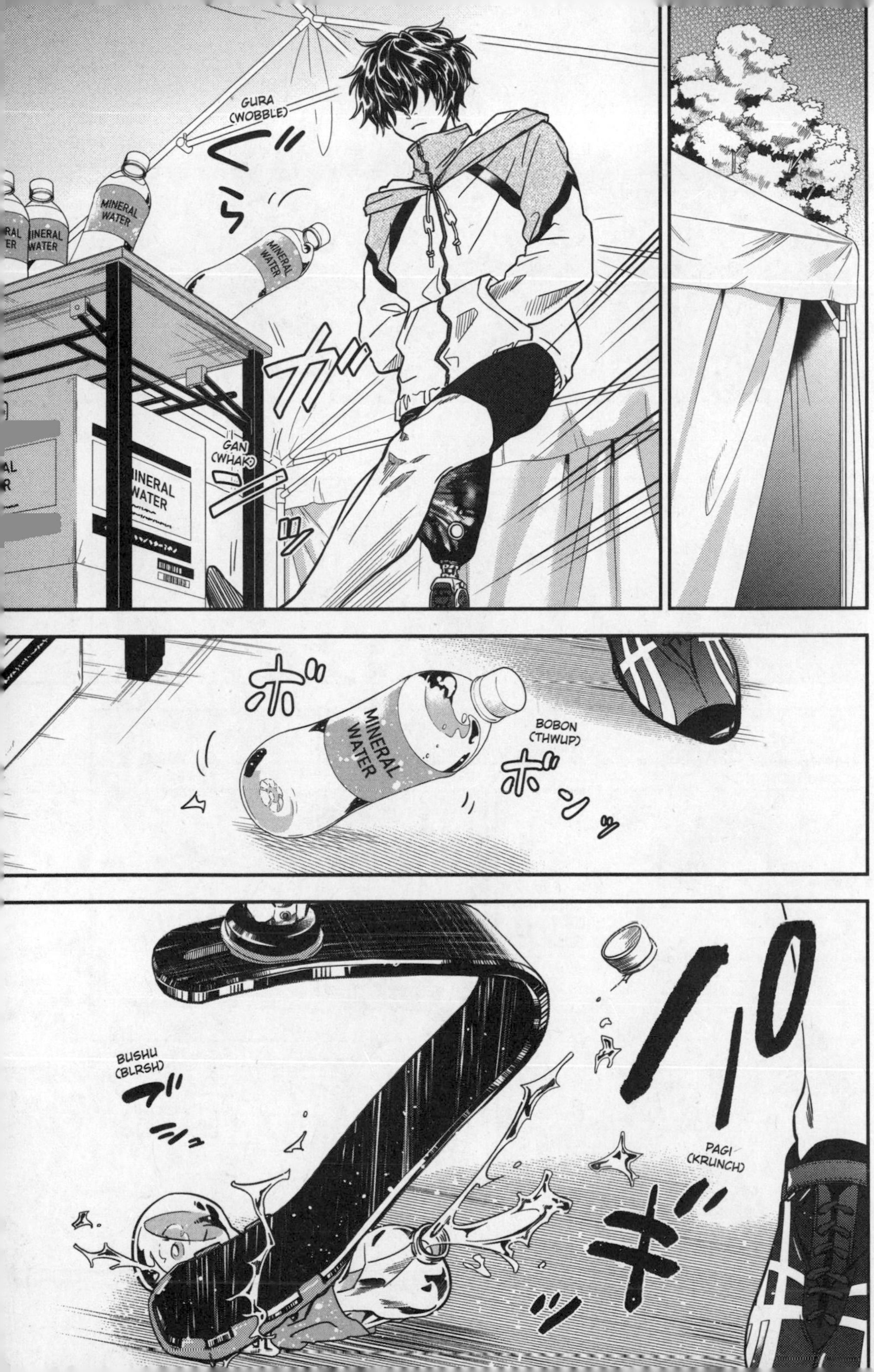
GURA (WOBBLE)
MINERAL WATER
MINERAL WATER
MINERAL WATER
MINERAL WATER
MINERAL WATER
GAN (WHAK)
BOBON (THWUP)
MINERAL WATER
PAGI (KRUNCH)
BUSHU (BLRSH)

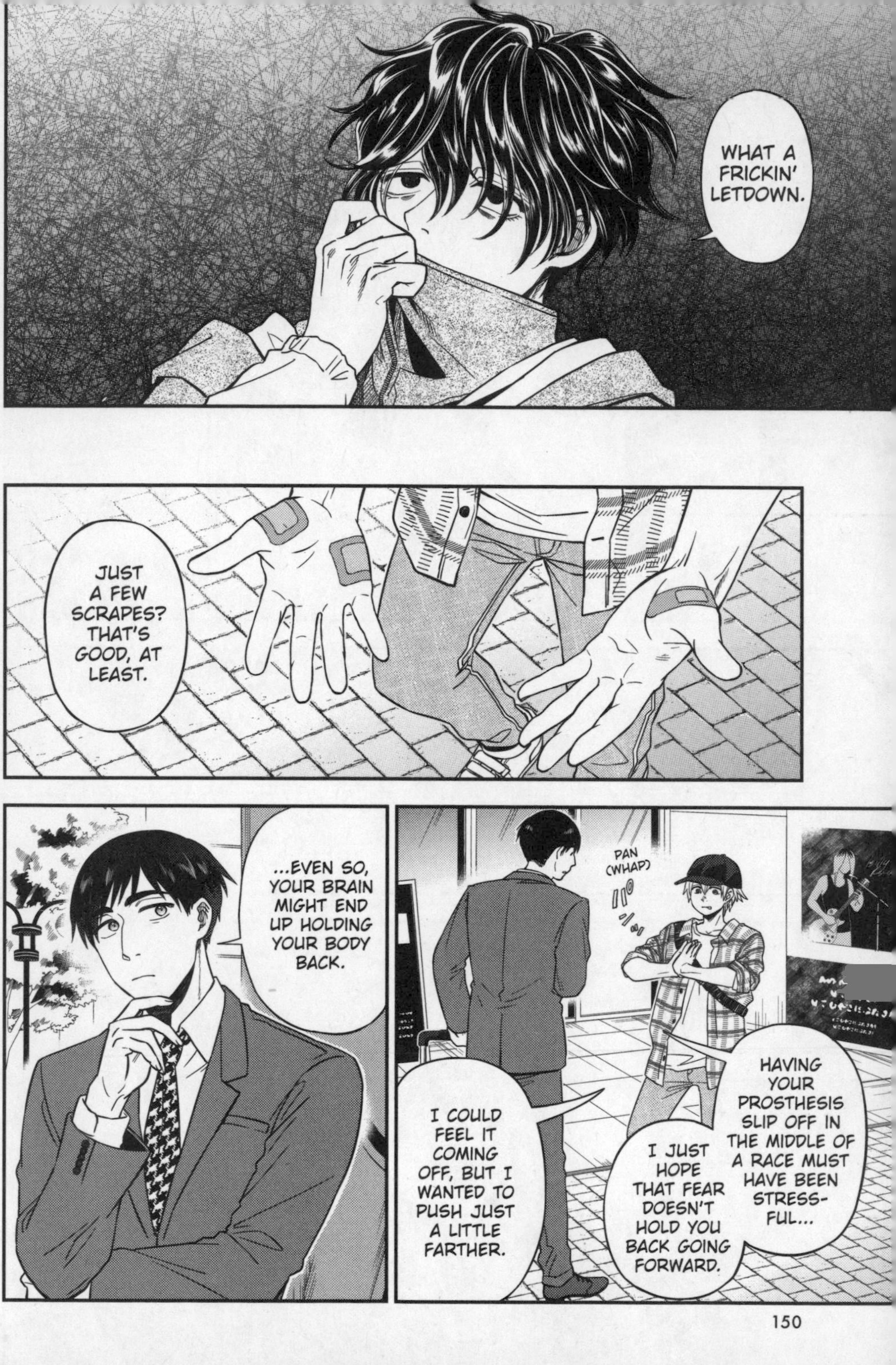
WHAT A FRICKIN' LETDOWN.
JUST A FEW SCRAPES? THAT'S GOOD, AT LEAST.
PAN (WHAP)
HAVING YOUR PROSTHESIS SLIP OFF IN THE MIDDLE OF A RACE MUST HAVE BEEN STRESS-FUL...
I JUST HOPE THAT FEAR DOESN'T HOLD YOU BACK GOING FORWARD.
I COULD FEEL IT COMING OFF, BUT I WANTED TO PUSH JUST A LITTLE FARTHER.
...EVEN SO, YOUR BRAIN MIGHT END UP HOLDING YOUR BODY BACK.

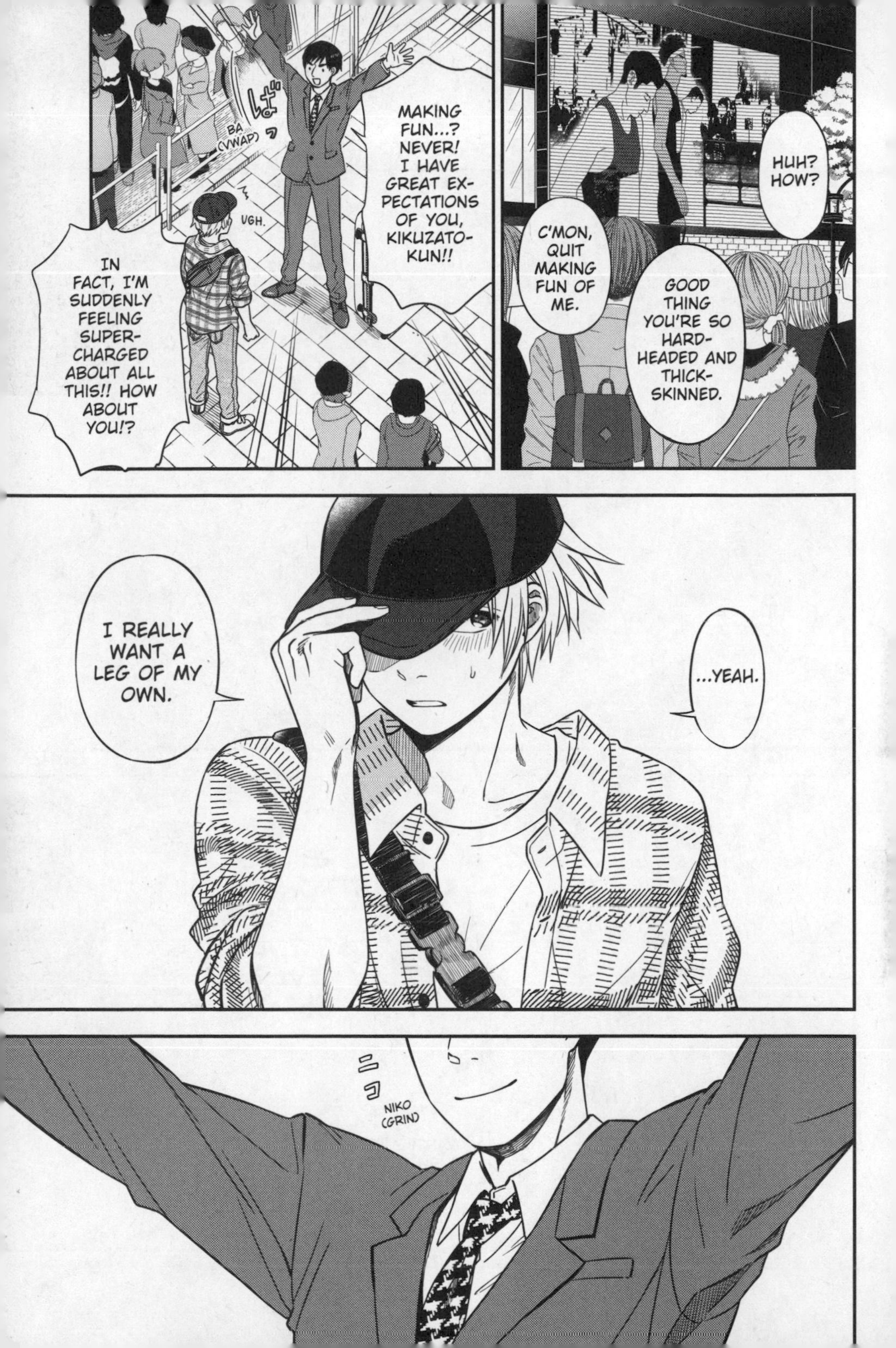
HUH? HOW?
C'MON, QUIT MAKING FUN OF ME.
GOOD THING YOU'RE SO HARD-HEADED AND THICK-SKINNED.
MAKING FUN...? NEVER! I HAVE GREAT EXPECTATIONS OF YOU, KIKUZATO-KUN!!
BA (VWAP)
UGH.
IN FACT, I'M SUDDENLY FEELING SUPER-CHARGED ABOUT ALL THIS!! HOW ABOUT YOU!?
...YEAH.
I REALLY WANT A LEG OF MY OWN.
NIKO (GRIN)

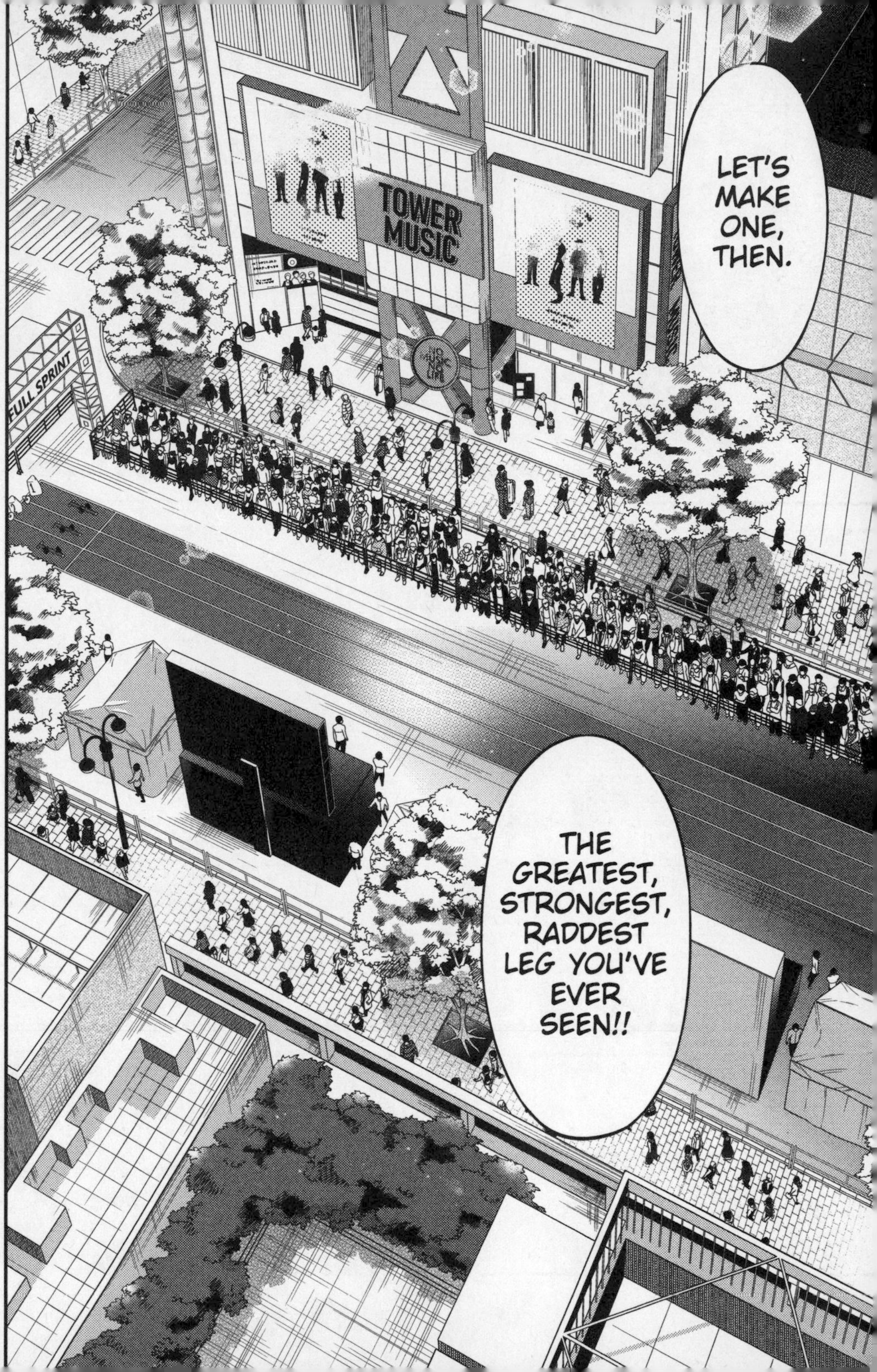
LET'S MAKE ONE, THEN.
THE GREATEST, STRONGEST, RADDEST LEG YOU'VE EVER SEEN!!
TOWER MUSIC
FULL SPRINT

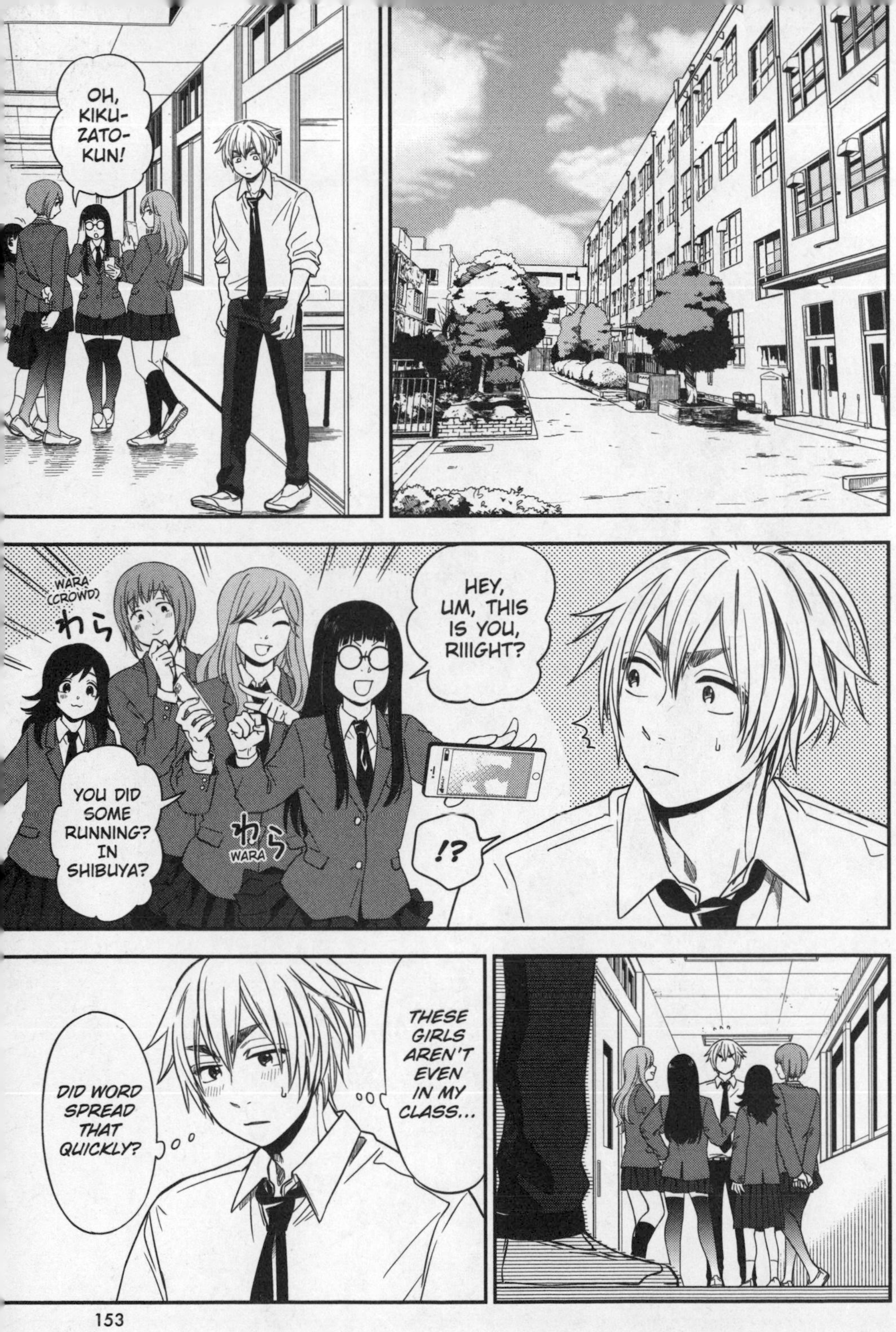

OH, KIKU-ZATO-KUN!
HEY, UM, THIS IS YOU, RIIIGHT?
!?
WARA (CROWD)
わら
わら
WARA
YOU DID SOME RUNNING? IN SHIBUYA?
THESE GIRLS AREN'T EVEN IN MY CLASS...
DID WORD SPREAD THAT QUICKLY?

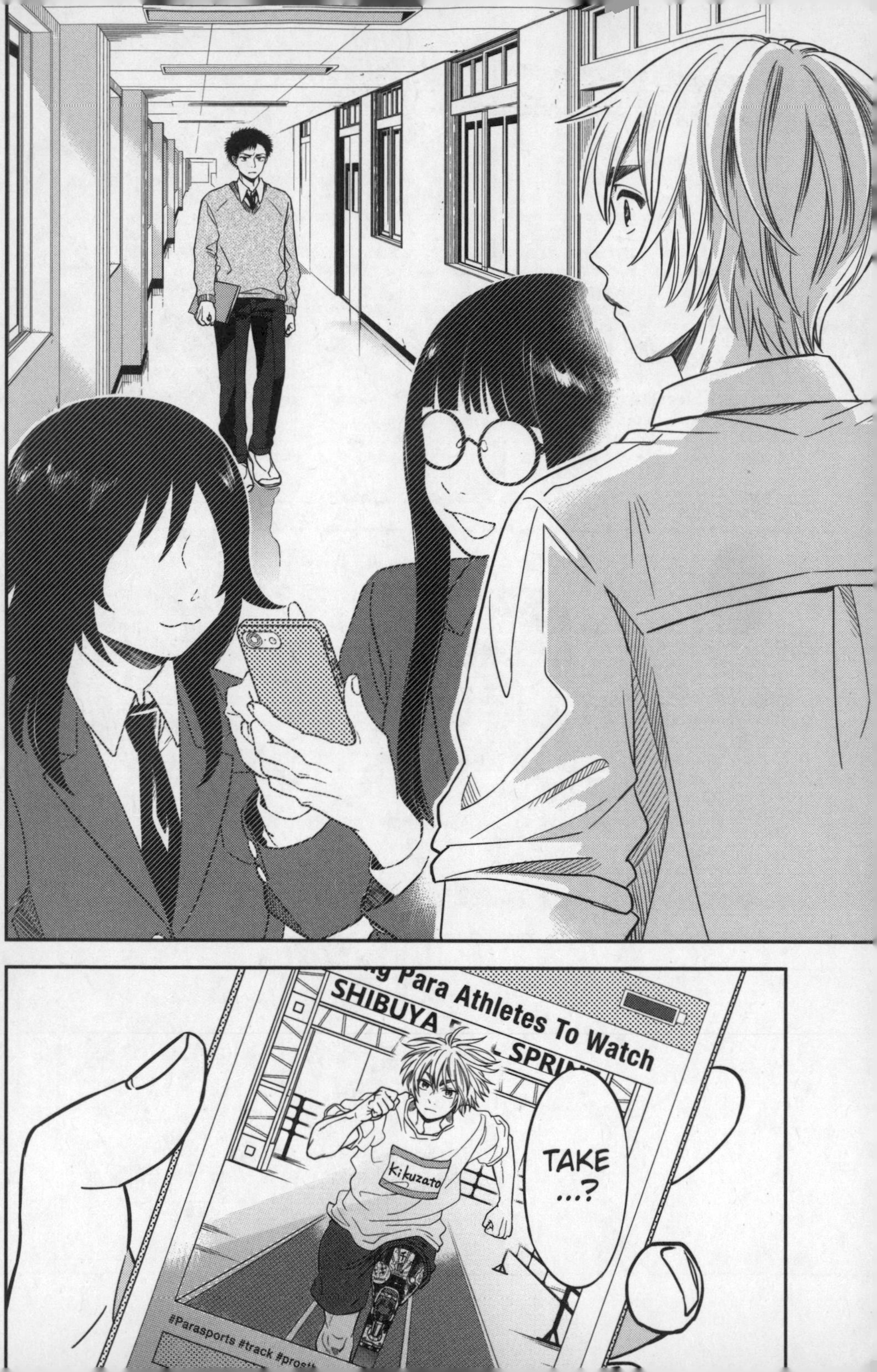
Para Athletes To Watch
SHIBUYA
Kikuzato
#Parasports #track
TAKE ...?

Run on Your New Legs, Vol. 1 : END

TRANSLATION NOTES

COMMON HONORIFICS
no honorific: Indicates familiarity or closeness; if used without permission or reason, addressing someone in this manner would constitute an insult.
-*san*: The Japanese equivalent of Mr./Mrs./Ms. This is the fail-safe honorific if politeness is required.
-*kun*: Used most often when referring to boys, this honorific indicates affection or familiarity. Occasionally used by older men among their peers, but it may also be used by anyone referring to a person of lower standing.
-*chan*: Affectionate honorific indicating familiarity used mostly in reference to girls; also used in reference to cute persons or animals of any gender.
-*sensei*: A respectful term for teachers, artists, or high-level professionals.
-*sama*: An honorific conveying great respect.

CURRENCY CONVERSION
While exchange rates fluctuate daily, a good approximation is ¥100 to 1 USD.

Page 59: The Radio **Kaikan** building is an iconic landmark of Akihabara, Tokyo.

Page 67: In Japanese culture, the symbol Chidori makes with his hand (touching thumb to tip of pointer finger) is code for "money." Chidori doesn't admit his motivation outright until later, but he's implying it with this gesture.

Page 70: Sennari are a brand of *dorayaki* sweets produced by Ryoguchiya-Korekiyo. *Dorayaki* consist of two pancake-like cakes encasing a sweet red-bean filling.

Page 75: Excepting classes with special equipment like phys ed or science labs, in Japanese high schools it is more common for students to remain in the same classroom all day while the teachers of various subjects rotate from room to room.

Page 157: The Japanese term for the houndstooth pattern is *chidori goushi* (literally, "thousand-bird lattice"), which explains why Chidori has chosen that pattern for his insoles as well as his necktie.

Special thanks
to all my consultants

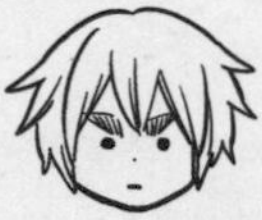

Athletes

Atsushi Yamamoto (Shin Nihon Jusetsu)
Junta Kosuda (Open House)
Mikio Ikeda (Digital Advertising Consortium)
Tomoki Yoshida (Nippon Sport Science University)

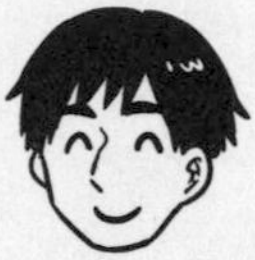

Companies
Industry Professionals

Xiborg
Otto Bock Japan
Okino Sports Prosthetics & Orthotics (Atsuo Okino)
D'ACTION (Shuji Miyake)
Naoto Yoshida (Writer)

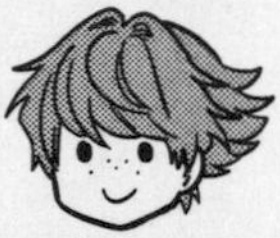

Assistants

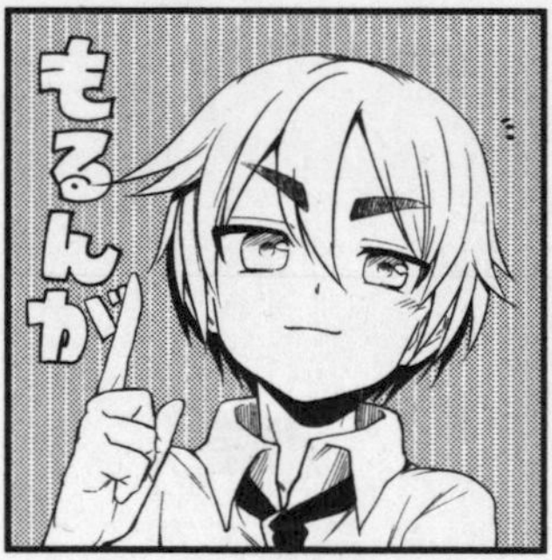
もるんが

Morunga

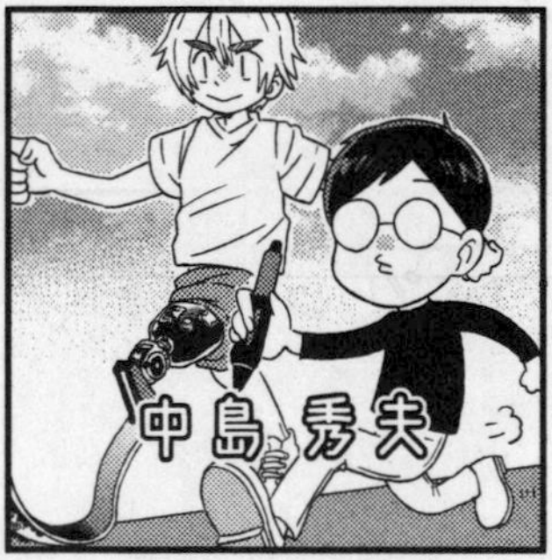
中島秀夫

Hideo Nakajima

Thank you to everyone else who
contributed to this book!

BONUS

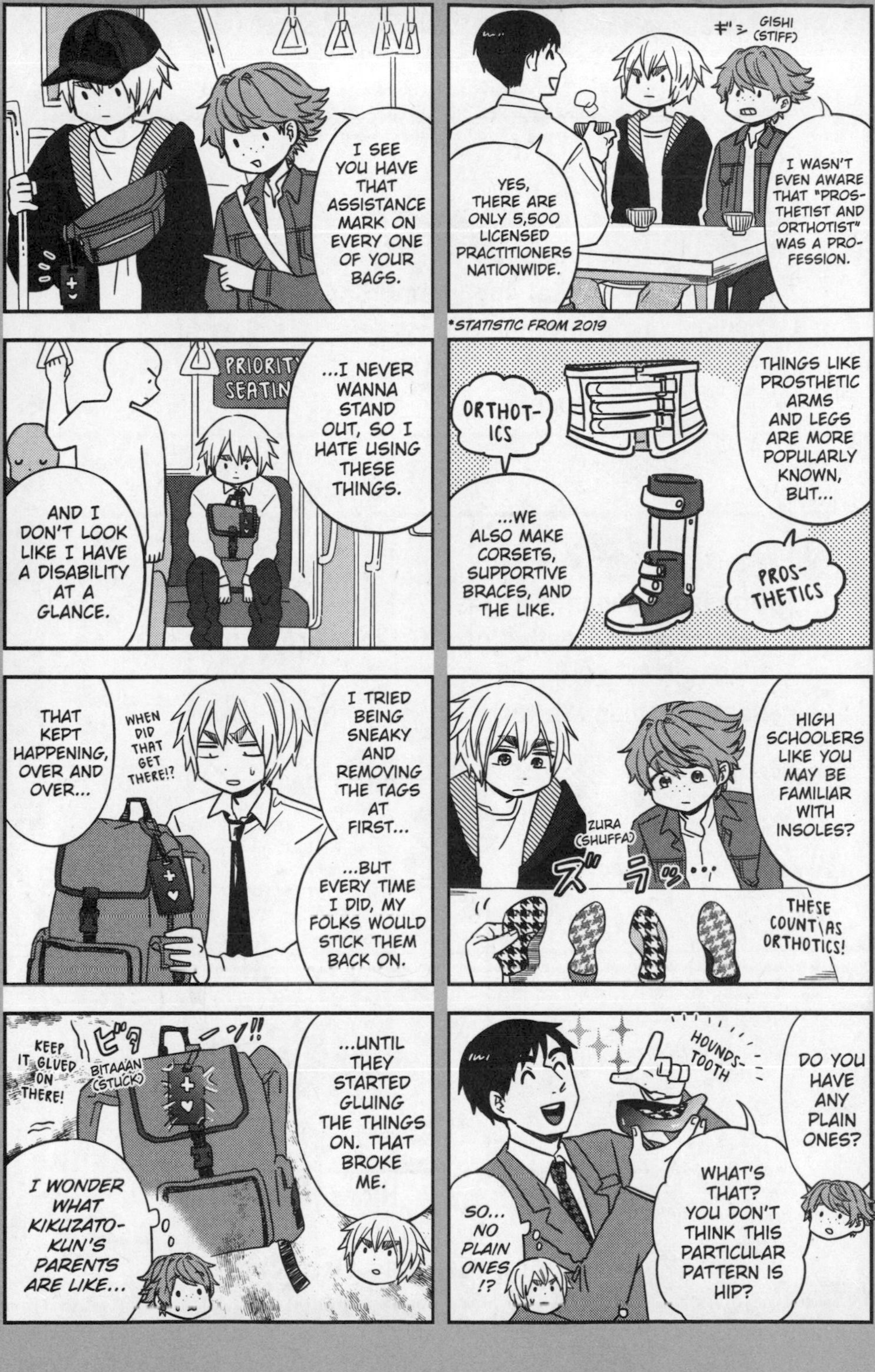
GISHI (STIFF)
I WASN'T EVEN AWARE THAT "PROSTHETIST AND ORTHOTIST" WAS A PROFESSION.
YES, THERE ARE ONLY 5,500 LICENSED PRACTITIONERS NATIONWIDE.
*STATISTIC FROM 2019
THINGS LIKE PROSTHETIC ARMS AND LEGS ARE MORE POPULARLY KNOWN, BUT...
PROSTHETICS
ORTHOTICS
...WE ALSO MAKE CORSETS, SUPPORTIVE BRACES, AND THE LIKE.
HIGH SCHOOLERS LIKE YOU MAY BE FAMILIAR WITH INSOLES?
ZURA (SHUFFA)
THESE COUNT AS ORTHOTICS!
DO YOU HAVE ANY PLAIN ONES?
HOUNDSTOOTH
WHAT'S THAT? YOU DON'T THINK THIS PARTICULAR PATTERN IS HIP?
SO... NO PLAIN ONES!?
I SEE YOU HAVE THAT ASSISTANCE MARK ON EVERY ONE OF YOUR BAGS.
...I NEVER WANNA STAND OUT, SO I HATE USING THESE THINGS.
AND I DON'T LOOK LIKE I HAVE A DISABILITY AT A GLANCE.
I TRIED BEING SNEAKY AND REMOVING THE TAGS AT FIRST...
...BUT EVERY TIME I DID, MY FOLKS WOULD STICK THEM BACK ON.
WHEN DID THAT GET THERE!?
THAT KEPT HAPPENING, OVER AND OVER...
...UNTIL THEY STARTED GLUING THE THINGS ON. THAT BROKE ME.
BITAAAN (STUCK)
KEEP IT GLUED ON THERE!
I WONDER WHAT KIKUZATO-KUN'S PARENTS ARE LIKE...

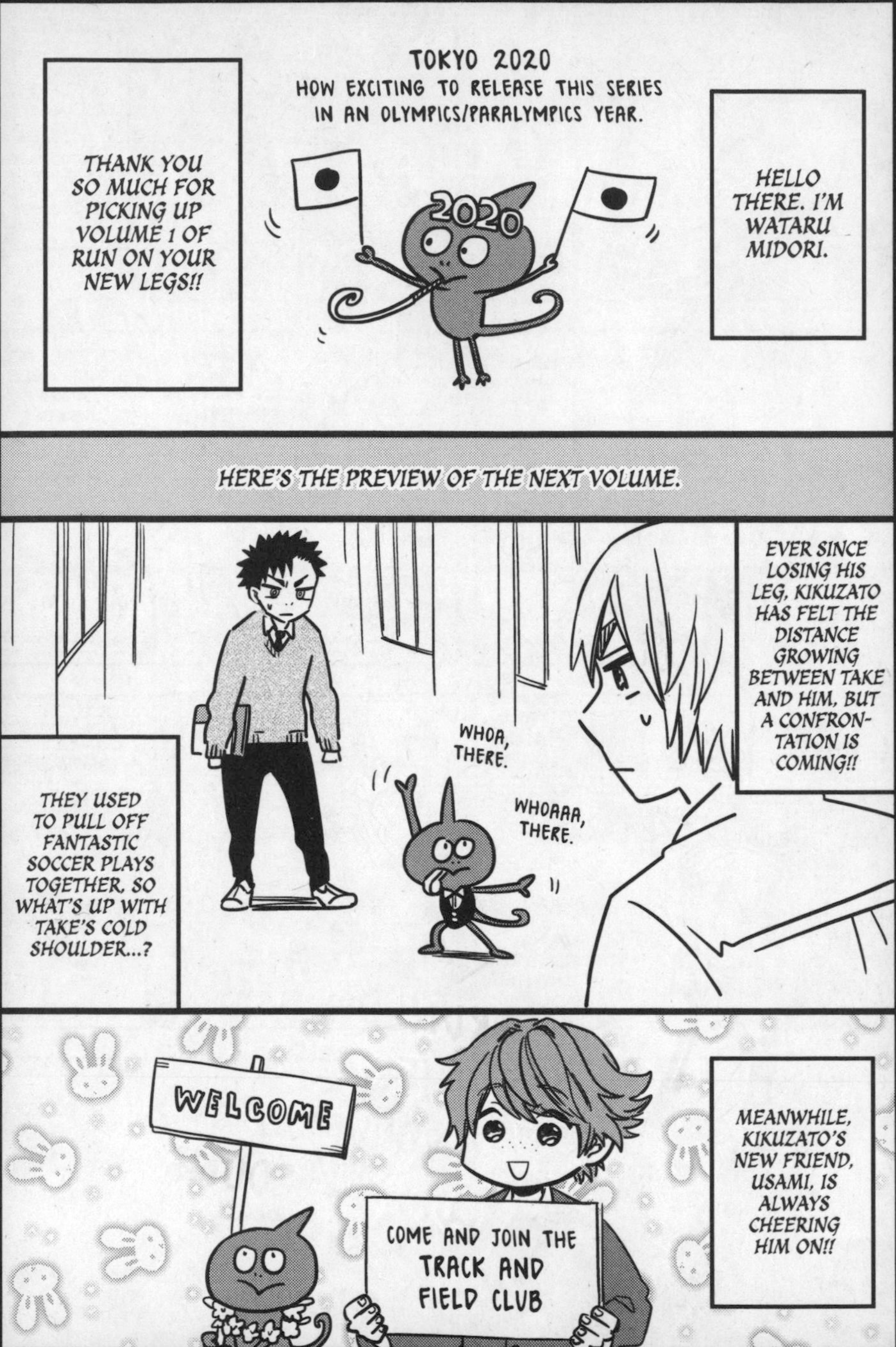
HELLO THERE. I'M WATARU MIDORI.
THANK YOU SO MUCH FOR PICKING UP VOLUME 1 OF RUN ON YOUR NEW LEGS!!
TOKYO 2020
HOW EXCITING TO RELEASE THIS SERIES IN AN OLYMPICS/PARALYMPICS YEAR.
2020
HERE'S THE PREVIEW OF THE NEXT VOLUME.
EVER SINCE LOSING HIS LEG, KIKUZATO HAS FELT THE DISTANCE GROWING BETWEEN TAKE AND HIM, BUT A CONFRONTATION IS COMING!!
WHOA, THERE.
WHOAAA, THERE.
THEY USED TO PULL OFF FANTASTIC SOCCER PLAYS TOGETHER, SO WHAT'S UP WITH TAKE'S COLD SHOULDER...?
MEANWHILE, KIKUZATO'S NEW FRIEND, USAMI, IS ALWAYS CHEERING HIM ON!!
COME AND JOIN THE TRACK AND FIELD CLUB
WELCOME

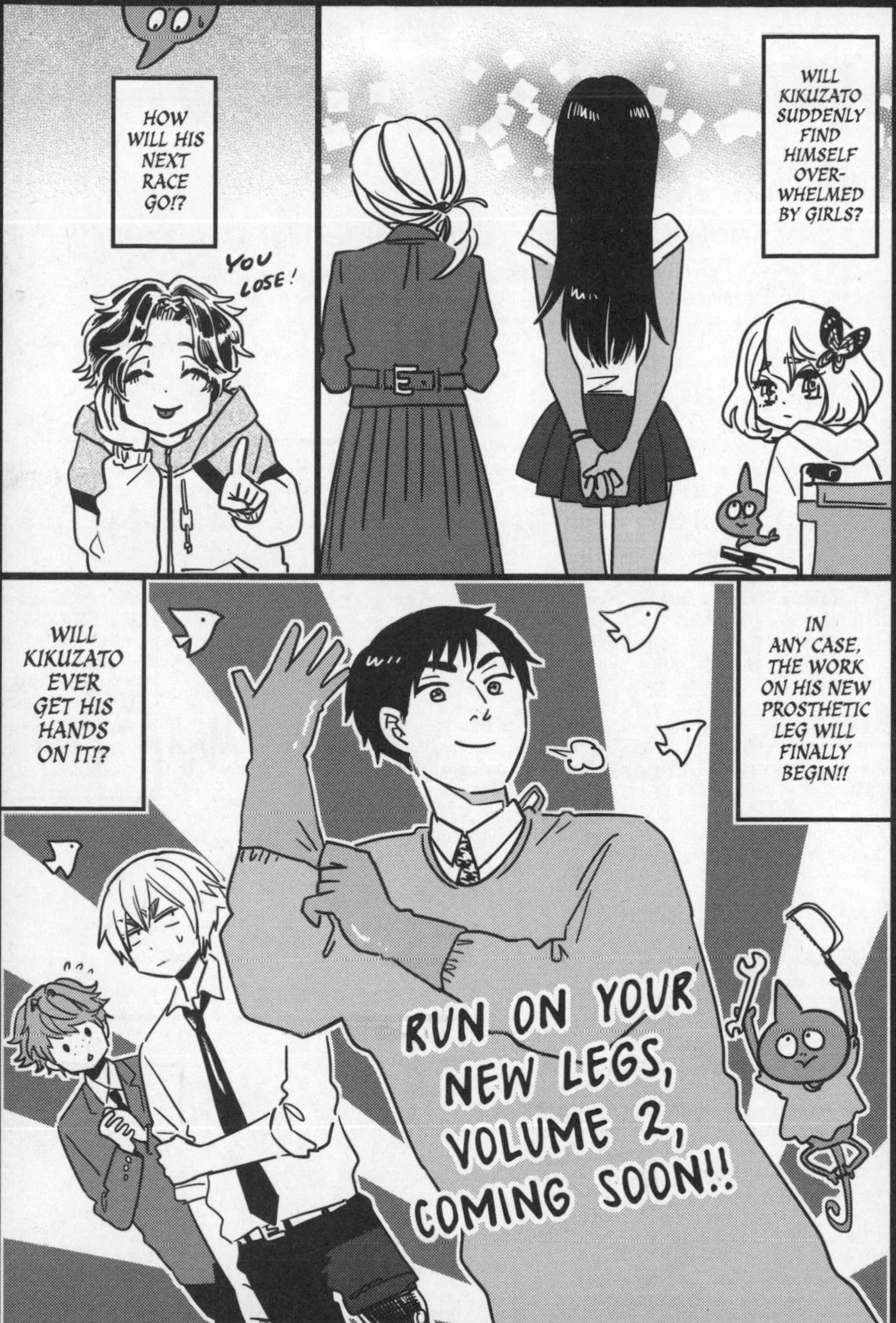
WILL KIKUZATO SUDDENLY FIND HIMSELF OVER-WHELMED BY GIRLS?
HOW WILL HIS NEXT RACE GO!?
YOU LOSE!
IN ANY CASE, THE WORK ON HIS NEW PROSTHETIC LEG WILL FINALLY BEGIN!!
WILL KIKUZATO EVER GET HIS HANDS ON IT!?
RUN ON YOUR NEW LEGS, VOLUME 2, COMING SOON!!

RUN ON YOUR NEW LEGS 1

WATARU MIDORI

TRANSLATION: Caleb Cook • LETTERING: Abigail Blackman

ATARASHII ASHI DE KAKENUKERO. Vol. 1
by Wataru MIDORI
© 2020 Wataru MIDORI
All rights reserved.
Original Japanese edition published by SHOGAKUKAN.
English translation rights in the United States of America, Canada, the United Kingdom, Ireland, Australia and New Zealand arranged with SHOGAKUKAN through Tuttle-Mori Agency, Inc.

Original Cover Design: Yoko AKUTA

Yen Press
150 West 30th Street, 19th Floor
New York, NY 10001

Visit us at yenpress.com
facebook.com/yenpress
twitter.com/yenpress
yenpress.tumblr.com
instagram.com/yenpress

First Yen Press Edition: March 2022

Yen Press is an imprint of Yen Press, LLC.
The Yen Press name and logo are trademarks of Yen Press, LLC.

The publisher is not responsible for websites (or their content) that are not owned by the publisher.

Library of Congress Control Number: 2021951359

ISBNs: 978-1-9753-3900-5 (paperback)
        978-1-9753-4569-3 (ebook)

10 9 8 7 6 5 4 3 2

WOR

Printed in the United States of America